Dick Francis, former National Hunt jockey, is the king of thriller writers, with **more** than thirty brilliant best-selling novels acclaimed across the world. In 1989 he received the Crime Writers' Association's prestigious award, the Cartier Diamond Dagger, in recognition of his outstanding contribution to the crime genre, and in May 1991 Tufts University of Boston awarded him an honorary Doctorate of Humane Letters.

Dick Francis

HOT MONEY

AND

IN THE FRAME

PAN BOOKS
IN ASSOCIATION WITH MICHAEL JOSEPH

Hot Money first published in Great Britain 1987 by Michael Joseph Ltd and first published by Pan Books Ltd 1988 in association with Michael Joseph Ltd.

In the Frame first published in Great Britain 1976 by Michael Joseph Ltd and first published by Pan Books Ltd 1978.

This edition published 1994 by Pan Books
a division of Macmillan General Books
Cavaye Place, London SW10 9PG
and Basingstoke
in association with Michael Joseph Ltd

Associated companies throughout the world

ISBN 0 330 34161 8

1 3 5 7 9 8 6 4 2

A CIP catalogue record for this book is available from
the British Library

Printed and bound in Great Britain by
Cox & Wyman Ltd, Reading, Berkshire

Hot Money

THE PEMBROKES

MALCOLM PEMBROKE

HIS WIVES
1 Vivien
2 Joyce
3 Alicia
4 Coochie
5 Moira

VIVIEN'S CHILDREN
1 Donald, married to Helen
2 Lucy, married to Edwin
3 Thomas, married to Berenice

JOYCE'S CHILD
1 Ian, unmarried

ALICIA'S CHILDREN
1 Gervase, married to Ursula
2 Ferdinand, married to Debs
3 Serena, unmarried

COOCHIE'S CHILDREN
1 Robin
2 Peter, dead

One

I intensely disliked my father's fifth wife, but not to the point of murder.

I, the fruit of his second ill-considered gallop up the aisle, had gone dutifully to the next two of his subsequent nuptials, the changes of 'mother' punctuating my life at six and fourteen.

At thirty however I'd revolted: wild horses couldn't have dragged me to witness his wedding to the sharp-eyed honey-tongued Moira, his fifth choice. Moira had been the subject of the bitterest quarrel my father and I ever had and the direct cause of a non-speaking wilderness which had lasted three years.

After Moira was murdered, the police came bristling with suspicion to my door, and it was by the merest fluke that I could prove I'd been geographically elsewhere when her grasping little soul had left her carefully tended body. I didn't go to her funeral, but I wasn't alone in that. My father didn't go either.

A month after her death he telephoned me, and it was so long since I'd heard his voice that it seemed that of a stranger.

'Ian?'

'Yes,' I said.

'Malcolm.'

'Hello,' I said.

'Are you doing anything?'

'Reading the price of gold.'

'No, dammit,' he said testily. 'In general, are you busy?'

'In general,' I said, 'fairly.'

The newspaper lay on my lap, an empty wine glass at my elbow. It was late evening, after eleven, growing cold. I had that day quit my job and put on idleness like a comfortable coat.

He sighed down the line. 'I suppose you know about Moira?'

1

'Front page news,' I agreed. 'The price of gold is on . . . er . . . page thirty-two.'

'If you want me to apologise,' he said, 'I'm not going to.'

His image stood sharp and clear in my mind: a stocky, grey-haired man with bright blue eyes and a fizzing vitality that flowed from him in sparks of static electricity in cold weather. He was to my mind stubborn, opinionated, rash and often stupid. He was also financially canny, intuitive, quick-brained and courageous, and hadn't been nicknamed Midas for nothing.

'Are you still there?' he demanded.

'Yes.'

'Well . . . I need your help.'

He said it as if it were an everyday requirement, but I couldn't remember his asking anyone for help ever before, certainly not me.

'Er . . .' I said uncertainly. 'What sort of help?'

'I'll tell you when you get here.'

'Where is "here"?'

'Newmarket,' he said. 'Come to the sales tomorrow afternoon.'

There was a note in his voice which couldn't be called entreaty but was far from a direct order, and I was accustomed only to orders.

'All right,' I said slowly.

'Good.'

He disconnected immediately, letting me ask no questions: and I thought of the last time I'd seen him, when I'd tried to dissuade him from marrying Moira, describing her progressively, in face of his implacable purpose, as a bad misjudgement on his part and as a skilful, untruthful manipulator and, finally, as a rapacious blood-sucking tramp. He'd knocked me down to the floor with one fast, dreadful blow, which he'd been quite capable of at sixty-five, three years ago. Striding furiously away, he'd left me lying dazed on my carpet and had afterwards behaved as if I no longer existed, packing into boxes everything I'd left in my old room in his house and sending them by public carrier to my flat.

Time had proved me right about Moira, but the unforgivable words had remained unforgiven to her death and, it had seemed, beyond. On this October evening, though, perhaps they were provisionally on ice.

I, Ian Pembroke, the fifth of my father's nine children, had from the mists of infancy loved him blindly through thunderous years of

2

domestic in-fighting which had left me permanently impervious to fortissimo voices and slammed doors. In a totally confused chaotic upbringing, I'd spent scattered unhappy periods with my bitter mother but had mostly been passed from wife to wife in my father's house as part of the furniture and fittings, treated by him throughout with the same random but genuine affection he gave to his dogs.

Only with the advent of Coochie, his fourth wife, had there been peace, but by the time she took over I was fourteen and world-weary, cynically expecting a resumption of hostilities within a year of the honeymoon.

Coochie, however, had been different. Coochie of all of them had been my only real mother, the only one who'd given me a sense of worth and identity, who'd listened and encouraged and offered good advice. Coochie produced twin boys, my half-brothers Robin and Peter, and it had seemed that at last Malcolm Pembroke had achieved a friendly family unit, albeit a sort of sunny clearing surrounded by jungle thickets of ex-wives and discontented siblings.

I grew up and left home but went back often, feeling never excluded. Coochie would have seen Malcolm into a happy old age but, when she was forty and the twins eleven, a hit-and-run driver swerved her car off the road and downhill onto rocks. Coochie and Peter had been killed outright. Robin, the elder twin, suffered brain damage. I had been away. Malcolm was in his office: a policeman went to him to tell him, and he let me know soon after. I'd learned the meaning of grief on that drizzly afternoon, and still mourned them all, their loss irreparable.

On the October evening of Malcolm's telephone call, I glanced at them as usual as I went to bed, their three bright faces grinning out from a silver frame on my chest of drawers. Robin lived – just – in serene twilight in a nursing home. I went to see him now and again. He no longer looked like the boy in the photograph, but was five years older, growing tall, empty-eyed.

I wondered what Malcolm could possibly want. He was rich enough to buy anything he needed, maybe – only maybe – excluding the whole of Fort Knox. I couldn't think of anything I could do for him that he couldn't get from anyone else.

Newmarket, I thought. The sales.

Newmarket was all very well for me because I'd been working as an assistant to a racehorse trainer. But Newmarket for Malcolm? Malcolm never gambled on horses, only on gold. Malcolm had made

3

several immense consecutive fortunes from buying and selling the hard yellow stuff, and had years ago reacted to my stated choice of occupation by saying merely, 'Horses? Racing? Good Lord! Well, if that's what you want, my boy, off you go. But don't expect me to know the first thing about anything.' And as far as I knew, he was still as ignorant of the subject as he'd been all along.

Malcolm and Newmarket bloodstock sales simply didn't mix. Not the Malcolm I'd known, anyway.

I drove the next day to the isolated Suffolk town whose major industry was the sport of kings, and among the scattered purposeful crowd found my father standing bareheaded in the area outside the sale-ring building, eyes intently focused on a catalogue.

He looked just the same. Brushed grey hair, smooth brown vicuna knee-length overcoat, charcoal business suit, silk tie, polished black shoes; confidently bringing his City presence into the casual sophistication of the country.

It was a golden day, crisp and clear, the sky a cold cloudless blue. I walked across to him in my own brand of working clothes: cavalry twill trousers, checked wool shirt, padded olive-green jacket, tweed cap. A surface contrast that went personality deep.

'Good afternoon,' I said neutrally.

He raised his eyes and gave me a stare as blue as the sky.

'So you came.'

'Well . . . yes.'

He nodded vaguely, looking me over. 'You look older,' he said.

'Three years.'

'Three years and a crooked nose.' He observed it dispassionately. 'I suppose you broke that falling off a horse?'

'No . . . You broke it.'

'Did I?' He seemed only mildly surprised. 'You deserved it.'

I didn't answer. He shrugged. 'Do you want some coffee?'

'OK.'

We hadn't touched each other, I thought. Not a hug, not a handshake, not a passing pat on the arm. Three years' silence couldn't easily be bridged.

He set off not in the direction of the regular refreshment room, but towards one of the private rooms set aside for the privileged. I followed in his footsteps, remembering wryly that it took him roughly two minutes any time to talk himself into the plushest recesses, wherever.

The Newmarket sales building was in the form of an amphitheatre, sloping banks of seats rising all round from the ground-level ring where each horse was led round while being auctioned. Underneath the seating and in a large adjacent building were rooms used as offices by auctioneers and bloodstock agents, and as entertainment rooms by commercial firms, such as Ebury Jewellers, Malcolm's present willing hosts.

I was used only to the basic concrete boxes of the bloodstock agents' offices. Ebury's space was decorated in contrast as an expensive showroom, with well-lit glass display cases round three walls shining with silver and sparkling with baubles, everything locked away safely but temptingly visible. Down the centre of the room, on brown wall-to-wall carpeting, stood a long polished table surrounded with armed, leather-covered dining chairs. Before each chair was neatly laid a leather-edged blotter alongside a gold-tooled tub containing pens, suggesting that all any client needed to provide here was his cheque-book.

A smooth young gentleman welcomed Malcolm with enthusiastic tact and offered drinks and goodies from the well-stocked buffet table which filled most of the fourth wall. Lunch, it seemed, was an all-day affair. Malcolm and I took cups of coffee and sat at the table, I, at any rate, feeling awkward. Malcolm fiddled with his spoon. A large loud lady came in and began talking to the smooth young man about having one of her dogs modelled in silver. Malcolm raised his eyes to them briefly and then looked down again at his cup.

'What sort of help?' I said.

I suppose I expected him to say he wanted help in some way with horses, in view of the venue he'd chosen, but it seemed to be nothing as straightforward.

'I want you beside me,' he said.

I frowned, puzzled. 'How do you mean?'

'Beside me,' he said. 'All the time.'

'I don't understand.'

'I don't suppose you do,' he said. He looked up at my face. 'I'm going to travel a bit. I want you with me.'

I made no fast reply and he said abruptly, explosively, 'Dammit, Ian, I'm not asking the world. A bit of your time, a bit of your attention, that's all.'

5

'Why now, and why me?'

'You're my son.' He stopped fiddling with the spoon and dropped it onto the blotter where it left a round stain. He leaned back in his chair. 'I trust you.' He paused. 'I need someone I can trust.'

'Why?'

He didn't tell me why. He said, 'Can't you get some time off from work? Have a holiday?'

I thought of the trainer I'd just left, whose daughter had made my job untenable because she wanted it for her fiancé. There was no immediate need for me to find another place, save for paying the rent. At thirty-three, I'd worked for three different trainers, and had lately come to feel I was growing too old to carry on as anyone's assistant. The natural progression was towards becoming a trainer myself, a dicey course without money.

'What are you thinking?' Malcolm asked.

'Roughly whether you would lend me half a million quid.'

'No,' he said.

I smiled. 'That's what I thought.'

'I'll pay your fares and your hotel bills.'

Across the room the loud lady was giving the smooth young man her address. A waitress had arrived and was busy unpacking fresh sandwiches and more alcohol onto the white-clothed table. I watched her idly for a few seconds, then looked back to Malcolm's face, and surprised there an expression that could only be interpreted as anxiety.

I was unexpectedly moved. I'd never wanted to quarrel with him: I'd wanted him to see Moira as I did, as a calculating, sweet-talking honeypot who was after his money, and who had used the devastation of Coochie's death to insinuate herself with him, turning up constantly with sympathy and offers to cook. Malcolm, deep in grief, had been helpless and grateful and seemed hardly to notice when she began threading her arm through his in company, and saying 'we'. I had for the whole three silent years wanted peace with my father, but I couldn't bear to go to his house and see Moira smirking in Coochie's place, even if he would have let me in through the door.

Now that Moira was dead, peace was maybe possible, and it seemed now as though he really wanted it also. I thought fleetingly that peace wasn't his prime object, that peace was only a preliminary necessary for some other purpose, but all the same it was enough.

6

'Yes,' I said, 'all right. I can take time off.'

His relief was visible. 'Good! Good! Come along then, I may as well buy a horse.' He stood up, full of sudden energy, waving his catalogue. 'Which do you suggest?'

'Why on earth do you want a horse?'

'To race, of course.'

'But you've never been interested . . .'

'Everyone should have a hobby,' he said briskly, though he'd never had one in his life. 'Mine is racing.' And, as an afterthought, he added, 'Henceforth,' and began to walk to the door.

The smooth young man detached himself from the dog lady and begged Malcolm to come back any time. Malcolm assured him he would, then wheeled round away from him again and marched across to one of the display cabinets.

'While I was waiting for you, I bought a cup,' he said to me over his shoulder. 'Want to see? One rather like that.' He pointed. 'It's being engraved.'

The cup in question was a highly-decorated and graceful elongated jug, eighteen inches tall and made undoubtedly of sterling silver.

'What's it for?' I asked.

'I don't know yet. Haven't made up my mind.'

'But . . . the engraving?'

'Mm. The Coochie Pembroke Memorial Challenge Trophy. Rather good, don't you think?'

'Yes,' I said.

He gave me a sidelong glance. 'I thought you'd think so.' He retraced his steps to the door. 'Right, then, a horse.'

Just like old times, I thought with half-forgotten pleasure. The sudden impulses which might or might not turn out to be thoroughly sensible, the intemperate enthusiasms needing instant gratification . . . and sometimes, afterwards, the abandoning of a débâcle as if it didn't exist. The Coochie Pembroke Memorial Challenge Trophy might achieve world-wide stature in competition or tarnish unpresented in an attic: with Malcolm it was always a toss-up.

I called him Malcolm, as all his children did, on his own instructions, and had grown up thinking it natural. Other boys might have Dad: I had my father, Malcolm.

Outside Ebury's room, he said, 'What's the procedure, then? How do we set about it?'

'Er . . .' I said. 'This is the first day of the Highflyer Sales.'

7

'Well?' he demanded as I paused. 'Go on.'

'I just thought you ought to know . . . the minimum opening bid today is twenty thousand guineas.'

It rocked him only slightly. 'Opening bid? What do they sell them for?'

'Anything from a hundred thousand up. You'll be lucky today to get a top-class yearling for under a quarter of a million. This is generally the most expensive day of the year.'

He wasn't noticeably deterred. He smiled. 'Come on, then,' he said. 'Let's go and start bidding.'

'You need to look up the breeding first,' I said. 'And then look at the animals, to see if you like them, and then get the help and advice of an agent . . .'

'Ian,' he said with mock sorrow, 'I don't know anything about the breeding, I can just about tell if a thing's got four legs, and I don't trust agents. So let's get on and bid.'

It sounded crazy to me, but it was his money. We went into the sale-ring itself where the auction was already in progress, and Malcolm asked me where the richest bidders could be found, the ones that really meant business.

'In those banks of seats on the left of the auctioneers, or here, in the entrance, or just round there to the left . . .'

He looked and listened and then led the way up to a section of seats from where we could watch the places I'd pointed out. The amphitheatre was already more than three-quarters full, and would later at times be crammed, especially whenever a tip-top lot came next.

'The very highest prices will probably be bid this evening,' I said, half teasing him, but all he said was, 'Perhaps we should wait, then.'

'If you buy ten yearlings,' I said, 'six might get to a racecourse, three might win a race and one might be pretty good. If you're lucky.'

'Cautious Ian.'

'You,' I said, 'are cautious with gold.'

He looked at me with half-shut eyes. 'Not many people say that.'

'You're fast and flamboyant,' I said, 'but you sit and wait for the moment.'

He merely grunted and began paying attention to the matter in hand, intently focusing not on the merchandise but on the bidders on the far side of the ring. The auctioneers in the box to our left were relaxed and polished, the one currently at the microphone elaborately

8

unimpressed by the fortunes passing. 'Fifty thousand, thank you, sir; sixty thousand, seventy . . . eighty? Shall I say eighty? Eighty, thank you, sir. Against you, sir. Ninety? Ninety. One hundred thousand. Selling now. I'm selling now. Against you, sir? No? All done? All done?' A pause for a sweep round to make sure no new bidder was frantically waving. 'Done, then. Sold to Mr Siddons. One hundred thousand guineas. The next lot . . .'

'Selling now,' Malcolm said. 'I suppose that means there was a reserve on it?'

I nodded.

'So until the fellow says "selling now", it's safe to bid, knowing you won't have to buy?'

'Yours might be the bid that reaches the reserve.'

He nodded. 'Russian roulette.'

We watched the sales for the rest of the afternoon, but he aimed no bullets at his own head. He asked who people were. 'Who is that Mr Siddons? That's the fourth horse he's bought.'

'He works for a bloodstock agency. He's buying for other people.'

'And that man in navy, scowling. Who's he?'

'Max Jones. He owns a lot of horses.'

'Every time that old woman bids, he bids against her.'

'It's a well-known feud.'

He sniffed. 'It must cost them fortunes.' He looked around the amphitheatre at the constantly changing audience of breeders, trainers, owners and the simply interested. 'Whose judgement would you trust most?'

I mentioned several trainers and the agents who might be acting on their behalf, and he told me to tell him when someone with good judgement was bidding, and to point them out. I did so many times, and he listened and passed no comment.

After a while, we went out for a break, an Ebury scotch, a sandwich and fresh air.

'I suppose you know,' Malcolm said casually, watching yearlings skittering past in the grasp of their handlers, 'that Moira and I were divorcing?'

'Yes, I heard.'

'And that she was demanding the house and half my possessions?'

'Mm.'

'And half my future earnings?'

'Could she?'

9

'She was going to fight for it.'

I refrained from saying that whoever had murdered Moira had done Malcolm a big favour, but I'd thought it several times.

I said instead, 'Still no clues?'

'No, nothing new.'

He spoke without regret. His disenchantment with Moira, according to his acid second wife, my own mother Joyce, had begun as soon as he'd stopped missing Coochie; and as Joyce was as percipient as she was catty, I believed it.

'The police tried damned hard to prove I did it,' Malcolm said.

'Yes, so I heard.'

'Who from? Who's your grapevine?'

'All of them,' I said.

'The three witches?'

I couldn't help smiling. He meant his three living ex-wives, Vivien, Joyce and Alicia.

'Yes, them. And all of the family.'

He shrugged.

'They were all worried that you might have,' I said.

'And were you worried?' he asked.

'I was glad you weren't arrested.'

He grunted noncommittally. 'I suppose you do know that most of your brothers and sisters, not to mention the witches, told the police you hated Moira?'

'They told me they'd told,' I agreed. 'But then, I did.'

'Lot of stinkers I've fathered,' he said gloomily.

Malcolm's personal alibi for Moira's death had been as unassailable as my own, as he'd been in Paris for the day when someone had pushed Moira's retroussé little nose into a bag of potting compost and held it there until it was certain she would take no more geranium cuttings. I could have wished her a better death, but it had been quick, everyone said. The police still clung to the belief that Malcolm had arranged for an assassin, but even Joyce knew that that was nonsense. Malcolm was a creature of tempest and volatility, but he'd never been calculatingly cruel.

His lack of interest in the horses themselves didn't extend to anything else at the sales: inside the sale-ring he had been particularly attentive to the flickering electronic board which lit up with the amount as each bid was made, and lit up not only in English currency but in dollars, yen, francs, lire and Irish punts at the current exchange

10

rates. He'd always been fascinated by the workings of money, and had once far more than doubled a million pounds simply by banking it in the United States at two dollars forty cents to the pound, waiting five years, and bringing it back when the rate stood at one dollar twenty cents, which neatly gave him twice the capital he'd started with and the interest besides. He thought of the money market, after gold, as a sort of help-yourself cornucopia.

None of his children had inherited his instinct for timing and trends, a lack he couldn't understand. He'd told me directly once or twice to buy this or sell that, and he'd been right, but I couldn't make money the way he did without his guidance.

He considered that the best years of his talent had been wasted: all the years when, for political reasons, the free movement of capital had been restricted and when gold bullion couldn't be bought by private Britons. Always large, Malcolm's income, once the controls were lifted, went up like a hot air balloon, and it was at the beginning of that period, when he'd woken to the possibilities and bought his first crock of gold for sixty pounds an ounce to sell it presently for over a hundred, that he'd first been called Midas.

Since then, he'd ridden the yellow roller-coaster several times, unerringly buying when the price sank ever lower, selling as it soared, but before the bubble burst, always seeming to spot the wobbling moment when the market approached trough or peak.

Coochie had appeared wearing ever larger diamonds. The three witches, Vivien, Joyce and Alicia, each with a nice divorce settlement agreed in less sparkling days, unavailingly consulted their lawyers.

There was a second electronic board outside the sale-ring showing the state of the sale inside. Malcolm concentrated on the flickering figures until they began to shine more brightly in the fading daylight, but he still paid no close attention to the merchandise itself.

'They all look very small,' he said reprovingly, watching a narrow colt pass on its way from stable to sale-ring.

'Well, they're yearlings.'

'One year old, literally?'

'Eighteen months, twenty months: about that. They race next year, when they're two.'

He nodded and decided to return to the scene of the action, and again found us seats opposite the big-money crowd. The amphitheatre had filled almost to capacity while we'd been outside, and soon, with

11

every seat taken, people shoved close-packed into the entrance and the standing-room sections: the blood of Northern Dancer and Nijinsky and of Secretariat and Lyphard was on its regal way to the ring.

A hush fell in the building at the entrance of the first of the legend-bred youngsters, the breath-held expectant hush of the knowledgeable awaiting a battle among financial giants. A fat cheque on this sales evening could secure a Derby winner and found a dynasty, and it happened often enough to tempt belief each time that this . . . *this* . . . was the one.

The auctioneer cleared his throat and managed the introduction without a quiver. 'Ladies and gentlemen, we now have Lot No 76, a bay colt by Nijinsky . . .' He recited the magical breeding as if bored, and asked for an opening bid.

Malcolm sat quiet and watched while the numbers flew high on the scoreboard, the price rising in jumps of fifty thousand; watched while the auctioneer scanned the bidding faces for the drop of an eyelid, the twitch of a head, the tiny acknowledgements of intent.

'. . . against you, sir. No more, then? All done?' The auctioneer's eyebrows rose with his gavel, remained poised in elevation, came smoothly, conclusively down. 'Sold for one million seven hundred thousand guineas to Mr Siddons . . .'

The crowd sighed, expelling collective breath like a single organism. Then came rustling of catalogues, movement, murmuring and rewound expectation.

Malcolm said, 'It's a spectator sport.'

'Addictive,' I agreed.

He glanced at me sideways. 'For one million . . . five million . . . there's no guarantee the colt will ever race, isn't that what you said? One could be throwing one's cash down the drain?'

'That's right.'

'It's a perfectly blameless way of getting rid of a lot of money very fast, wouldn't you say?'

'Well . . .' I said slowly, 'is that what you're at?'

'Do you disapprove?'

'It's your money. You made it. You spend it.'

He smiled almost secretively at his catalogue and said, 'I can hear the "but" in your voice.'

'Mm. If you want to enjoy yourself, buy ten next-best horses instead of one super-colt, and get interested in them.'

'And pay ten training fees instead of one?'

I nodded. 'Ten would drain the exchequer nicely.'

He laughed in his throat and watched the next half-grown blue-blood reach three million guineas before Mr Siddons shook his head. '. . . sold for three million and fifty thousand guineas to Mrs Terazzini . . .'

'Who's she?' Malcolm asked.

'She owns a world-wide bloodstock empire.'

He reflected. 'Like Robert Sangster?'

'Yep. Like him.'

He made a noise of understanding. 'An industry.'

'Yes.'

The following lot, a filly, fetched a more moderate sum, but the hush of expectancy returned for the next offering. Malcolm, keenly tuned by now to the atmosphere, watched the bidders as usual, not the nervous chestnut colt.

The upward impetus stopped at a fraction over two million and the auctioneer's eyebrows and gavel rose. 'All done?'

Malcolm raised his catalogue.

The movement caught the eye of the auctioneer, who paused with the gavel raised, using his eyebrows as a question, looking at Malcolm with surprise. Malcolm sat in what could be called the audience, not with the usual actors.

'You want to bid, sir?' asked the auctioneer.

'And fifty,' Malcolm said clearly, nodding.

There was a fluttering in the dovecot of auctioneers as head bent to head among themselves, consulting. All round the ring, necks stretched to see who had spoken, and down in the entrance-way the man who'd bid last before Malcolm shrugged, shook his head and turned his back to the auctioneer. His last increase had been for twenty thousand only: a last small raise over two million, which appeared to have been his intended limit.

The auctioneer himself seemed less than happy. 'All done, then?' he asked again, and with no further replies, said, 'Done then. Sold for two million and seventy thousand guineas to . . . er . . . the bidder opposite.'

The auctioneer consulted with his colleagues again and one of them left the box, carrying a clipboard. He hurried down and round the ring to join a minion on our side, both of them with their gaze fastened on Malcolm.

13

'Those two auctioneers won't let you out of their sight,' I observed. 'They suffered badly from a vanishing bidder not so long ago.'

'They look as if they're coming to arrest me,' Malcolm said cheerfully; and both of the auctioneers indeed made their way right to his sides, handing him the clipboard and politely requiring him to sign their bill of sale, in triplicate and without delay. They retired to ground level but were still waiting for us with steely intent when, after three further sales had gone through as expected, we made our way down.

They invited Malcolm civilly to the quieter end of their large office, and we went. They computed what he owed and deferentially presented the total. Malcolm wrote them a cheque.

They politely suggested proof of identity and a reference. Malcolm gave them an American Express card and the telephone number of his bank manager. They took the cheque gingerly and said that although Mr ... er ... Pembroke should if he wished arrange insurance on his purchase at once, the colt would not be available for removal until ... er ... tomorrow.

Malcolm took no offence. He wouldn't have let anyone he didn't know drive off with a horsebox full of gold. He said tomorrow would be fine, and in high good spirits told me I could ferry him back to his Cambridge hotel, from where he'd come that morning in a taxi, and we would have dinner together.

After we'd called in at an insurance agent's office and he'd signed some more papers and another cheque, we accordingly walked together to the car-park from where people were beginning to drift home. Night had fallen, but there were lights enough to see which car was which, and as we went I pointed out the row ahead where my wheels stood.

'Where are you going to send your colt?' I asked, walking.

'Where would you say?'

'I should think,' I said ... but I never finished the answer, or not at that actual moment.

A car coming towards us between two rows of parked cars suddenly emitted two headlight beams, blinding us; and at the same moment it seemed to accelerate fiercely, swerving straight towards Malcolm.

I leaped ... flung myself ... at my father, my flying weight spinning him off balance, carrying him off his feet, knocking him down. I fell on top of him, knowing that the pale speeding bulk of the

14

car had caught me, but not sure to what extent. There was just a bang and a lot of lights curving like arcs, and a whirling view of gleams on metal, and a fast crunch into darkness.

We were on the ground then between two silent parked cars, our bodies heavy with shock and disorientation, in a sort of inertia.

After a moment, Malcolm began struggling to free himself from under my weight, and I rolled awkwardly onto my knees and thankfully thought of little but bruises. Malcolm pushed himself up until he was sitting with his back against a car's wheel, collecting his wits but looking as shaken as I felt.

'That car,' he said eventually, between deep breaths, 'was aiming ... to kill me.'

I nodded speechlessly. My trousers were torn, thigh grazed and bleeding.

'You always had ... quick reactions,' he said. 'So now ... now you know ... why I want you beside me ... all the time.'

Two

It was the second time someone had tried to kill him, he said.

I was driving towards Cambridge a shade more slowly than usual, searching anxiously in the rear-view mirrors for satanically-minded followers but so far thankfully without success. My right leg was stiffening depressingly from the impact of twenty minutes ago, but I was in truth fairly used to that level of buffet through having ridden over the years in three or four hundred jump races, incurring consequent collisions with the ground.

Malcolm didn't like driving for reasons Coochie had deftly diagnosed as impatience. Coochie hadn't liked his driving either, for reasons (she said) of plain fear, and had taken over as family chauffeur. I too had been used to driving Malcolm from the day I gained my licence: I would need to have been delirious to ask him to take the wheel just because of some grazed skin.

The second time someone had tried to kill him . . .

'When was the first time?' I asked.

'Last Friday.'

It was currently Tuesday evening. 'What happened?' I said.

He took a while over answering. When he did there was more sadness in his voice than anger, and I listened to his tone behind the words and slowly understood his deepest fears.

'One moment I was walking the dogs . . . well, I think I was, but that's it, I don't really remember.' He paused. 'I think I had a bang on the head . . . Anyway, the last thing I remember is calling the dogs and opening the kitchen door. I meant to take them through the garden to that field with the stream and the willows. I don't know how far I went. I shouldn't think far. Anyway, I woke up in Moira's car in the garage . . . it's still there . . . and it's damn lucky I woke up at all . . . the engine was running . . .' He stopped for a few moments.

16

'It's funny how the mind works. I knew absolutely at once that I had to switch off the engine. Extraordinary. Like a flash. I was in the back seat, sort of tumbled . . . toppled over . . . half lying. I got up and practically fell through between the front seats to reach the key in the ignition, and when the engine stopped I just lay there, you know, thinking that I was bloody uncomfortable but not having any more energy to move.'

'Did anyone come?' I said, when he paused.

'No . . . I felt better after a while. I stumbled out of the car and was sick.'

'Did you tell the police?'

'Sure, I told them.' His voice sounded weary at the recollection. 'It must have been about five when I set off with the dogs. Maybe seven by the time I called the police. I'd had a couple of stiff drinks by then and stopped shaking. They asked me why I hadn't called them sooner. Bloody silly. And it was the same lot who came after Moira. They think I did it, you know. Had her killed.'

'I know.'

'Did the witches tell you that too?'

'Joyce did. She said you couldn't have. She said you might have . . . er . . . .' I baulked from repeating my mother's actual words, which were 'throttled the little bitch in a rage', and substituted more moderately, '. . . been capable of killing her yourself, but not of paying someone else to do it.'

He made a satisfied noise but no comment, and I added, 'That seems to be the family concensus.'

He sighed. 'It's not the police concensus. Far from it. I don't think they believed anyone had tried to kill me. They made a lot of notes and took samples . . . I ask you . . of my vomit, and dusted over Moira's car for fingerprints, but it was obvious they were choked with doubts. I think they thought I'd been going to commit suicide and thought better of it . . . or else that I'd staged it in the hope people would believe I couldn't have killed Moira if someone was trying to kill *me* . . .' He shook his head. 'I'm sorry I told them at all, and that's why we're not reporting tonight's attempt either.'

He had been adamant, in the sales car-park, that we shouldn't.

'What about the bump on your head?' I asked.

'I had a swelling above my ear. Very tender, but not very big. The word I heard the police use about that was "inconclusive".'

17

'And if you'd died . . .' I said thoughtfully.

He nodded. 'If I'd died, it would have wrapped things up nicely for them. Suicide. Remorse. Implicit admission of guilt.'

I drove carefully towards Cambridge, appalled and also angry. Moira's death hadn't touched me in the slightest, but the attacks on my father showed me I'd been wrong. Moira had had a right to live. There should have been rage, too, on her behalf.

'What happened to the dogs?' I said.

'What? Oh, the dogs. They came back . . . they were whining at the kitchen door. I let them in while I was waiting for the police. They were muddy . . . heaven knows where they'd been. They were tired anyway. I fed them and they went straight to their baskets and went to sleep.'

'Pity they couldn't talk.'

'What? Yes, I suppose so. Yes.' He fell into silence, sighing occasionally as I thought over what he'd told me.

'Who,' I said eventually, 'knew you were going to Newmarket Sales?'

'Who?' He sounded surprised at the question, and then understood it. 'I don't know.' He was puzzled. 'I've no idea. I didn't know myself until yesterday.'

'Well, what have you been doing since the police left you last Friday night?'

'Thinking.' And the thoughts, it was clear, had been melancholic: the thoughts now saddening his voice.

'Mm,' I said, 'along the lines of why was Moira killed?'

'Along those lines.'

I said it plainly. 'To stop her taking half your possessions?'

He said unwillingly, 'Yes.'

'And the people who had a chief interest in stopping her were your likely heirs. Your children.'

He was silent.

I said, 'Also perhaps their husbands and wives, also perhaps even the witches.'

'I don't want to believe it,' he said. 'How could I have put a murderer into the world.'

'People do,' I said.

'*Ian!*'

The truth was that, apart from poor Robin, I didn't know my half-brothers and half-sisters well enough to have any certainty about any of them. I was usually on speaking terms with them all, but didn't seek them out. There had been too much fighting, too many rows: Vivien's children disliked Alicia's, Alicia's disliked them and me, Vivien hated Joyce and Joyce hated Alicia very bitterly indeed. Under Coochie's reign, the whole lot had been banned from sleeping in the house, if not from single-day visits, with the result that a storm of collective resentment had been directed at me whom she had kept and treated as her own.

'Apart from thinking,' I said, 'what have you been doing since Friday night?'

'When the police had gone, I . . . I . . .' he stopped.

'The shakes came back?' I suggested.

'Yes. Do you understand that?'

'I'd have been scared silly,' I said. 'Stupid not to be. I'd have felt that whoever had tried to kill me was prowling about in the dark waiting for me to be alone so he could have another go.'

Malcolm audibly swallowed. 'I telephoned to the hire firm I use now and told them to send a car to fetch me. Do you know what panic feels like?'

'Not that sort, I guess.'

'I was sweating, and it was cold. I could feel my heart thumping . . . banging away at a terrible rate. It was awful. I packed some things . . . I couldn't concentrate.'

He shifted in his seat as the outskirts of Cambridge came up in the headlights and began to give me directions to the hotel where he said he'd spent the previous four nights.

'Does anyone know where you're staying?' I asked, turning corners. 'Have you seen any of your old chums?'

Malcolm knew Cambridge well, had been at university there and still had friends at high tables. It must have seemed to him a safe city to bolt to, but it was where I would have gone looking for him, if not much else failed.

'Of course I have,' he said in answer to my question. 'I spent Sunday with the Rackersons, dined with old Digger in Trinity last night . . . it's nonsense to think they could be involved.'

'Yes,' I agreed, pulling up outside his hotel. 'All the same, go and pack and check out of here, and we'll go somewhere else.'

'It's not necessary,' he protested.

'You appointed me as minder, so I'm minding,' I said.

He gave me a long look in the dim light inside the car. The

19

doorman of the hotel stepped forward and opened the door beside me, an invitation to step out.

'Come with me,' my father said.

I was both astounded by his fear and thought it warranted. I asked the doorman where I should park, and turned at his suggestion through an arch into the hotel's inner courtway. From there, through a back door and comfortable old-fashioned hallways, Malcolm and I went up one flight of red-carpeted stairs to a lengthy winding corridor. Several people we passed glanced down at my torn trouser-leg with the dried-blood scenery inside, but no one said anything: was it still British politeness, I wondered, or the new creed of not getting involved? Malcolm, it seemed, had forgotten the problem existed.

He brought his room key out of his pocket and, with it raised, said abruptly, 'I suppose *you* didn't tell anyone I would be at the sales.'

'No, I didn't.'

'But you knew.' He paused. 'Only you knew.'

He was staring at me with the blue eyes and I saw all the sudden fear-driven question marks rioting through his mind.

'Go inside,' I said. 'The corridor isn't the place for this.'

He looked at the key, he looked wildly up and down the now empty corridor, poised, almost, to run.

I turned my back on him and walked purposefully away in the direction of the stairs.

'*Ian*,' he shouted.

I stopped and turned round.

'Come back,' he said.

I went back slowly. 'You said you trusted me,' I said.

'I haven't seen you for three years . . . and I broke your nose . . .'

I took the key out of his hand and unlocked the door. I supposed I might have been suspicious of me if I'd been attacked twice in five days, considering I came into the high-probability category of son. I switched on the light and went forward into the room which was free from lurking murderers that time at least.

Malcolm followed, only tentatively reassured, closing the door slowly behind him. I drew the heavy striped curtains across the two windows and briefly surveyed the spacious but old-fashioned accommodation: reproduction antique furniture, twin beds, pair of armchairs, door to bathroom.

20

No murderer in the bathroom.

'Ian . . .' Malcolm said.

'Did you bring any scotch?' I asked. In the old days, he'd never travelled without it.

He waved a hand towards a chest of drawers where I found a half-full bottle nestling among a large number of socks. I fetched a glass from the bathroom and poured him enough to tranquillise an elephant.

'For God's sake . . .' he said.

'Sit down and drink it.'

'You're bloody arrogant.'

He did sit down, though, and tried not to let the glass clatter against his teeth from the shaking of his hand.

With much less force, I said, 'If I'd wanted you dead, I'd have let that car hit you tonight. I'd have jumped the other way . . . out of trouble.'

He seemed to notice clearly for the first time that there had been any physical consequences to our escape.

'Your leg,' he said, 'must be all right?'

'Leg is. Trousers . . . can I borrow a pair of yours?'

He pointed to a cupboard where I found a second suit almost identical to the one he was wearing. I was three inches taller than he and a good deal thinner but, belted and slung round the hips, whole cloth was better than holey.

He silently watched me change and made no objection when I telephoned down to the reception desk and asked them to get his bill ready for his departure. He drank more of the scotch, but nowhere was he relaxed.

'Shall I pack for you?' I asked.

He nodded, and watched some more while I fetched his suitcase, opened it on one of the beds and began collecting his belongings. The things he'd brought spoke eloquently of his state of mind when he'd packed them: about ten pairs of socks but no other underwear, a dozen shirts, no pyjamas, two towelling bath-robes, no extra shoes. The clearly new electric razor in the bathroom still bore a stick-on price tag, but he had brought his antique gold-and-silver-backed brushes, all eight of them, including two clothes brushes. I put everything into the case, and closed it.

'Ian,' he said.

'Mm?'

'People can pay assassins . . . You could have decided not to go through with it tonight . . . at the last moment . . .'

'It wasn't like that,' I protested. Saving him had been utterly instinctive, without calculation or counting of risks: I'd been lucky to get off with a graze.

He said almost beseechingly, with difficulty, 'It wasn't you, was it, who had Moira . . . Or me, in the garage . . . ? Say it wasn't you.'

I didn't know really how to convince him. He'd known me better, lived with me longer than with any of his other children, and if his trust was this fragile then there wasn't much future between us.

'I didn't have Moira killed,' I said. 'If you believe it of me, you could believe it of yourself.' I paused. 'I don't want you dead, I want you alive. I could never do you harm.'

It struck me that he really needed to hear me say I loved him, so although he might scoff at the actual words, and despite the conditioned inhibitions of my upbringing, I said, feeling that desperate situations needed desperate remedies, 'You're a great father . . . and . . . er . . . I love you.'

He blinked. Such a declaration pierced him, one could see. I'd probably overdone it, I thought, but his distrust had been a wound for me too.

I said much more lightly, 'I swear on the Coochie Pembroke Memorial Challenge Trophy that I would never touch a hair on your head . . . nor Moira's either, though I did indeed loathe her.'

I lifted the suitcase off the bed.

'Do I go on with you or not?' I said. 'If you don't trust me, I'm going home.'

He was looking at me searchingly, as if I were a stranger, which I suppose in some ways I was. He had never before, I guessed, had to think of me not as a son but as a man, as a person who had led a life separate from his, with a different outlook, different desires, different values. Sons grew from little boys into their own adult selves: fathers tended not to see the change clearly. Malcolm, I was certain, thought of me basically as still having the half-formed personality I'd had at fifteen.

'You're different,' he said.

'I am the same. Trust your instinct.'

Some of the tension at last slackened in his muscles. His instinct had been trust, an instinct strong enough to carry him to the telephone after three silent years. He finished the scotch and stood up, filling his lungs with a deep breath as if making resolves.

'Come with me, then,' he said.

I nodded.

He went over to the chest of drawers and from the bottom drawer, which I hadn't checked, produced a briefcase. I might have guessed it would be there somewhere: even in the direst panic, he wouldn't have left behind the lists of his gold shares or his currency exchange calculator. He started with the briefcase to the door, leaving me to bring the suitcase, but on impulse I went over again to the telephone and asked for a taxi to be ready for us.

'But your car's here,' Malcolm said.

'Mm. I think I'll leave it here, for now.'

'But why?'

'Because if I didn't tell anyone you were going to Newmarket Sales, and nor did you, then it's probable you were followed there, from . . . er . . . here. If you think about it . . . the car that tried to kill you was waiting in the sales car-park, but you didn't have a car. You went there by taxi. Whoever drove at you must have seen you and me together, and known who I was, and guessed you might leave with me, so although I didn't see anyone following us tonight from Newmarket, whoever-it-was probably knew we would come here, to this hotel, so . . . well . . . so they might be hanging about in the courtyard where we parked, where it's nice and dark outside the back door, waiting to see if we come out again.'

'My God!'

'It's possible,' I said. 'So we'll leave through the front with the doorman in attendance, don't you think?'

'If you say so,' he said weakly.

'From now on,' I said, 'we take every exaggerated precaution we can think of.'

'Well, where are we going in this taxi?'

'How about somewhere where we can rent a car?'

The taxi-driver, however, once we'd set off without incident from the hotel, bill paid, luggage loaded, doorman tipped, informed us doubtfully that nine o'clock on a Tuesday night wasn't going to be easy. All the car-hire firms' offices would be closed.

'Chauffeur-driven car, then,' Malcolm said. 'Fellows who do weddings, that sort of thing. Twenty quid in it for you if you fix it.'

Galvanised by this offer, the taxi-driver drove us down some back

23

streets, stopped outside an unpromising little terraced house and banged on the door. It opened, shining out a melon-slice of light, and gathered the taxi-driver inside.

'We're going to be mugged,' Malcolm said.

The taxi-driver returned harmlessly, however, accompanied by a larger man buttoning the jacket of a chauffeur's uniform and carrying a reassuring peaked cap.

'The firm my brother-in-law works for does mostly weddings and funerals,' the taxi-driver said. 'He wants to know where you want to go.'

'London,' I said.

London appeared to be no problem at all. The driver and his brother-in-law climbed into the front of the taxi which started off, went round a corner or two, and pulled up again outside a lock-up garage. We sat in the taxi as asked while the two drivers opened the garage, disclosing its contents. Which was how Malcolm and I proceeded to London in a very large highly-polished black Rolls-Royce, the moonlighting chauffeur separated from us discreetly by a glass partition.

'Why did you go to the sales at all?' I asked Malcolm. 'I mean, why Newmarket? Why the sales?'

Malcolm frowned. 'Because of Ebury's, I suppose.'

'The jewellers?'

'Yes . . . well . . . I knew they were going to have a showroom there. They told me so last week when I went to see them about Coochie's jewellery. I mean, I know them pretty well, I bought most of her things from there. I was admiring a silver horse they had, and they said they were exhibiting this week at Newmarket Sales. So then yesterday when I was wondering what would fetch you . . . where you would meet me . . . I remembered the sales were so close to Cambridge, and I decided on it not long before I rang you'

I pondered a bit. 'How would you set about finding where someone was, if you wanted to, so to speak?'

To my surprise he had a ready answer. 'Get the fellow I had for tailing Moira.'

'Tailing . . .'

'My lawyer said to do it. It might save me something, he said, if Moira was having a bit on the side, see what I mean?'

'I do indeed,' I agreed dryly. 'But I suppose she wasn't?'

'No such luck.' He glanced at me. 'What do you have in mind?'

'Well . . . I just wondered if he could check where everyone in the family was last Friday and tonight.'

'Everyone!' Malcolm exclaimed. 'It would take weeks.'

'It would put your mind at rest.'

He shook his head gloomily. 'You forget about assassins.'

'Assassins aren't so frightfully easy to find, not for ordinary people. How would you set about it, for instance, if you wanted someone killed? Put an ad in *The Times*?'

He didn't seem to see such a problem as I did, but he agreed that 'the fellow who tailed Moira' should be offered the job of checking the family.

We discussed where we should stay that night: in which hotel, in fact, as neither of us felt like returning home. Home, currently, to me, was a rather dull suburban flat in Epsom, not far from the stable I'd been working for. Home for Malcolm was still the house where I'd been raised, from which Moira had apparently driven him, but to which he had returned immediately after her death. 'Home' for all the family was that big house in Berkshire which had seen all five wives come and go: Malcolm himself had been brought up there, and I could scarcely imagine what he must have felt at the prospect of losing it.

'What happened between you and Moira?' I said.

'None of your goddam business.'

We travelled ten miles in silence. Then he shifted, sighed, and said, 'She wanted Coochie's jewellery and I wouldn't give it to her. She kept on and on about it, rabbit, rabbit. Annoyed me, do you see? And then . . . well . . .' he shrugged, 'she caught me out.'

'With another woman?' I said without surprise.

He nodded, unashamed. He'd never been monogamous and couldn't understand why it should be expected. The terrible rows in my childhood had all been centred on his affairs: while he'd been married to Vivien and then to Joyce, he had maintained Alicia all the time as his mistress. Alicia bore him two children while he was married to Vivien and Joyce, and also one subsequently, when he'd made a fairly honest woman of her, at her insistence.

I liked to think he had been faithful finally to Coochie, but on the whole it was improbable, and I was never going to ask.

Malcolm favoured our staying at the Dorchester, but I persuaded him he was too well known there, and we settled finally on the Savoy.

25

'A suite,' Malcolm said at the reception desk. 'Two bedrooms, two bathrooms and a sitting-room, and send up some Bollinger right away.'

I didn't feel like drinking champagne, but Malcolm did. He also ordered scrambled eggs and smoked salmon for us both from room-service, with a bottle of Hine Antique brandy and a box of Havana cigars for comforts.

Idly I totted up the expenses of his day: one solid silver trophy, one two-million-guinea thoroughbred, insurance for same, Cambridge hotel bill, tip for the taxi-driver, chauffeured Rolls-Royce, jumbo suite at the Savoy with trimmings. I wondered how much he was really worth, and whether he intended to spend the lot.

We ate the food and drank the brandy still not totally in accord with each other. The three years' division had been, it seemed, a chasm not as easy to cross as I'd thought. I felt that although I'd meant it when I said I loved him, it was probably the long memories of him that I really loved, not his physical presence here and now, and I could see that if I was going to stay close to him, as I'd promised, I would be learning him again and from a different viewpoint; that each of us, in fact, would newly get to know the other.

'Any day now,' Malcolm said, carefully dislodging ash from his cigar, 'we're going to Australia.'

I absorbed the news and said, 'Are we?'

He nodded. 'We'll need visas. Where's your passport?'

'In my flat. Where's yours?'

'In the house.'

'Then I'll get them both tomorrow,' I said, 'and you stay here.' I paused. 'Are we going to Australia for any special reason?'

'To look at gold mines,' he said. 'And kangaroos.'

After a short silence, I said, 'We don't just have to escape. We do have to find out who's trying to kill you, in order to stop them succeeding.'

'Escape is more attractive,' he said. 'How about a week in Singapore on the way?'

'Anything you say. Only ... I'm supposed to ride in a race at Sandown on Friday.'

'I've never understood why you like it. All those cold wet days. All those falls.'

'You get your rush from gold,' I said.

'Danger?' His eyebrows rose. 'Quiet, well-behaved, cautious Ian? Life is a bore without risk, is that it?'

'It's not so extraordinary,' I said.

I'd ridden always as an amateur, unpaid, because something finally held me back from the total dedication needed for turning professional. Race riding was my deepest pleasure, but not my entire life, and in consequence I'd never developed the competitive drive necessary for climbing the pro ladder. I was happy with the rides I got, with the camaraderie of the changing-room, with the wide skies and the horses themselves, and yes, one had to admit it, with the risk.

'Staying near me,' Malcolm said, 'as you've already found out, isn't enormously safe.'

'That's why I'm staying,' I said.

He stared. He said, 'My God,' and he laughed. 'I thought I knew you. Seems I don't.'

He finished his brandy, stubbed out his cigar and decided on bed; and in the morning he was up before me, sitting on a sofa in one of the bathrobes and reading the *Sporting Life* when I ambled out in the underpants and shirt I'd slept in.

'I've ordered breakfast,' he said. 'And I'm in the paper — how about that?'

I looked where he pointed. His name was certainly there, somewhere near the end of the detailed lists of yesterday's sales. 'Lot 79, ch. colt, 2,070,000 gns. Malcolm Pembroke'.

He put down the paper, well pleased. 'Now, what do we do today?'

'We summon your private eye, we fix a trainer for the colt, I fetch our passports and some clothes, and you stay here.'

Slightly to my surprise, he raised no arguments except to tell me not to be away too long. He was looking rather thoughtfully at the healing graze down my right thigh and the red beginnings of bruising around it.

'The trouble is,' he said, 'I don't have the private eye's phone number. Not with me.'

'We'll get another agency, then, from the yellow pages.'

'Your mother knows it, of course. Joyce knows it.'

'How does she know it?'

'She used him,' he said airily, 'to follow me and Alicia.'

There was nothing, I supposed, which should ever surprise me about my parents.

'When the lawyer fellow said to have Moira tailed, I got the private eye's name from Joyce. After all, he'd done a good job on me and Alicia all those years ago. Too bloody good, when you think of it. So get through to Joyce, Ian, and ask her for the number.'

Bemused, I did as he said.

'Darling,' my mother shrieked down the line. 'Where's your father?'

'I don't know,' I said.

'Darling, do you know what he's bloody *done*?'

'No . . . what?'

'He's given a *fortune*, darling, I mean literally *hundreds* of *thousands*, to some wretched little film company to make some absolutely *ghastly* film about tadpoles or something. Some bloody fool of a man telephoned to find out where your father was, because it seems he promised them even *more* money which they'd like to have . . . I ask you! I know you and Malcolm aren't talking, but you've got to do something to stop him.'

'Well,' I said, 'it's his money.'

'Darling, don't be so *naive*. Someone's going to inherit it, and if only you'd swallow all that bloody pride, as I've told you over and over, it would be *yours*. If you go on and on with this bloody quarrel, he'll leave it all to Alicia's beastly brood, and I cannot *bear* the prospect of her gloating for ever more. So make it up with Malcolm *at once*, darling, and get him to see sense.'

'Calm down,' I said. 'I have.'

'*What?*'

'Made it up with him.'

'Thank God, at *last*!' my mother shrieked. 'Then, darling, what are you waiting for? Get onto him *straight* away and stop him spending your inheritance.'

Three

Malcolm's house, after three years of Moira's occupancy, had greatly changed.

Malcolm's Victorian house was known as 'Quantum' because of the Latin inscription carved into the lintel over the front door. QUANTUM IN ME FUIT – roughly, 'I did the best I could.'

I went there remembering the comfortable casualness that Coochie had left and not actually expecting that things would be different: and I should have known better, as each wife in turn, Coochie included, had done her best to eradicate all signs of her predecessor. Marrying Malcolm had, for each wife, involved moving into his house, but he had indulged them all, I now understood, in the matter of ambience.

I let myself in through the kitchen door with Malcolm's keys and thought wildly for a moment that I'd come to the wrong place. Coochie's pinewood and red-tiled homeliness had been swept away in favour of glossy yellow walls, glittering white appliances and shelves crowded with scarlet and deep pink geraniums cascading from white pots.

Faintly stunned, I looked back through time to the era before Coochie, to Alicia's fluffy occupancy of broderie anglaise frills on shimmering white curtains with pale blue work-tops and white floor tiles; and back further still to the starker olive and milk-coffee angularities chosen by Joyce. I remembered the day the workmen had torn out my mother's kitchen, and how I'd gone howling to Malcolm: he'd packed me off to Joyce immediately for a month, which I didn't like either, and when I returned I'd found the white frills installed, and the pale blue cupboards, and I thought them all sissy, but I'd learned not to say so.

For the first time ever, I wondered what the kitchen had looked like in Vivien's time, when forty-five or so years ago young Malcolm had brought her there as his first bride. Vivien had been dispossessed and resentful by the time I was born, and I'd seldom seen her smiling. She seemed to me the least positive of the five wives and the least intelligent but, according to her photographs, she had been in her youth by streets the most beautiful. The dark sweep of her eyebrows and the high cheekbones remained, but the thick black hair had thinned now in greying, and entrenched bitterness had soured the once sweet mouth. Vivien's marriage, I'd guessed, had died through Malcolm's boredom with her, and although they now still met occasionally at events to do with their mutual children and grandchildren, they were more apt to turn their backs than to kiss.

Vivien disliked and was plaintively critical of almost everybody while at the same time unerringly interpreting the most innocent general remarks of others as being criticism of herself. It was impossible to please her often or for long, and I, like almost all the extended family, had long ago stopped trying. She had indoctrinated her three offspring with her own dissatisfactions to the point where they were nastily disparaging of Malcolm behind his back, though not to his face, hypocrites that they were.

Malcolm had steadfastly maintained them through young adulthood and then cast them loose, each with a trust fund that would prevent them from actually starving. He had treated all seven of his normally surviving children in the same way; his eighth child, Robin, would be looked after for ever. None of us seven could have any complaints: he had given us all whatever vocational training we'd chosen and afterwards the cushion against penury, and at that point in each of our lives had considered his work done. Whatever became of us in the future, he said, had to be in our own hands.

With the family powerfully in mind, I went from the kitchen into the hall where I found that Moira had had the oak panelling painted white. Increasingly amused, I thought of the distant days when Alicia had painstakingly bleached all the old wood, only to have Coochie stain it dark again: and I supposed that perhaps Malcolm enjoyed change around him in many ways, not just in women.

His own private room, always called the office although more like a comfortable cluttered sitting-room, seemed to have escaped the latest refit except in the matter of gold velvet curtains replacing the old green. Otherwise, the room as always seemed filled with his strong personality, the walls covered with dozens of framed photographs, the deep cupboards bulging with files, the bookshelves crammed, every surface bearing mementoes of his journeyings and achievements, nothing very tidy.

I went over to the desk to find his passport and half-expected to hear his voice at any minute even though I'd left him forty miles away persuasively telephoning to 'the fellow who tailed Moira'.

His passport, he'd said, was in the second drawer down on the right-hand side, and so it was, among a large clutter of bygone travel arrangements and expired medical insurances. Malcolm seldom threw much away, merely building another cupboard for files. His filing system was such that no one but he had the slightest idea where any paper or information could be found, but he himself could put his finger on things unerringly. His method, he'd told me once long ago, was always to put everything where he would first think of looking for it; and as a child, I'd seen such sense in that that I had copied him ever since.

Looking around again, it struck me that although the room was crammed with objects, several familiar ones were missing. The gold dolphin, for instance, and the gold tree bearing amethysts, and the Georgian silver candelabras. Perhaps at last, I thought, he had stored them prudently in the bank.

Carrying the passport, I went upstairs to fetch clothes to add to his sketchy packing and out of irresistible curiosity detoured into the room which had been mine. I expected a bright Moira-style transformation, but in fact nothing at all had been changed, except that nothing of me remained.

The room was without soul; barren. The single bed, stripped, showed a bare mattress. There were no cobwebs, no dust, no smell of neglect, but the message was clear: the son who had slept there no longer existed.

Shivering slightly, I closed the door and wondered whether the absolute rejection had been Malcolm's or Moira's and, shrugging, decided I didn't now mind which.

Moira's idea of the perfect bedroom turned out to be plum and pink with louvred doors everywhere possible. Malcolm's dressing-room next door had received the same treatment, as had their joint bathroom, and I set about collecting his belongings with a strong feeling of intruding upon strangers.

I found Moira's portrait only because I kicked it while searching for pyjamas: it was underneath Malcolm's chest of drawers in the

31

dressing-room. Looking to see what I'd damaged, I pulled out a square gold frame which fitted a discoloured patch on the wall and, turning it over, found the horrible Moira smiling at me with all her insufferable complacency.

I had forgotten how young she had been, and how pretty. Thirty years younger than Malcolm; thirty-five when she'd married him and, in the painting anyway, unlined. Reddish-gold hair, pale unfreckled skin, pointed chin, delicate neck. The artist seemed to me to have caught the calculation in her eyes with disconcerting clarity, and when I glanced at the name scrawled at the bottom I understood why. Malcolm might not have given her diamonds, but her portrait had been painted by the best.

I put her back face down under the chest of drawers as I'd found her, where Malcolm, I was sure, had consigned her.

Fetching a suitcase from the boxroom (no decor changes there), I packed Malcolm's things and went downstairs, and in the hall came face to face with a smallish man carrying a large shotgun, the business end pointing my way.

I stopped abruptly, as one would.

'Put your hands up,' he said hoarsely.

I set the suitcase on the floor and did as he bid. He wore earth-stained dark trousers and had mud on his hands, and I asked him immediately, 'Are you the gardener?'

'What if I am? What are you doing here?'

'Collecting clothes for my father . . . er . . . Mr Pembroke. I'm his son.'

'I don't know you. I'm getting the police.' His voice was belligerent but quavery, the shotgun none too steady in his hands.

'All right,' I said.

He was faced then with the problem of how to telephone while aiming my way.

I said, seeing his hesitation, 'I can prove I'm Mr Pembroke's son, and I'll open the suitcase to show you I'm not stealing anything. Would that help?'

After a pause, he nodded. 'You stay over there, though,' he said.

I judged that if I alarmed him there would be a further death in my father's house, so I very slowly and carefully opened the suitcase, removed the underpants and the rest, and laid them out on the hall floor. After that, I equally slowly took my own wallet out of my pocket, opened it, removed a credit card and laid it on the floor face

32

upwards. Then I retreated backwards from the exhibits, ending with my back against the closed and locked front door.

The elderly gardener came suspiciously forward and inspected the show, dropping his eyes only in split seconds, raising them quickly, giving me no chance to jump him.

'That's his passport,' he said accusingly.

'He asked me to fetch it.'

'Where is he?' he said. 'Where's he gone?'

'I have to meet him with his passport. I don't know where he's going.' I paused. 'I really am his son. You must be new here. I haven't seen you before.'

'Two years,' he said defensively. 'I've worked here two years.' He seemed to come quite suddenly to a decision to believe me, and almost apologetically lowered the gun. 'This house is supposed to be locked up,' he said. 'Then I see you moving about upstairs.'

'Upsetting,' I agreed.

He gestured to Malcolm's things. 'You'd better pack them again.'

I began to do so under his still watchful eye.

'It was brave of you to come in here,' I said, 'if you thought I was a burglar.'

He braced his shoulders in an old automatic movement. 'I was in the army once.' He relaxed and shrugged. 'Tell you the truth, I was coming in quietly-like to phone the police, then you started down the stairs.'

'And . . . the gun?'

'Brought it with me just in case. I go after rabbits . . . I keep the gun handy.'

I nodded. It was the gardener's own gun, I thought. Malcolm had never owned one, as far as I knew.

'Has my father paid you for the week?' I said.

His eyes at once brightened hopefully. 'He paid me last Friday, same as usual. Then Saturday morning he phoned my house to tell me to come round here to see to the dogs. Take them home with me, same as I always do when he's away. So I did. But he was gone off the line before I could ask him how long he'd be wanting me to have them.'

I pulled out my cheque-book and wrote him a cheque for the amount he specified. Arthur Bellbrook, he said his name was. I tore out the cheque and gave it to him and asked him if there was anyone else who needed wages.

He shook his head. 'The cleaner left when Mrs Pembroke was done in . . . er . . . murdered. Said she didn't fancy the place any more.'

'Where exactly was Mrs Pembroke . . . er . . . murdered?'

'I'll show you if you like.' He stored the cheque away in a pocket. 'Outside in the greenhouse.'

He took me, however, not as I'd imagined to the rickety old familiar greenhouse sagging against a mellowed wall in the kitchen garden, but to a bright white octagonal wrought-iron construction like a fancy bird-cage set as a summer-house on a secluded patch of lawn. From far outside, one could clearly see the flourishing geraniums within.

'Well, well,' I said.

Arthur Bellbrook uttered 'Huh' as expressing his disapproval and opened the metal-and-glass door.

'Cost a fortune to heat, will this place,' he observed. 'And it got too hot in the summer. The only thing as will survive in it is geraniums. Mrs Pembroke's passion, geraniums.'

An almost full sack of potting compost lay along one of the work surfaces, the top side of it slit from end to end to make the soil mixture easy to reach. A box of small pots stood nearby, some of them occupied by cuttings.

I looked at the compost with revulsion. 'Is that where . . .?' I began.

'Yes,' he said. 'Poor lady. There's no one ought to die like that, however difficult they could be.'

'No,' I agreed. A thought struck me. 'It was you who found her, wasn't it?'

'I went home like always at four o'clock, but I was out for a stroll about seven, and I thought I would just come in to see what state she'd left the place in. See, she played at gardening. Never cleaned the tools, things like that.' He looked at the boarded floor as if still seeing her there. 'She was lying face down, and I turned her over. She was dead all right. She was white like always but she had these little pink dots in her skin. They say you get those dots from asphyxiation. They found potting compost in her lungs, poor lady.' He had undoubtedly been shocked and moved at the time, but there was an echo of countless repetitions in his voice now and precious little feeling.

'Thank you for showing me,' I said.

He nodded and we both went out, shutting the door behind us.

34

'I don't think Mr Pembroke liked this place much,' he said unexpectedly. 'Last spring, when she chose it, he said she could have it only if he couldn't see it from the house. Otherwise he wouldn't pay the bill. I wasn't supposed to hear, of course, but there you are, I did. They'd got to shouting, you see.'

'Yes,' I said, 'I do see.' Shouting, slammed doors, the lot.

'They were all lovey-dovey when I first came here,' he said, 'but then I reckon her little ways got to him, like, and you could see it all going downhill like a runaway train. I'm here all day long, see, and in and out of the house, and you couldn't miss it.'

'What little ways?' I asked casually.

He glanced at me sideways with reawakening suspicions. 'I thought you were his son. You must have known her.'

'I didn't come here. I didn't like her.'

He seemed to find that easily believable.

'She could be as sweet as sugar...' He paused, remembering. 'I don't know what you'd call it, really, what she was. But for instance last year, as well as the ordinary vegetables for the house, I grew a special little patch separately ... fed them, and so on ... to enter in the local show. Just runner beans, carrots and onions, for one of the produce classes. I'm good at that, see? Well, Mrs Pembroke happened to spot them a day or two before I was ready to harvest. On the Thursday, with the show on the Saturday. "What huge vegetables," she says, and I tell her I'm going to exhibit them on Saturday. And she looks at me sweet as syrup and says, "Oh no, Arthur. Mr Pembroke and I both like vegetables, as you know. We'll have some of these for dinner tomorrow and I'll freeze the rest. They are *our* vegetables, aren't they, Arthur? If you want to grow vegetables to show, you must do it in your own garden in your own time." And blow me, when I came to work the next morning, the whole little patch had been picked over, beans, carrots, onions, the lot. She'd taken them, right enough. Pounds and pounds of them, all the best ones. Maybe they ate some, but she never did bother with the freezing. On the Monday, I found a load of the beans in the dustbin.'

'Charming,' I said.

He shrugged. 'That was her sort of way. Mean, but within her rights.'

'I wonder you stayed,' I said.

'It's a nice garden, and I get on all right with Mr Pembroke.'

35

'But after he left?'

'He asked me to stay on to keep the place decent. He paid me extra, so I did.'

Walking slowly, we arrived back at the kitchen door. He smelled faintly of compost and old leaves and the warm fertility of loam, like the gardener who'd reigned in this place in my childhood.

'I grew up here,' I said, feeling nostalgia.

He gave me a considering stare. 'Are you the one who built the secret room?'

Startled, I said, 'It's not really a room. Just a sort of triangular-shaped space.'

'How do you open it?'

'You don't.'

'I could use it,' he said obstinately, 'for an apple store.'

I shook my head. 'It's too small. It's not ventilated. It's useless, really. How do you know of it?'

He pursed his lips and looked knowing. 'I could see the kitchen garden wall looked far too thick from the back down at the bottom corner and I asked old Fred about it, who used to be gardener here before he retired. He said Mr Pembroke's son once built a sort of shed there. But there's no door, I told him. He said it was the son's business, he didn't know anything about it himself, except that he thought it had been bricked up years ago. So if it was you who built it, how do you get in?'

'You can't now,' I said. 'I did brick it up soon after I built it to stop one of my half-brothers going in there and leaving dead rats for me to find.'

'Oh.' He looked disappointed. 'I've often wondered what was in there.'

'Dead rats, dead spiders, a lot of muck.'

He shrugged. 'Oh well, then.'

'You've been very helpful,' I said. 'I'll tell my father.'

His lined face showed satisfaction. 'You tell him I'll keep the dogs and everything in good nick until he comes back.'

'He'll be grateful.'

I picked up the suitcase from inside the kitchen door, gave a last look at Moira's brilliant geraniums, vibrantly alive, shook the grubby hand of Arthur Bellbrook, and (in the car hired that morning in London) drove away towards Epsom.

Collecting my own things from my impersonal suburban flat took half the time. Unlike Malcolm, I liked things bare and orderly and, meaning always to move to somewhere better but somehow never going out to search, I hadn't decked the sitting-room or the two small bedrooms with anything brighter than new patterned curtains and a Snaffles print of Sergeant Murphy winning the 1923 Grand National.

I changed from Malcolm's trousers into some of my own, packed a suitcase and picked up my passport. I had no animals to arrange for, nor any bills pressing. Nothing anywhere to detain me.

The telephone answering machine's button glowed red, announcing messages taken. I rewound the tape and listened to the disembodied voices while I picked out of the fridge anything that would go furry and disgusting before my return.

Something, since I'd left the day before, had galvanised the family into feverish activity, like stirring an anthill with a stick.

A girlish voice came first, breathless, a shade anxious. 'Ian, this is Serena. Why are you always out? Don't you sleep at home? Mummy wants to know where Daddy is. She knows you and he aren't speaking, she's utterly thick to expect you to know, but anyway she insisted I ask you. So if you know, give me a ring back, OK?'

Serena, my half-sister, daughter of Alicia, the one child born to Alicia in wedlock. Serena, seven years my junior, lay in my distant memory chiefly as a small fair-haired charmer who'd followed me about like a shadow, which had flattered my twelve-year-old ego disgracefully. She liked best to sit on Malcolm's lap, his arms protectively around her, and from him, it had seemed to me, she could conjure a smile when he was angry and pretty dresses when she had a cupboardful.

Alicia, in sweeping out of the house when Serena was six, taking with her not only Serena but her two older boys, had left me alone in the suddenly quiet house, alone in the frilly kitchen, alone and untormented in the garden. There had been a time then when I would positively have welcomed back Gervase, the older boy, despite his dead rats and other rotten tricks; and it had actually been in the vacuum after his departure that I contrived the bricking up of my kitchen-wall room, not while he was there to jeer at it.

Grown up, Gervase still displayed the insignia of a natural bully: mean tightening of the mouth, jabbing forefinger, cold patronising stare down the nose, visible enjoyment of others' discomfiture. Serena, now tall and slim, taught aerobic dancing for a living, bought clothes still by the cartload and spoke to me only when she wanted something done.

'Mummy wants to know where Daddy is . . .' The childish terms sat oddly in the ear, somehow, coming from someone now twenty-six; and she alone of all his children had resisted calling Malcolm, Malcolm.

The next caller was Gervase himself. He started crossly, 'I don't like these message contraptions. I tried to get you all evening yesterday and I hear nothing but your priggish voice telling me to leave my name and telephone number, so this time I'm doing it, but under protest. This is your brother Gervase, as no doubt you realise, and it is imperative we find Malcolm at once. He has gone completely off his rocker. It's in your own interest to find him, Ian. We must all bury our differences and stop him spending the family money in this reckless way.' He paused briefly. 'I suppose you do know he has given half a million . . . *half a million* . . . to a busload of retarded children? I got a phone call from some stupid gushing female who said, "Oh Mr Pembroke, however can we thank you?" and when I asked her what for, she said wasn't I *the* Mr Pembroke who had solved all their problems, Mr Malcolm Pembroke? Madam, I said, what are you talking about? So she told me. *Half a million pounds*. Are you listening, Ian? He's irresponsible. It's out of proportion. He's got to be prevented from giving way to such ridiculous impulses. If you ask me, it's the beginning of senility. You must find him and tell us where he's got to, because so far as I can discover he hasn't answered his telephone since last Friday morning when I rang him to say Alicia's alimony had not been increased by the rate of inflation in this last quarter. I expect to hear from you without delay.'

His voice stopped abruptly on the peremptory order and I pictured him as he was now, not the muscular thick-set black-haired boy but the flabbier, overweight thirty-five-year-old stockbroker, over-bearingly pompous beyond his years. In a world increasingly awash with illegitimate children, he increasingly resented his own illegit-imacy, referring to it ill-temperedly on inappropriate occasions and denigrating the father who, for all his haste into bed with Alicia, had accepted Gervase publicly always as his son, and given him his surname with legal adoption.

Gervase had nonetheless been taunted early on by cruel school-mates, developing an amorphous hatred then which later focused itself on me, Ian, the half-brother who scarcely valued or understood the distinction between his birth and mine. One could understand why he'd lashed out in those raw adolescent days, but a matter of regret, I thought, that he'd never outgrown his bitterness. It remained with him, festering, colouring his whole personality, causing people often to wriggle away from his company, erupting in didactic outbursts and wretched unjustified jealousies.

Yet his wife appeared to love him forgivingly, and had produced two children, both girls, the first of them appearing a good three years after the well-attended marriage. Gervase had said a little too often that he himself would never in any circumstances have burdened a child with what he had suffered. Gervase, to my mind, would spend his last-ever moments worrying that the word 'illegitimate' would appear on his death certificate.

Ferdinand, his brother, was quite different, taking illegitimacy as of little importance, a matter of paperwork, no more.

Three years younger than Gervase, a year younger than myself, Ferdinand looked more like Malcolm than any of us, a living testimony to his parentage. Along with the features, he'd inherited the financial agility but lacking Malcolm's essential panache had carved himself a niche in an insurance company, not a multi-million fortune.

Ferdinand and I had been friends while we both lived in the house as children, but Alicia had thoroughly soured all that when she'd taken him away, dripping into all her children's ears the relentless spite of her dispossession. Ferdinand now looked at me with puzzlement as if he couldn't quite remember why he disliked me, and then Alicia would remind him sharply that if he wasn't careful I would get my clutches on his, Gervase's and Serena's rightful shares of Malcolm's money, and his face would darken again into unfriendliness.

It was a real pity about Ferdinand, I thought, but I never did much about it.

After Gervase on my answering machine came my mother, Joyce, very nearly incoherent with rage. Someone, it appeared, had already brought the *Sporting Life* to her notice. She couldn't *believe* it, she said. Words failed her. (They obviously didn't.) How *could* I have done anything as stupid as taking Malcolm to Newmarket Sales, because obviously I would have been there with him, it wasn't his scene otherwise, and why had I been so *deceitful* that morning when

I'd talked to her, and would I without fail ring her *immediately*, this was a *crisis*, Malcolm had got to be stopped.

The fourth and last message, calmer after Joyce's hysteria, was from my half-brother Thomas, the third of Malcolm's children, born to his first wife, Vivien.

Thomas, rising forty, prematurely bald, pale skinned, sporting a gingerish moustache, had married a woman who acidly belittled him every time she opened her mouth. ('Of course, Thomas is absolutely useless when it comes to . . .' [practically anything] and 'if only poor Thomas was capable of commanding a suitable salary' and 'Dear Thomas is one of life's failures, aren't you, darling?') Thomas bore it all with hardly a wince, though after years of it I observed him grow less effective and less decisive, not more, almost as if he had come to believe in and to act out his Berenice's opinion of him.

'Ian,' Thomas said in a depressed voice, 'this is Thomas. I've been trying to reach you since yesterday lunchtime but you seem to be away. When you've read my letter, please will you ring me up.'

I'd picked up his letter from my front doormat but hadn't yet opened it. I slit the envelope then and found that he too had a problem. I read:

Dear Ian,

Berenice is seriously concerned about Malcolm's wicked selfishness. She, well, to be honest, she keeps on and on about the amounts he's throwing away these days, and to be honest the only thing which has pacified her for a long time now is the thought of my eventual share of Malcolm's money, and if he goes on spending at this rate, well my life is going to be pretty *intolerable*, and I wouldn't be telling you this if you weren't my brother and the best of the bunch, which I suppose I've never said until now, but sometimes I think you're the only sane one in the family even if you do ride in those dangerous races, and, well, can you do anything to reason with Malcolm, as you're the only one he's likely to listen to, even though you haven't been talking for ages, which is unbelievable considering how you used to be with each other, and I blame that money-grubbing Moira, I really do, though Berenice used to think that anything or anyone who came between you and Malcolm could only be to my benefit, because Malcolm might with luck cut you out of his will. Well, I didn't mean to say that, old chap, but it's what Berenice thought, to be honest, until

Moira was going to take half of everything in the divorce settlement, and I really thought Berenice would have a seizure when she heard that, she was so furious. It really would save my sanity, Ian, if you could make Malcolm see that we all _NEED_ that money. I don't know what will happen if he goes on spending it at this rate. I do _BEG_ you, old chap, to stop him.

Your brother Thomas.

I looked at the letter's general incoherence and at the depth of the plea in the last few sentences with their heavily underlined words and thought of the non-stop barrage of Berenice's disgruntlement, and felt more brotherly towards Thomas than ever before. True, I still thought he should tell his wife to swallow her bile, not spill it all out on him, corroding his self-confidence and undermining his prestige with everyone within earshot; but I did at least and perhaps at last see how he could put up with it, by soothing her with the syrup of prosperity ahead.

I understood vaguely why he didn't simply ditch her and decamp: he couldn't face doing what Malcolm had done, forsaking wife and children when the going got rough. He had been taught from a very young age to despise Malcolm's inconstancy. He stayed grimly glued to Berenice and their two cheeky offspring and suffered for his virtue; and it was from fear of making the same calamitous mistake, I acknowledged, that I had married no one at all.

Thomas's was the last message on the tape. I took it out of the machine and put it in my pocket, inserting a fresh tape for future messages. I also, after a bit of thought, sorted through a boxful of family photographs, picking out groups and single pictures until I had a pretty comprehensive gallery of Pembrokes. These went into my suitcase along with a small cassette player and my best camera.

I did think of answering some of the messages, but decided against it. The arguments would all have been futile. I did truly believe in Malcolm's absolute right to do what he liked with the money he had made by his own skill and diligence. If he chose to give it in the end to his children, that was our good luck. We had no rights to it; none at all. I would have had difficulty in explaining that concept to Thomas or Joyce or Gervase or Serena, and apart from not wanting to, I hadn't the time.

I put my suitcase in the car, along with my racing saddle, helmet, whip and boots and drove back to the Savoy, being relieved to find Malcolm still there, unattacked and unharmed.

He was sitting deep in an armchair, dressed again as for the City, drinking champagne and smoking an oversize cigar. Opposite him, perched on the front edge of an identical armchair, sat a thin man of much Malcolm's age but with none of his presence.

'Norman West,' Malcolm said to me, waving the cigar vaguely at his visitor; and to the visitor he said, 'My son, Ian.'

Norman West rose to his feet and shook my hand briefly. I had never so far as I knew met a private detective before, and it wouldn't have been the occupation I would have fitted to this damp-handed nervous threadbare individual. Of medium height, he had streaky grey hair overdue for a wash, dark-circled brown eyes, greyish unhealthy skin and a day's growth of greying beard. His grey suit looked old and uncared for and his shoes had forgotten about polish. He looked as much at home in a suite in the Savoy as a punk rocker in the Vatican.

As if unerringly reading my mind he said, 'As I was just explaining to Mr Pembroke, I came straight here from an all-night observation job, as he was most insistent that it was urgent. This rig fitted my observation point. It isn't my normal gear.'

'Clothes for all seasons?' I suggested.

'Yes, that's right.'

His accent was the standard English of bygone radio announcers, slightly plummy and too good to be true. I gestured to him to sit down again, which he did as before, leaning forward from the front edge of the seat cushion and looking enquiringly at Malcolm.

'Mr West had just arrived when you came,' Malcolm said. 'Perhaps you'd better explain to him what we want.'

I sat on the spindly little sofa and said to Norman West that we wanted him to find out where every single member of our extended family had been on the previous Friday from, say, four o'clock in the afternoon onwards, and also on Tuesday, yesterday, all day.

Norman West looked from one to the other of us in obvious dismay.

'If it's too big a job,' Malcolm said, 'bring in some help.'

'It's not really *that*,' Norman West said unhappily. 'But I'm afraid there may be a conflict of interest.'

'What conflict of interest?' Malcolm demanded.

Norman West hesitated, cleared his throat and hummed a little.

Then he said, 'Last Saturday morning I was hired by one of your family to find *you*, Mr Pembroke. I've already been working, you see, for one of your family. Now you want me to check up on *them*. I don't think I should, in all conscience, accept your proposition.'

'*Which* member of my family?' Malcolm demanded.

Norman West drummed his fingers on his knee, but decided after inner debate to answer.

'Mrs Pembroke,' he said.

Four

Malcolm blinked. 'Which one?' he asked.

'Mrs Pembroke,' Norman West repeated, puzzled.

'There are nine of them,' I said. 'So which one?'

The detective looked uncomfortable. 'I spoke to her only on the telephone. I thought . . . I assumed . . . it was the Mrs Malcolm Pembroke for whom I worked once before, long ago. She referred me to that case, and asked for present help. I looked up my records . . .' He shrugged helplessly. 'I imagined it was the same lady.'

'Did you find Mr Pembroke,' I asked, 'when you were looking for him?'

Almost unwillingly, West nodded. 'In Cambridge. Not too difficult.'

'And you reported back to Mrs Pembroke?'

'I really don't think I should be discussing this any further.'

'At least, tell us how you got back in touch with Mrs Pembroke to tell her of your success.'

'I didn't,' he said. 'She rang me two or three times a day, asking for progress reports. Finally on Monday evening, I had news for her. After that, I proceeded with my next investigation, which I have now concluded. This left me free for anything Mr Pembroke might want.'

'I want you to find out which Mrs Pembroke wanted to know where I was.'

Norman West regretfully shook his unkempt head. 'A client's trust . . .' he murmured.

'A client's trust, poppycock!' Malcolm exploded. 'Someone who knew where to find me damn near killed me.'

Our detective looked shocked but rallied quickly. 'I found you, sir, by asking Mrs Pembroke for a list of places you felt at home in, as in my experience missing people often go to those places, and she gave me a list of five such possibilities, of which Cambridge was number

44

three. I didn't even go to that city looking for you. As a preliminary, I was prepared to telephone to all the hotels in Cambridge asking for you, but I tried the larger hotels first, as being more likely to appeal to you, sir, and from only the third I got a positive response. If it was as easy as that for me to find you, it was equally easy for anyone else. And, sir, if I may say so, you made things easy by registering under your own name. People who want to stay lost shouldn't do that.'

He spoke with a touching air of dignity ill-matched to his seedy appearance and for the first time I thought he might be better at his job than he looked. He must have been pretty efficient, I supposed, to have stayed in the business so long, even if catching Malcolm with his trousers off couldn't have taxed him sorely years ago.

He finished off the glass of champagne that Malcolm had given him before my arrival, and refused a refill.

'How is Mrs Pembroke paying you?' I asked.

'She said she would send a cheque.'

'When it comes,' I said, 'you'll know which Mrs Pembroke.'

'So I will.'

'I don't see why you should worry about a conflict of interests,' I said. 'After all, you've worked pretty comprehensively for various Pembrokes. You worked for my mother, Joyce Pembroke, to catch my father with the lady who gave her grounds for divorce. You worked for my father, to try to catch his fifth wife having a similar fling. You worked for the unspecified Mrs Pembroke to trace my father's whereabouts. So now he wants you to find out where all his family were last Friday and yesterday so as to be sure it was none of his close relatives who tried to kill him, as it would make him very unhappy if it were. If you can't square that with your conscience, of course with great regret he'll have to retain the services of someone else.'

Norman West eyed me with a disillusionment which again encouraged me to think him not as dim as he looked. Malcolm was glimmer-eyed with amusement.

'Pay you well, of course,' he said.

'Danger money,' I said, nodding.

Malcolm said, 'What?'

'We don't want him to step on a rattlesnake, but in fairness he has to know he might.'

Norman West looked at his short and grimy nails. He didn't seem unduly put out, nor on the other hand eager.

'Isn't this a police job?' he asked.

'Certainly,' I said. 'My father called them in when someone tried to kill him last Friday, and he'll tell you all about it. And you have to bear in mind that they're also enquiring into the murder of Moira Pembroke, whom you followed through blameless days. But you would be working for my father, not for the police, if you take his cash.'

'Pretty decisive, aren't you, sir?' he said uneasily.

'Bossy,' Malcolm agreed, 'in his quiet way.'

All those years, I thought, of getting things done in a racing stable, walking a tightrope between usurping the power of the head lad on one hand and the trainer himself on the other, like a lieutenant between a sergeant-major and a colonel. I'd had a lot of practice, one way and another, at being quietly bossy.

Malcolm unemotionally told West about his abortive walk with the dogs and the brush with carbon monoxide, and after that described also the near-miss at Newmarket.

Norman West listened attentively with slowly blinking eyes and at the end said, 'The car at Newmarket could have been accidental. Driver looking about for cigarettes, say. Not paying enough attention. Seeing you both at the last minute ... swerving desperately.'

Malcolm looked at me. 'Did it seem like that to you?'

'No.'

'Why not?' West asked.

'The rate of acceleration, I suppose.'

'Foot on accelerator going down absent-mindedly during search for cigarettes?'

'Headlights, full beam,' I said.

'A sloppy driver? Had a few drinks?'

'Maybe.' I shook my head. 'The real problem is that if the car *had* hit us – or Malcolm – there might have been witnesses. The driver might have been stopped before he could leave the sales area. The car number might have been taken.'

West smiled sorrowfully. 'It's been done successfully before now, in broad daylight in a crowded street.'

'Are you saying,' Malcolm demanded of me, 'that the car *wasn't* trying to kill me?'

'No, only that the driver took a frightful risk.'

'Did any witnesses rush to pick us up?' Malcolm asked forcefully.

'Did anyone so much as pass a sympathetic remark? No, they damned well didn't. Did anyone try to stop the driver or take his number? The hell they did.'

'All the same,' West said, 'your son is right. Hit-and-run in a public place has its risks. If it was tried here, and sirs, I'm not saying it wasn't, the putative gain must have outweighed the risk, or, er, in other words – '

'In other words,' Malcolm interrupted with gloom, 'Ian is right to think they'll try again.'

Norman West momentarily looked infinitely weary, as if the sins of the world were simply too much to contemplate. He had seen, I supposed, as all investigators must, a lifetime's procession of sinners and victims; and, moreover, he looked roughly seventy and hadn't slept all night.

'I'll take your job,' he said without enthusiasm, radiating minimum confidence, and I glanced at Malcolm to see if he really thought this was the best we could do in detectives, signs of intelligence or not. Malcolm appeared to have no doubts, however, and spent the next five minutes discussing fees which seemed ominously moderate to me.

'And I'll need a list,' West said finally, 'of the people you want checked. Names and addresses and normal habits.'

Malcolm showed unexpected discomfort, as if checking that amorphous entity 'the family' was different from checking each individual separately, and it was I who found a piece of Savoy writing paper to draw up the list.

'OK,' I said, 'first of all there's Vivien, my father's first wife. Mrs Vivien Pembroke.'

'Not her,' Malcolm objected. 'It's ridiculous.'

'Everyone,' I said firmly. 'No exceptions. That makes it fair on everyone ... because there are going to be some extremely angry relations when they all realise what's happening.'

'They won't find out,' Malcolm said.

Fat chance, I thought.

To West, I said, 'They all telephone each other all the time, not by any means always out of friendship but quite often out of spite. They won't gang up against you because they seldom form alliances among themselves. Some of them are pretty good liars. Don't believe everything they say about each other.'

'*Ian!*' Malcolm said protestingly.

'I'm one of them, and I know,' I said.

After Vivien's name on the list I wrote the names of her children:

   Donald

   Lucy

   Thomas

'Thomas,' I said, 'is married to Berenice.' I added her name beside his. 'He is easy to deal with, she is not.'

'She's a five-star cow,' Malcolm said.

West merely nodded.

'Lucy,' I said, 'married a man called Edwin Bugg. She didn't like that surname, and persuaded him to change it to hers, and she is consequently herself a Mrs Pembroke.'

West nodded.

'Lucy is a poet,' I said. 'People who know about poetry say her stuff is the real thing. She makes a big production of unworldliness which Edwin, I think, has grown to find tiresome.'

'Huh,' Malcolm said. 'Edwin's an out-and-out materialist, always tapping me for a loan.'

'Do you give them to him?' I said interestedly.

'Not often. He never pays me back.'

'Short of money, are they?' West asked.

'Edwin Bugg,' Malcolm said, 'married Lucy years ago because he thought she was an heiress, and they've scraped along ever since on the small income she gets from a trust fund I set up for her. Edwin's never done a stroke of work in his parasitic life and I can't stand the fellow.'

'They have one teenage schoolboy son,' I said, smiling, 'who asked me the last time I saw him how to set about emigrating to Australia.'

West looked at the list and said to Malcolm, 'What about Donald, your eldest?'

'Donald,' said his father, 'married a replica of his mother, beautiful and brainless. A girl called Helen. They live an utterly boring virtuous life in Henley-on-Thames and are still billing and cooing like newlyweds although Donald must be nearly forty-five, I suppose.'

No one commented. Malcolm himself, rising sixty-nine, could bill and coo with the best, and with a suppressed shiver I found myself thinking for the first time about the *sixth* marriage, because certainly, in the future, if Malcolm survived, there would be one. He had never in the past lived long alone. He liked rows better than solitude.

'Children?' Norman West asked into the pause.

'Three,' Malcolm said. 'Pompous little asses.'

West glanced at me questioningly, and yawned.

'Are you too tired to take all this in?' I asked.

'No, go ahead.'

'Two of Donald's children are too young to drive a car. The eldest, a girl at art school, is five foot two and fragile, and I cannot imagine her being physically capable of knocking Malcolm out and carrying his body from garden to garage and inserting him into Moira's car.'

'She hasn't the courage either,' Malcolm said.

'You can't say that,' I disagreed. 'Courage can pop up anywhere and surprise you.'

West gave me a noncommittal look. 'Well,' he said, taking the list himself and adding to it, 'this is what we have so far. Wife number one: Vivien Pembroke. Her children: Donald (44), wife Helen, three offspring. Lucy, husband Edwin (né Bugg), school-age son. Thomas, wife Berenice . . .?'

'Two young daughters.'

'Two young daughters,' he repeated, writing.

'My grandchildren,' Malcolm protested, 'are all too young to have murdered anybody.'

'Psychopaths start in the nursery,' West said laconically. 'Any sign in any of them of abnormal violent behaviour? Excessive cruelty, that sort of thing? Obsessive hatreds?'

Malcolm and I both shook our heads but with a touch of uncertainty; his maybe because of something he did know, mine because of all I didn't know, because of all the things that could be hidden.

'Does greed, too, begin in the nursery?' I said.

'I wouldn't say so, would you?' West answered.

I shook my head again. 'I'd say it was nastily adult and grows with opportunity. The more there is to grab, the greedier people get.'

Malcolm said, only half as a question, 'My fortune corrupts . . . geometrically?'

'You're not alone,' I said dryly. 'Just think of all those multi-billionaire families where the children have already had millions settled on them and still fight like cats over the pickings when their father dies.'

'Bring it down to thousands,' West said unexpectedly. 'Or to hundreds. I've seen shocking spite over hundreds. And the lawyers rub their hands and syphon off the cream.' He sighed, half disillusionment, half weariness. 'Wife number two?' he asked, and answered his own question, 'Mrs Joyce Pembroke.'

'Right,' I said. 'I'm her son. She had no other children. And I'm not married.'

West methodically wrote me down.

'Last Friday evening,' I said, 'I was at work in a racing stable at five o'clock with about thirty people as witnesses, and last night I was certainly not driving the car that nearly ran us over.'

West said stolidly, 'I'll write you down as being cleared of primary involvement. That's all I can do with any of your family, Mr Pembroke.' He finished the sentence looking at Malcolm who said, 'Hired assassin' between his teeth, and West nodded. 'If any of them hired a good professional, I doubt if I'll discover it.'

'I thought good assassins used rifles,' I said.

'Some do. Most don't. They pick their own way. Some use knives. Some garotte. I knew of one who used to wait at traffic lights along his victim's usual route to work. One day, the lights would be red, the victim would stop. The assassin tapped on the window, asking a question . . . or so it's supposed. The victim wound down the window and the assassin shot him point blank in the head. By the time the lights turned green and the cars behind started tooting their horns, the assassin had long gone.'

'Did they ever catch him?' I asked.

West shook his head. 'Eight prominent businessmen were killed that way within two years. Then it stopped. No one knows why. My guess is the assassin lost his nerve. It happens in every profession.'

I thought of jump jockeys to whom it had happened almost overnight, and I supposed it occurred in stockbrokers also. Any profession, as he said.

'Or someone bumped him off because he knew too much,' Malcolm said.

'That too is possible.' West looked at the list. 'After Mrs Joyce?'

Malcolm said sourly, 'The lady you so artfully photographed me with at the instigation of, as you call her, Mrs Joyce.'

The West eyebrows slowly rose. 'Miss Alicia Sandways? With, if I remember, two little boys?'

'The little boys are now thirty-five and thirty-two,' I said.

'Yes.' He sighed. 'As I said, I recently dug out that file. I didn't realise that . . . er . . . Well, so we have wife number three, Mrs Alicia Pembroke. And her children?'

50

Malcolm said, 'The two boys, Gervase and Ferdinand. I formally adopted them when I married their mother, and changed their surname to Pembroke. Then we had little Serena,' his face softened, 'and it was for her I put up with Alicia's tantrums the last few years we were together. Alicia was a great mistress but a rotten wife. Don't ask me why. I indulged her all the time, let her do what she liked with my house, and in the end nothing would please her.' He shrugged. 'I gave her a generous divorce settlement, but she was very bitter. I wanted to keep little Serena . . . and Alicia screamed that she supposed I didn't want the boys because they were illegitimate. She fought in the courts for Serena, and she won . . . She filled all her children's heads with bad feelings for me.' The old hurt plainly showed. 'Serena did suggest coming back to look after me when Coochie was killed, but it wasn't necessary because Moira was there. When Moira was killed, she offered again. It was kind of Serena. She's a nice girl, really, but Alicia tries to set her against me.'

West, in a pause that might or might not have been sympathetic, wrote after Alicia's name:

Gervase. Illegitimate at birth, subsequently adopted
Ferdinand. The same
Serena. Legitimate

'Are they married?' he asked.

'Gervase has a wife called Ursula,' I said. 'I don't know her well, because when I see them they're usually together and it's always Gervase who does the talking. They too, like Thomas, have two little girls.'

West wrote it down.

'Ferdinand,' I said, 'has married two raving beauties in rapid succession. The first, American, has gone back to the States. The second one, Deborah, known as Debs, is still in residence. So far, no children.'

West wrote.

'Serena,' I said, 'is unmarried.'

West completed that section of the list. 'So we have wife number three, Mrs Alicia Pembroke. Her children are Gervase, wife Ursula, two small daughters. Ferdinand, current wife Debs, no children. Serena, unmarried . . . er . . . , a fiancé, perhaps? Live-in lover?'

'I don't know of one,' I said, and Malcolm said he didn't know either.

'Right,' West said. 'Wife number four?'

There was a small silence. Then I said, 'Coochie. She's dead. She had twin sons. One was killed with her in a car crash, the other is brain-damaged and lives in a nursing home.'

'Oh.' The sound carried definite sympathy this time. 'And wife number five, Mrs Moira Pembroke, did she perhaps have any children from a previous marriage?'

'No,' Malcolm said. 'No previous marriage, no children.'

'Right.' West counted up his list. 'That's three ex-wives . . . er, by the way, did any of them remarry?'

I answered with a faint smile, 'They would lose their alimony if they did. Malcolm was pretty generous in their settlements. None of them has seen any financial sense in remarrying.'

'They all should have done,' Malcolm grumbled. 'They wouldn't be so warped.'

West said merely, 'Right. Then, er, six sons, two daughters. Four current daughters-in-law, one son-in-law. Grand-children . . . too young. So, er, discounting the invalid son and Mr Ian here, there are fourteen adults to be checked. That will take me a week at least. Probably more.'

'As fast as you can,' I said.

He looked actually as if he had barely enough strength or confidence to get himself out of the door let alone embark on what was clearly an arduous task.

'Can I tell them all why I'm making these enquiries?' he asked.

'Yes, you damned well can,' Malcolm said positively. 'If it's one of them, and I hope to God it isn't, it might put the wind up them and frighten them off. Just don't tell them where to find me.'

I looked down at the list. I couldn't visualise any of them as being criminally lethal, but then greed affected otherwise rational people in irrational ways. All sorts of people . . . I knew of a case when two male relatives had gone into a house where an old woman had been reported newly dead, and taken the bedroom carpet off the floor, rolling it up and making off with it and leaving her lying alone in her bed above bare boards, all to seize her prize possession before the rest of the family could get there. Unbelievable, I'd thought it. The old woman's niece, who cleaned my flat every week, had been most indignant, but not on her aunt's account. 'It was the only good carpet in the house,' she vigorously complained. 'Nearly new. The only thing worth having. It should have come to me, by rights. Now I'll never get it.'

'I'll need all their addresses,' West said.

Malcolm waved a hand. 'Ian can tell you. Get him to write them down.'

Obediently I opened my suitcase, took out my address book and wrote the whole list, with telephone numbers. Then I got out the pack of photographs and showed them to West.

'Would they help you?' I asked. 'If they would, I'll lend them to you, but I want them back.'

West looked through them one by one, and I knew that he could see, if he were any detective at all, all the basic characters of the subjects. I liked taking photographs and preferred portraits, and somehow taking a camera along gave me something positive to do whenever the family met. I didn't like talking to some of them; photography gave me a convincing reason for disengagements and drifting around.

If there was one common factor in many of the faces it was discontent, which I thought was sad. Only in Ferdinand could one see real lightheartedness, and even in him, as I knew, it could come and go; and Debs, his second wife, was a stunning blonde, taller than her husband, looking out at the world quizzically as if she couldn't quite believe her eyes, not yet soured by disappointment.

I'd caught Gervase giving his best grade-one bullying down-the-nose stare, and saw no good purpose in ever showing him the reflection of his soul. Ursula merely looked indeterminate and droopy and somehow guilty, as if she thought she shouldn't even have her photo taken without Gervase's permission.

Berenice, Thomas's wife, was the exact opposite, staring disapprovingly straight into the lens, bold and sarcastic, unerringly destructive every time she uttered. And Thomas, a step behind her, looking harried and anxious. Another of Thomas alone, smiling uneasily, defeat in the sag of his shoulders, desperation in his eyes.

Vivien, Joyce and Alicia, the three witches, dissimilar in features but alike in expression, had been caught when they weren't aware of the camera, each of them watching someone else with disfavour.

Alicia, fluffy and frilly, still wore her hair brought youthfully high to a ribbon bow on the crown, from where rich brown curls tumbled in a cascade to her shoulders. Nearly sixty, she looked in essence younger than her son Gervase, and she would still have been pretty but for the pinched hardness of her mouth.

She had been a fair sort of mother to me for the seven years of her reign, seeing to my ordinary needs like food and new clothes and treating me no different from Gervase and Ferdinand, but I'd never felt like going to her for advice or comfort. She hadn't loved me, nor I her, and after the divorce we had neither felt any grief in separation. I'd detested what she'd done afterwards to Gervase, Ferdinand and Serena, twisting their minds with her own spite. I would positively have liked to have had friendly brothers and sisters as much as Malcolm would have valued friendly children. After nearly twenty years, Alicia's intense hurt still spread suffering outward in ripples.

Serena's picture showed her as she had been a year earlier, before aerobic dancing had slimmed her further to a sexless-looking leanness. The fair hair of childhood had slightly darkened, and was stylishly cut in a short becoming cap-shape which made her look young for her twenty-six years. A leggy Peter Pan, I thought, not wanting to grow up: a girl-woman with a girlish voice saying 'Mummy and Daddy', and an insatiable appetite for clothes. I wondered briefly whether she were still a virgin and felt faintly surprised to find that I simply didn't know and, moreover, couldn't tell.

'These are very interesting,' West said, glancing at me. 'I should certainly like to borrow them.' He shuffled them around and sorted them out. 'Who are these? You haven't put their names on the back, like the others.'

'That's Lucy and Edwin, and that's Donald and Helen.'

'Thanks.' He wrote the identification carefully in small neat letters.

Malcolm stretched out a hand for the photographs which West gave him. Malcolm looked through them attentively and finally gave them back.

'I don't remember seeing any of these before,' he said.

'They're all less than three years old.'

His mouth opened and shut again. He gave me a brooding look, as if I'd just stabbed him unfairly in the ribs.

'What do you think of them?' I asked.

'A pity children grow up.'

West smiled tiredly and collected the lists and photographs together.

'Right, Mr Pembroke. I'll get started.' He stood up and swayed slightly, but when I took a step forward to steady him he waved me away. 'Just lack of sleep.' On his feet, he looked even nearer to exhaustion, as if the outer greyness had penetrated inwards to the core. 'First thing in the morning, I'll be checking the Pembrokes.'

It would have been churlish to expect him to start that afternoon, but I can't say I liked the delay. I offered him another drink and a reviving lunch, which he declined, so I took him to the hotel's front door and saw him safely into a taxi, watching him sink like a collapsing scarecrow into the seat cushions.

Returning to the suite, I found Malcolm ordering vodka and Beluga caviar from room service with the abandon to which I was becoming accustomed. That done, he smoothed out the *Sporting Life* and pointed to one section of it.

'It says the Arc de Triomphe race is due to be run this Sunday in Paris.'

'Yes, that's right.'

'Then let's go.'

'All right,' I said.

Malcolm laughed. 'We may as well have some fun. There's a list here of the runners.'

I looked where he pointed. It was a bookmaker's advertisement showing the ante-post prices on offer.

'What are the chances,' Malcolm said, 'of my buying one of these horses?'

'Er,' I said. 'Today, do you mean?'

'Of course. No good buying one *after* the race, is there?'

'Well . . .'

'No, of course not. The winner will be worth millions and the others peanuts. *Before* the race, that's the thing.'

'I don't suppose anyone will sell,' I said, 'but we can try. How high do you want to go? The favourite won the Epsom Derby and is reported to be going to be syndicated for ten million pounds. You'd have to offer a good deal more than that before they'd consider selling him now.'

'Hm,' Malcolm said. 'What do you think of him as a horse?'

I smothered a gasp or two and said with a deadpan face, 'He's a very good horse but he had an exceptionally exhausting race last time out. I don't think he's had enough time to recover, and I wouldn't back him this time.'

'Have you backed him before?' Malcolm asked curiously.

'Yes, when he won the Derby, but he was favourite for that, too.'

'What do you think will win the Arc de Triomphe, then?'

'Seriously?' I said.

'Of course seriously.'

'One of the French horses, Meilleurs Voeux.'

'Can we buy him?'

'Not a hope. His owner loves his horses, loves winning more than profit and is immensely rich.'

'So am I,' Malcolm said simply. 'I can't help making money. It used to be a passion, now it's a habit. But this business about Moira jolted me, you know. It struck me that I may not have a hell of a lot of time left, not with enough health and strength to enjoy life. I've spent all these years amassing the stuff, and for what? For my goddam children to murder me for? Sod that for a sad story. You buy me a good horse in this race on Sunday and we'll go and yell it home, boy, at the top of our lungs.'

It took all afternoon and early evening to get even a tinge of interest from anyone. I telephoned to the trainers of the English – or Irish – runners, asking if they thought their owners might sell. I promised each trainer that he would go on training the horse, and that my father would send him also the two-million-guinea colt he'd bought yesterday. Some of the trainers were at the Newmarket Sales and had to be tracked down to hotels, and once tracked, had to track and consult with their owners. Some simply said no, forget it.

Finally, at seven forty-five, a trainer from Newmarket rang back to say his owner would sell a half-share if his price was met. I relayed the news and the price to Malcolm.

'What do you think?' he said.

'Um . . . the horse is quite good, the price is on the high side, the trainer's in the top league.'

'OK.' Malcolm said. 'Deal.'

'My father accepts,' I said. 'And, er, the colt is still in the Sales stables. Can you fetch it tomorrow, if we clear it with the auctioneers?'

Indeed he could. He sounded quite cheerful altogether. He would complete his paperwork immediately if Malcolm could transfer the money directly to his bloodstock account, bank and account number supplied. I wrote the numbers to his dictation. Malcolm waved a hand and said, 'No problem. First thing in the morning. He'll have it by afternoon.'

'Well,' I said, breathing out as I put the receiver down, 'you now own half of Blue Clancy.'

'Let's drink to it,' Malcolm said. 'Order some Bollinger.'

I ordered it from room service, and while we waited for it to arrive I told him about my encounter with his gardener, Arthur Bellbrook.

'Decent chap,' Malcolm said, nodding. 'Damned good gardener.'

I told him wryly about Moira and the prize vegetables, which he knew nothing about.

'Silly bitch,' he said. 'Arthur lives in a terrace house with a pocket handkerchief garden facing north. You couldn't grow prize stuff there. If she'd asked me I'd have told her that, and told her to leave him alone. Good gardeners are worth every perk they get.'

'He seemed pretty philosophical,' I said, 'and, incidentally, pretty bright. He'd spotted that the kitchen garden wall is thicker than it should be at the corner. He'd asked old Fred, and heard about the room I built there. He wanted to know how to get in, so he could use it as an apple store.'

Malcolm practically ejected from his armchair, alarm widening his eyes, his voice coming out strangled and hoarse. 'My God, you didn't tell him, did you?'

'No, I didn't,' I said slowly. 'I told him it was empty and was bricked up twenty years ago.' I paused. 'What have you put in there?'

Malcolm subsided into his chair, not altogether relieved of anxiety.

'Never you mind,' he said.

'You forget that I could go and look.'

'I don't forget it.'

He stared at me. He'd been interested, all those summers ago, when I'd designed and built the pivoting brick door. He'd come down the garden day after day to watch, and had patted me often on the shoulder, and smiled at the secret. The resulting wall looked solid, felt solid, *was* solid. But at one point there was a thick vertical steel rod within it, stretching from a concrete underground foundation up into the beam supporting the roof. Before I'd put the new roof on, I'd patiently drilled round holes in bricks (breaking many) and slid them into the rod, and arranged and mortared the door in neat courses, so that the edges of it dovetailed into the fixed sections next to it.

To open the room, when I'd finished everything, one had first to remove the wedge-like wooden sill which gave extra support to the bottom course of the door when it was closed, and then to activate the spring latch on the inner side by poking a thin wire through a tiny hole in the mortar at what had been my thirteen-year-old waist height. The design of the latch hadn't been my own, but something I'd read in a book: at any rate, when I'd installed it, it worked obligingly at once.

It had pleased me intensely to build a door that Gervase would never find. No more dead rats. No more live birds, shut in and fluttering with fright. No more invasions of my own private place.

Gervase had never found the door and nor had anyone else and, as the years passed, grass grew long in front of the wall, and nettles, and although I'd meant to give the secret to Robin and Peter some day, I hadn't done so by the time of the crash. Only Malcolm knew how to get in — and Malcolm had used the knowledge.

'What's in there?' I repeated.

He put on his airiest expression. 'Just some things I didn't want Moira to get her hands on.'

I remembered sharply the objects missing from his study.

'The gold dolphin, the amethyst tree, the silver candelabra ... those?'

'You've been looking,' he accused.

I shook my head. 'I noticed they were gone.'

The few precious objects, all the same, hardly accounted for the severity of his first alarm.

'What else is in there?' I said.

'Actually,' he said, calmly now, 'quite a lot of gold.'

Five

'Some people buy and sell gold without ever seeing it,' he said. 'But I like possessing the actual stuff. There's no fun in paper transactions. Gold is beautiful on its own account, and I like to see it and feel it. But it's not all that easy to store it in banks or safety deposits. Too heavy and bulky. And insurance is astronomical. Takes too much of the profit. I never insure it.'

'You're storing it there in the wall . . . waiting for the price to rise?'

'You know me, don't you?' He smiled. 'Buy low, bide your time, sell high. Wait a couple of years, not often more. The price of gold itself swings like a pendulum, but there's nothing, really, like gold shares. When gold prices rise, gold shares often rise by two or three times as much. I sell the gold first and the shares a couple of months later. Psychological phenomenon, you know, that people go on investing in gold mines, pushing the price up, when the price of gold itself is static or beginning to drop. Illogical, but invaluable to people like me.'

He sat looking at me with the vivid blue eyes, teaching his child.

'Strategic Minerals, now. There never was anything like the Strategic Minerals Corporation of Australia. This year, the price of gold itself rose twenty-five per cent, but Strats – shares in Strategic Minerals – rose nearly a thousand per cent before they dropped off the top. Incredible. I got in near the beginning of those and sold at nine hundred and fifty per cent profit. But don't be fooled, Strats happen only once or twice in a lifetime.'

'How much,' I said, fascinated, 'did you invest in Strats?'

After a brief pause he said, 'Five million. I had a feeling about them . . . they just smelled right. I don't often go in so deep, and I didn't expect them to fly so high, no one could, but there you are, all gold shares rose this year, and Strats rose like a skylark.'

'How are they doing now?' I asked.

'Don't know. I'm concerned with the present. Gold mines, you see, don't go on for ever. They have a life: exploration, development, production, exhaustion. I get in, wait a while, take a profit, forget them. Never stay too long with a rising gold share. Fortunes are lost by selling too late.'

He did truly trust me, I thought. If he'd doubted me still, he wouldn't have told me there was gold behind the brick door, nor that even after tax he had made approximately thirty million pounds on one deal. I stopped worrying that he was overstretching himself in buying the colt and a half-share in Blue Clancy. I stopped worrying about practically everything except how to keep him alive and spending.

I'd talked to someone once whose father had died when she was barely twenty. She regretted that she hadn't ever known him adult to adult, and wished she could meet him again, just to talk. Watching Malcolm, it struck me that in a way I'd been given her wish: that the three years' silence had been a sort of death, and that I could talk to him now adult to adult, and know him as a man, not as a father.

We spent a peaceful evening together in the suite, talking about what we'd each done during the hiatus, and it was difficult to imagine that outside, somewhere, a predator might be searching for the prey.

At one point I said, 'You gave Joyce's telephone number on purpose to the film man, didn't you? And Gervase's number to the retarded-children lady? You wanted me with you to see you buy the colt . . . You made sure that the family knew all about your monster outlays as soon as possible, didn't you?'

'Huh,' he said briefly, which after a moment I took as admission. One misdirected telephone call had been fairly possible: two stretched credibility too far.

'Thomas and Berenice,' I said, 'were pretty frantic over some little adventure of yours. What did you do to stir *them* up?'

'How the hell do you know all this?'

I smiled and fetched the cassette player, and re-ran for him the message tape from my telephone. He listened grimly but with an undercurrent of amusement to Serena, Gervase and Joyce and then read Thomas's letter, and when he reached Thomas's intense closing appeal I waited for explosions.

They didn't come. He said wryly, 'I suppose they're what I made them.'

60

'No,' I said.

'Why not?'

'Personality is mysterious, but it's born in you, not made.'

'But it can be brainwashed.'

'Yes, OK,' I said. 'But you didn't do it.'

'Vivien and Alicia did . . . because of me.'

'Don't wallow in guilt so much. It isn't like you.'

He grinned. 'I don't feel guilty, actually.'

Joyce, I thought, had at least played fair. A screaming fury she might have been on the subject of Alicia, but she'd never tried to set me against Malcolm. She had agreed in the divorce settlement when I was six that he should have custody of me: she wasn't basically maternal, and infrequent visits from her growing son were all she required. She'd never made great efforts to bind me to her, and it had always been clear to me that she was relieved every time at my departure. Her life consisted of playing, teaching, and writing about bridge, a game she played to international tournament standard, and she was often abroad. My visits had always disrupted the acute concentration she needed for winning, and as winning gave her the prestige essential for lecture tours and magazine articles, I had more often raised impatience in her than comradeship, a feeling she had dutifully tried to stifle.

She had given me unending packs of cards to play with and had taught me a dozen card games, but I'd never had her razor memory of any and every card played in any and every game, a perpetual disappointment to her and a matter for impatience in itself. When I veered off to make my life in a totally different branch of the entertainment industry, she had been astonished at my choice and at first scornful, but had soon come round to checking the racing pages during the steeplechase season to see if I was listed as riding.

'What did you tell Thomas and Berenice?' I asked Malcolm again, after a pause.

With satisfaction he said, 'I absentmindedly gave their telephone number to a wine merchant who was to let me know the total I owed him for the fifty or so cases of 1979 Pol Roger he was collecting for me to drink.'

'And, er, roughly how much would that cost?'

'The 1979, the Winston Churchill vintage, is quite exceptional, you know.'

'Of course it would be,' I said.

'Roughly twenty-five thousand pounds, then, for fifty cases.'

Poor Thomas, I thought.

'I also made sure that Alicia knew I'd given about a quarter of a million pounds to fund scholarships for bright girls at the school Serena went to. Alicia and I haven't been talking recently. I suppose she's furious I gave it to the school and not to Serena herself.'

'Well, why did you?'

He looked surprised. 'You know my views. You must all carve your own way. To make you all rich too young would rob you of incentive.'

I certainly did know his views, but I wasn't sure I always agreed with them. I would have had bags of incentive to make a success of being a racehorse trainer if he'd lent, advanced or given me enough to start, but I also knew that if he did, he'd have to do as much for the others (being ordinarily a fair man), and he didn't believe in it, as he said.

'Why did you want them all to know how much you've been spending?' I asked. 'Because of course they all will know by now. The telephone wires will have been red hot.'

'I suppose I thought ... um ... if they believed I was getting rid of most of it there would be less point in killing me ... do you see?'

I stared at him. 'You must be crazy,' I said. 'It sounds to me like an invitation to be murdered without delay.'

'Ah well, that too has occurred to me of late.' He smiled vividly. 'But I have you with me now to prevent that.'

After a speechless moment I said, 'I may not always be able to see the speeding car.'

'I'll trust your eyesight.'

I pondered. 'What else have you spent a bundle on, that I haven't heard about?'

He drank some champagne and frowned, and I guessed that he was trying to decide whether or not to tell me. Finally he sighed and said, 'This is for your ears only. I didn't do it for the same reason, and I did it earlier ... several weeks ago, in fact, before Moira was murdered.' He paused. 'She was angry about it, though she'd no right to be. It wasn't her money. She hated me to give anything to anyone else. She wanted everything for herself.' He sighed. 'I don't know how you knew right from the beginning what she was like.'

'Her calculator eyes,' I said.

62

He smiled ruefully. He must have seen that look perpetually, by the end.

'The nursing home where Robin is,' he said unexpectedly, 'needed repairs. So I paid for them.'

He wasn't talking, I gathered, in terms of a couple of replaced window-frames.

'Of course, you know it's a private nursing home?' he said. 'A family business, basically.'

'Yes.'

'They needed a new roof. New wiring. A dozen urgent upgradings. They tried raising the residential fees too high and lost patients, familiar story. They asked my advice about fund-raising. I told them not to bother. I'd get estimates, and all I'd want in return was that they'd listen to a good business consultant who I'd send them.' He shifted comfortably in his armchair. 'Robin's settled there. Calm. Any change upsets him, as you know. If the whole place closed and went out of business, which was all too likely, I'd have to find somewhere else for him, and he's lost enough . . .'

His voice tapered off. He had delighted in Robin and Peter when they'd been small, playing with them on the carpet like a young father, proud of them as if they were his first children, not his eighth and ninth. Good memories: worth a new roof.

'I know you still go to visit him,' he said. 'The nurses tell me. So you must have seen the place growing threadbare.'

I nodded, thinking about it. 'They used to have huge vases of fresh flowers everywhere.'

'They used to have top quality everything, but they've had to compromise to patch up the building. Country houses are open money drains when they age. I can't see the place outliving Robin, really. You will look after him, when I've gone?'

'Yes,' I said.

He nodded, taking it for granted. 'I appointed you his trustee when I set up the fund for him, do you remember? I've not altered it.'

I was glad that he hadn't. At least, somewhere, obscurely, things had remained the same between us.

'Why don't we go and see him tomorrow?' he said. 'No one will kill me there.'

'All right,' I agreed: so we went in the hired car in the morning, stopping in the local town to buy presents of chocolate and simple toys designed for three-year-olds, and I added a packet of balloons to the pile while Malcolm paid.

'Does he like balloons?' he asked, his eyebrows rising.

'He gets frustrated sometimes. I blow the balloons up, and he bursts them.'

Malcolm looked surprised and in some ways disturbed. 'I didn't know he could feel frustration.'

'It seems like that. As if sometimes he half remembers us . . . but can't quite.'

'Poor boy.'

We drove soberly onwards and up the drive of the still splendid-looking Georgian house which lay mellow and symmetrical in the autumn sunshine. Inside, its near fifty rooms had been adapted and transformed in the heyday of private medicine into a highly comfortable hospital for mostly chronic, mostly old, mostly rich patients. Short-stay patients came and went, usually convalescing after major operations performed elsewhere, but in general one saw the same faces month after month: the same faces ageing, suffering, waiting for release. Dreadfully depressing, I found it, but for Robin, it was true, it seemed the perfect haven, arrived at after two unsuccessful stays in more apparently suitable homes involving other children, bright colours, breezy nurses and jollying atmospheres. Robin seemed better with peace, quiet and no demands, and Malcolm had finally acted against professional advice to give them to him.

Robin had a large room on the ground floor with french doors opening on to a walled garden. He seldom went out into the garden, but he preferred the doors open in all weathers, including snow-storms. Apart from that, he was docile and easy to deal with, and if anyone had speculated on the upheavals that might happen soon if puberty took its natural course, they hadn't mentioned it in my hearing.

He looked at us blankly, as usual. He seldom spoke, though he did retain the ability to make words: it was just that he seemed to have few thoughts to utter. Brain damage of that magnitude was idiosyncratic, we'd been told, resulting in behaviour individual to each victim. Robin spoke rarely and then only to himself, in private, when he didn't expect to be overheard: the nurses sometimes heard him, and had told us, but said he stopped as soon as he saw them. I'd asked them what he said, but they didn't know, except for words like 'shoes' and 'bread' and 'floor': ordinary words. They didn't know why he wouldn't speak at other times. They were sure, though, that he understood a fair amount of what others said, even if in a haze.

We gave him some pieces of chocolate which he ate, and unwrapped the toys for him which he fingered but didn't play with. He looked at the balloon packet without emotion. It wasn't a frustration day: on those, he looked at the packet and made blowing noises with his mouth.

We sat with him for quite a while, talking, telling him who we were while he wandered around the room. He looked at our faces from time to time, and touched my nose once with his finger as if exploring that I was really there, but there was no connection with our minds. He looked healthy, good looking, a fine boy: heartbreaking, as always.

A nurse came in the end, middle-aged, kind-faced, to take him to a dining-room for lunch, and Malcolm and I transferred to the office where my father was given a saviour's welcome and offered a reviving scotch.

'Your son, slow progress, I'm afraid.' Earnest, dedicated people. Malcolm nodded. No progress would have been more accurate.

'We do our best for him always.'

'Yes, I know.' Malcolm drank the scotch, shook their hands, made our farewells. We left, as I always left, in sadness, silence and regret.

'So bloody unfair,' Malcolm said halfway back to London. 'He ought to be laughing, talking, roaring through life.'

'Yes.'

'I can't bear to see him, and I can't bear not to. I'd give all my money to have him well again.'

'And make a new fortune afterwards,' I said.

'Well, yeah, why not?' He laughed, but still with gloom. 'It would have been better if he'd died with the others. Life's a bugger, sometimes, isn't it?'

The gloom lasted back to the Savoy and through the next bottle of Bollinger, but by afternoon Malcolm was complaining of the inactivity I'd thrust upon him and wanting to visit cronies in the City. Unpredictability be our shield, I prayed, and kept my eyes open for speeding cars; but we saw the day out safely in offices, bars, clubs and a restaurant, during which time Malcolm increased his wealth by gambling a tenner at evens on the day's closing price of gold which fell by two pounds when the trend was upwards. 'It'll shoot right up next year, you watch.'

On Friday, despite my pleas for sanity, he insisted on accompanying me to Sandown Park races.

'You'll be safer here,' I protested, 'in the suite.'

'I shan't *feel* safer.'

'At the races, I can't stay beside you.'

'Who's to know I'll be there?'

I gazed at him. 'Anyone who guesses we are now together could know. They'll know how to find *me*, if they look in the papers.'

'Then don't go.'

'I'm going. You stay here.'

I saw, however, that the deep underlying apprehension which he tried to suppress most of the time would erupt into acute nervous anxiety if I left him alone in the suite for several hours, and that he might, out of boredom, do something much sillier than going to the races, like convincing himself that anyone in his family would keep a secret if he asked it.

Accordingly I drove him south of London and took him through the jockeys' entrance gate to the weighing-room area where he made his afternoon a lot safer by meeting yet another crony and being instantly invited to lunch in the holy of holies.

'Do you have cronies all over the world?' I asked.

'Certainly,' he said, smiling broadly. 'Anyone I've known for five minutes is a crony, if I get on with them.'

I believed him. Malcolm wasn't easy to forget, nor was he hard to like. I saw the genuine pleasure in his immediate host's face as they walked away together, talking, and reflected that Malcolm would have been a success in whatever career he had chosen, that success was part of his character, like generosity, like headlong rashness.

I was due to ride in the second race, a steeplechase for amateurs, and as usual had arrived two prudent hours in advance. I turned away from watching Malcolm and looked around for the owner of the horse I was about to partner, and found my path blocked by a substantial lady in a wide brown cape. Of all the members of the family, she was the last I would have expected to see on a racecourse.

'Ian,' she said accusingly, almost as if I'd been pretending to be someone else.

'Hello.'

'Where have you been? Why don't you answer your telephone?'

Lucy, my elder half-sister. Lucy, the poet.

Lucy's husband Edwin was, as always, to be found at her side, rather as if he had no separate life. The leech, Malcolm had called him unkindly in the past. From a Bugg to a leech.

Lucy was blessed with an unselfconsciousness about her weight which stemmed both from unworldliness and an overbelief in health foods. 'But nuts and raisins are *good* for you,' she would say, eating them by the kilo. 'Bodily vanity, like intellectual arrogance, is a sickness of the soul.'

She was forty-two, my sister, with thick straight brown hair uncompromisingly cut, large brown eyes, her mother's high cheek-bones and her father's strong nose. She was as noticeable in her own way as Malcolm was himself, and not only because of her shapeless clothes and dedicated absence of cosmetics. Malcolm's vitality ran in her too, though in different directions, expressing itself in vigour of thought and language.

I had often, in the past, wondered why someone as talented and strongminded as she shouldn't have made a marriage of equal minds, but in recent years had come to think she had settled for a nonentity like Edwin because the very absence of competition freed her to be wholly herself.

'Edwin is concerned,' she said, 'that Malcolm is leaving his senses.'

For Edwin, read Lucy, I thought. She had a trick of ascribing her own thoughts to her husband if she thought they would be unwelcome to her audience.

Edwin stared at me uneasily. He was a good-looking man in many ways, but mean spirited, which if one were tolerant one would excuse because of the perpetual knife-edge state of his and Lucy's finances. I wasn't certain any more whether it was he who had actually failed to achieve employment, or whether Lucy had in some way stopped him from trying. In any event, she earned more prestige than lucre for her writing, and Edwin had grown tired of camouflaging the frayed elbows of his jackets with oval patches of thin leather badly sewn on.

Edwin's concern, it seemed, was real enough although if it had been his alone they wouldn't have come.

'It isn't fair of him,' he said, meaning Malcolm. 'Lucy's trust fund was set up years ago before inflation and doesn't stretch as far as it used to. He really ought to put that right. I've told him so several times, and he simply ignores me. And now he's throwing his money away in this profligate way as if his heirs had no rights at all.' Indignation shook in his voice, along with, I could see, a very definite fear of a rocky future if the fortune he'd counted on for so long should be snatched away in the last furlong, so to speak.

I sighed and refrained from saying that I thought that Malcolm's heirs had no rights while he was alive. I said merely, soothingly, 'I'm sure he won't let you starve.'

'That's not the point,' Edwin said with thin fury. 'The point is that he's given an *immense* amount of money to Lucy's old college to establish post-graduate scholarships for poets.'

I looked from his pinch-lipped agitated mouth to Lucy's face and saw shame where there should perhaps have been pride. Shame, I thought, because she found herself sharing Edwin's views when they ran so contrary to her normal disdain for materialism. Perhaps even Lucy, I thought, had been looking forward to a comfortably off old age.

'You should be honoured,' I said.

She nodded unhappily. 'I am.'

'No,' Edwin said. 'It's disgraceful.'

'The Lucy Pembroke Scholarships,' I said slowly.

'Yes. How did you know?' Lucy asked.

And there would be the Serena Pembroke Scholarships, of course. And the Coochie Pembroke Memorial Challenge Trophy . . .

'What are you smiling at?' Lucy demanded. 'You can't say you've made much of a success of your life so far, can you? If Malcolm leaves us all nothing, you'll end up carting horse-muck until you drop from senility.'

'There are worse jobs,' I said mildly.

There were horses around us, and racecourse noises, and a skyful of gusty fresh air. I could happily spend my life, I knew, in almost any capacity that took me to places like Sandown Park.

'You've wasted every talent you have,' Lucy said.

'My only talent is riding horses.'

'You're blind and stupid. You're the only male Pembroke with decent brains and you're too lazy to use them.'

'Well, thanks,' I said.

'It's not a compliment.'

'No, so I gathered.'

'Joyce says you're sure to know where Malcolm is as you've finally made up your quarrel, though you'll lie about it as a matter of course,' Lucy said. 'Joyce said you would be here today on this spot at this time, if I wanted to reach you.'

'Which you did, rather badly.'

'Don't be so obtuse. You've got to stop him. You're the only one who can, and Joyce says you're probably the only one who won't try . . . and you *must* try, Ian, and succeed, if not for yourself, then for the rest of the family.'

'For you?' I asked.

'Well . . .' She couldn't openly abandon her principles, but they were bending, it seemed. 'For the others,' she said stalwartly.

I looked at her with new affection. 'You're a hypocrite, my dear sister,' I said.

In smarting retaliation, she said sharply, 'Vivien thinks you're trying to cut the rest of us out and ingratiate yourself again with Malcolm.'

'I expect she would,' I said. 'I expect Alicia will think it also, when Vivien has fed it to her.'

'You really are a bastard.'

'No,' I said, my lips twitching, 'that's Gervase.'

'*Ian!*'

I laughed. 'I'll tell Malcolm you're concerned. I promise I will, somehow. And now I've got to change my clothes and ride in a race. Are you staying?'

Lucy hesitated but Edwin said, 'Will you win?'

'I don't think so. Save your money.'

'You're not taking it seriously,' Lucy said.

I looked straight at her eyes. 'Believe me,' I said, 'I take it very seriously indeed. No one had a right to murder Moira to stop her taking half Malcolm's money. No one has a right to murder Malcolm to stop him spending it. He is fair. He will leave us all provided for, when the time comes, which I hope may be twenty years from now. You tell them all to stop fretting, to ease off, to have faith. Malcolm is teasing you all and I think it's dangerous, but he is dismayed by everyone's greed, and is determined to teach us a lesson. So you tell them, Lucy, tell Joyce and Vivien and everyone, that the more we try to grab, the less we will get. The more we protest, the more he will spend.'

She looked back silently. Eventually she said, 'I am ashamed of myself.'

'Rubbish,' Edwin said to me vehemently. 'You must stop Malcolm. You must.'

Lucy shook her head. 'Ian's right.'

'Do you mean Ian won't even try?' Edwin demanded incredulously.

'I'm positive he won't,' Lucy said. 'Didn't you hear what he said? Weren't you listening?'

'It was all rubbish.'

Lucy patted my arm. 'We may as well see you race, while we're here. Go and get changed.'

It was a more sisterly gesture and tone than I was used to, and I reflected with a shade of guilt that I'd paid scant attention to her own career for a couple of years.

'How is the poetry going?' I asked. 'What are you working on?'

The question caught her unprepared. Her face went momentarily blank and then filled with what seemed to be an odd mixture of sadness and panic.

'Nothing just now,' she said. 'Nothing for quite a while,' and I nodded almost apologetically as if I had intruded, and went into the weighing-room and through to the changing-room reflecting that poets, like mathematicians, mostly did their best work when young. Lucy wasn't writing; had maybe stopped altogether. And perhaps, I thought, the frugality she had for so long embraced had begun to seem less worthy and less worth it, if she were losing the inner sustaining comfort of creative inspiration.

Poor Lucy, I thought. Life could be a bugger, as Malcolm said. She had already begun to value the affluence she had long despised or she wouldn't have come on her mission to Sandown Park, and I could only guess at the turmoil in her spiritual life. Like a nun losing her faith, I thought. But no, not a nun. Lucy, who had written explicitly of sex in a way I could never believe had anything to do with Edwin (though one could be wrong), wouldn't ever have been a nun.

With such random thoughts, I took off my ordinary clothes and put on white breeches and a scarlet jersey with blue stripes on the sleeves, and felt the usual battened-down excitement which made me breathe deeply and feel intensely happy. I rode in about fifty races a year, if I was lucky . . . and I would have to get another job fairly soon, I reflected, if I were to ride exercise regularly and stay fit enough to do any good.

Going outside, I talked for a while to the trainer and owner of the horse I was to ride, a husband and wife who had themselves ridden until twenty years earlier in point-to-point races and who liked to re-live it all vicariously through me. The husband, George, was now a public trainer on a fairly grand scale, but the wife, Jo, still preferred to run her own horses in amateur races. She currently owned three steeplechasers, all pretty good. It did me no harm at all to be seen on them and to be associated in racing minds with that stable.

'Young Higgins is jumping out of his skin,' Jo said.

Young Higgins was the name of that day's horse. Young Higgins was thirteen, a venerable gentleman out to disprove rumours of retirement. We all interpreted 'jumping out of his skin' as meaning fit, sound and pricking his ears with enthusiasm, and at his age one couldn't ask for much more. Older horses than he had won the Grand National, but Young Higgins and I had fallen in the great race the only time we'd tried it, and to my regret Jo had decided on no more attempts.

'We'll see you in the parade ring, then, Ian, before the race,' George said, and Jo added, 'And give the old boy a good time.'

I nodded, smiling. Giving all of us a good time was the point of the proceedings. Young Higgins was definitely included.

The minute George and Jo turned away to go off towards the grandstands, someone tapped me on the back of the shoulder. I turned round to see who it was and to my total astonishment found myself face to face with Lucy's older brother, Malcolm's first child, my half-brother Donald.

'Good heavens,' I said. 'You've never been to the races in your life.'

He often told me he hadn't, saying rather superciliously that he didn't approve of the sordid gambling.

'I haven't come for the races,' he said crossly. 'I've come to see you about Malcolm's taking leave of his senses.'

'How . . . er . . .?' I stopped. 'Did Joyce send you?' I said.

'What if she did? We are all concerned. She told us where to find you, certainly.'

'Did she tell the whole family?' I asked blankly.

'How do I know? She telephoned us. I daresay she telephoned everyone she could get hold of. You know what she's like. She's your mother, after all.'

Even so late in his life, he couldn't keep out of his voice the old resentments, and perhaps also, I reflected, they were intensifying with age. My mother had supplanted his, he was saying, and any indiscretion my mother ever committed was in some way my fault.

He had thought in that illogical way for as long as I'd been aware of him, and nothing had changed.

Donald was, in the family's opinion, the brother nearest in looks to myself, and I wasn't sure I liked it. Irrefutably, he was the same height and had blue eyes less intense in colour than Malcolm's. Agreed, Donald had middling brown curly hair and shoulders wider than his hips. I didn't wear a bushy moustache though, and I just hoped I didn't walk with what I thought of as a self-important strut; and I sometimes tried to make sure, after I'd been in Donald's company, that I absolutely didn't.

Donald's life had been so disrupted when Malcolm had ousted Vivien, Donald always told us, that he had never been able to decide properly on a career. It couldn't have been easy, I knew, to survive such an upheaval, but Donald had only been nine at the time, a bit early for life decisions. In any event, as an adult he had drifted from job to job in hotels, coming to harbour at length as secretary of a prestigious golf club near Henley-on-Thames, a post which I gathered had proved ultimately satisfactory in social standing, which was very important to his self-esteem.

I didn't either like or dislike Donald particularly. He was eleven years older than I was. He was *there*.

'Everyone insists you stop Malcolm squandering the family money,' he said, predictably.

'It's *his* money, not the family's,' I said.

'What?' Donald found the idea ridiculous. 'What you've got to do is explain that he owes it to us to keep the family fortune intact until we inherit it. Unfortunately we know he won't listen to any of us except you, and now that you appear to have made up your quarrel with him, you are elected to be our spokesman. Joyce thinks we have to convince you first of the need to stop Malcolm, but I told her it was ridiculous. You don't need convincing, you want to be well off one day just the same as the rest of us, of course you do, it's only natural.'

I was saved from both soul-searching and untrue disclaimers by the arrival of Helen, Donald's wife, who had apparently been buying a racecard.

'We're not staying,' Donald said disapprovingly, eyeing it.

She gave him a vague smile. 'You never know,' she said.

Beautiful and brainless, Malcolm had said of her, and perhaps he was right. Tall and thin, she moved with natural style and made cheap clothes look expensive: I knew they were cheap because she had a habit of saying where they'd come from and how much she'd paid for them, inviting admiration of her thriftiness. Donald always tried to shut her up.

'Do tell us where to watch the races from,' she said.

'We're not here for that,' Donald said.

'No, dear, we're here because we need money now that the boys have started at Eton.'

'No, dear,' Donald said sharply.

'But you know we can't afford . . .'

'Do be quiet, dear,' Donald said.

'Eton costs a bomb,' I said mildly, knowing that Donald's income would hardly stretch to one son there, let alone two. Donald had twin boys, which seemed to run in the family.

'Of course it does,' Helen said, 'but Donald puts such store by it. "My sons are at Eton," that sort of thing. Gives him *standing* with the people he deals with in the golf club.'

'Helen, dear, do be quiet.' Donald's embarrassment showed, but she was undoubtedly right.

'We thought Donald might have inherited before the boys reached thirteen,' she said intensely. 'As he hasn't, we're borrowing every penny we can to pay the fees, the same as we borrowed for the prep school and a lot of other things. But we've borrowed against Donald's expectations . . . so you see it's essential for us that there really is plenty to inherit, as there are so many people to share it with. We'll be literally bankrupt if Malcolm throws too much away . . . and I don't think Donald could face it.'

I opened my mouth to answer her but no sound came out. I felt as if I'd been thrust into a farce over which I had no control.

Walking purposefully to join us came Serena, Ferdinand and Debs.

Six

'Stay right here,' I said to all of them. 'I have to go into the weighing-room to deal with a technicality. Stay right here until I come out.'

They nodded with various frowns, and I dived into privacy in a desperate search for a sheet of paper and an envelope.

I wrote to Malcolm:

Half the family have turned up here, sent by Joyce. For God's sake stay where you are, keep out of sight and wait until I come to fetch you.

I stuck the note into the envelope, wrote Malcolm's name on the outside, and sought out an official who had enough rank to send someone to deliver it.

'My father is lunching in the Directors' dining-room,' I said. 'And it's essential that he gets this note immediately.'

The official was obliging. He was going up to the Stewards' room anyway, he said, and he would take it himself. With gratitude and only a minor lessening of despair – because it would be just like Malcolm to come down contrarily to confront the whole bunch – I went out again into the sunlight and found the five of them still faithfully waiting exactly where I'd left them.

'I say,' Debs said, half mocking, 'you do look dashing in all that kit.'

Donald looked at her in surprise, and I had a vivid impression of his saying soon in his golf club, 'My brother, the amateur jockey . . .', knowing that if I'd been a professional he would have hushed it up if he could. A real snob, Donald: but there were worse sins.

Debs, Ferdinand's second wife, had come to the races in a black leather coat belted at the waist, with shoulder-length blond hair above and long black boots below. Her eyelids were purple, like her fingernails. The innocence I'd photographed in her a year ago was in danger of disappearing.

Ferdinand, shorter than Debs and more like Malcolm than ever, appeared to be in his usual indecision over whether I was to be loved or hated. I smiled at him cheerfully and asked what sort of a journey he'd had.

'A lot of traffic,' he said lamely.

'We didn't come here to talk about traffic,' Serena said forbiddingly. 'We want to know where Daddy is.'

Malcolm's little Serena, now taller than he, was dressed that day in royal blue with white frills at neck and wrists, a white woollen hat with a pompom on top covering her cap of fair hair. She looked a leggy sixteen, not ten years older. Her age showed only in the coldness of her manner towards me, which gave no sign of thawing.

In her high-pitched, girlish voice she said, 'We want him to settle very substantial sums on us all right now. Then he can go to blazes with the rest.'

I blinked. 'Who are you quoting?' I asked.

'Myself,' she said loftily, and then more probably added, 'Mummy too. And Gervase.'

It had Gervase's thuggish style stamped all over it.

Donald and Helen looked distinctly interested in the proposal. Ferdinand and Debs had of course heard it before.

'Gervase thinks it's the best solution,' Ferdinand said, nodding.

I doubted very much that Malcolm would agree, but said only, 'I'll pass on your message next time he gets in touch with me.'

'But Joyce is sure you know where he is,' Donald objected.

'Not exactly,' I said. 'Do you know that Lucy and Edwin are here too?'

They were satisfactorily diverted, looking over their shoulders to see if they could spot them in the growing crowds.

'Didn't Joyce tell you she was sending so many of you here?' I asked generally, and it was Ferdinand, sideways, his face turned away, who answered.

'She told Serena to come here. She told Serena to tell me, which she did, so we came together. I didn't know about Donald and Helen or Lucy and Edwin. I expect she wanted to embarrass you.'

His eyes swivelled momentarily to my face, wanting to see my reaction. I don't suppose my face showed any. Joyce might call me 'darling' with regularity but could be woundingly unkind at the same time, and I'd had a lifetime to grow armour.

Ferdinand happened to be standing next to me. I said on impulse into his ear, 'Ferdinand, who killed Moira?'

He stopped looking for Lucy and Edwin and transferred his attention abruptly and wholly to me. I could see calculations going on in the pause before he answered, but I had no decoder for his thoughts. He was the most naturally congenial to me of all my brothers, yet the others were open books compared with him. He was secretive, as perhaps I was myself. He had wanted to build his own kitchen-wall hidey-hole when I'd built mine, only Malcolm had said we must share, that one was enough. Ferdinand had sulked and shunned me for a while, and smirked at Gervase's dead rats. I wondered to what extent people remained the same as they'd been when very young: whether it was safe to assume they hadn't basically changed, to believe that if one could peel back the layers of living one would come to the known child. I wanted Ferdinand to be as I had known him at ten, eleven, twelve – a boy dedicated to riding a bicycle while standing on his head on the saddle – and not in a million years a murderer.

'I don't know who killed Moira,' he said finally. 'Alicia says you did. She told the police it *had* to be you.'

'I couldn't have.'

'She says the police could break your alibi if they really tried.'

I knew that they had really tried: they'd checked every separate five minutes of my day, and their manner and their suspicions had been disturbing.

'And what do *you* think?' I asked curiously.

His eyelids flickered. 'Alicia says . . .'

I said abruptly, 'Your mother says too damned much. Can't you think for yourself?'

He was offended, as he would be. He hooked his arms through those of Debs and Serena and made an announcement. 'We three are going to have a drink and a sandwich. If you fall off and kill yourself, no one will miss you.'

I smiled at him, though his tone had held no joke.

'And don't be so bloody forgiving,' he said.

He whirled the girls away from me and marched them off. I wondered how he'd got the day off from work, though I supposed most people could if they tried. He was a statistician, studying to be an actuary in his insurance company. What were the probabilities, I wondered, of a thirty-two-year-old statistician whose wife had purple fingernails being present when his brother broke his neck at Sandown Park?

Donald and Helen said that they too would run a sandwich to earth (Donald's words) and Helen added earnestly that *she* would care that I finished the race safely, whatever Ferdinand said.

'Thanks,' I said, hoping I could believe her, and went back into the changing-room for an interval of thought.

Lucy and Edwin might leave before the end of the afternoon, and so might Donald and Helen, but Ferdinand wouldn't. He liked going racing. He'd said on one mellow occasion that he'd have been quite happy being a bookmaker; he was lightning fast at working out relative odds.

The problem of how to extract Malcolm unseen from the racecourse didn't end, either, with those members of the family I'd talked to. If they were all so certain I knew where Malcolm was, one of the others, more cunning, could be hiding behind trees, waiting to follow me when I left.

There were hundreds of trees in Sandown Park.

The first race came and went, and in due course I went out to partner Young Higgins in the second.

Jo as usual had red cheeks from pleasure and hope. George was being gruffly businesslike, also as usual, telling me to be especially careful at the difficult first fence and to go easy up the hill past the stands the first time.

I put Malcolm out of my mind, and also murder, and it wasn't difficult. The sky was a clear distant blue, the air crisp with the coming of autumn. The leaves on all those trees were yellowing, and the track lay waiting, green and springy, with the wide fences beckoning to be flown. Simple things; and out there one came starkly face to face with oneself, which I mostly found more exhilarating than frightening. So far, anyway.

Jo said, 'Only eight runners, just a perfect number,' and George said, as he always did, 'Don't lie too far back coming round the last long bend.'

I said I would try not to.

Jo's eyes were sparkling like a child's in her sixty-year-old face, and I marvelled that she had never in all that time lost the thrill of expectation in moments like these. There might be villains at every level in horse racing, but there were also people like Jo and George whose goodness and goodwill shone out like searchlights, who made the sport overall good fun and wholesome.

. Life and death might be serious in the real world, but life and death on a fast steeplechaser on a Friday afternoon in the autumn sunshine was a lighthearted toss-up, an act of health on a sick planet.

I fastened the strap of my helmet, was thrown up on Young Higgins and rode him out onto the track. Perhaps if I'd been a professional and ridden up to ten times as often I would have lost the swelling joy that that moment always gave me: one couldn't grin like a maniac, even to oneself, at a procession of bread-and-butter rides on cold days, sharp tracks, bad horses.

Young Higgins was living up to his name, bouncing on his toes and tossing his head in high spirits. We lined up with the seven others, all of whose riders I happened to know from many past similar occasions. Amateurs came in all guises: there was a mother, an aunt and a grandfather riding that afternoon, besides a journalist, an earl's son, a lieutenant-colonel, a show-jumper and myself. From the stands, only a keen eye could have told one from the other without the guidance of our colours, and that was what amateur racing was all about: the equality, the levelling anonymity of the starting gate.

The tapes went up and we set off with three miles to go, almost two whole circuits, twenty-two jumps and an uphill run to the winning post.

The aunt's horse, too strong for her, took hold of the proceedings and opened up an emphatic lead, which no one else bothered to cut down. The aunt's horse rushed into the difficult downhill first fence and blundered over it, which taught him a lesson and let his rider recover control, and for about a mile after that there were no dramatic excitements. The first race I'd ever ridden in had seemed to pass in a whirling heaving flurry leaving me breathless and exhausted, but time had stretched out with experience until one could watch and think and even talk.

'Give me room, blast you,' shouted the lieutenant-colonel on one side of me.

'Nice day,' said the earl's son chattily on the other, always a clown who enlivened his surroundings.

'Shift your *arse*!' yelled the mother to her horse, giving him a crack round that part of his anatomy. She was a good rider, hated slow horses, hated not to win, weighed a muscular ten stone and was scornful of the show-jumper, whom she had accused often of incompetence.

The show-jumper, it was true, liked to set his horse right carefully before jumps, as in the show-ring, and hadn't managed to speed up in the several steeplechase races he'd ridden so far. He wasn't in consequence someone to follow into a fence and I avoided him whenever possible.

The journalist was the best jockey in the race, a professional in all but status, and the grandfather was the worst but full of splendid reckless courage. More or less in a bunch, the whole lot of us came round the bottom bend and tackled the last three jumps of the first circuit. The aunt was still in front, then came the lieutenant-colonel, myself and the earl's son in a row, then the mother just behind, with the show-jumper and the grand-father beside her. I couldn't see the journalist: somewhere in the rear, no doubt, biding his wily time.

The lieutenant-colonel's mount made a proper hash of the last of the three fences, jogging both of his rider's feet out of the irons and tipping the military backside into the air somewhere in the region of the horse's mane. Landing alongside and gathering my reins, I saw that the lieutenant-colonel's balance was hopelessly progressing down the horse's galloping shoulder as he fought without success to pull himself back into the saddle.

I put out an arm, grasped his jersey and yanked him upwards and backwards, shifting his disastrous centre of gravity into a more manageable place and leaving him slowing and bumping in my wake as he sat down solidly in the saddle, trying to put his feet back into his flying stirrups, which was never very easy at thirty miles an hour.

He had breathing space to collect things going up the hill, though, as we all did, and we swept round the top bend and down to the difficult fence again with not much change in order from the first time.

Someone had once long ago pulled me back into the saddle in that same way: it was fairly common in jump racing. Someone had also once tipped me straight into the air with an upward wrench of my heel, but that was another story. The lieutenant-colonel was saying 'Thanks' and also 'Move over, you're crowding me,' more or less in the same breath.

After crossing the water jump for the second time over on the far side of the track, the show-jumper made a spurt to the front and then slowed almost to a standstill on landing over the next fence, having jumped especially pedantically, and the aunt crashed into the back of him with some singularly un-aunt-like language.

'Lovely lady,' said the earl's son, appreciatively, as we passed the débâcle. 'How are you going yourself?'

'Not bad,' I said. 'How are you?'

We jumped the last of the seven far-side fences together and in front, and put all our energies into staying there round the long last bend and over the three last fences. I could hear horses thudding behind me and the mother's voice exhorting her slowcoach. Approaching the Pond fence, I could sense the earl's son's horse beginning to tire, I could see that precious winning post far ahead and the way to it clear, and for at least a few moments I thought I might win. But then the lieutenant-colonel reappeared fast at my elbow, still shouting for room, and between the last two fences, as I'd feared he would, the journalist materialised from the outback and made it look easy, and Young Higgins tired into Middle-Aged Higgins on the hill.

He and I finished third, which wasn't too bad, with the earl's son, persevering, not far away fourth.

'A nice afternoon out,' he said happily as we trotted back together, and I looked at the lights in his eyes and saw it was the same for him as for me, a high that one couldn't put into words, an adventure of body and spirit that made of dismounting and walking on the ground a literal coming down to earth.

Jo was pleased enough, patting Young Higgins hard. 'Ran a great race, didn't you, old boy? Jumped like a stag.'

'You'd have been second,' said George, who had good binoculars, 'if you'd let the lieutenant-colonel fall off.'

'Yeah, well,' I said, unbuckling the griths, 'there were a lot of hooves down there.'

George smiled. 'Don't forget to weigh in.' (He said it every time.) 'Come for a drink in the Owners' bar when you've changed.'

I accepted. It was part of the ritual, part of the bargain. They liked to re-live Young Higgins' outing fence for fence in return for having given me the ride. They were still standing in the unsaddling enclosure talking to friends when I went out again in street clothes, and with welcoming smiles waved me into their group. None of my own family being in sight, I went with them without problems and, over glasses of Jo's favourite brandy and ginger ale, earned my afternoon's fun by describing it.

I returned to the weighing-room area afterwards and found that not only were all the same family members still on the racecourse, but that they had coalesced into an angry swarm and had been joined by one of the queen bees herself, my mother Joyce.

Joyce, in fur and a green hat, was a rinsed blonde with greenish eyes behind contact lenses which seldom missed a trick in life as in cards. Dismayed but blank-faced, I gave her a dutiful peck on her smooth cheek which, it seemed, she was in no mood to receive.

'Darling,' she said, the syllables sizzling with displeasure, 'did you or did you not send that weasel Norman West to check up on my whereabouts last Friday?'

'Er,' I said.

'Did you or did you not send him sniffing round Vivien on the same errand?'

'Well,' I said, half smiling, 'I wouldn't have put it as crudely, but I suppose so, yes.'

The battery of eyes from the others was as friendly as napalm.

'Why?' Joyce snapped.

'Didn't Norman West tell you?'

She said impatiently, 'He said something nonsensical about Malcolm being attacked. I told him if Malcolm had been attacked, I would have heard of it.'

'Malcolm was very nearly killed,' I said flatly. 'He and I asked Norman West to make sure that none of you could have done it.'

Joyce demanded to be told what had happened to Malcolm, and I told her. She and all the others listened with open mouths and every evidence of shock, and if there was knowledge, not ignorance, behind any of the horrified eyes, I couldn't discern it.

'Poor Daddy!' Serena exclaimed. 'How *beastly*.'

'A matter for the police,' Donald said forcefully.

'I agree,' I said. 'I'm surprised they haven't been to see all of you already, as they did when Moira died.'

Edwin said, with a shake of the head, 'How near, how near,' and then, hearing the regret in his voice as clearly as I did, added hurriedly, 'What a blessing he woke up.'

'When the police make their enquiries,' I said, 'they don't exactly report the results to Malcolm. He wants to make sure for himself that none of the family was at Quantum last Friday afternoon. If you cooperate with Norman West when he gets to you, you'll set Malcolm's mind at rest.'

'And what if we can't prove where we were?' Debs asked.

'Or even remember?' Lucy said.

'Malcolm will have to live with it,' Joyce said crisply.

'Living with it would present him less problem,' I said dryly. 'It's dying he wants to avoid.'

They stared at me in silence. The reality of Moira's murder had been to them, I guessed, as to me, a slow-burning fuse, with seemingly no bad consequences at first, but with accelerating worries as time passed. Perhaps they, as I had done, had clung to the motiveless-intruder-from-outside theory at first because the alternative was surely unthinkable, but in the weeks since then, they must at least have begun to wonder. The fuse would heat soon into active suspicions, I saw, which might tear apart and finally scatter for ever the fragile family fabric.

Would I mind, I thought? Not if I still had Malcolm ... and perhaps Ferdinand ... and Joyce ... and maybe Lucy, or Thomas ... Serena ... would I care if I never again laid eyes on Gervase?

The answer, surprisingly enough, was yes, I would mind. Imperfect, quarrelsome, ramshackle as it was, the family were origins and framework, the geography of living. Moira, ungrieved, was already rewriting that map, and if her murderer remained for ever undiscovered, if Malcolm himself – I couldn't think of it – were killed, there would be no healing, no reforming, no telephone network for information, no contact, just a lot of severed galaxies moving inexorably apart.

The big bang, I thought, still lay ahead. The trick was to smother the fuse before the explosion, and that was all very well, but where was the burning point, and how long had we got?

'Buy me a drink, darling,' Joyce commanded. 'We're in deep trouble.'

She began to move off, but the others showed no signs of following. I looked at the seven faces all expressing varying degrees of anxiety and saw them already begin to move slightly away from each other, not one cohesive group, but Donald and Helen as a couple, Lucy and Edwin, a pair, and Ferdinand, Debs and Serena, the youngest trio.

'I'll tell Malcolm your fears,' I said. 'And your needs.'

'Oh yes, please do,' Helen said intensely.

'And Gervase's plan,' Ferdinand added.

'Do come on, darling,' Joyce said peremptorily over her shoulder. 'Which way is the bar?'

'Run along, little brother,' Lucy said with irony. Serena said, 'Mumsie's waiting,' and Debs fairly tittered. I thought of sticking my toes in and making Joyce come back, but what did it matter? I could put up with the jibes, I'd survived them for years, and I understood what prompted them. I shrugged ruefully and went after Joyce, and could feel the pitying smiles on the back of my neck.

I steered Joyce into the busy Members' bar which had a buffet table along one side with salads and breads and a large man in chef's clothes carving from turkeys, haunches of beef and hams on the bone. I was hungry after riding and offered Joyce food, but she waved away the suggestion as frivolity. I bought her instead a large vodka and tonic with a plain ginger ale for myself, and we found spare seats at a table in a far corner where, after the merest glance around to make sure she wouldn't be overheard among the general hubbub, she leaned forward until the brim of the green hat was practically touching my forehead and launched into her inquisition.

'Where is your father?' she said.

'When did you last see your father?' I amended.

'What on earth are you talking about?'

'That picture by Orchardson.'

'Stop playing games. Where is Malcolm?'

'I don't know,' I said.

'You're lying.'

'Why do you want to find him?'

'*Why?*' She was astonished. 'Because he's out of his mind.' She dug into her capacious handbag and brought out an envelope, which she thrust towards me. 'Read that.'

I opened the envelope and found a small piece of newspaper inside, a snipped paragraph without headline or provenance.

It said:

Second-string British contender is Blue Clancy, second in last year's Derby and winner this year of Royal Ascot's King Edward VII Stakes. Owner Ramsey Osborn yesterday hedged his Arc bets by selling a half-share in his four-year-old colt to arbitrageur Malcolm Pembroke, who launched into bloodstock only this week with a two million guineas yearling at the Premium Sales.

Ouch, I thought.

'Where did it come from?' I asked.

'What does it matter where it came from? That new "Racing Patter" column in the *Daily Towncrier*, as a matter of fact. I was drinking coffee this morning when I read it and nearly choked. The point is, is it true?'

'Yes,' I said.

'*What?*'

'Yes,' I said again. 'Malcolm bought half of Blue Clancy. Why shouldn't he?'

'Sometimes,' my mother said forcefully, 'you are so stupid I could hit you.' She paused for breath. 'And what exactly is an arbitrageur?'

'A guy who makes money by buying low and selling high.'

'Oh. Gold.'

'And foreign currencies. And shares. And maybe racehorses.'

She was unmollified. 'You know perfectly well he's just throwing his money away to spite everybody.'

'He didn't like Moira being killed. He didn't like being attacked himself. I shouldn't think he'll stop spending until he knows whether we have or haven't a murderer in the family, and even then . . .' I smiled, 'he's getting a taste for it.'

Joyce stared. 'Moira was murdered by an intruder,' she said.

I didn't answer.

She took a large swallow of her vodka and tonic and looked at me bleakly. She had been barely twenty when I was born, barely nineteen when Malcolm had whisked her headlong from an antique shop in Kensington and within a month installed her in his house with a new wedding ring and too little to do.

Malcolm, telling me now and again about those days, had said, 'She understood figures, you see. And she could beat me at cards. And she looked so damned demure. So young. Not bossy at all, like she was later. Her people thought me an upstart, did you know? Their ancestors traced back to Charles II, mine traced back to a Victorian knife-grinder. But her people weren't rich, you know. More breeding than boodle. It was an impulse, marrying Joyce. There you are, I admit it. Turned out she didn't like sex much, more's the pity. Some women are like that. No hormones. So I went on seeing Alicia. Well, I would, wouldn't I? Joyce and I got on all right, pretty polite to each other and so on, until she found out about Alicia. Then we had fireworks, all hell let loose for months on end,

84

do you remember? Don't suppose you remember, you were only four or five.'

'Five and six, actually.'

'Really? Joyce liked being mistress of the house, you know. She learned about power. Grew up, I suppose. She took up bridge seriously, and started voluntary work. She hated leaving all that, didn't much mind leaving me. She said Alicia had robbed her of her self-esteem and ruined her position in the local community. She's never forgiven her, has she?'

Joyce had returned to the small Surrey town where her parents had lived and later died, their social mantle falling neatly onto her able shoulders. She bullied the local people into good works, made continual bridge-tournament forays, earned herself a measure of celebrity, and no, had never forgiven Alicia.

In the bar at Sandown she was dressed, as always, with a type of businesslike luxury: mink jacket over grey tailored suit, neat white silk shirt, long strings of pearls, high-heeled shoes, green felt hat, polished calf handbag. 'A well-dressed, well-bred, brassy blonde' Alicia had once called her, which was both accurate and unfair, as was Joyce's tart tit-for-tat opinion of Alicia as 'White meat of chicken aboard the gravy train'.

Joyce drank most of the rest of her vodka and said, 'Do you really think one of the family is capable of murder?'

'I don't know.'

'But *who*?'

'That's the question.'

'It isn't possible,' she insisted.

'Well,' I said. 'Take them one by one. Tell me why it's impossible in each individual case, according to each person's character. Start at the beginning, with Vivien.'

'No, Ian,' she protested.

'Yes,' I said. 'Help me. Help Malcolm. Help us all.'

She gave me a long worried look, oblivious to the movement and noise going on all around us. The next race was already in progress but without noticeable thinning of the crowd who were watching it on closed circuit television above our heads.

'Vivien,' I prompted.

'Impossible, just impossible. She's practically dim-witted. If she was ever going to murder anybody, it would have been long ago and it would have been Alicia. Alicia ruined Vivien's marriage, just like mine. Vivien's a sniffler, full of self-pity. And why would she do it? For those three wimpish offspring?'

'Perhaps,' I said. 'They all need money. She hasn't enough herself to bail them out of their holes.'

'It's still impossible.'

'All right,' I said. 'How about Donald? And Helen?'

Donald had been ten, more than half Joyce's age, when she had married Malcolm, and he had been in and out of Quantum, as had Lucy and Thomas, whenever Malcolm had exercised his joint-custody rights and had them to stay. Joyce's lack of interest in children had definitely extended to her step-children, whom she'd found noisy, bad tempered and foul mannered, though Malcolm disagreed.

'Donald's a pompous, snobbish ass,' she said now, 'and as insecure as hell under the bluster. Malcolm thinks Helen's as brainless as she's pretty, but I'd say you don't need brains to murder, rather the opposite. I'd think Helen would fight like a fury to save her cubs from physical harm. But Moira wasn't threatening her cubs, not directly. I'd think Helen could be only a hot-blood killer, but so could most people, driven hard enough to defend themselves or their young.'

I wondered if she knew about the school-fees crisis: if they hadn't directly told her, she had got them remarkably right.

'Lucy?' I said.

'Lucy thinks everyone is inferior to herself, especially if they have more money.'

Poor Lucy, I thought. 'And Edwin?' I said.

Joyce frowned. 'Edwin . . .'

'Edwin isn't impossible?' I asked.

'He never gets time off from running errands. Not enough time anyway for waiting around to catch Moira alone in her glass house.'

'But in character?'

'I don't know enough about him,' Joyce confessed. 'He yearns for money, that's for sure, and he's earned it, picking up after Lucy all these years. I don't know his impatience level.'

'All right then,' I said, 'what about Thomas?'

'Thomas!' Joyce's face looked almost sad. 'He wasn't as insufferable as Donald and Lucy when he was little. I liked him best of the three. But that damned Vivien screwed him up properly, didn't she?

God knows why he married Berenice. She'll badger him into the grave before he inherits, and then where will she be?'

Joyce finished the vodka and said, 'I don't like doing this, Ian, and I'm stopping right here.'

Thomas, I thought. She wasn't sure about Thomas, and she doesn't want to say so. The analysis had all of a sudden come to an unwelcome, perhaps unexpected, abyss.

'Another drink?' I suggested.

'Yes. Gervase is drinking, did you know?'

'He always drinks.'

'Ursula telephoned me to ask for advice.'

'Did she really?' I was surprised. 'Why didn't she ask Alicia?'

'Ursula detests her mother-in-law,' Joyce said. 'We have that in common. Ursula and I have become quite good friends.'

Amazing, I thought, and stood up to fetch the refills.

Joyce's eyes suddenly widened in disbelief, looking beyond me.

'I knew you were lying,' she said bitterly. 'There's Malcolm.'

Seven

I turned, not knowing whether to be frightened or merely irritated.

Malcolm hadn't seen Joyce, and he wasn't looking for her or for me but solely for a drink. I made my way to the bar to meet him there and took him by the arm.

'Why aren't you bloody upstairs?' I said.

'I was outstaying my welcome, old chap. It was getting very awkward. They had an ambassador to entertain. I've been up there three bloody hours. Why didn't you come and fetch me?'

'Joyce,' I said grimly, 'is sitting over there in the corner. I am buying her a drink, and she saw you come in.'

'Joyce!' He turned round and spotted her as she looked balefully in our direction. 'Damn it.'

'Prowling around outside we also have Donald and Helen, Lucy and Edwin, Ferdinand and Debs, and Serena.'

'Christ,' he said. 'Hunting in pairs.'

'You may joke,' I said, 'and you may be right.'

'I couldn't stay up there. They were waiting for me to leave, too polite to tell me to go.'

He looked apprehensive, as well he might.

'Will Joyce tell them all that I'm here?'

'We'll see if we can stop it,' I said. 'What do you want to drink? Scotch?'

He nodded and I squeezed through the throng by the bar and eventually got served. He helped me carry the glasses and bottles back to the table, and sat where I'd been sitting, facing Joyce. I fetched another chair from nearby and joined my ever non-loving parents.

'Before you start shouting at each other,' I said, 'can we just take two things for granted? Joyce wants Malcolm to stop scattering largesse, Malcolm wants to go on living. Both ends are more likely to be achieved if we discover who murdered Moira, in case it is Moira's murderer who wishes also to kill Malcolm.' I paused. 'OK for logic?'

They both looked at me with the sort of surprise parents reserve for unexpected utterances from their young.

Malcolm said, 'Surely it's axiomatic that it's Moira's murderer who's trying to kill me?'

I shook my head. 'Ever heard of copycat crime?'

'My God,' he said blankly. 'One possible murderer in the family is tragedy. Two would be . . .'

'Statistically improbable,' Joyce said.

Malcolm and I looked at her with respect.

'She's right,' Malcolm said, sounding relieved, as if one killer were somehow more manageable than two.

'OK,' I agreed, wondering what the statistical probabilities really were, wondering whether Ferdinand could work them out, 'OK, the police failed to find Moira's murderer although they tried very hard and are presumably still trying . . .'

'Trying to link me with an assassin,' muttered Malcolm darkly.

'We might, as a family,' I said, 'have been able to overcome Moira's murder by making ourselves believe in the motiveless unknown outside-intruder theory . . .'

'Of course we believe it,' Joyce said faintly.

'Not now, we can't. Two unknown outside-intruder motiveless murders – because Malcolm was meant to die – are so statistically improbable as to be out of sight. The police haven't found Moira's murderer, but we have now got to try to do it ourselves. It's no longer safe not to, which is why we engaged Norman West.' I looked directly at Joyce. 'Stop fussing over what Malcolm is spending and start thinking of ways to save his life, if only so that he can make more money, which he can do, but only if he's alive.'

'Ian . . .' She was shocked.

'You roused the whole family this morning on the telephone, telling them where to find me, and now seven of them that we know of are here, and others may be who've kept out of sight. Much though we hate the idea, Moira's murderer may be here.'

'No, no,' Joyce exclaimed.

'Yes,' I said. 'Malcolm's primary defence against being murdered is staying out of reach of lethal instruments, which means people not knowing where to find him. Well, you, my darling mother, brought the whole pack here to the races, so now you'd better help Malcolm to leave before they catch him.'

'I didn't know he'd be here,' she protested.

'No, but he is. It's time to be practical.'

No one pointed out that if she *had* known he'd be there, she would have sent everyone with even more zeal.

'Do you have any ideas?' Malcolm asked me hopefully.

'Yes, I do. But we have to have Joyce's help, plus her promise of silence.'

My mother was looking less than her normal commanding self and gave assurances almost meekly.

'This is not a private bar,' I said, 'and if any of the family have bought Club passes, they may turn up in here at any moment, so we'd best lose no time. I'm going to leave you both here for a few minutes, but I'll be back. Stay in this corner. Whatever happens, stay right here. If the family find you, still stay here. OK?'

They both nodded, and I left them sitting and looking warily at each other in the first tête-à-tête they'd shared for many a long year.

I went in search of the overall catering director whom I knew quite well because one of his daughters rode against me regularly in amateur races, and found him by sending urgent messages via the manager of the Members' bar.

'Ian,' he said ten slow minutes later, coming to the bar from the back, where the bottles were, 'what's the trouble?'

He was a company director, head of a catering division, a capable man in his fifties, sprung from suburbia, upwardly mobile from merit, grown worldly wise.

I said the trouble was private, and he led me away from the crowds, through the back of the bar and into a small area of comparative quiet, out of sight of the customers.

My father, I told him, badly needed an immediate inconspicuous exit from the racecourse and wanted to know if a case of vintage Bollinger would ease his passage.

'Not skipping his bookie, I hope?' the caterer said laconically.

'No, he wants to elope with my mother, his ex-wife, from under the eyes of his family.'

The caterer, amused, agreed that Bollinger might be nice. He also laughed at my plan, told me to put it into operation, he would see it went well, and to look after his Rosemary whenever she raced.

I went back through the bar to collect Malcolm and to ask Joyce to

90

fetch her car and to drive it to where the caterers parked their vans, giving her directions. The two of them were still sitting alone at the table, not exactly gazing into each other's eyes with rapture but at least not drawn apart in frost. They both seemed relieved at my reappearance, though, and Joyce picked up her handbag with alacrity to go to fetch her car.

'If you see any of the others,' I said, 'just say you're going home.'

'I wasn't born yesterday, darling,' she replied with reviving sarcasm. 'Run along and play games, and let me do my part.'

The game was the same one I'd thought of earlier in the changing-room, modified only by starting from a different point. It was just possible that the wrong eyes had spotted Malcolm in his brief passage outside from the exit door of the Directors' rooms to the entrance door of the bar, but even if so, I thought we could fool them.

In the quiet private space at the rear of the bar, the catering director was watching the large chef remove his white coat and tall hat.

'A case of vintage Bollinger for the caterer, a handout for the chef,' I murmured in Malcolm's ear. 'Get Joyce to drop you at a railway station, and I'll see you in the Savoy. Don't move until I get there.'

Malcolm, looking slightly dazed, put on the chef's coat and hat and pulled out his wallet. The chef looked delighted with the result and went back to slicing his turkeys in temporary shirtsleeves. Malcolm and the catering director left through the bar's rear door and set off together through the racecourse buildings to go outside to the area where the caterers' vans were parked. I waited quite a long anxious time in the bar, but eventually the catering director returned, carrying the white disguise, which he restored to its owner.

'Your father got off safely,' he assured me. 'He didn't see anyone he knew. What was it all about? Not really an elopement, was it?'

'He wanted to avoid being assassinated by his disapproving children.'

The caterer smiled, of course not believing it. I asked where he would like the fizz sent and he took out a business card, writing his private address on the back.

'Your father lunched with the Directors, didn't he?' he said. 'I thought I saw him up there.' His voice implied that doing favours for people who lunched with the Directors was doubly vouched for, like

91

backing up a cheque with a credit card, and I did my best to reinforce further his perception of virtue.

'He's just bought a half share in an Arc de Triomphe runner,' I said. 'We're going over for the race.'

'Lucky you,' he said, giving me his card. He frowned suddenly, trying to remember. 'Didn't Rosemary tell me something about your father's present wife being pointlessly murdered some weeks ago? His late wife, I suppose I should say. Dreadful for him, dreadful.'

'Yes,' I said. 'Well . . . some people connected with her turned up here today unexpectedly, and he wanted to escape meeting them.'

'Ah,' he said with satisfied understanding. 'In that case, I'm glad to have been of help.' He chuckled. 'They didn't really look like elopers.'

He shook my hand and went away, and with a couple of deep breaths I left the Members' bar and walked back to the weighing-room to pick up my gear. There was still one more race to be run but it already felt like a long afternoon.

George and Jo were there when I came out carrying saddle, helmet, whip and holdall, saying they'd thought they'd catch me before I left.

'We've decided to run Young Higgins again two weeks tomorrow at Kempton,' Jo said. 'You'll be free for that, won't you?'

'Yes, indeed.'

'And Park Railings, don't forget, at Cheltenham next Thursday.'

'Any time, any place,' I said, and they laughed, conspirators in addiction.

It occurred to me as they walked away, looking back and waving, that perhaps I'd be in Singapore, Australia or Timbuktu next week or the week after; life was uncertain, and that was its seduction.

I saw none of the family on my way to the exit gate, and none between there and my car. With a frank sigh of relief, I stowed my gear in the boot and without much hurry set off towards Epsom, a detour of barely ten miles, thinking I might as well pick up my mail and listen to messages.

The telephone answering machine did have a faculty for listening to messages from afar, but it had never worked well, and I'd been too lazy to replace the remote controller which, no doubt, needed new batteries anyway.

With equally random thoughts I drove inattentively onwards, and it wasn't until I'd gone a fair distance that I realised that every time I glanced in the rear-view mirror I could see the same car two or three cars back. Some cars passed me: it never did, nor closed a gap to catch up.

I sat up, figuratively and literally, and thought, 'What do you know?' and felt my heart beat as at the starting gate.

What I didn't know was whose car it was. It looked much like the hired one I was driving, a middle-rank four-door in underwashed cream; ordinary, inconspicuous, no threat to Formula One.

Perhaps, I thought sensibly, the driver was merely going to Epsom, at my own pace, so at the next traffic lights I turned left into unknown residential territory, and kept on turning left at each crossroads thereafter, reasoning that in the end I would complete the circle and end up facing where I wanted to go. I didn't hurry nor continually look in the rear-view mirror, but when I was back again on a road – a different one – with signposts to Epsom, the similar car was still somewhere on my tail, glimpsed tucked in behind a van.

If he had only a minimal sense of direction, I thought, he would realise what I had done and guess I now knew he was following. On the other hand, the back roads between Sandown Park and Epsom were a maze, like most Surrey roads, and he might possibly not have noticed, or thought I was lost, or . . .

Catching at straws, I thought. Face facts. I knew he was there and he knew I knew and what should I do next?

We were already on the outskirts of Epsom and almost automatically I threaded my way round corners, going towards my flat. I had no reason not to, I thought. I wasn't leading my follower to Malcolm, if that was what he had in mind. I also wanted to find out who he was, and thought I might outsmart him through knowing some ingenious short cuts round about where I lived.

Many of the houses in that area, having been built in the thirties without garages, had cars parked permanently on both sides of the streets. Only purpose-built places, like my block of flats, had adequate parking, except for two or three larger houses converted to flats which had cars where once there had been lawns.

I drove on past my home down the narrow roadway and twirled fast into the driveway of one of the large houses opposite. That particular house had a narrow exit drive also into the next tree-lined avenue: I drove straight through fast, turned quickly, raced round two more corners and returned to my own road to come up behind the car which had been following me.

He was there, stopped, awkwardly half-parked in too small a

space with his nose to the kerb, rear sticking out, brake lights still shining: indecision showing all over the place. I drew to a halt right behind him, blocking his retreat, put on my brakes, climbed out, took three or four swift strides and opened the door on the driver's side.

There was a stark moment of silence.

Then I said, 'Well, well, well,' and after that I nodded up towards my flat and said, 'Come on in,' and after that I said, 'If I'd known you were coming, I'd have baked a cake.'

Debs giggled. Ferdinand, who had been driving, looked sheepish. Serena, unrepentant, said, 'Is Daddy here?'

They came up to my flat where they could see pretty clearly that no, Daddy wasn't. Ferdinand looked down from the sitting-room window to where his car was now parked beside mine in neat privacy, and then up at the backs of houses opposite over a nearby fence.

'Not much of a view,' he said disparagingly.

'I'm not here much.'

'You knew I was following you, didn't you?'

'Yes,' I said. 'Like a drink?'

'Well . . . scotch?'

I nodded and poured him some from a bottle in the cupboard.

'No ice,' he said, taking the glass. 'After that drive, I'll take it neat.'

'I didn't go fast,' I said, surprised.

'Your idea of fast and mine round those goddam twisty roads are about ten miles an hour different.'

The two girls were poking about in the kitchen and bedrooms and I could hear someone, Serena no doubt, opening doors and drawers in a search for residues of Malcolm.

Ferdinand shrugged, seeing my unconcern. 'He hasn't been here at all, has he?' he said.

'Not for three years.'

'Where is he?'

I didn't answer.

'We'll have to torture you into telling,' said Ferdinand. It was a frivolous threat we'd used often in our childhood for anything from 'Where are the cornflakes' to 'What is the time' and Ferdinand himself looked surprised that it had surfaced.

'Mm,' I said. 'As in the tool shed?'

'Shit,' Ferdinand said. 'I didn't mean . . .'

94

'I should absolutely hope not.'

We both remembered, though, the rainy afternoon when Gervase had put the threat into operation, trying to make me tell him where I'd hidden my new cricket bat which he coveted. I hadn't told him, out of cussedness. Ferdinand had been there, too frightened of Gervase to protest, and also Serena, barely four, wide-eyed and uncomprehending.

'I thought you'd forgotten,' Ferdinand said. 'You've never mentioned it.'

'Boys will be bullies.'

'Gervase still is.'

Which of us, I thought, was not as we had been in the green garden? Donald, Lucy, Thomas, Gervase, Ferdinand, Serena – all playing there long ago, children's voices calling through the bushes, the adults we would become already forming in the gangling limbs, smooth faces, groping minds. None of those children . . . *none of us*. . . I thought protestingly, could have killed.

Serena came into the sitting-room carrying a white lace negligée and looking oddly shocked.

'You've had a woman here!' she said.

'There's no law against it.'

Debs, following her, showed a more normal reaction. 'Size ten, good perfume, expensive tastes, classy lady,' she said. 'How am I doing?'

'Not bad.'

'Her face cream's in the bathroom,' Serena said. 'You didn't tell us you had a . . . a . . .'

'Girl-friend,' I said. 'And do you have . . . a boy-friend?'

She made an involuntary face of distaste and shook her head. Debs put a sisterly arm round Serena's shoulders and said, 'I keep telling her to go to a sex therapist or she'll end up a dry old stick, but she won't listen, will you love?'

Serena wriggled free of Debs' arm and strode off with the negligée towards the bedrooms.

'Has anyone ever assaulted her?' I asked Ferdinand. 'She has that look.'

'Not that I know of.' He raised his eyebrows. 'She's never said so.'

'She's just scared of sex,' Debs said blithely. 'You wouldn't think anyone would be, these days. Ferdinand's not, are you, bunny?'

Ferdinand didn't react, but said, 'We've finished here, I think.' He drained his scotch, put down his glass and gave me a cold stare as if to announce that any semi-thaw I might have perceived during the afternoon's exchanges was now at an end. The ice-curtain had come down again with a clang.

'If you cut us out with Malcolm,' he said, 'you'll live to regret it.'

Hurt, despite myself, and with a touch of acid, I asked, 'Is that again what Alicia says?'

'Damn you, Ian,' he said angrily, and made for the door, calling, 'Serena, we're going,' giving her no choice but to follow.

Debs gave me a mock gruesome look as she went in their wake. 'You're Alicia's number one villain, too bad, lovey. You keep your hooks off Malcolm's money or you won't know what hit you.'

There was a fierce last-minute threat in her final words, and I saw, as the jokey manner slipped, that it was merely a façade which hid the same fears and furies of all the others, and her eyes, as she went, were just as unfriendly.

With regret, I watched from the window as the three of them climbed into Ferdinand's car and drove away. It was an illusion to think one could go back to the uncorrupted emotions of childhood, and I would have to stop wishing for it. I turned away, rinsed out Ferdinand's glass, and went into my bedroom to see how Serena had left it.

The white negligée was lying on my bed. I picked it up and hung it in its cupboard, rubbing my cheek in the fabric and smelling the faint sweet scent of the lady who came occasionally for lighthearted interludes away from a husband who was all but impotent but nevertheless loved. We suited each other well: perfectly happy in ephemeral passion, with no intention of commitment.

I checked round the flat, opened a few letters and listened to the answering machine: there was nothing of note. I spent a while thinking about cars. I had arranged on the telephone two days earlier that the hotel in Cambridge would allow my own car to remain in their park for a daily fee until I collected it, but I couldn't leave it there for ever. If I took a taxi to Epsom station, I thought, I could go up to London by train. In the morning, I would go by train to Cambridge, fetch my car, drive back to the flat, change to the hired car and drive that back to London. It might even be a shade safer, I thought, considering that Ferdinand, and through him the others, would know its colour, make and number, to turn that car in and hire a different one.

The telephone rang. I picked up the receiver and heard a familiar voice, warm and husky, coming to the point without delay.

'How about now?' she said. 'We could have an hour.'

I could seldom resist her. Seldom tried.

'An hour would be great. I was just thinking of you.'

'Good,' she said. 'See you.'

I stopped worrying about cars and thought of the white lace negligée instead; more enticing altogether. I put two wine glasses on the table by the sofa and looked at my watch. Malcolm would scarcely have reached the Savoy, I thought, but it was worth a try; and in fact he picked up the telephone saying he had that minute walked into the suite.

'I'm glad you're safely back,' I said. 'I've been a bit detained. I'll be two or three hours yet. Don't get lost.'

'Your mother is a cat,' he said.

'She saved your skin.'

'She called me a raddled old roué done up like a fifth-rate pastrycook.'

I laughed and could hear his scowl down the line.

'What do you want after caviar,' he said, 'if I order dinner?'

'Chef's special.'

'God rot you, you're as bad as your mother.'

I put the receiver down with amusement and waited through the twenty minutes it would take until the doorbell rang.

'Hello,' she said, as I let her in. 'How did the races go?'

I kissed her. 'Finished third.'

'Well done.'

She was older than I by ten or twelve years, also slender, auburn-haired and unselfconscious. I fetched the always-waiting champagne from the refrigerator, popped off the cork and poured our drinks. They were a ritual preliminary, really, as we'd never yet finished the bottle and, as usual, after half a glass, there was no point in sitting around on the sofa making small talk.

She exclaimed over the long black bruise down my thigh. 'Did you fall off a horse?'

'No, hit a car.'

'How careless.'

I drew the bedroom curtains to dim the setting western sun and lay with her naked between the sheets. We were practised lovers and comfortable with each other, philosophical over the fact that the

97

coupling was usually better for one than the other, rarely earth-moving for both simultaneously. That day, like the time before, it turned out ecstatic for her, less so for me, and I thought the pleasure of giving such pleasure enough in itself.

'Was it all right for you?' she said finally.

'Yes, of course.'

'Not one of your great times.'

'They don't come to order. Not your turn, my turn. It's luck.'

'A matter of friction and angles,' she teased me, repeating what I'd once said. 'Who's showering first?'

She liked to return clean to her husband, acknowledging the washing to be symbolic. I showered and dressed, and waited for her in the sitting-room. She was an essential part of my life, a comfort to the body, a contentment in the mind, a bulwark against loneliness. I usually said goodbye with regret, knowing she would return, but on that particular afternoon I said, 'Stay,' knowing all the same that she couldn't.

'What's the matter?' she said.

'Nothing.'

'You shivered.'

'Premonition.'

'What of?' She was preparing to go, standing by the door.

'That this will be the last time.'

'Don't be silly,' she said. 'I'll be back.'

She kissed me with what I knew was gratitude, the way I too kissed her. She smiled into my eyes. 'I'll be back.'

I opened the door for her and she went away lightheartedly, and I knew that the premonition had been not for her, but for myself.

I ferried the cars in the morning, going from London to Cambridge and Epsom and back to the hire firm, and no one followed me anywhere, as far as I could see.

When I'd departed, Malcolm had been full of rampaging indignation over the non-availability of first-class seats on any flight going to Paris the following day for the Arc de Triomphe.

'Go economy,' I said, 'it's only half an hour.'

It appeared that there were no economy seats either. I left him frowning but returned to find peace. He had chartered a private jet. He told me that snippet later, because he was currently engaged with Norman West who had called to give a progress report. The detective still seemed alarmingly frail but the grey on-the-point-of-death look had abated to fawn. The dustbin clothes had been replaced by an ordinary dark suit, and the greasy hair, washed, was revealed as almost white and neatly brushed.

I shook his hand: damp, as before.

'Feeling better, Mr West?' I asked.

'Thank you, yes.'

'Tell my son what you've just said,' Malcolm commanded. 'Give him the bad news.'

West gave me a small apologetic smile and then looked down at the notepad on his knee.

'Mrs Vivien Pembroke can't remember what she did on the Friday,' he said. 'And she spent Tuesday alone at home sorting through piles of old magazines.'

'What's bad news about that?' I asked.

'Don't be obtuse,' Malcolm said impatiently. 'She hasn't an alibi. None of the whole damn bunch has an alibi.'

'Have you checked them all?' I said, surprised. 'You surely haven't had time.'

'I haven't,' he agreed.

'Figure of speech.' Malcolm waved a hand. 'Go on telling him, Mr West.'

'I called on Mrs Berenice Pembroke.' West sighed expressively. 'She found me unwelcome.'

Malcolm chuckled sourly. 'Tongue like a rhinoceros-hide whip.'

West made a small squirming movement as if still feeling the lash, but said merely, with restraint, 'She was completely uncooperative.'

'Was Thomas there, when you called?' I asked.

'No, sir, he wasn't. Mrs Pembroke said he was at work. I later telephoned his office, to the number you gave me, hoping he could tell me where both his wife and himself had been at the relevant times, and a young lady there said that Mr Pembroke left the firm several weeks ago, and she knew nothing of his present whereabouts.'

'Well,' I said, stumped. 'I didn't know.'

'I telephoned Mrs Pembroke again to ask where her husband worked now, and she told me to ... er ... drop dead.'

Thomas, I thought, had worked for the same firm of biscuit makers from the day he'd finished a course in book-keeping and accountancy. Berenice referred disparagingly to his occupation as 'storekeeping' but Thomas said he was a quantity surveyor whose job it was to estimate the raw materials needed for each large contract, and cost them, and pass the information to the management. Thomas's promotions within the firm had been minor, such as from second assistant to first assistant, and at forty he could see, I supposed, that he would never be boardroom material. How bleak, I thought, to have to face his mid-life limitations with Berenice cramming them down his throat at every turn. Poor old Thomas . . .

'Mrs Joyce Pembroke,' West said, 'is the only one who is definite about her movements. On each relevant day, she was playing bridge. She didn't like me snooping, as she called it, and she wouldn't say who she was playing bridge with as she didn't want those people bothered.'

'You can leave Mrs Joyce Pembroke out,' I said.

'Huh?' Malcolm said.

'You know perfectly well,' I told him, 'that Joyce wouldn't kill you. If you'd had any doubts, you wouldn't have gone off in a car with her yesterday.'

'All right, all right,' he said, grumbling. 'Cross Joyce off.'

I nodded to West, and he put a line through Joyce.

'Yesterday I called on Mrs Alicia Pembroke and then later on Mrs Ursula Pembroke.' West's face showed no joy over the encounters. 'Mrs Alicia Pembroke told me to mind my own business, and Mrs Ursula Pembroke had been crying and wouldn't speak to me.' He lifted his hands out in a gesture of helplessness. 'I couldn't persuade either of them of the advantage of establishing alibis.'

'Did you get any impression,' I asked, 'that the police had been there before you, asking the same questions?'

'None at all.'

'I told you,' Malcolm said. 'They didn't believe I was attacked. They thought I'd just staged the whole thing.'

'Even so . . .'

'They checked everyone out over Moira, as you no doubt remember, and came up with a load of clean slates. They're just not bothering to do it again.'

'Do you happen to have their telephone number with you?'

'Yes I do,' he said, bringing a diary out of an inner pocket and flicking over the pages. 'But they won't tell you anything. It's like talking to a steel door.'

I dialled the number all the same and asked for the superintendent.

'In what connection, sir?'

'About the attempted murder of Mr Malcolm Pembroke a week ago yesterday.'

'One moment, sir.'

Time passed, and a different voice came on the line, plain and impersonal.

'Can I help you, sir?'

'About the attempted murder of Mr Malcolm Pembroke . . .'

'Who are you, sir?'

'His son.'

'Er . . . which one?'

'Ian.'

There was a brief rustling of paper.

'Could you tell me your birth date, as proof of identity?' Surprised, I gave it.

Then the voice said, 'Do you wish to give information, sir?'

'I wanted to find out how the investigation was going.'

'It isn't our custom to discuss that.'

'But . . .'

'But I can tell you, sir, that investigations into the alleged attack are being conducted with thoroughness.'

'*Alleged!*' I said.

'That's right, sir. We can find no evidence at all that there was another party involved.'

'I don't believe it.'

With slightly exaggerated patience but also a first flicker of sympathy, he said, 'I can tell you, sir, that there was no evidence of Mr Pembroke being dragged from the garden to the garage, which he alleged must have happened. No marks on the path. No scrapes on the heels of Mr Pembroke's shoes, which we examined at the time. There were no fingerprints except his own on the door handles of the car, no fingerprints except his anywhere. He showed no signs of carbon monoxide poisoning, which he explained was because he had delayed calling us. We examined the scene thoroughly the following morning, after Mr Pembroke had left home, and we found nothing at all to indicate the presence of an assailant. You can be sure we are not closing the case, but we are not at this time able to find grounds for suspicion of any other person.'

'He was nearly killed,' I said blankly.

'Yes, sir, well I'm sorry, sir, but that's how things stand.' He paused briefly. 'I can understand your disbelief, sir. It can't be easy for you.' He sounded quite human, offering comfort.

'Thank you at least for talking to me,' I said.

'Right, sir. Goodbye.'

'Goodbye,' I said slowly, but he had already gone.

'*Now* what's the matter?' Malcolm asked, watching my face.

I repeated what I'd just heard.

'Impossible!' Malcolm said explosively.

'No.'

'What then?'

'Clever.'

Eight

'Which door did you go out of, with the dogs?' I asked.

'The kitchen door, like I always do.'

'The kitchen door is about five steps along that covered way from the rear door into the garage.'

'Yes, of course it is,' Malcolm said testily.

'You told me that you set off down the garden with the dogs, and I suppose you told the police the same thing?'

'Yes, of course I did.'

'But you can't really remember actually going. You remember that you meant to, isn't that what you told me?'

He frowned. 'I suppose it is.'

'So what if you never made it to the garden, but were knocked out right there by the kitchen door? And what if you weren't dragged from there into the garage, but *carried*?'

His mouth opened. 'But I'm ...'

'You're not too heavy,' I said. 'I could carry you easily in a fireman's lift.'

He was five foot seven, stocky but not fat. He weighed ten stone something, I would have guessed.

'And the fingerprints?' Norman West asked.

'In a fireman's lift,' I said, 'you sling the person you want to carry over your left shoulder, don't you, with his head hanging down your back. Then you grasp his knees with your left arm, and hold his right wrist in your own right hand, to stop him slipping off?'

They both nodded.

'So if you're holding someone's wrist, you can put his hand easily onto any surface you like, including car door handles ... particularly,' I said, thinking, 'if you've opened the doors yourself first with gloves on, so that your victim's prints will be on top of any smudges you have made.'

103

'You should have been an assassin,' Malcolm said. 'You'd have been good at it.'

'So now we have Malcolm slumped in the back seat, half lying, like you said. So next you switch on the engine and leave the doors open so that all the nice fumes pour into the car quickly.'

'Doors?' Malcolm interrupted.

'The driver's door and one of the rear doors, at the least.'

'Oh, yes.'

'And then you have,' I said, 'a suicide.'

'And when I woke up,' Malcolm said gloomily, 'I put my prints all over the place. On the ignition key . . . everywhere.'

'No one could have counted on that.'

'It just looked bad to the police.'

We contemplated the scenario.

'If it happened like that,' West said, 'as indeed it could have done, whoever attacked you had to know that you would go out of the kitchen door at around that time.'

Malcolm said bleakly, 'If I'm at home, I always go for a walk with the dogs about then. Take them out, bring them back, give them their dinners, pour myself a drink. Routine.'

'And . . . er . . . is there anyone in your family who doesn't know when you walk the dogs?'

'Done it all my life, at that time,' Malcolm said.

There was a short silence, then I said, 'I wish I'd known all this when that car nearly killed us at Newmarket. We really ought to have told the police.'

'I was fed up with them,' Malcolm said. 'I've spent hours and hours with the suspicious buggers since Moira's death. I'm allergic to them. They bring me out in a rash.'

'You can't blame them, sir. Most murdered wives are killed by their husbands,' West said. 'And frankly, you appeared to have an extremely strong motive.'

'Rubbish,' Malcolm said. 'I don't see how people can kill people they've loved.'

'Unfortunately it's common.' West paused. 'Do you want me to continue with your family, sir, considering how little progress I've been able to make with them?'

'Yes,' Malcolm said heavily. 'Carry on. I'll get Joyce to tell them all to answer your questions. She seems to be able to get them to do what she wants.'

To get them to do what *they* want, I thought. She couldn't stir them into courses they didn't like.

Norman West put his notebook into his jacket pocket and shifted his weight forward on his chair.

'Before you go,' I said, 'I thought you might like to know that I asked the telephonist of the Cambridge hotel if anyone besides yourself had asked if a Mr Pembroke was staying there last weekend. She said they'd definitely had at least three calls asking for Mr Pembroke, two men and a woman, and she remembered because she thought it odd that no one wanted to talk to him, or would leave a message; they only wanted to know if he was there.'

'*Three!*' Malcolm exclaimed.

'One would be Mr West,' I pointed out. To West, I said, 'In view of that, could you tell us who asked you to find my father?'

West hesitated. 'I don't positively know which Mrs Pembroke it was. And . . . er . . . even if I became sure during these investigations, well, no sir, I don't think I could.'

'Professional ethics,' Malcolm said, nodding.

'I did warn you, sir,' West said to me, 'about a conflict of interests.'

'So you did. Hasn't she paid you yet, then? No name on any cheque?'

'No, sir, not yet.'

He rose to his feet, no one's idea of Atlas, though world-weary all the same. He shook my hand damply, and Malcolm's, and said he would be in touch. When he'd gone, Malcolm sighed heavily and told me to pour him some scotch.

'Don't you want some?' he said, when I gave him the glass.

'Not right now.'

'What did you think of Mr West?'

'He's past it.'

'You're too young. He's experienced.'

'And no match for the female Pembrokes.'

Malcolm smiled with irony. 'Few are,' he said.

We flew to Paris in the morning in the utmost luxury and were met by a chauffeured limousine which took its place with regal slowness in the solid traffic jam moving as one entity towards Longchamp.

The French racecourse, aflutter with flags, seemed to be swallowing *tout le monde* with insatiable appetite, until no one could walk in a straight line through the public areas where the crowds were heavy with guttural vowels and garlic.

Malcolm's jet/limousine package also included, I found, an invitation from the French Jockey Club, passes to everywhere and a Lucullan lunch appointment with the co-owner of Blue Clancy, Mr Ramsey Osborn.

Ramsey Osborn, alight with the *joie de vivre* gripping the whole place, turned out to be a very large sixtyish American who towered over Malcolm and took to him at once. Malcolm seemed to see the same immediate signals. They were cronies within two minutes.

'My son, Ian,' Malcolm said eventually, introducing me.

'Glad to know you.' He shook my hand vigorously. 'The one who fixed the sale, right?' His eyes were light grey and direct. 'Tell you the truth, there's a colt and a filly I want to buy for next year's Classics, and this way Blue Clancy will finance them very nicely.'

'But if Blue Clancy wins the Arc?' I said.

'No regrets, son.' He turned to Malcolm. 'You've a cautious boy, here.'

'Yeah,' Malcolm said. 'Cautious like an astronaut.'

The Osborn grey eyes swivelled back my way. 'Is that so? Do you bet?'

'Cautiously, sir.'

He laughed, but it wasn't unalloyed good humour. Malcolm, I thought, was much more to his liking. I left them sitting down at table together and, confident enough that no assassin would penetrate past the eagle-eyed doorkeepers of the upper citadel of the French Jockey Club, went down myself to ground level, happier to be with the action.

I had been racing in France a good deal, having for some years been assistant to a trainer who sent horses across the Channel as insouciantly as to York. Paris and Deauville were nearer anyway, he used to say, despatching me from Epsom via nearby Gatwick airport whenever he felt disinclined to go himself. I knew in consequence a smattering of racecourse French and where to find what I wanted, essential assets in the vast stands bulging with hurrying, vociferous, uninhibited French racegoers.

I loved the noise, the smell, the movement, the quick angers, the gesticulations, the extravagance of ground-level French racing. British jockeys tended to think French racegoers madly aggressive, and certainly once I'd actually had to defend with my fists a jockey who'd lost on a favourite I'd brought over. Jockeys in general had been insulted and battered to the extent that they no longer had to walk through crowds when going out or back from races at many tracks, and at Longchamp made the journey from weighing-room to horse by going up an elevator enclosed with plastic walls like a tunnel, across a bridge, and down a similar plastic-tunnel escalator on the other side.

I wandered around, greeting a few people, watching the first race from the trainers' stand, tearing up my losing pari-mutuel ticket, wandering some more, and feeling finally, without any work to do, without any horse to saddle, purposeless. It was an odd feeling. I couldn't remember when I'd last gone racing without being actively involved. Racing wasn't my playground, it was my work; without work it felt hollow.

Vaguely depressed, I returned to Malcolm's eyrie and found him blossoming in his new role as racehorse owner. He was referring to Le Prix de l'Arc de Triomphe familiarly as 'the Arc' as if it hadn't swum into his consciousness a bare half-week earlier, and discussing Blue Clancy's future with Ramsey Osborn as if he knew what he was talking about.

'We're thinking of the Breeders' Cup,' he said to me, and I interpreted the glint in his eyes as a frantic question as well as an instant decision.

'If he runs well today,' Osborn put in, qualifying it.

'It's a long way to California,' I said, agreeing with him. 'To the world championships, one might say.'

Malcolm was grateful for the information and far from dismayed by it. Pretty well the opposite, I saw. It would be to California we would go on the way to Australia, I guessed, rather than Singapore.

Lunch seemed to be continuing all afternoon, in the way French lunches do, with tidy circles of chateaubriand appearing, the empty plates to be cleared before small bundles of beans and carrots were served, followed by fresh little cheeses rolled in chopped nuts, and tiny strawberry tartlets with vanilla coulis. According to the menu, I had through my absence missed the *écrevisses*, the consommé, the *crêpes de volaille*, the *salade verte* and the sorbet. Just as well, I thought, eyeing the *friandises* which arrived with the coffee. Even amateur jockeys had to live by the scales.

Malcolm and Ramsey Osborn passed mellowly to cognac and cigars and watched the races on television. No one was in a hurry:

the Arc was scheduled for five o'clock and digestion could proceed until four-thirty.

Ramsey Osborn told us he came from Stamford, Connecticut, and had made his money by selling sports clothes. 'Baseball caps by the million,' he said expansively. 'I get them made, I sell them to retail outlets. And shoes, shirts, jogging suits, whatever goes. Health is big business, we'd be nowhere without exercise.'

Ramsey looked as if he didn't exercise too much himself, having pads of fat round his eyes, a heavy double chin and a swelling stomach. He radiated goodwill, however, and listened with kind condescension as Malcolm said reciprocally that he himself dealt modestly in currency and metal.

Ramsey wasn't grasping Malcolm's meaning, I thought, but then for all his occasional flamboyance Malcolm never drew general attention to his wealth. Quantum was a large comfortable Victorian family house, but it wasn't a mansion: when Malcolm had reached mansion financial status, he'd shown no signs of wanting to move. I wondered briefly whether that would change in future, now that he'd tasted prodigality.

In due course, the three of us went down to the saddling boxes and met both Blue Clancy and his trainer. Blue Clancy looked aristocratic, his trainer more so. Malcolm was visibly impressed with the trainer, as indeed was reasonable, as he was a bright young star, now rising forty, who had already trained six Classic winners and made it look easy.

Blue Clancy was restless, his nostrils quivering. We watched the saddling ritual and the final touches; flick of oil to shine the hooves, sponging of nose and mouth to clean and gloss, tweaking of forelock and tack to achieve perfection. We followed him into the parade ring and were joined by his English jockey who was wearing Ramsey's white, green and crimson colours and looking unexcited.

Malcolm was taking with alacrity to his first taste of big-time ownership. The electricity was fairly sparking. He caught my eye, saw what I was thinking, and laughed.

'I used to think you a fool to choose racing,' he said. 'Couldn't understand what you saw in it.'

'It's better still when you ride.'

'Yes . . . I saw that at Sandown. And about time, I suppose.'

Ramsey and the trainer claimed his attention to discuss tactics with the jockey, and I thought of the summer holidays when we were children, when Gervase, Ferdinand and I had all learned to ride. We'd learned on riding-school ponies, cycling to the nearby stables and spending time there grooming, feeding and mucking out. We'd entered local gymkhanas, and booted the poor animals in pop-the-balloon races. We'd ridden them backwards, bareback and with our knees on the saddle, and Ferdinand, the specialist, standing briefly on his head. The ponies had been docile and no doubt tired to death, but for two or three years we had been circus virtuosi: and Malcolm had paid the bills uncomplainingly, but had never come to watch us. Then Gervase and Ferdinand had been whisked away by Alicia, and in the lonely vacuum afterwards I'd ridden almost every possible morning, laying down a skill without meaning it seriously, not realising, in the flurry of academic school examinations, that it was the holiday pastime that would beckon me for life.

Blue Clancy looked as well as any of the others, I thought, watching the runners walk round, and the trainer was displaying more confidence than uncertainty. He thanked me for fixing the sale (from which he'd made a commission) and assured me that the two-million-guinea yearling was now settled snugly in a prime box in his yard. He'd known me vaguely until then as another trainer's assistant, a dogsbody, but as son and go-between of a new owner showing all signs of being severely hooked by the sport, I was now worth cultivation.

I was amused and far from minding. Life was like that. I might as well make the most of Malcolm's coat-tails while I was on them, I thought. I asked if I could see round the trainer's yard next time I was in Newmarket, and he said sure, he'd like it, and almost seemed to mean it.

'I'm sometimes there with George and Jo,' I said. 'Schooling their few jumpers. I ride them in amateur 'chases.' Everyone in Newmarket knew who George and Jo were: they were the equivalent of minor royalty.

'Oh, that's you, is it?' He put a few things together. 'Didn't realise that was you.'

'Mm.'

'Then come any time.' He sounded warmer, more positive. 'I mean it,' he said.

The way upwards in racing, I thought, ironic at myself, could lead along devious paths. I thanked him without effusiveness, and said 'Soon.'

Blue Clancy went out to the parade and the rest of us moved to the owners' and trainers' stand, which was near the core of things and buzzing with other similar groups locked in identical tensions.

'What chance has he got?' Malcolm demanded of me. 'Seriously.' His eyes searched my face as if for truth, which wasn't what I thought he wanted to hear.

'A bit better than he had on Thursday, since the second favourite has been scratched.' He wanted me to tell him more, however unrealistic, so I said, 'He's got a good chance of being placed. Anything can happen. He could win.'

Malcolm nodded, not knowing whether or not to believe me, but wanting to. Well and truly hooked, I thought, and felt fond of him.

I thought in my heart of hearts that the horse would finish sixth or seventh, not disgraced but not in the money. I'd backed him on the pari-mutuel but only out of loyalty: I'd backed the French horse Meilleurs Voeux out of conviction.

Blue Clancy moved well going down to the start. This was always the best time for owners, I thought, while the heart beat with expectation and while the excuses, explanations, disappointments were still ten minutes away. Malcolm lifted my binoculars to his eyes with hands that were actually trembling.

The trainer himself was strung up, I saw, however he might try to disguise it. There was only one 'Arc' in a year, of course, and too few years in a lifetime.

The horses seemed to circle for an interminable time at the gate but were finally fed into the slots to everyone's satisfaction. The gates crashed open, the thundering rainbow poured out, and twenty-six of Europe's best thoroughbreds were out on the right-hand circuit straining to be the fastest, strongest, bravest over one and a half miles of grass.

'Do you want your binoculars?' Malcolm said, hoping not.

'No. Keep them, I can see.'

I could see Ramsey Osborn's colours on the rails halfway back in the field, the horse moving easily, as were all the others at that point of the race. In the 'Arc', the essentials were simple: to be in the first ten coming round the last long right-hand bend, not to swing too wide into the straight and, according to the horse's stamina, pile on the pressure and head for home. Sometimes in a slow-starting 'Arc', one jockey would slip the field on the bend and hang on to his lead; in others, there would be war throughout to a whisker verdict. Blue

110

Clancy's 'Arc' seemed to be run at give-no-quarter speed, and he came into the finishing straight in a bunch of flying horses, lying sixth or eighth, as far as I could see.

Malcolm shouted 'Come on,' explosively as if air had backed up in his lungs from not breathing, and the ladies around us in silk dresses and hats, and the men in grey morning suits, infected by the same urgency, yelled and urged and cursed in polyglot babel. Malcolm put down the raceglasses and yelled louder, totally involved, rapt, living through his eyes.

Blue Clancy was doing his bit, I thought. He hadn't blown up. In fact, he was hanging on to fifth place. Going faster. Fourth . . .

The trainer, more restrained than owners, was now saying, 'Come on, come *on*' compulsively under his breath, but two of the horses already in front suddenly came on faster than Blue Clancy and drew away from the field, and the real hope died in the trainer with a sigh and a sag to the shoulders.

The finish the crowd watched was a humdinger which only a photograph could decide. The finish Malcolm, Ramsey, the trainer and I watched was two lengths further back, where Blue Clancy and his jockey, never giving up, were fighting all out to the very end, flashing across the line absolutely level with their nearest rival, only the horse's nose in front taking his place on the nod.

'On the nod,' the trainer said, echoing my thought.

'What does that mean?' Malcolm demanded. He was high with excitement, flushed, his eyes blazing. 'Were we third? Say we were third.'

'I think so,' the trainer said. 'There'll be a photograph.'

We hurried down from the stand to get to the unsaddling enclosure, Malcolm still short of breath and slightly dazed. 'What does on the nod mean?' he asked me.

'A galloping horse pokes his head out forward with each stride in a sort of rhythm, forward, back, forward, back. If two horses are as close as they were, and one horse's nose is forward when it passes the finishing line, and the other horse's happens to be back . . . well, that's on the nod.'

'Just luck, you mean?'

'Luck.'

'My God,' he said, 'I never thought I'd feel like that. I never thought I'd *care*. I only did it for a jaunt.'

He looked almost with wonderment at my face, as if I'd been

111

before him into a far country and he'd now discovered the mystery for himself.

Ramsey Osborn, who had roared with the best, beamed with pleasure when an announcement confirmed Blue Clancy's third place, saying he was sure glad the half-share sale had turned out fine. There were congratulations all round, with Malcolm and Ramsey being introduced to the owners of the winner, who were Italian and didn't understand Ramsey's drawl. Press photographers flashed like popping suns. There were television cameras, enquiring journalists, speeches, presentations. Malcolm looked envious of the Italian owners: third was fine but winning was better.

The four of us went for a celebratory drink; champagne, of course.

'Let's go for it,' Ramsey said. 'The Breeders' Cup. All the way.'

'We'll have to see how he is after today,' the trainer said warningly. 'He had a hard race.'

'He'll be all right,' Ramsey said with hearty confidence. 'Did you see the distance? Two lengths behind the winner. That's world class and no kidding.'

The trainer looked thoughtful but didn't argue. The favourite, undeniably world class, had finished second, victory snatched away no doubt by his earlier exhausting outing. He might not come back at all after his gruelling 'Arc'. The French favourite (and mine), Meilleurs Voeux, had finished fifth which made Blue Clancy better than I'd thought. Maybe he wouldn't be disgraced in the Breeders' Cup, if we went. I hoped we would go, but I was wary of hope.

The afternoon trickled away with the champagne, and Malcolm, almost as tired as his horse, sank euphorically into the limousine going back to the airport and closed his eyes in the jet.

'My first ever runner,' he said sleepily. 'Third in the "Arc". Not bad, eh?'

'Not bad.'

'I'm going to call the yearling Chrysos.'

'Why Chrysos?' I said.

He smiled without opening his eyes. 'It's Greek for gold.'

Malcolm was feeling caged in the Savoy.

On Sunday night, when we returned from Paris, he'd hardly had the energy to undress. By Monday morning, he was pacing the carpet

112

with revitalised energy and complaining that another week in the suite would drive him bonkers.

'I'm going back to Quantum,' he said. 'I miss the dogs.'

I said with foreboding, 'It would take the family half a day at most to find out you were there.'

'I can't help it. I can't hide for ever. You can come and stay close to me there.'

'Don't go,' I said. 'You're safe here.'

'Keep me safe at Quantum.'

He was adamant and began packing, and short of roping him to the bedstead, I couldn't stop him.

Just before we left, I telephoned Norman West and found him at home – which didn't bode well for the investigations. He was happy to tell me, he said, that it was now certain Mrs Deborah Pembroke, Ferdinand's wife, couldn't have been at Newmarket Bloodstock Sales, as on that day she had done a photo-modelling session. He had checked up with the magazine that morning, as Mrs Deborah had told me he could, and they had provided proof.

'Right,' I said. 'What about Ferdinand himself?'

'Mr Ferdinand was away from his office on both those days. Working at home on the Friday. The next week, he attended a course on the statistical possibilities of insurance fraud. He says that after registration on the Monday, they kept no record of attendance. I checked there too, and no one clearly remembers, they're all half strangers to each other.'

I sighed. 'Well . . . my father and I are going back to Quantum.'

'That's not wise, surely.'

'He's tired of imprisonment. Report to us there, will you?'

He said he would, when he had more news.

Cross off Debs, I thought. Bully for Debs.

I drove us down to Berkshire, stopping at Arthur Bellbrook's house in the village to collect the dogs. The two full-grown Dobermanns greeted Malcolm like puppies, prancing around him and rubbing against his legs as he slapped and fondled them. Real love on both sides, I saw. Uncomplicated by greed, envy or rejection.

Malcolm looked up and saw me watching him.

'You should get a dog,' he said. 'You need something to love.'

He could really hit home, I thought.

He bent back to his friends, playing with their muzzles, letting them try to snap at his fingers, knowing they wouldn't bite. They weren't guard dogs as such: he liked Dobermanns for their muscular agility, for their exuberance. I'd been brought up with relays of them around me, but it wasn't the affection of dogs I wanted, and I'd never asked for one of my own.

I thought of the afternoon he'd let them out of the kitchen and then been hit on the head. The dogs must have seen or sensed someone there. Though not guard dogs, they should still have warned Malcolm.

'Do those two dogs bark when strangers call?' I asked.

'Yes, of course.' Malcolm straightened, still smiling, letting the lithe bodies press against his knees. 'Why?'

'Did they bark a week last Friday, when you set out to walk them?'

The smile died out of his face. With almost despair he said, 'No. I don't think so. I don't remember. No ... not especially. They were pleased to be going out.'

'How many of the family do they know well?' I said.

'Everyone's been to the house several times since Moira died. All except you. I thought at first it was to support me, but ...' he shrugged with disillusion, 'they were all busy making sure none of the others ingratiated themselves with me and cut them out.'

Every possibility led back to the certainty we couldn't accept.

Malcolm shuddered and said he would walk through the village with the dogs. He would meet people he knew on the way, and there were people in that village who'd been close friends with Vivien, Alicia and Joyce and had sided with them, and had since fed them inflammatory half-lies about Malcolm's doings.

'You know the village grapevine is faster than telex,' I said. 'Put the dogs in the car.'

He wouldn't listen. It was only six days since the second time someone had tried to kill him, but he was already beginning to believe there would be no more attempts. Well, no more that morning, I supposed. He walked a mile and a half with the dogs, and I drove slowly ahead, looking back, making sure at each turn that he was coming into sight. When he reached the house safely, he said I was being over-protective.

'I thought that was what you wanted,' I said.

'It is and it isn't.'

Surprisingly, I understood him. He was afraid and ashamed of it, and in consequence felt urged to bravado. Plain straightforward fear, I thought, would have been easier to deal with. At least I got him to

114

wait outside with the dogs for company while I went into the house to reconnoitre, but no one had been there laying booby traps, no one was hiding behind doors with raised blunt instruments, no one had sent parcel bombs in the post.

I fetched him, and we unpacked. We both took it for granted I would sleep in my old room, and I made up the bed there. I had bought provisions in London to the extent of bread, milk, lemons, smoked salmon and caviar, a diet both of us now considered normal. There was champagne in the cellar and a freezer full of post-Moira TV dinners in cardboard boxes. We weren't going to starve, I thought, inspecting them, though we might get indigestion.

Malcolm spent the afternoon in his office opening letters and talking to his stockbroker on the telephone, and at the routine time proposed to give the dogs their pre-dinner walk.

'I'll come with you,' I said.

He nodded without comment, and in the crisp early October air we set off down the garden, through the gate into the field, and across to the willow-lined stream he had been aiming for ten days earlier.

We had all sailed toy boats down that stream when we'd been children, and picked watercress there, and got thoroughly wet and muddy as a matter of course. Alicia had made us strip, more than once, before she would let us into her bridal-white kitchen.

'Last Monday,' Malcolm said casually, watching the dogs sniff for water rats round the tree roots, 'I made a new will.'

'Did you?'

'I did. In Cambridge. I thought I might as well. The old one left a lot to Moira. And then, after that Friday . . . well, I wanted to put things in order, in case . . . just in case.'

'What did you do with it?' I asked.

He seemed amused. 'The natural question is surely, "What's in it? What have you left to *me*?" '

'Mm,' I said dryly. 'I'm not asking that, ever. What I'm asking is more practical.'

'I left it with the solicitor in Cambridge.'

We were wandering slowly along towards the stream, the dogs quartering busily. The willow leaves, yellowing, would fall in droves in the next gale, and there was bonfire smoke drifting somewhere in the still air.

'Who knows where your will is?' I asked.

'I do. And the solicitor.'

'Who's the solicitor?'

'I saw his name on a brass plate outside his office and went in on impulse. I've got his card somewhere. We discussed what I wanted, he had it typed up, and I signed it with witnesses in his office and left it there for safekeeping.'

'For a brilliant man,' I said peaceably, 'you're as thick as two planks.'

Nine

Malcolm said explosively, 'You're bloody rude,' and, after a pause, 'In what way am I thick? A new will was essential.'

'Suppose you died without telling me or anybody else you'd made it, or where it could be found?'

'Oh.' He was dismayed, then brightened. 'The solicitor would have produced it.'

'If he knew you by reputation, if he had any idea of the sums involved, if he heard you were dead, if he were conscientious, and if he knew who to get in touch with. If he were lazy, he might not bother, he's under no obligation. Within a month, unless you boasted a bit about your wealth, he'll have forgotten your will's in his files.'

'You seem to know an awful lot about it.'

'Joyce worked for years for the Citizens Advice Bureau, do you remember? I used to hear lurid tales of family squabbles because no one knew where to find a will they were sure had been made. And equally lurid tales of family members knowing where the will was and burning it before anyone else could find it, if they didn't like what was in it.'

'That's why I left it in safekeeping,' Malcolm said. 'Precisely because of that.'

We reached the far boundary of the field. The stream ran on through the neighbour's land, but we at that point turned back.

'What should I do then?' he asked. 'Any ideas?'

'Send it to the probate office at Somerset House.'

'How do you mean?'

'Joyce told me about it, one time. You put your will in a special envelope they'll send you if you apply for it, then you take it or send it to the central probate office. They register your will there and keep it safe. When anyone dies and any solicitor anywhere applies for probate, the central probate office routinely checks its files. If it has ever registered a will for that person, that's the envelope that will be opened, and that's the will that will be proved.'

He thought it over. 'Do you mean, if I registered a will with the probate office, and then changed my mind and wrote a new one, it wouldn't be any good?'

'You'd have to retrieve the old will and re-register the new one. Otherwise the old will would be the one adhered to.'

'Good God. I didn't know any of this.'

'Joyce says not enough people know. She says if people would only register their wills, they couldn't be pressured into changing them when they're gaga or frightened or on their deathbeds. Or at least, wills made like that would be useless.'

'I used to laugh, rather, at Joyce's voluntary work. Felt indulgent.' He sighed. 'Seems it had its uses.'

The Citizens Advice Bureau, staffed by knowledgeable armies of Joyces, could steer one from the cradle to the grave, from marriage to divorce to probate, from child allowance to old age supplements. I'd not always listened attentively to Joyce's tales, but I'd been taken several times to the Bureau, and I seemed to have absorbed more than I'd realised.

'I kept a copy of my new will,' Malcolm said. 'I'll show it to you when we go in.'

'You don't need to.'

'You'd better see it,' he said.

I didn't argue. He whistled to the dogs who left the stream reluctantly, and we made our way back to the gate into the garden.

'Just wait out here while I check the house,' I said.

He was astonished. 'We've only been out for half an hour. And we locked the doors.'

'You regularly go out for half an hour at this time. And how many of the family still have keys to the house?'

He was silent. All of the people who had ever lived there could have kept their keys to the house, and there had never been any need, before now, to change the locks.

'Stay here, then?' I asked, and he nodded sadly.

The kitchen door was still locked. I let myself in and went all through the house again, but it was quiet and undisturbed, and doors that I'd set open at certain angles were still as I'd left them.

I called Malcolm and he came into the kitchen and began getting the food for the dogs.

'Are you going through this checking rigmarole every single time we leave the house?' he said, sounding as if he didn't like it.

'Yes, until we get the locks changed.'

He didn't like that either, but expressed his disapproval only in a frown and a rather too vigorous scraping of dog food out of a tin.

'Fill the water bowls,' he said rather crossly, and I did that and set them down again on the floor.

'It isn't so easy to change the locks,' he said. 'They're all mortice locks, as you know, set into the doors. The one on the front door is antique.'

The front door keys were six inches long and ornate, and there had never been more than three of them, as far as I knew.

'All right,' I said. 'If we keep the front door bolted and the keys in your safe, we won't change that one.'

A little pacified, he put the filled dinner bowls on the floor, wiped his fingers and said it was time for a noggin. I bolted the kitchen door on the inside and then followed him through the hall to the office, where he poured scotch into two glasses and asked if I wanted to desecrate mine with ice. I said yes and went back to the kitchen to fetch some. When I returned, he had taken some sheets of paper from his open briefcase and was reading them.

'Here you are. Here's my will,' he said, and passed the papers over.

He had made the will, I reflected, before he had telephoned me to put an end to our quarrel, and I expected not to figure in it in consequence, but I'd done him an injustice. Sitting in an armchair and sipping the whisky, I read through all the minor bequests to people like Arthur Bellbrook, and all the lawyerly gobbledegook 'upon trust' and without commas, and came finally to the plain language.

'To each of my three divorced wives Vivien Joyce and Alicia I bequeath the sum of five hundred thousand pounds.

'My son Robin being provided for I direct that the residue of my estate shall be divided equally among my children Donald Lucy Thomas Gervase Ian Ferdinand and Serena.'

A long clause followed with provisions for 'if any of my children shall pre-decease me', leaving 'his or her share' to the grandchildren.

Finally came two short sentences:

'I bequeath to my son Ian the piece of thin wire to be found on my desk. He knows what he can do with it.'

Surprised and more moved than I could say, I looked up from the last page and saw the smile in Malcolm's eyes deepen to a throaty chuckle.

'The lawyer chap thought the last sentence quite obscene. He said I shouldn't put that sort of thing in a will.'

I laughed. 'I didn't expect to be in your will at all.'

'Well . . .' He shrugged. 'I'd never have left you out. I've regretted for a long while . . . hitting you . . . everything.'

'Guess I deserved it.'

'Yes, at the time.'

I turned back to the beginning of the document and re-read one of the preliminary paragraphs. In it, he had named me as his sole executor, when I was only his fifth child. 'Why me?' I said.

'Don't you want to?'

'Yes. I'm honoured.'

'The lawyer said to name someone I trusted.' He smiled lopsidedly. 'You got elected.'

He stretched out an arm and picked up from his desk a leather pot holding pens and pencils. From it, he pulled a wire about ten inches long and about double the thickness, of the sort used by florists for stiffening flower stalks.

'If this one should get lost,' he said, 'just find another.'

'Yes. All right.'

'Good.' He put the wire back in the pot and the pot back in the desk.

'By the time you pop off,' I said, 'the price of gold might have risen out of sight and all I'd find in the wall would be spiders.'

'Yeah, too bad.'

I felt more at one with him than at any time since he'd telephoned, and perhaps he with me. I hoped it would be a very long time before I would have to execute his will.

'Gervase,' I said, 'suggests that you should distribute some of your money now, to . . . er . . . reduce the estate tax.'

'Does he? And what do you think?'

'I think,' I said, 'that giving it to the family instead of to scholarships and film companies and so on might save your life.'

The blue eyes opened wide. 'That's immoral.'

'Pragmatic.'

'I'll think about it.'

We dined on the caviar, but the fun seemed to have gone out of it.

120

'Let's have shepherd's pie tomorrow,' Malcolm said. 'There's plenty in the freezer.'

We spent the next two days uneventfully at Quantum being careful, but with no proof that care was needed.

Late on Tuesday afternoon, out with the dogs and having made certain that Arthur Bellbrook had gone home, we walked round behind the kitchen wall and came to the treasure house.

A veritable sea of nettles guarded the door. Malcolm looked at them blankly. 'The damn things grow overnight.'

I pulled my socks over the bottoms of my trousers and assayed the traverse; stamped down an area by the bottom of the door and with fingers all the same stinging felt along to one end of the wooden sill and with some effort tugged it out. Malcolm leaned forward and gave me the piece of wire, and watched while I stood up and located the almost invisible hole. The wire slid through the tiny tube built into the mortar and, under pressure, the latch inside operated as smoothly as it had when I'd installed it. The wire dislodged a metal rod out of a slot, allowing the latch to spring open.

'I oiled it,' Malcolm said. 'The first time I tried, it was as rusty as hell.'

I pushed the edge of the heavy narrow door and it opened inwards, its crenellated edges disengaging from the brick courses on each side with faint grating noises but with no pieces breaking off.

'You built it well,' Malcolm said. 'Good mortar.'

'You told me how to mix the mortar, if you remember.'

I stepped into the small brick room which was barely four feet across at the far end and about eight feet long, narrowing in a wedge-shape towards the door which was set into one of the long walls. The wider end wall was stacked to waist height with flat wooden boxes like those used for château-bottled wines. In front, there were two large cardboard boxes with heavily taped-down tops. I stepped further in and tried to open one of the wine-type boxes, but those were nailed shut. I turned round and took a couple of steps back and stood in the doorway, looking out.

'Gold at the back, treasures in front,' Malcolm said, watching me with interest.

'I'll take your word for it.'

The air in the triangular room smelled faintly musty. There was no

121

ventilation, as I'd told Arthur Bellbrook, and no damp course, either. I reset the rod into the latch on the inside, as it wouldn't shut unless one did, and stepped outside. My teenage design limitations meant that one had to go down on one's knees to close the door the last few inches, hooking one's fingers into a hollow under the bottom row of bricks and pulling hard. The door and walls fitted together again like pieces of jigsaw, and the latch inside clicked into place. I replaced the sill under the door, kicking it home, and tried to encourage the crushed nettles to stand up again.

'They'll be flourishing again by morning,' Malcolm said. 'Rotten things.'

'Those cardboard boxes are too big to come out through the door,' I observed, rubbing stings on my hands and wrists.

'Oh, sure. I took them in empty and flat, then set them up, and filled them bit by bit.'

'You could take those things out again now.'

There was a pause, then he said, 'I'll wait. As things are at present, they might as well stay there.'

I nodded. He whistled to the dogs and we went on with the walk. We had given up referring explicitly to fear of the family, but it still hung around us like grief. On our return from the field, Malcolm waited outside without comment until I checked through the house, and prosaically began feeding the dogs on my report of all clear.

Neither of us discussed how long all the precautions were going to have to go on. Norman West's latest report had been as inconclusive as his first, and by Wednesday evening the pitiful summary I'd been making of his results read as follows:

DONALD:	busy about the golf club. Cannot pinpoint any times.
HELEN:	working at home making Henley souvenirs.
LUCY:	reading, walking, writing, meditating.
EDWIN:	housework, shopping for groceries, going to public library.
THOMAS:	looking for new job, suffering headaches.
BERENICE:	housekeeping, looking after children, uncooperative.
GERVASE:	commuting to London, in and out of his office, home late.
URSULA:	looking after daughters, unhappy.

122

FERDINAND:	on statistics course, no attendance records.
DEBS:	photo-session vouched for on Newmarket Sales day.
SERENA:	teaching aerobics mornings and most evenings, shopping for clothes afternoons.
VIVIEN:	pottering about, can't remember.
ALICIA:	probably the same, unhelpful.
JOYCE:	playing bridge.

All one could say, I thought, was that no one had made any effort to produce alibis for either relevant time. Only Debs had a firm one, which had been arranged and vouched for by others. All the rest of the family had been moving about without timing their exits and entrances: normal behaviour for innocent people.

Only Joyce and I lived beyond half an hour's drive from Quantum. All of the others, from Donald at Henley to Gervase at Maidenhead, from Thomas near Reading to Lucy near Marlow, from Ferdinand in Wokingham to Serena in Bracknell, and even Vivien in Twyford and Alicia near Windsor, all of them seemed to have put down roots in a ring round the parent house like thistledown blown on the wind and reseeding.

The police had remarked on it when investigating Moira's murder, and had checked school runs and train timetables until they'd been giddy. They had apparently caught no one lying, but that seemed to me inconclusive in a family which had had a lot of practice in misrepresentation. The fact had been, and still was, that anybody could have got to Quantum and home again without being missed.

I spent a short part of that Wednesday wandering around Moira's greenhouse, thinking about her death.

The greenhouse was invisible from the house, as Arthur Bellbrook had said, set on a side lawn which was bordered with shrubs. I wondered whether Moira had been alarmed to see her killer approach. Probably not. Quite likely, she had herself arranged the meeting, stating time and place. Malcolm had once mentioned that she didn't like casual callers, preferring them to telephone first. Perhaps it had been an unforeseen killing, an opportunity seized. Perhaps there had been a quarrel. Perhaps a request denied. Perhaps one of Moira's specials in acid-sweet triumphs, like picking Arthur Bellbrook's vegetables.

Moira in possession of Quantum, about to take half of everything

Malcolm owned. Moira smugly satisfied, oblivious to her danger. I doubted if she had believed in her nightmare death even while it was happening.

Malcolm spent the day reading the *Financial Times* and making phone calls: yen, it appeared from snatches I overheard, were behaving gruesomely from Malcolm's point of view.

Although making calls outward, neither of us was keen to answer inward calls since that morning, when Malcolm had been drenched by a shower of recriminations from Vivien, all on the subject of meanness. He had listened with wry pain and given me a resumé once Vivien had run out of steam.

'One of the cats in the village told her we were here, so now the whole family will know,' he said gloomily. 'She says Donald is bankrupt, Lucy is starving and Thomas got the sack and can't deal with unemployment. Is it all true? It can't be. She says I should give them twenty thousand pounds each immediately.'

'It wouldn't hurt,' I said. 'It's Gervase's idea watered down.'

'But I don't believe in it.'

I explained about Donald's school fees crisis, Lucy's crumbling certainties, Thomas with Berenice chipping away at his foundations. He said their troubles lay in their own characters, which was true enough. He said if he gave those three a hand-out, he would have to do it for us all, or there would be a shooting civil war among Vivien, Joyce and Alicia. He made a joke of it, but he was stubborn. He had provided for us through our trust funds. The rest was up to us. He hadn't changed his mind. He'd thought over Vivien's suggestion, and the answer was no.

He telephoned back to Vivien and to her fury told her so. I could hear her voice calling him wicked, mean, cruel, vindictive, petty, sadistic, tyrannical and evil. He took offence, shouted at her to shut up, shut up, and finally slammed down the receiver while she was still in full flood.

All Vivien had achieved, I thought, was to make him dig his toes in further.

I thought him pig-headed, I thought him asking to be murdered. I looked at the unrelenting blue eyes daring me to argue, and wondered if he thought giving in would be weakness, if he thought baling out his children would diminish his own self-respect.

I said nothing at all. I was in a bad position to plead for the others, as I stood to gain myself. I hoped for many reasons that he would be

124

able to change his mind, but it had to come from inside. I went out to Moira's greenhouse to give him time to calm down, and when I returned neither of us mentioned what had passed.

On the dogs' walk that afternoon, I reminded him that I was due to ride at Cheltenham the following day, and asked if he had any cronies in that direction with whom he could spend the time.

'I'd like to see you ride again,' he said.

He constantly surprised me.

'What if the family come too?'

'I'll dress up as another chef.'

I didn't know that it was wise, but again he had his own way, and I persuaded myself he would come to no harm on a racecourse. When we got there, I introduced him to George and Jo who congratulated him on Blue Clancy and took him off to lunch.

I looked around apprehensively all afternoon for brothers, sisters, mother and step-mothers, but saw none. The day was cold and windy with everyone turning up collars and hunching shoulders to keep warm, with hats on every head, felt, tweed, wool and fur. If anyone had wanted to hide inside their clothes, the weather was great for it.

Park Railings gave me a splendid ride and finished fourth, less tired than his jockey, who hadn't sat on a horse for six days. George and Jo were pleased enough, and Malcolm, who had been down the track with them to watch one of the other steeplechases from beside one of the jumps, was thoughtful.

'I didn't realise you went so fast,' he said, going home. 'Such speed over those jumps.'

'About thirty miles an hour.'

'I suppose I could buy a steeplechaser,' he said, 'if you'd ride it.'

'You'd better not. It would be favouritism.'

'Huh.'

We went thirty miles towards Berkshire and came to a hostelry he liked where we stopped for the late afternoon noggins (Arthur Bellbrook was taking the dogs home with him for the night) and waited lazily until dinner.

We talked about racing, or rather Malcolm asked questions and I answered them. His interest seemed inexhaustible, and I wondered if it would die as fast as it had sprung up. He couldn't wait to find out what Chrysos might do next year.

We ate without hurrying, lingering over coffee, and went on home, pulling up yawning outside the garage, sleepy from fresh air and French wine.

'I'll check the house,' I said without enthusiasm.

'Oh, don't bother, it's late.'

'I'd better check it. Honk the horn if you see something you don't like.'

I left him in the car, let myself into the kitchen and switched on the lights. The door to the hall was closed as usual, to keep the dogs, when they were there, from roaming through the house. I opened the door to the hall and switched on the hall lights.

I stopped there briefly, looking round.

Everything looked quiet and peaceful, but my skin began to crawl just the same, and my chest felt tight from suddenly suspended breath.

The door to the office and the door to the sitting-room were not as I had left them. The door to the office was more than half open, the door to the sitting-room all but closed; neither standing at the precise narrow angle at which I'd set them every time we'd been out.

I tried to remember whether I'd actually set the doors before leaving that morning, or whether I'd forgotten. But I *had* set them. I knew I had. I'd picked up my saddle and other gear in the hall after doing it, and shut the hall-to-kitchen door, and locked the outside door, leaving the dogs with Arthur Bellbrook in the garden.

I hadn't until then thought of myself as a coward, but I felt dead afraid of going further into the house. It was so large, so full of dark corners. There were two cellars, and the several unlit attic bedrooms of long-gone domestic servants, and the boxroom deep with shadows. There were copious cupboards everywhere and big empty wardrobes. I'd been round them all three or four times during the past few days, but not at night, and not with the signals standing at danger.

With an effort, I took a few steps into the hall, listening. I had no weapon. I felt nakedly vulnerable. My heart thumped uncomfortably. The house was silent.

The heavy front door, locked and bolted like a fortress, had not been touched. I went over to the office, reached in with an arm, switched on the light and pushed the half-open door wider.

There was no one in there. Everything was as Malcolm had left it in the morning. The windows shone blackly, like threats. Taking a deep breath, I repeated the procedure with the sitting-room, but also checking the bolts on the french windows, and after that with the dining-room, and the downstairs cloakroom, and then with worse trepidation went down the passage beside the stairs to the big room that had been our playroom when we were children and a billiard room in times long past.

The door was shut. Telling myself to get on with it, I opened the door, switched on the light, pushed the door open.

There was no one there. It wasn't really a relief, because I would have to go on looking. I checked the storeroom opposite, where there were stacks of garden furniture, and also the door at the end of the passage, which led out into the garden: securely bolted on the inside. I went back to the hall and stood at the bottom of the stairs, looking upward.

It was stupid to be so afraid, I thought. It was home, the house I'd been brought up in. One couldn't be frightened by home.

One was.

I swallowed. I went up the stairs. There was no one in my bedroom. No one in five other bedrooms, nor in the boxroom, no one in the bathrooms, no one in the plum and pink lushness of Malcolm's own suite. By the end, I was still as scared as I'd been at the beginning, and I hadn't started on cellars or attics or small hiding places.

I hadn't looked under the beds. Demons could be waiting anywhere to jump out on me, yelling. Giving in, I switched off all the upstairs lights and went cravenly back to the hall.

Everything was still quiet, mocking me.

I was a fool, I thought.

Leaving the hall and kitchen lights on, I went back to Malcolm who started to get out of the car when he saw me coming. I waved him back and slid in beside him, behind the driving wheel.

'What's the matter?' he said.

'Someone may be here.'

'What do you mean?'

I explained about the doors.

'You're imagining things.'

'No. Someone has used their key.'

We hadn't yet been able to have the locks changed, although the carpenter was due to be bringing replacements the following morning. He'd had difficulty finding good new locks to fit into such

127

old doors, he'd said, and had promised them for Thursday, but I'd put him off until Friday because of Cheltenham.

'We can't stay out here all night,' Malcolm protested. 'It's bound to be the wind or something that moved the doors. Let's go to bed, I'm whacked.'

I looked at my hands. They weren't actually shaking. I thought for a while until Malcolm grew restless.

'I'm getting cold,' he said. 'Let's go in, for God's sake.'

'No . . . we're not sleeping here.'

'What? You can't mean it.'

'I'll lock the house, and we'll go and get a room somewhere else.'

'At this time of night?'

'Yes.' I made to get out of the car and he put a hand on my arm to catch my attention.

'Fetch some pyjamas, then, and washing things.'

I hesitated. 'No, I don't think it's safe.' I didn't say I couldn't face it, but I couldn't.

'Ian, all this is crazy.'

'It would be crazier still to be murdered in our beds.'

'But just because two doors . . .'

'Yes. Because.'

He seemed to catch some of my own uneasiness because he made no more demur, but when I was headed again for the kitchen he called after me, 'At least bring my briefcase from the office, will you?'

I made it through the hall again with only a minor tremble in the gut; switched on the office light, fetched his briefcase without incident and set the office door again at its usual precise angle. I did the same to the sitting-room door. Perhaps they would tell us in the morning, I thought, whether or not we had had a visitor who had hidden from my approach.

I went back through the hall, switched the lights off, shut the hall-to-kitchen door, let myself out, left the house dark and locked and put the briefcase on the car's back seat.

On the basis that it would be easiest to find a room in London, particularly at midnight, for people without luggage, I drove up the M4 and on Malcolm's instructions pulled up at the Ritz. We might be refugees, he said, but we would be staying in no camp, and he explained to the Ritz that he'd decided to stay overnight in London as he'd been delayed late on business.

'Our name is Watson,' I said impulsively, thinking suddenly of Norman West's advice and picking out of the air the first name I could think of. 'We will pay with travellers' cheques.'

Malcolm opened his mouth, closed it again, and kept blessedly quiet. One could write whatever name one wanted onto travellers' cheques.

The Ritz batted no eyelids, offered us connecting rooms (no double suites available) and promised razors, toothbrushes and a bottle of scotch.

Malcolm had been silent for most of the journey, and so had I, feeling with every heart-calming mile that I had probably over-reacted, that maybe I hadn't set the doors, that if any of the family had let themselves into the house while we were out, they'd been gone long before we returned. We had come back hours later than anyone could have expected, if they were judging the time it would take us to drive from Cheltenham.

I could have sat at the telephone in the house and methodically checked with all the family to make sure they were in their own homes. I hadn't thought of it, and I doubted if I could have done it, feeling as I had.

Malcolm, who held that sleeping pills came a poor second to scotch, put his nightcap theory to the test and was soon softly snoring. I quietly closed the door between our two rooms and climbed between my own sheets, but for a long time lay awake. I was ashamed of my fear in the house which I now thought must have been empty. I had risked my neck without a qualm over big fences that afternoon: I'd been petrified in the house that someone would jump out on me from the dark. The two faces of courage, I thought mordantly: turn one face to the wall.

We went back to Berkshire in the morning and couldn't reach Quantum by car because the whole village, it seemed, was out and blocking the road. Cars and people everywhere: cars parked along the roadsides, people walking in droves towards the house.

'What on earth's going on?' Malcolm said.

'Heaven knows.'

In the end I had to stop the car, and we finished the last bit of the journey on foot.

We had to push through crowds and were unpopular until people recognised Malcolm, and made way for him, and finally we reached the entrance to the drive ... and there literally rocked to a stop.

To start with there was a rope stretched across it, barring our way, with a policeman guarding it. In front of the house, there were ambulances, police cars, fire-engines ... swarms of people in uniform moving purposefully about.

Malcolm swayed with shock, and I felt unreal, disconnected from my feet. Our eyes told us: our brains couldn't believe.

There was an immense jagged gaping hole in the centre of Quantum.

People standing near us in the gateway, round-eyed, said, 'They say it was the gas.'

Ten

We were in front of the house, talking to policemen. I couldn't remember walking up the drive.

Our appearance on the scene had been a shock to the assembled forces, but a welcome one. They had been searching for our remains in the rubble.

They told us that the explosion had happened at four-thirty in the morning, the *wumph* and reverberation of it waking half the village, the shockwaves breaking windows and setting dogs howling. Several people had called the police, but when the force had reached the village, everything had seemed quiet. No one knew where the explosion had occurred. The police drove round the extended neighbourhood until daylight, and it was only then that anyone saw what had happened to Quantum.

The front wall of the hall, the antique front door with it, had been blown out flat onto the drive, and the centre part of the upper storey had collapsed into the hall. The glass in all the windows had disappeared.

'I'm afraid it's worse at the back,' a policeman said phlegmatically. 'Perhaps you'd come round there, sir. We can at least tell everyone there are no bodies.'

Malcolm nodded mechanically and we followed the policeman round to the left, between the kitchen and garage, through to the garden and along past the dining-room wall. The shock when we rounded onto the terrace was, for all the warning, horrific and sickening.

Where the sitting-room had been, there was a mountain of jumbled dusty bricks, plaster, beams and smashed furniture spilling outwards onto the grass. Malcolm's suite, which had been above the sitting-room, had vanished, had become part of the chaos. Those of the attic rooms that had been above his head had come down too. The roof, which had looked almost intact from the front, had at the

131

rear been stripped of tiles, the old sturdy rafters standing out against the sky like picked ribs.

My own bedroom had been on one side of Malcolm's bedroom: all that remained of it were some shattered spikes of floorboards, a strip of plaster cornice and a drunken mantle clinging to a cracked wall overlooking a void.

Malcolm began to shake. I took off my jacket and put it round his shoulders.

'We don't have gas,' he said to the policeman. 'My mother had it disconnected sixty years ago because she was afraid of it.'

There was a slight spasmodic wind blowing, enough to lift Malcolm's hair and leave it awry. He looked suddenly frail, as if the swirling air would knock him over.

'He needs a chair,' I said.

The policeman gestured helplessly to the mess. No chairs left.

'I'll get one from the kitchen. You look after him.'

'I'm quite all right,' Malcolm said faintly.

'The outside kitchen door is locked, sir, and we can't allow you to go in through the hall.'

I produced the key, showed it to him, and went along and in through the door before he could stop me. In the kitchen, the shiny yellow walls themselves were still standing, but the door from the hall had blown open, letting in a glacier tongue of bricks and dust. Dust everywhere, like a veil. Lumps of plaster had fallen from the ceiling. Everything glass, everything china in the room had cracked apart. Moira's geraniums, fallen from their shelves, lay in red farewell profusion over her all-electric domain.

I picked up Malcolm's pine armchair, the one thing he had insisted on keeping through all the changes, and carried it out to where I'd left him. He sank into it without seeming to notice it and put his hand over his mouth.

There were firemen and other people tugging at movable parts of the ruins, but the tempo of their work had slowed since they'd seen we were alive. Several of them came over to Malcolm, offering sympathy, but mostly wanting information, such as were we certain there had been no one else in the house?

As certain as we could be.

Had we been storing any gas in the house? Bottled gas? Butane? Propane? Ether?

No.

Why ether?

It could be used for making cocaine.

We looked at them blankly.

They had already discovered, it seemed, that there had been no mains gas connected. They were asking about other possibilities because it nevertheless looked like a gas explosion.

We'd had no gas of any sort.

Had we been storing any explosive substances whatsoever?

No.

Time seemed disjointed.

Women from the village, as in all disasters, had brought hot tea in thermos flasks for the men working. They gave some to Malcolm and me, and found a red blanket for Malcolm so that I could have my jacket back in the chill gusty air. There was grey sheet cloud overhead: the light was grey, like the dust.

A thick ring of people from the village stood in the garden round the edges of the lawn, with more arriving every minute across the fields and through the garden gate. No one chased them away. Many were taking photographs. Two of the photographers looked like Press.

A police car approached, its siren wailing ever louder as it made slow progress along the crowded road. It wailed right up the drive, and fell silent, and presently a senior-looking man not in uniform came round to the back of the house and took charge.

First, he stopped all work on the rubble. Then he made observations and wrote in a notebook. Then he talked to the chief of the firemen. Finally he came over to Malcolm and me.

Burly and black moustached, he said, as to an old acquaintance, 'Mr Pembroke.'

Malcolm similarly said, 'Superintendent,' and everyone could hear the shake he couldn't keep out of his voice. The wind died away for a while, though Malcolm's shakes continued within the blanket.

'And you, sir?' the superintendent asked me.

'Ian Pembroke.'

He pursed his mouth below the moustache, considering me. He was the man I'd spoken to on the telephone, I thought.

'Where were you last night, sir?'

'With my father in London,' I said. 'We've just . . . returned.'

I looked at him steadily. There were a great many things to be said, but I wasn't going to rush into them.

133

He said noncommittally, 'We will have to call in explosive experts as the damage here on preliminary inspection, and in the absence of any gas, seems to have been caused by an explosive device.'

Why didn't he say bomb, I thought irritably. Why shy away from the word? If he'd expected any reaction from Malcolm or me, he probably got none as both of us had come to the same conclusion from the moment we'd walked up the drive.

If the house had merely been burning, Malcolm would have been dashing about, giving instructions, saving what he could, dismayed but full of vigour. It was the implications behind a bomb which had knocked him into shivering lassitude: the implications and the reality that if he'd slept in his own bed, he wouldn't have risen to bath, read the *Sporting Life*, go to his bank for travellers' cheques and eat breakfast at the Ritz.

And nor, for that matter, would I.

'I can see you're both shocked,' the superintendent said unemotionally. 'It's clearly impossible to talk here, so I suggest you might come to the police station.' He spoke carefully, giving us at least theoretically the freedom of refusing.

'What about the house?' I said. 'It's open to the four winds. Apart from this great hole, all the windows are broken everywhere else. There's a lot of stuff still inside . . . silver . . . my father's papers in his office . . . some of the furniture.'

'We will keep a patrol here,' he said. 'If you'll give the instructions, we'll suggest someone to board up the windows, and we'll contact a construction firm with a tarpaulin large enough for the roof.'

'Send me the bill,' Malcolm said limply.

'The firms concerned will no doubt present their accounts.'

'Thanks anyway,' I said.

The superintendent nodded.

A funeral for Quantum, I thought. Coffin windows, pall roof. Lowering the remains into the ground would probably follow. Even if any of the fabric of the house should prove sound enough, would Malcolm have the stamina to rebuild, and live there, and remember?

He stood up, the blanket clutched around him, looking infinitely older than his years, a sag of defeat in the cheeks. Slowly, in deference to the shaky state of his legs, Malcolm, the superintendent and I made our way along past the kitchen and out into the front drive.

The ambulances had departed, also one of the fire-engines, but the rope across the gateway had been overwhelmed, and the front garden was full of people, one young constable still trying vainly to hold them back.

A bunch in front of the rest started running in our direction as soon as we appeared, and with a feeling of unreality I saw they were Ferdinand, Gervase, Alicia, Berenice, Vivien, Donald, Helen . . . I lost count.

'Malcolm,' Gervase said loudly, coming to a halt in front of us, so that we too had to stop. 'You're alive!'

A tiny flicker of humour appeared in Malcolm's eyes at this most obvious of statements, but he had no chance of answering as the others set up a clamour of questions.

Vivien said, 'I heard from the village that Quantum had blown up and you were both dead.' Her strained voice held a complaint about having been given erroneous news.

'So did I,' Alicia said. 'Three people telephoned . . . so I came at once, after I'd told Gervase and the others, of course.' She looked deeply shocked, but then they all did, mirroring no doubt what they could see on my own face but also suffering from the double upset of misinformation.

'Then when we all get here,' Vivien said, 'we find you *aren't* dead.' She sounded as if that too were wrong.

'What did happen?' Ferdinand asked. 'Just look at Quantum.'

Berenice said, 'Where were you both, then, when it exploded?'

'We thought you were dead,' Donald said, looking bewildered.

More figures pushed through the crowd, horror opening their mouths. Lucy, Edwin and Serena, running, stumbling, looking alternately from the wounded house to me and Malcolm.

Lucy was crying, 'You're alive, you're alive!' Tears ran down her cheeks. 'Vivien said you were dead.'

'I was told they were dead,' Vivien said defensively. Dim-witted . . . Joyce's judgement came back.

Serena was swaying, pale as pale. Ferdinand put an arm round her and hugged her. 'It's all right, girl, they're not dead after all. The old house's a bit knocked about, eh?' He squeezed her affectionately.

'I don't feel well,' she said faintly. 'What happened?'

'Too soon to say for certain,' Gervase said assertively. 'But I'd say one can't rule out a bomb.'

They repudiated the word, shaking their heads, covering their ears. Bombs were for wars, for wicked schemes in aeroplanes, for bus stations in far places, for cold-hearted terrorists . . . for other people. Bombs weren't for a family house outside a Berkshire village, a house surrounded by quiet green fields, lived in by an ordinary family.

Except that we weren't an ordinary family. Ordinary families didn't have fifth wives murdered while planting geraniums. I looked around at the familiar faces and couldn't see on any of them either malice or dismay that Malcolm had escaped. They were all beginning to recover from the shock of the wrongly reported death and also beginning to realise how much damage had been done to the house.

Gervase grew angry. 'Whoever did this shall pay for it!' He sounded pompous more than effective.

'Where's Thomas?' I asked.

Berenice shrugged waspishly. 'Dear Thomas went out early on one of his useless job-hunting missions. I've no idea where he was going. Vivien telephoned after he'd left.'

Edwin said, 'Is the house insured against bombs, Malcolm?'

Malcolm looked at him with dislike and didn't answer.

Gervase said masterfully, 'You'd better come home with me, Malcolm. Ursula will look after you.'

None of the others liked that. They all instantly made counter-proposals. The superintendent, who had been listening with attentive eyes, said at this point that plans to take Malcolm home would have to be shelved for a few hours.

'Oh, really?' Gervase stared down his nose. 'And who are you?'

'Detective Superintendent Yale, sir.'

Gervase raised his eyebrows but didn't back down. 'Malcolm's done nothing wrong.'

'I want to talk to the superintendent myself,' Malcolm said. 'I want him to find out who tried to destroy my house.'

'Surely it was an accident,' Serena said, very upset.

Ferdinand still had his arm round her. 'Face facts, girl.' He hesitated, looking at me. 'Vivien and Alicia told everyone you were both living here again . . . so how come you escaped being hurt?'

'Yes,' Berenice said. 'That's what I asked.'

'We went to London for a night out and stayed there,' I said.

'Very lucky,' Donald said heartily, and Helen, who stood at his elbow and hadn't spoken so far at all, nodded a shade too enthusiastically and said, 'Yes, yes.'

'But if we'd been in the office,' I said, 'we would have been all right.'

136

They looked along the front of the house to the far corner where the office windows were broken but the walls still stood.

'You wouldn't be in the office at four-thirty in the morning,' Alicia said crossly. 'Why should you be?'

Malcolm was growing tired of them. Not one had hugged him, kissed him, or made warm gestures over his survival. Lucy's tears, if they were genuine, had come nearest. The family obviously could have accommodated his death easily, murmuring regrets at his graveside, maybe even meaning them, but looking forward also with well-hidden pleasure to a safely affluent future. Malcolm dead could spend no more. Malcolm dead would free them to spend instead.

'Let's go,' he said to the superintendent, 'I'm cold.'

An unwelcome thought struck me. 'Did any of you,' I asked the family, 'tell Joyce . . . about the house?'

Donald cleared his throat. 'Yes, I . . . er . . . broke it to her.'

His meaning was clear. 'You told her we were dead?'

'Vivien said you were dead,' he said, sounding as defensive as she had. 'She said I should tell Joyce, so I did.'

'My God,' I said to the superintendent, 'Joyce is my mother. I'll have to phone her at once.'

I turned instinctively back to the house, but the superintendent stopped me, saying the telephones weren't working.

He, I and Malcolm began to move towards the gate, but we had gone only halfway when Joyce herself pushed through the crowd and ran forward, frantically, fearfully distraught.

She stopped when she saw us. Her face went white and she swayed as Serena had done, and I sprinted three or four long strides and caught her upright before she fell.

'It's all right,' I said, holding her. 'It's all right. We're alive.'

'Malcolm . . .'

'Yes, we're both fine.'

'Oh, I thought . . . Donald said . . . I've been crying all the way here, I couldn't see the road . . .' She put her face against my jacket and cried again with a few deep gulps, then pushed herself off determinedly and began searching her tailored pockets for a handkerchief. She found a tissue and blew her nose. 'Well, darling,' she said, 'as you're alive, what the hell's been going on?'

She looked behind Malcolm and me and her eyes widened.

'The whole bloody tribe come to the wake?' To Malcolm she said, 'You've the luck of the devil, you old bugger.'

Malcolm grinned at her, a distinct sign of revival.

The three ex-wives eyed each other warily. Any mushy idea that the near-death of the man they'd all married and the near-destruction of the house they'd all managed might have brought them to sisterly sympathy was a total non-starter.

'Malcolm can come and stay with me,' Joyce said.

'Certainly not,' Alicia said instantly, clearly alarmed. 'You can take your precious Ian. Malcolm can go with Gervase.'

'I won't have it,' Vivien said sharply. 'If Malcolm's going anywhere, it's fitting he should stay with Donald, his eldest son.'

Malcolm looked as if he didn't know whether to laugh or scream.

'He's staying with me,' I said. 'If he wants to.'

'In your flat?' Ferdinand asked.

I had an appalling vision of my flat disintegrating like Quantum but, unlike Quantum, killing people above and below.

'No, not there,' I said.

'Then where, darling?' Joyce asked.

'Wherever we happen to be.'

Lucy smiled. It was the sort of thing she was happy with. She pulled her big brown cloak closer round her large form and said that it sounded a thoroughly sensible proposal. The others looked at her as if she were retarded instead of the brains of the tribe.

'I'll go wherever I want to,' Malcolm said flatly, 'and with Ian.'

I collected a battery of baleful glares, all of them as ever afraid I would scoop their shares of the pool: all except Joyce, who wanted me to.

'As that's settled,' she said with a hint of maternal smugness which infuriated all the others, 'I want to see just how bad the damage is to the house.' She looked at me briefly. 'Come along, darling, you can show me.'

'Run along, mummy's boy,' Gervase said spitefully, smarting from having been spurned by Malcolm.

'Poor dear Ian, tied to mummy's apron strings.' Berenice's effort came out thick with detestation. 'Greedy little Ian.'

'It isn't fair,' Serena said plaintively. 'Ian gets everything, always. I think it's beastly.'

'Come on, darling,' Joyce said. 'I'm waiting.'

I felt rebellious, tried to smother it, and sought for a different solution.

'You can all come,' I said to them. 'Come and see what really happened here.'

The superintendent had in no way tried to break up the family party but had listened quietly throughout. I happened to catch his eye at that point, and he nodded briefly and walked back beside Malcolm as everyone slowly moved round to the rear of the house.

The extent and violence of the damage there silenced even Gervase. All of the mouths gaped: in all eyes, horrified awe.

The chief fireman came over and with a certain professional relish began in a strong Berkshire accent to point out the facts.

'Blast travels along the lines of least resistance,' he said. 'This is a good strong old house, which I reckon is why so much of it is still standing. The blast, see, travelled outwards, front and back from a point somewhere near the centre of the main upper storey. Some of the blast went upwards into the roof, bringing down some of those little attic bedrooms, and a good bit of blast, I'd reckon, blew downwards, making a hole that the upper storey and part of the attic just collapsed into, see what I mean?'

Everyone saw.

'There's this wall here,' he pointed to the one between what had been the sitting-room and what was still the dining-room, 'this wall here, with the chimney built into it, this is one of the main load-bearing walls. It goes right up to the roof. Same the other side, more or less. Those two thick walls stopped the blast travelling sideways, except a bit through the doorways.' He turned directly to Malcolm. 'I've seen a lot of wrecked buildings, sir, mostly burned, it's true, but some gas explosions, and I'd say, and mind you, you'd have to get a proper survey dóne, but I'd say, on looking at this house, that although it got a good shaking you could think of rebuilding it. Good solid Victorian house, otherwise it would have folded up like a pack of cards.'

'Thank you,' Malcolm said faintly.

The fireman nodded. 'Don't you let any fancy demolition man tell you different, sir. I don't like people being taken advantage of when they're overcome by disasters. I've seen too much of that, and it riles me. What I'm telling you is a straight opinion. I've nothing to gain one way or the other.'

'We're all grateful,' I said.

He nodded, satisfied, and Gervase finally found his voice.

'What sort of bomb was it?' he asked.

139

'As to that, sir, I wouldn't know. You'd have to wait for the experts.' The fireman turned to the superintendent. 'We shut off the electricity at the meter switch in the garage when we got here, and likewise turned off the mains water under a man-hole cover out by the gate. The storage tank in the roof had emptied through the broken pipes upstairs and water was still running when we got here, and all that water's now underneath the rubble. There's nothing I can see can start a fire. If you want to go into the upper storey at the sides, you'll need ladders, the staircase is blocked. I can't vouch for the dividing walls up there, we looked through the windows but we haven't been inside, you'd have to go carefully. We didn't go up to the attic much, bar a quick look from up the ladder. But down here, you should be all right in the dining-room and in that big room the other side of this mess, and also in the kitchen and the front room on the far side.'

'My office,' Malcolm said.

The superintendent nodded, and I reflected that he already knew the layout of the house well from earlier repeated visits.

'We've done as much as we can here,' the fireman said. 'All right if we shove off now?'

The superintendent, agreeing, went a few steps aside with him in private consultation and the family began to come back from suspended animation.

The Press photographers moved in closer, and took haphazard pictures of us, and a man and a woman from different papers approached with insistent questions. Only Gervase seemed to find those tolerable and did all the answering. Malcolm sat down again on the pine chair, which was still there, and gathered his blanket around him, retreating into it up to his eyes like a Red Indian.

Vivien, spotting him, went over and told him she was tired of standing and needed to sit down and it was typically selfish of him to take the only seat, and an insult to her, as she was the senior woman present. Glancing at her with distaste, Malcolm got to his feet and moved a good distance away, allowing her to take his place with a self-satisfied smirk. My dislike of Vivien rose as high as her cheekbones and felt as shrewish as her mouth.

Alicia, recovered, was doing her fluttery feminine act for the reporters, laying out charm thickly and eclipsing Serena's little-girl ploy. Seeing them together, I thought that it must be hard for Serena to have a mother who refused to mature, who in her late fifties still dressed and behaved like an eighteen-year-old, who for years had blocked her daughter's natural road to adulthood. Girls needed a motherly mother, I'd been told, and Serena didn't have one. Boys needed one too, and Joyce wasn't one, but I'd had a father all the time and in the end I'd also had Coochie, and Serena hadn't had either, and there lay all the difference in the world.

Edwin was having as hard a time as Donald in putting on a show of rejoicing over Malcolm's deliverance.

'It's all very well for you,' he said to me bitterly, catching my ironic look in his direction. 'Malcolm despises me – and don't bother to deny it, he makes it plain enough – and I don't see why I should care much for him. Of course, I wouldn't wish him dead . . .'

'Of course not,' I murmured.

'. . . but, well, if it had happened . . .' he stopped, not actually having the guts to say it straight out.

'You'd have been glad?' I said.

'No.' He cleared his throat. 'I could have faced it,' he said.

I almost laughed. 'Bully for you, Edwin,' I said. 'Hang in there, fellow.'

'I could have faced your death, too,' he said stuffily.

Oh well, I thought. I asked for that.

'How much do you know about bombs?' I asked.

'That's a ridiculous question,' he said, and walked off, and I reflected that Norman West had reported Edwin as spending an hour most days in the public library, and I betted one could find out how to make bombs there, if one persevered.

Berenice said to me angrily, 'It's all your fault Thomas is out of work.'

I blinked. 'How do you make that out?'

'He's been so worried about Malcolm's behaviour that he couldn't concentrate and he made mistakes. He says you could get Malcolm to help us, but of course I tell him you won't, why should you, you're Malcolm's pet.' She fairly spat the last word, the rage seething also in her eyes and tightening all the cords in her neck.

'You told Thomas that?' I said.

'It's true,' she said furiously. 'Vivien says you've always been Malcolm's favourite and he's never been fair to Thomas.'

'He's always been fair to all of us,' I said positively, but of course she didn't believe it.

She was older than Thomas by four or five years and had married him when she was well over thirty and (Joyce had said cattily) desperate for any husband that offered. Ten years ago, when I'd been to their wedding, she had been a thin, moderately attractive woman lit up by happiness. Thomas had been proud of himself and proprietary. They had looked, if not an exciting couple, stable and full of promise, embarking on a good adventure.

Ten years and two daughters later, Berenice had put on weight and outward sophistication and lost whatever illusions she'd had about marriage. I'd long supposed it was basic disappointment which had made her so destructive of Thomas, but hadn't bothered to wonder about the cause of it. Time I did, I thought. Time I understood the whole lot of them, because perhaps in that way we might come to know who could and who couldn't murder.

To search through character and history, not through alibis. To listen to what they said and didn't say, to learn what they could control, and what they couldn't.

I knew, as I stood there looking at the bunch of them, that only someone in the family itself could go that route, and that if I didn't do it, no one else would.

Norman West and Superintendent Yale could dig into facts. I would dig into the people. And the problem with that, I thought, mocking my own pretension, was that the people would do anything to keep me out.

I had to recognise that what I was going to do could produce more trouble than results. Spotting the capability of murder could elude highly-trained psychiatrists, who had been known to advise freedom for reformed characters only to have them go straight out and kill. A highly-trained psychiatrist I was not. Just someone who could remember how we *had* been, and could learn how we were now.

I looked at the monstrously gutted house and shivered. We had returned unexpectedly on Monday; today was Friday. The speed of planning and execution was itself alarming. Never again were we likely to be lucky. Malcolm had survived three attacks by sheer good fortune, but Ferdinand wouldn't have produced healthy statistics about a fourth. The family looked peacefully normal talking to the reporters, and I was filled with a sense of urgency and foreboding.

Eleven

One of Malcolm's dogs came bounding across the grass towards him, followed a few seconds later by the other. Malcolm put a hand out of his blanket and patted them, but with more absentmindedness than welcome. After them came Arthur Bellbrook with a face of consternation and concern which lightened considerably when he set eyes on Malcolm. In his grubby trousers and ancient tweed jacket, he came at a hobbling run in old army boots and fetched up very out of breath at Malcolm's side.

'Sir! You're alive! I went to Twyford to fetch some weedkiller. When I got back, they told me in the village . . .'

'Gross exaggeration,' Malcolm said, nodding.

Arthur Bellbrook turned to me, panting. 'They said you were both dead. I couldn't get down the road . . . had to come across the fields. Look at the house!'

I explained about our going to London, and asked him what time he'd gone home the previous day.

'Four o'clock, same as always. Say three-forty, then. About then.' He was beginning to get his breath back, his eyes round with disbelief as he stared at the damage.

Nearer to three-thirty, I privately reckoned, if he was admitting to going home early at all.

'Did you go in the house at any time during the day?' I asked.

. He switched his gaze from the ruins to me and sounded aggrieved. 'No, I didn't. You know I couldn't have. You've been locking the place like it's a fortress since you came back, and I didn't have a key. Where could I have got a key from?'

I said placatingly, 'It's just that we're anxious . . . someone got in, they must have.'

'Not me.' He was slightly mollified. 'I was working in the kitchen garden all day, digging potatoes and such like. I had the two dogs

143

with me, tied up on their leads. If anyone had tried to get in the house, they'd have barked for sure, but they didn't.'

Malcolm said, 'Arthur, could you keep the dogs with you for another day or two?'

'Yes, I . . .' He looked helplessly at the heap of rubble spilling out across the terrace and onto the lawn. 'What do you want me to do about the garden?'

'Just . . . carry on,' Malcolm said. 'Keep it tidy.' It didn't seem incongruous to him to polish the setting, though I thought that perhaps, left to its own, nature would scatter leaves and grow longer grass and soften the raw brutality of the jagged edges.

The superintendent, seeing Arthur Bellbrook, came across to him and asked the same questions that I had. Again, they seemed to know each other well, undoubtedly from Moira's investigations, and if there didn't seem to be friendship, there was clearly a mutual respect.

The reporters, having sucked the nectar from Gervase, advanced on Malcolm and on the gardener and the superintendent. I moved away, leaving them to it, and tried to talk to Ferdinand.

He was unfriendly and answered with shrugs and monosyllables.

'I suppose,' I said bitterly, 'you would rather I was lying in shreds and bloody tatters under all that lot.'

He looked at the tons of fallen masonry. 'Not really,' he said coolly.

'That's something.'

'You can't expect us to like it that you've an inside edge with Malcolm.'

'You had three years,' I pointed out, 'during which he wouldn't speak to me. Why did you waste them? Why didn't you get an inside edge yourself?'

'We couldn't get past Moira.'

I half smiled. 'Nor could I.'

'It's now we're talking about,' he said. He looked greatly like Malcolm, right down to the stubbornness in the eyes.

'What do you want me to do, walk away and let him be murdered?' I said.

'Walk away . . .?'

'That's why he wants me with him, to try to keep him safe. He asked me to be his bodyguard, and I accepted.'

Ferdinand stared. 'Alicia said . . .'

'Alicia is crazy,' I interrupted fiercely. 'So are you. Take a look at yourself. Greed, jealousy and spite, you've let them all in. I won't cut you out with Malcolm, I'd never attempt it. Try believing that instead, brother, and save yourself a lot of anxiety.'

I turned away from him in frustration. They were all illogical, I thought. They had almost begged me to use any influence I had with Malcolm to stop him spending and bale them out, and at the same time they believed I would ditch them to my own advantage. But then people had always been able to hold firmly to two contradictory ideas at the same time, as when once, in racing's past, Stewards, Press and public alike had vilified one brilliant trainer as 'most crooked', and elected one great jockey as 'most honest', blindly and incredibly ignoring that it was the self-same trusted jockey who for almost all of his career rode the brilliant trainer's horses. I'd seen a cartoon once that summed it up neatly: 'Entrenched belief is never altered by the facts.'

I wished I hadn't lashed out at Ferdinand. My idea of detection from the inside wasn't going to be a riotous success if I let my own feelings get in the way so easily. I might think the family unjust, they might think me conniving: OK, I told myself, accept all that and forget it. I'd had to put up with their various resentments for much of my life and it was high time I developed immunity.

Easier said than done, of course.

Superintendent Yale had had enough of the reporters. The family had by this time divided into two larger clumps, Vivien's and Alicia's, with Joyce and I hovering between them, belonging to neither. The superintendent went from group to group asking that everyone should adjourn to the police station. 'As you are all here,' he was saying, 'we may as well take your statements straight away, to save you being bothered later.'

'Statements?' Gervase said, eyebrows rising.

'Your movements yesterday and last night, sir.'

'Good God,' Gervase said. 'You don't think any of us would have done this, do you?'

'That's what we have to find out.'

'It's preposterous.'

None of the others said anything, not even Joyce.

The superintendent conferred with a uniformed colleague who was busy stationing his men round the house so that the ever-increasing spectators shouldn't get too close. The word must have spread, I thought. The free peepshow was attracting the next villages, if not Twyford itself.

Much of the family, including Malcolm, Joyce and myself, packed into the three police cars standing in the front drive, and Gervase, Ferdinand and Serena set off on foot to go back to the transport they had come in.

'I wouldn't put it past Alicia,' Joyce said darkly to the superintendent as we drove past them towards the gate, 'to have incited that brood of hers to blow up Quantum.'

'Do you have any grounds for that statement, Mrs Pembroke?'

'Statement? It's an opinion. She's a bitch.'

In the front passenger seat, Yale's shoulders rose and fell in a sigh.

The road outside was still congested with cars, with still more people coming on foot. Yale's driver stopped beside Joyce's car, which she'd left in the centre of the road in her haste, and helped to clear room for her to turn in. With her following, we came next to the hired car Malcolm and I had arrived in, but as it was hopelessly shut in on three sides by other locked vehicles, we left it there and went on in the police car.

In his large modern police station with its bullet-proofed glass enquiry desk, the superintendent ushered us through riot-proofed doors to his office and detailed a policewoman to take Joyce off for some tea. Joyce went protestingly, and Yale with another sigh sat us down in his bare-looking Scandinavian-type place of business.

He looked at us broodingly from behind a large desk. He looked at his nails. He cleared his throat. Finally he said to Malcolm, 'All right. You don't have to say it. I do not believe you would blow up your house just to make me believe that someone is trying to kill you.'

There was a long pause.

'That being so,' he said, as we both sat without speaking, 'we must take the attack in the garage more seriously.'

He was having a hard time, I thought. He ran a finger and thumb down his large black moustache and waited for comments from us that still didn't come.

He cleared his throat again. 'We will redouble our efforts to find Mrs Moira Pembroke's killer.'

Malcolm finally stirred, brought out his cigar case, put a cigar in his mouth and patted his pockets to find matches. There was a plastic notice on Yale's desk saying NO SMOKING. Malcolm, his glance resting on it momentarily, lit the match and sucked the flame into the tobacco.

Yale decided on no protest and produced a glass ashtray from a lower drawer in his desk.

'I would be dead twice over,' Malcolm said, 'if it weren't for Ian.' He told Yale about the car roaring straight at us at Newmarket.

'Why didn't you report this, sir?' Yale said, frowning.

'Why do you think?'

Yale groomed his moustache and didn't answer.

Malcolm nodded. 'I was tired of being disbelieved.'

'And . . . er . . . last night?' Yale asked.

Malcolm told him about our day at Cheltenham, and about Quantum's inner doors. 'I wanted to sleep in my own bed. I was tired. Ian absolutely wouldn't have it, and drove us to London.'

Yale looked at me steadily. 'Did you have a premonition?'

'No, I don't think so.' I hadn't felt a shiver, as I had in my flat. Perhaps the premonition in the flat had been for the house. 'I was just . . . frightened,' I said.

Malcolm glanced at me with interest.

Yale said, 'What of?'

'Not of bombs,' I said. 'I never considered that. Frightened there was someone in the house. I couldn't have slept there, that's all.' I paused. 'I saw the way the car drove at my father at Newmarket – it hit my leg, after all – and I believed him, of course, about being attacked and gassed in the garage. I knew he wouldn't have murdered Moira, or have had her murdered by anyone else. I believe absolutely in his extreme danger. We've been moving around, letting no one know where to find us, until this week.'

'My fault,' Malcolm said gloomily. 'I insisted on coming back here. Ian didn't want to.'

'When the doors were moved,' I said, 'it was time to go.'

Yale thought it over without comment for a while and then said, 'When you were in the house looking round, did you see anything unusual except for the doors?'

'No, nothing.'

'Nothing where it shouldn't be? Or absent from where it should have been?'

I thought back to that breathless heart-thumping search. Whoever had moved the doors must at least have looked into the office and the sitting-room. I hadn't bothered with the position of any of the other

147

doors except closing the one from the kitchen to the hall. Someone could have looked into all the rooms in the house, for all I knew.

'No,' I said in the end. 'Nothing else seemed out of place.'

Yale sighed again. He sighed a lot, it seemed to me. 'If you think of anything later, let me know.'

'Yes, all right.'

'The time-frame we're looking at,' he said, 'is between about three-forty p.m., when the gardener went home taking the dogs, and ten-thirty p.m., when you returned from Cheltenham.' He pursed his lips. 'If you hadn't stayed out to dinner, what time would you have been home?'

'We meant to stay out to dinner,' Malcolm said. 'That's why Arthur had the dogs.'

'Yes, but if . . .'

'About six-thirty,' I said. 'If we'd gone straight home after the last race.'

'We had a drink at the racecourse after the last race,' Malcolm said. 'I had scotch, Ian had some sort of fizzy gut-rot.' He tapped ash into the ashtray. He was enjoying having Yale believe him at last, and seemed to be feeling expansive.

'Ian thinks,' he said, 'that I was probably knocked out just outside the kitchen door that day, and that I was carried from there straight into the garage, not dragged, and that it was someone the dogs knew, as they didn't bark. They were jumping up and down by the kitchen door, I can remember that, as they do if someone they know has come. But they do that anyway when it's time for their walk, and I didn't give it a thought.' He inhaled a lot of smoke and let it out into the superintendent's erstwhile clean air. 'Oh yes, and about the fingerprints . . .' He repeated what I'd said about firemen's lifts.

Yale looked at me neutrally and polished his moustache. He was difficult to read, I thought, chiefly because he didn't want to be read. All policemen, I supposed, raised barriers and, like doctors and lawyers, tended not to trust what they were told, which could be bitterly infuriating to the truthful.

He must have been forty or forty-five, I supposed, and had to be competent to have reached that rank. He looked as if he habitually had too little exercise and too many sandwiches, and gave no impression of wallowing in his own power. Perhaps now he'd dropped his over-smart suspicions of Malcolm, he could actually solve his case, though I'd heard the vast majority of criminals were in jail because of having been informed on, not detected. I did very much want him to succeed. I wished he could spontaneously bring himself to share what he was thinking, but I supposed he'd been trained not to. He kept his counsel anyway on that occasion, and I kept mine, and perhaps it was a pity.

A policewoman came in and said, looking harassed, that she didn't know where to put the Pembroke family.

Yale thought briefly and told her to show them all to his office. Malcolm said, 'Oh God,' and dragged on his cigar, and presently the whole troop arrived.

I got to my feet and Alicia immediately sat on my chair. Vivien and Joyce both glared at Malcolm, still seated, willing him to rise, which he didn't. Which of them could he possibly give his chair to, I thought, stifling laughter, without causing exmarital bloodshed?

With a straight face, Yale asked the policewoman to fetch two more chairs, and I couldn't even tell if he were amused or simply practical. When Vivien and Joyce were suitably enthroned, he looked around and counted us all: thirteen.

'Who's missing?' he asked.

He got various answers: 'My wife, Debs', 'Thomas, my husband', 'Ursula, of course.'

'Very well. Now, if any of you know anything or guess anything about the explosion at Quantum House, I want to hear about it.'

'Terrorists,' Vivien said vaguely.

Everyone ignored her and no one else made any suggestion.

'While you are here,' Yale said, 'I'll ask you all to answer certain questions. I'll have my personnel write down your answers, and of course after that you can leave. The questions are, what were you doing yesterday between three in the afternoon and midnight, what were you doing a week last Tuesday between the same hours, and what were you doing two weeks ago today, Friday, also between three p.m. and midnight.'

Edwin said crossly, 'We've already answered most of those questions for that wretched man, West. It's too much to go over it all again.'

Several of the others nodded.

Yale looked blank. 'Who is West?'

'A detective,' Berenice said. 'I sent him away with a flea in his ear, I can tell you.'

'He was awfully persistent,' Helen said, not liking the memory. 'I

149

told him I couldn't possibly remember exactly, but he went on prying.'

'Dreadful little man,' Serena said.

'He said I was illegitimate,' Gervase complained sourly. 'It's thanks to Joyce that he knew.'

Yale's mouth opened and closed again and he took a deep breath. 'Who is West?' he asked intensely.

'Fellow I hired,' Malcolm said. 'Private detective. Hired him to find out who was trying to kill me, as I reckoned the police weren't getting anywhere.'

Yale's composure remained more or less intact. 'All the same,' he said, 'please answer the questions again. And those of you without husband and wife here, please answer for them as best you can.' He looked around at all the faces, and I would have sworn he was puzzled. I looked to see what he had seen, and I saw the faces of ordinary people, not murderers. Ordinary people with problems and hang-ups, with quirks and grievances. People anxious and disturbed by the blasting of the house that most had lived in and all had visited. Not one of them could possibly be a murderer, I thought. It had after all to be someone from outside.

I felt a lot of relief at this conclusion until I realised I was raising any excuse not to have to find a murderer among ourselves; yet we did have to find one, if Malcolm were to live. The dilemma was permanent.

'That's all for now,' Yale said, rising to his feet. 'My staff will take your statements in the interview rooms. And Mr Pembroke senior, will you stay here a moment? And Mr Ian Pembroke also? There are the arrangements to be made about the house.'

The family left me behind with bad grace. 'It's my job, not Ian's, to see to things. I am the eldest.' That was Donald. 'You need someone with know-how.' That was Gervase, heavily. 'It's not Ian's house.' Petulance from Edwin.

Yale managed however to shovel them all out, and immediately the door had closed, I said, 'While they're all in the interview rooms, I'm taking my father out of here.'

'The house . . .' Malcolm began.

'I'll see to the house later. We're leaving here now, this minute. If Superintendent Yale will lend us a police car, fine; otherwise we'll catch buses or taxis.'

'You can have a police car within reason,' Yale said.

'Great. Then . . . um . . . just take my father to the railway station. I'll stay here.'

'All right.'

To Malcolm, I said, 'Go to London. Go to where we were last night. Use the same name. Don't telephone anyone. Don't for God's sake let anyone know where you are.'

'You're bloody arrogant.'

'Yes. This time, listen to me.'

Malcolm gave me a blue glare, stubbed out his cigar, stood up and let the red blanket drop from his shoulders to the floor.

'Where will you be?' Yale asked him.

'Don't answer,' I said brusquely.

Malcolm looked at me, then at the superintendent. 'Ian will know where I am. If he doesn't want to tell you, he won't. Gervase tried to burn some information out of him once, and didn't succeed. He still has the scars . . .' he turned to me '. . . don't you?'

'Malcolm!' I protested.

Malcolm said to Yale, 'I gave Gervase a beating he'll never forget.'

'And he's never forgiven me,' I said.

'Forgiven you? For what? You didn't snitch to me. Serena did. She was so young she didn't really understand what she'd been seeing. Gervase could be a proper bully.'

'Come on,' I said, 'we're wasting time.'

Superintendent Yale followed us out of his office and detailed a driver to take Malcolm.

'I'll come in the car, once I can move it,' I said to him. 'Don't go shopping, I'll buy us some things later. Do be sensible, I beg you.'

'I promise,' he said; but promises with Malcolm weren't necessarily binding. He went out with the driver and I stood on the police station steps watching his departure and making sure none of the family had seen him or could follow.

Yale made no comment but waved me back to his office. Here he gave me a short list of reputable building contractors and the use of his telephone. I chose one of the firms at random and explained what was needed, and Yale took the receiver himself and insisted that they were to do minimum weather-proofing only, and were to move none of the rubble until the police gave clearance.

'When the driver returns from taking your father,' he said to me, disconnecting, 'we can spare him to ferry you back to your car.'

'Thank you.'

151

'I'm trusting you, you know, to maintain communications between me and your father.'

'I'll telephone here every morning, if you like.'

'I'd much rather know where he is.'

I shook my head. 'The fewer people know, the safer.'

He couldn't exactly accuse me of taking unreasonable precautions, so he left it, and asked instead, 'What did your half-brother burn you with?'

'A cigarette. Nothing fancy.'

'And what information did he want?'

'Where I'd hidden my new cricket bat,' I answered: but it hadn't been about cricket bats, it had been about illegitimacy, which I hadn't known at the time but had come to understand since.

'How old were you both?'

'I was eleven. Gervase must have been thirteen.'

'Why didn't you give him the bat?' Yale asked.

'It wasn't the bat I wouldn't give him. It was the satisfaction. Is this part of your enquiries?'

'Everything is,' he said laconically.

The hired car was movable when I got back to it and as it was pointing in that direction I drove it along to Quantum. There were still amazing numbers of people there, and I couldn't get past the now more substantial barrier across the drive until the policeman guarding it had checked with Superintendent Yale by radio.

'Sorry, sir,' one of them said, finally letting me in. 'The superintendent's orders.'

I nodded and drove on, parking in front of the house beside two police cars which had presumably returned from taking the many family members to their various cars.

I had already grown accustomed to the sight of the house; it still looked as horrific but held no more shocks. Another policeman walked purposefully towards me as I got out of the car and asked what I wanted. To look through the downstairs windows, I said.

He checked by radio. The superintendent replied that I could look through the windows as long as the constable remained at my side, and as long as I would point out to him anything I thought looked wrong. I readily agreed to that. With the constable beside me, I walked towards the place where the hall could still be discerned,

152

skirting the heavy front door, which had been blown outwards, frame and all, when the brickwork on either side of it had given way.

QUANTUM IN ME FUIT lay face downwards on the gravel. I did the best I could. Someone's best, I thought, grateful to be alive, hadn't quite been good enough.

'Don't go in, sir,' the young constable said warningly. 'There's more could come down.'

I didn't try to go in. The hall was full of ceilings and floors and walls from upstairs, though one could see daylight over the top of the heap, the daylight from the back garden. Somewhere in the heap were all of Malcolm's clothes except the ones he'd worn to Cheltenham, all his vicuna coats and handmade shoes, all of the gold-and-silver brushes he'd packed on his flight to Cambridge, and somewhere, too, the portrait of Moira.

Jagged arrows of furniture stuck up from the devastation like the arms of the drowning, and pieces of dusty unrecognisable fabric flapped forlornly when a gust of wind took them. Tangled there, too, was everything I'd brought with me from my flat, save only my racing kit – saddle, helmet and holdall – which was still in the boot of the car along with Malcolm's briefcase. Everything was replaceable, I supposed; and I felt incredibly glad I hadn't thought of bringing the silver-framed picture of Coochie and the boys.

There was glass everywhere along the front of the house, fallen from the shattered windows. With the constable in tow, I crunched along towards the office, passing the ruins of the downstairs cloakroom on the way, where a half-demolished wall had put paid to the plumbing.

The office walls themselves, like those of the kitchen, were intact, but the office door that I'd set at such a careful angle was wide open with another brick and plaster glacier spilling through it. The shockwave that must have passed through the room to smash its way out through the windows had lifted every unweighted sheet of paper and redistributed it on the floor. Most of the pictures and countless small objects were down there also, including, I noticed, the pen pot holding the piece of wire. Apart from the ancient bevelled glass of a splendid breakfront bookcase which stood along one wall, everything major looked restorable, though getting rid of the dust would be a problem in itself.

I spent a good deal of time gazing through the open spaces of the office windows, but in the end had to admit defeat. The positions of too much had been altered for me to see anything inexplicably wrong. I'd seen nothing significant in there the previous evening when I'd fetched Malcolm's briefcase, when I'd been wide awake with alarm to such things.

Shaking my head I moved on round the house, passing the still shut and solidly bolted garden door which marked the end of the indoor passage. The blast hadn't shifted it, had dissipated on nearer targets. Past it lay the long creeper-covered north wall of the old playroom, and I walked along there and round into the rear garden.

The police had driven stakes into the lawn and tied ropes to them, making a line for no one to cross. Behind the rope the crowd persisted, open-eyed, chattering, pointing, coming to look and moving away to trail back over the fields. Among them Arthur Bellbrook, the dogs at his side, was holding a mini-court in a semicircle of respectful listeners. The reporters and Press photographers seemed to have vanished but other cameras still clicked in a barrage. There was a certain restrained orderliness about everything which struck me hard as incongruous.

Turning my back to the gawpers, I looked through the playroom window, seeing it, like the office, from the opposite angle to the previous night. Apart from the boxroom and my bedroom, it was the only room unmetamorphosed by Moira, and it still looked what it had been for forty years, the private domain of children.

The old battered armchairs were still there, and the big table that with a little imagination had been fort, boat, spaceship and dungeon in its time. The long shelves down the north wall still bore generations of train sets, building sets, board games and stuffed toys. Robin and Peter's shiny new bicycles were still propped there, that had been the joy of their lives in the week before the crash. There were posters of pop groups pinned to the walls and a bookcase bulging with reprehensible tastes.

The explosion on the other side of the thick load-bearing wall had done less damage to the playroom than to anywhere else I'd seen; only the broken windows and the ubiquitous dust, which had flooded in from the passage, showed that anything had happened. A couple of teddy bears had tumbled off the shelves, but the bicycles were still standing.

Anything there that shouldn't be there, anything not there that should be, Yale had said. I hadn't seen anything the night before in those categories, and I still couldn't.

154

With a frustrated shrug, I skirted the poured-out guts of the house and on the far side looked through the dining-room windows. Like the playroom, the dining-room was relatively undamaged, though here the blast had blown in directly from the hall, leaving the now familiar tongue of rubble and covering everything with a thick grey film. For ever after, I would equate explosions with dust.

The long table, primly surrounded by high-backed chairs, stood unmoved. Some display plates held in wires on the wall had broken and fallen off. The sideboard was bare, but then it had been before. Malcolm had said the room had hardly been used since he and Moira had taken to shouting.

I continued round to the kitchen and went in through the door, to the agitation of the constable. I told him I'd been in there earlier to fetch the pine chair, which someone had since brought back, and he relaxed a very little.

'That door,' I said, pointing to one in a corner, 'leads to the cellars. Do you know if anyone's been down there?'

He didn't think so. He was pretty sure not. He hadn't heard anyone mention cellars.

The two underground rooms lay below the kitchen and dining-room, and without electric lights I wasn't keen to go down there. Still . . . what excuse did I have not to?

Malcolm kept some claret in racks there, enough to grieve him if the bottles were broken. Coochie had used the cellars romantically for candlelit parties with red-checked tablecloths and gypsy music, and the folding tables and chairs were still stacked there, along with the motley junk of ages that was no longer used but too valuable to throw away.

'Do you have a torch, constable?' I asked.

No, he hadn't. I went to fetch the one I'd installed by habit in the hired car and, in spite of his disapproval, investigated downstairs. He followed me, to do him justice.

To start with, the cellars were dry, which was a relief as I'd been afraid the water from the storage tank and the broken pipes would have drained down and flooded them.

None of Malcolm's bottles was broken. The chimney wall, continuing downwards as sturdy foundations, had sheltered everything on its outer side as stalwartly below as it had above.

The dire old clutter of pensioned-off standard lamps, rocking-chair, pictures, tin trunk, tiger skin, bed headboard, tea-trolley, all took brief life in the torchlight and faded back to shadow. Same old junk, undisturbed.

All that one could say again was that nothing seemed to be there in the cellar that shouldn't be, and nothing not there that should. Shrugging resignedly, I led the way upstairs and closed the door.

Outside again, I looked into the garage, which seemed completely untouched, and walked round behind it to the kitchen garden. The glass in the old greenhouse was broken, and I supposed Moira's little folly, away on the far side of the garden, would have suffered the same fate.

I dearly wanted to go down to the far end of the kitchen garden to make sure the gold store was safe, but was deterred by the number of interested eyes already swivelled my way, and particularly by Arthur Bellbrook's.

The wall itself looked solid enough. The crowds were nowhere near it, as it was away to the left, while they were coming in from the fields on the right.

The constable stood by my side, ready to accompany me everywhere.

Shrugging, I retreated. Have faith, I thought, and drove away to London.

Twelve

Malcolm had achieved a double suite at the Ritz with views of Green Park. He had lunched on Strasbourg pâté and Dover sole, according to the remains on the white-clothed room-service table, and had reached the lower half of a bottle of Krug.

'How are the shakes?' I said, putting his briefcase down beside him.

'Were you followed here?' he asked.

'I was not.'

He was doing his best to pretend he had regained total command of himself, yet I guessed the train journey had been an anxious and lonely ordeal. It was difficult for me to imagine the escalating trauma within him. How could anyone be the target of deadly unrelenting virulence and not in the end break down? I'd got to invent something better for him, I thought, than cooping him up in millionaire cells. Make him safe, give him back his lightheartedness, set him free.

'Um,' I said, 'I hope your passport's still in your briefcase.'

'Yes, it is.' He had taken it in his briefcase to Paris.

'Good.'

An unfortunate thought struck him. 'Where's yours?' Malcolm asked.

'In the rubble. Don't worry, I'll get a replacement. Do you have a visa for America?'

'Yes. I also had one for Australia once, but they only last a year. If we go, we'll have to get new visas from Australia House.'

'How about if you go to America tomorrow?' I said.

'*Tomorrow?* How can I?'

'I'll take you safely to Heathrow and see you off.'

'Dammit, that's not what I meant.'

'No,' I said. 'Well . . . the Breeders' Cup races are three weeks tomorrow at Santa Anita. Why don't we phone Ramsey Osborn?

157

Why don't we phone Blue Clancy's trainer? Why don't you fly to Los Angeles tomorrow and have a fine old time at the races for three weeks? They have racing every day on the same track. If I know you, you'll be cronies with the racetrack committee immediately. Ramsey Osborn will send introductions. You can stay where the Breeders' Cup organisers do, at the Beverly Wilshire hotel which I've heard is right at the end of Rodeo Drive where there's a man's shop so expensive you have to make an appointment to be let in. Buy a few shirts there, it'll make a nice dent in your bankroll. Forget Quantum. Forget the bloody family. They won't know where you are and they'll never find you.'

I stopped only a fraction for breath, not long enough for him to raise objections. 'On the Tuesday after the Breeders' Cup, they're running the Melbourne Cup in Melbourne, Australia. That's their biggest race. The whole country stops for it. A lot of the people from the Breeders' Cup will go on to Australia. You'll have made cronies among them by the dozen. I've heard it's all marvellous. I've never been, and I'd love to. I'll join you as soon as my passport's renewed and I'll go on minding your back – if you still want me to.'

He had listened at first with apathy, but by the end he was smiling. I'd proposed the sort of impulsive behaviour that had greatly appealed to him in the past, and it still did, I was grateful to see.

'A damn sight better than rotting at the Ritz,' he announced.

'Great,' I said. 'Get out your diary for the numbers.'

It was soon settled. Blue Clancy would go over for the Breeders' Cup as long as he was fit. Ramsey Osborn, booming away in Stamford, Connecticut, promised introductions galore to a score of very dear friends he'd met a couple of times out West. Why didn't Malcolm stop off at Lexington on the way and feast his eyes on some real bloodstock? Ramsey had some very good friends in Lexington who would be delighted to have Malcolm stay with them. Ramsey would call them and fix it. Stay by the phone, you guys, he said. He would fix it and call back. It was breakfast time in Connecticut, he said. It would be an hour earlier in Lexington. He would see if the lazy so and so's were out of bed.

Whether they were or they weren't, Ramsey phoned back within twenty minutes. As before, Malcolm talked on the sitting-room telephone, I on the extension in my bedroom.

'All set,' Ramsey said. 'They're expecting you, Malcolm, tomorrow, and I'm flying down Sunday. They're real sweet guys, you'll love them. Dave and Sally Cander. Dogwood Drift Farm, outside of Lexington.' He read out the telephone number. 'You got that?'

Malcolm had got it.

Ramsey asked where Malcolm was planning to stay for the Breeders' Cup. 'Beverly Wilshire? Couldn't be better. Centre of the universe. I'll make reservations right away.'

Malcolm explained he needed a two-bedroom suite for himself and me. Sure thing, Ramsey agreed. No problem. See you, he said. We had made his day, he said, and to have a good one.

The sitting-room seemed smaller and quieter when he'd gone off the line, but Malcolm had revitalised remarkably. We went at once by taxi to Australia House where Malcolm got his visa without delay, and on the way back stopped first at his bank for more travellers' cheques and then in Piccadilly a little short of the Ritz to shop in Simpson's for replacement clothes from the skin up, not forgetting suitcases to pack them in. Malcolm paid for all of mine with his credit card, which was a relief. I hardly liked to ask him outright for my fare to California, but he'd thought of my other finances himself already and that evening gave me a bumper cheque to cover several additional destinations.

'Your fare and so on. Pay Arthur Bellbrook. Pay Norman West. Pay the contractors for weatherproofing Quantum. Pay for the hired car. Pay your own expenses. Anything else?'

'Tickets to Australia?'

'We'll get those in the morning. I'll pay for them here, with mine to Lexington. If we can get you a Los Angeles ticket without a date on, I can pay for that, too.'

We made plans about telephone calls. He was not to phone me, I would phone him.

We dined in good spirits, the dreadful morning at least overlaid. He raised his glass: 'To Blue Clancy' and 'To racing' and 'To life.'

'To life,' I said.

I drove him to Heathrow in the morning safely as promised, and saw him on his way to Lexington via New York and Cincinnati. He was fizzing at least at half strength and gave me a long blue look before he departed.

'Don't think I don't know what I owe you,' he said.

'You owe me nothing.'

'Bloody Moira,' he said unexpectedly, and looked back and waved as he went.

Feeling good about him, I telephoned from the airport to Superintendent Yale but got one of his assistants: his chief was out at Quantum and had left a message that if I phoned I was to be asked if I could join him. Yes, I could, I agreed, and arrived in the village about forty minutes later.

The road to the house wasn't as congested as the day before, but fresh waves of sightseers still came and went continuously. I drove up to the gate and after radio consultation the constable there let me pass. Another policeman was at my side the moment I stopped in front of the house. Different men, both of them, from the day before.

Superintendent Yale appeared from the direction of the kitchen, having been alerted by the gateman, I surmised.

'How is Mr Pembroke?' he asked, shaking hands with every sign of having adopted humanity as a policy.

'Shaken,' I said.

He nodded understandingly. He was wearing an overcoat and looked cold in the face, as if he'd been out of doors for some time. The mild wind of yesterday had intensified rawly and the clouds looked more threatening, as if it would rain. Yale glanced with anxiety at the heavens and asked me to go round with him to the back garden.

The front of the house looked sad and blind, with light brown plywood hammered over all the windows and a heavy black tarpaulin hanging from under the roof to hide the hole in the centre. At the rear, the windows were shuttered and the bare roof rafters were covered but the devastated centre was still open to the elements. Several men in hard hats and overalls were working there, slowly picking up pieces from the huge jumble and carrying them to throw them into a rubbish skip which stood a short distance away across the lawn.

'Do they propose to move all that by hand?' I asked.

'As much as is necessary,' Yale said. 'We've got a surprise for you.' He waved to a man in beige overalls with a blue hard hat who came over to us and asked me my name.

'Ian Pembroke,' I said obligingly.

He unzipped the front of his overalls, put a hand inside and drew out a battered navy-blue object which he held out to me with a small satisfied smile. 'You may need this,' he said.

160

Never a truer word. It was my passport.

'Where on earth did you find it?' I said, delighted.

He shrugged and pointed to the mess. 'We always come across a few things unharmed. We're making a pile of them for you, but don't get your hopes up.'

I zipped the passport into my new Simpson's Barbour and thought gratefully that I wouldn't have to trail around getting a new one.

'Have you found any gold-and-silver-backed brushes?' I asked.

'Not so far.'

'They're my father's favourite things.'

'We'll look out for them,' he said. 'Now, we'd like you to help us in return.'

'Anything I can.'

He was a lean, highly professional sort of man, late forties I guessed, giving an impression of army. He said his name was Smith. He was an explosives expert.

'When you first came here yesterday morning,' he said, 'did you smell anything?'

I was surprised. I thought back.

'Brick dust,' I said. 'The wind was stirring it up. It was in my throat.'

He grunted. 'This looks like a gas explosion, but you're quite certain, aren't you, that there was no gas in the house?'

'Absolutely certain.'

'Do you know what cordite smells like?' he asked.

'Cordite? Like after a gun's been fired, do you mean?'

'That's right.'

'Well, yes, I know what it smells like.'

'And you didn't smell that here yesterday morning?'

I looked at him, puzzled. 'No one was shot,' I said.

He smiled briefly. 'Do you know what cordite is?' he asked.

'Not really.'

'It was used very commonly as a general explosive,' he said, 'before Nobel invented dynamite in 1867. It's less fierce than dynamite. It's sort of high-grade gunpowder, and it's still used in some types of quarries. It explodes comparatively slowly, at about two thousand five hundred metres per second, or a little over. It explodes like a gas. It doesn't punch small holes through walls like a battering ram. It's rather like an expanding balloon that knocks them flat.'

I looked at the house.

'Yes, like that,' Smith said.

'Cordite . . .' I frowned. 'It means nothing.'

'Its strong smell lingers,' he said.

'Well . . . we didn't get here until ten, and the explosion was at four-thirty in the morning, and it was fairly windy, though not as rough as today. I should think any smell had blown away.' I paused. 'What about all the people who were here before us? What do they say?'

'They're not here today,' Smith said succinctly. 'I haven't asked them.'

'No one said anything to me about a smell,' I said.

Smith shrugged. 'We'll do microscopic tests. We would do, anyway. But it looks to me as if cordite is a strong possibility.'

'Can you buy cordite?' I asked vaguely. 'Can anyone?'

'No, they definitely can't,' Smith said with decision. 'Twenty years or so ago, maybe, but not now. Since terrorism became a part of life, most sorts of explosives are highly regulated. It's extremely difficult for the general public to get hold of them. There are a few explosive substances on the open market, but detonators to set them off are not.'

I found I was thinking of cordite in terms of the small quantities used in firearms, whereas to knock down half a house . . .

'How much cordite would that have taken?' I asked, gesturing to the results.

'I haven't yet worked it out. A good deal.'

'What would it have been in?'

'Anything.'

'What does it look like? Is it like jelly?'

'No, you're thinking of high-explosive TNT. That's liquid when it's fed into bomb cases, then it gels inside. Bombs dropped from aircraft are that sort. Cordite is loose grains, like gunpowder. To get a useful result, you have to compress it. Confine it. Then you need heat to start off the chemical reaction, which proceeds at such a rate that the ingredients appear to explode.'

'Appear!' I said, and added hastily, 'OK, I take your word for it, don't explain.'

He gave me a slightly pitying look but let up on the lecture and went back to searching in the ruins. Superintendent Yale asked if any of the Pembrokes had ever had any connection whatever with quarries. None that I knew of, I said. It was most improbable.

162

'Or had friends who had quarries, or who worked in quarries?'

I didn't know. I'd never heard of any.

My gaze wandered away from Smith and his fellow diggers after truth, and I became more aware of the audience beyond the rope in the garden. There weren't anything like as many as the day before, but clearly the work in progress was a draw in itself.

Arthur Bellbrook was there again, talking away. He must enjoy the celebrity, I thought. He'd been the one who'd found Moira, and now there was the house . . . Arthur was talking as if he owned the news, rocking back on his heels and sticking his stomach out. The dogs on their leads patiently waited. It didn't matter to them, I supposed, that Arthur was into maybe the twentieth account of life and death with the Pembrokes.

A stray piece of memory connected Arthur to the smell of cordite, and I couldn't think why that should be until I remembered him carrying his shotgun into the house on the day he'd thought I was a burglar.

I cast the stray thought out but it sauntered back, telling me it was nothing to do with Arthur and shotguns.

What then?

I frowned, trying to remember.

'What's the matter?' Yale said, watching me.

'Nothing, really.'

'You've thought of something. One of your family does have a quarry connection, is that it?'

'Oh no,' I half laughed. 'Not that. The smell of cordite . . .'

The smell of cordite on a misty morning, and the gardener . . . not Arthur, but old Fred before him . . . telling us children to keep out of the way, to go right back out of the field, he didn't want our heads blown off . . .

I remembered abruptly, like a whole scene springing to life on a film screen. I walked across to where Smith in his hard blue hat bent to his task and said, without preamble, 'Does cordite have another name?'

He straightened, with a piece of brick and plaster in his hand.

'I suppose so,' he said. 'It's commonly called "black powder".'

Black powder.

'Why?' he said.

'Well, we had some here once. But long ago, when we were

163

children. Twenty years ago at least, probably more. But I suppose . . . some of the family could have remembered . . . as I just have.'

Yale, who had followed me to listen, said, 'Remember what?'

'There used to be four or five great old willow trees down by the stream, across the field.' I pointed. 'Those you can see now are only twenty years old or so. They grow very fast . . . they were planted after they took the old trees down. They were splendid old trees, huge, magnificent.'

Yale made hurrying-up motions with his hands, as if to say the state of long-gone willows, however patrician, was immaterial.

'They were at the end of their lives,' I said. 'If there was a gale, huge branches would crack off. Old Fred, who was the gardener for years here before Arthur, told my father they weren't safe and they'd have to come down, so he got some foresters to come and fell them. It was dreadful seeing them come down . . .' I didn't think I'd tell Yale that half the family had been in tears. The trees had been friends, playground, climbing frames, deepest purple imaginary rain forests: and, afterwards, there was too much daylight and the dead bodies being sawn up for firewood and burned on bonfires. The stream hadn't looked the same when open to bright sunshine; rather ordinary, not running through dappled mysterious shade.

'Go on,' Yale said with half-stifled impatience. 'What's all this about trees?'

'The stumps,' I said. 'The tree men sawed the trees off close to the ground but left the stumps, and no one could get them out. A tractor came from a nearby farm and tried . . .' We'd had a great time then, having rides all day. 'Anyway, it failed. Nothing else would move the stumps, and Fred didn't want to leave them there to rot, so he decided to blow them up . . . with black powder.'

'Ah,' Yale said.

Black powder had sounded, somehow, as if it ought to belong to pirates. We'd been most impressed. Fred had got his powder and he'd dug a hole down below the stubborn roots of the first stump, and filled it and set off one enormous explosion. It was just as well he'd cleared us out of the field first because the blast had knocked Fred himself flat although he'd been about a hundred feet away. The first tree stump had come popping out of the ground looking like a cross between an elephant and an octopus, but Malcolm, who came running in great alarm to see what had happened, forbade Fred to blow up the others.

As I told the gist of this to Yale and Smith, the second reel of the film was already unrolling in my mind, and I stopped fairly abruptly when I realised what I was remembering.

'Fred,' I said, 'carried the box of black powder back to the tool shed and told us never to touch it. We were pretty foolish but not that crazy. We left it strictly alone. And there the box stayed until it got covered over with other junk and we didn't notice it or think of it any more . . .' I paused, then said, 'Wouldn't any explosive be useless after all this time?'

'Dynamite wouldn't last much more than a year in a tool shed,' Smith said. 'One hot summer would ruin it. But black powder – cordite – is very stable, and twenty years is immaterial.'

'What are we waiting for?' Yale said, and walked towards the tool shed which lay behind the garage on the near side of the kitchen garden.

The tool shed was a place I hadn't thought of looking into the day before: but even if I had, I doubted if I would have remembered the black powder. Its memory had been too deep.

'Where is this box?' Yale asked.

I looked at the contents of the tool shed in perplexity. I hadn't been in there for years, and in that time it had passed from Fred to Arthur. Fred had had an upturned orange box to sit on while he waited through heavy showers: Arthur had an old fireside chair. Fred had had a tray with a cracked mug and a box of sugar cubes and had come indoors to fetch his tea: Arthur had an electric kettle. Fred had tended old tools lovingly: Arthur had shiny new ones with paint still on the handles.

Beyond the tools and the chair, in the centre section of the spacious shed, were things like mowers, chainsaws and hedgeclippers and, at the furthest shadowy end, the flotsam by-passed by time, like the stuff in the cellar, stood in forgotten untidy heaps.

It all looked unpromisingly undisturbed, but Yale called up a pair of young policemen and told them to take everything out of the tool shed and lay each object separately on the ground. Smith went back to the rubble, but Yale and I watched the policemen and so did Arthur Bellbrook, who came hurrying across the moment he saw what was happening.

'What's going on?' he said suspiciously.

'When did you last clean out the tool shed?' Yale asked.

Arthur was put out and beginning to bridle.

'Just say,' I said to him. 'We just want to know.'

'I've been meaning to,' he said defensively. 'That's Fred's old rubbish, all that at the back.'

The superintendent nodded, and we all watched the outgoing procession of ancient, rusting, broken and neglected tat. Eventually one of the men came out with a dirty wooden box which I didn't recognise at first because it was smaller than I'd seen in my memory. He put it on the ground beside other things, and I said doubtfully, 'I think that's it.'

'Mr Smith,' Yale called.

Mr Smith came. Yale pointed at the box, which was about the size of crates used for soft drink bottles, and Smith squatted beside it.

The lid was nailed shut. With an old chisel, Smith prised it open and peeled back the yellowish paper which was revealed. Inside the paper, half-filling the box, there was indeed black powder.

Smith smelled it and poked it around. 'It's cordite, all right, and in good condition. But as it's here, it obviously hasn't been used. And anyway, there wouldn't have been anything like enough in this box to have caused that much damage to the house.'

'Well,' I said weakly, 'it was only an idea.'

'Nothing wrong with the idea,' Smith said. He looked around at the growing collection of discards. 'Did you find any detonators?'

He had everyone open every single packet and tin: a lot of rusty staples and nails saw daylight, and old padlocks without keys and rotting batteries, but nothing he could identify as a substance likely to set off an explosion.

'Inconclusive,' he said, shrugging, and returned to his rubble.

Yale told Arthur to leave the cordite where it was and do what he liked with the rest, and Arthur began throwing the decaying rubbish into the skip.

I tried to apologise for all the waste of time, but the superintendent stopped me.

'When you saw the tree stump blown up, which of your brothers and sisters were there?'

I sighed, but it had to be faced. 'Gervase, Ferdinand and I were always together at that time, but some of the older ones were there too. They used to come for weekends still after they were grown up. Vivien used to make them, so that Malcolm wouldn't cut them out. Alicia hated it. Anyway, I know Lucy was there, because she wrote a poem about roots shrieking blindly to the sky.'

Yale looked sceptical.

'She's a poet,' I said lamely. 'Published.'

'The roots poem was published?'

'Yes.'

'All right, then. She was there. Who else?'

'Someone was carrying Serena on his shoulders when we had to leave the field for the explosion. I think it must have been Thomas. He used to make her laugh.'

'How old were you all at that time?' Yale asked.

'I don't know exactly.' I thought back. Alicia had swept out not very long after. 'Perhaps I was thirteen. Gervase is two years older, Ferdinand one year younger. Lucy would have been ... um ... twenty-two, about, and Thomas nineteen. Serena must have been six, at that rate, and Donald ... I don't know if he was there or not ... he would have been twenty-four.'

Yale thoughtfully pulled out his notebook and asked me to repeat the ages, starting with Donald.

'Donald twenty-four, Lucy twenty-two, Thomas nineteen, Gervase fifteen, myself thirteen, Ferdinand twelve, Serena six.'

'Right,' he said, putting a full-stop.

'But what does it matter, if the cordite is still here?' I said.

'They all saw the force of the explosion,' he said. 'They all saw it knock the gardener over from a hundred feet away, isn't that what you said?'

I looked at the shattered house and said forlornly, 'None of them could have done it.'

Yale put his notebook away. 'You might be right,' he said.

Smith again came over to join us. 'You've given me an idea,' he said to me. 'You and your tree roots. Can you draw me a plan of where the rooms were, exactly, especially those upstairs?'

I said I thought so, and the three of us went into the garage out of the wind, where I laid a piece of paper on the bonnet of Moira's car and did my best.

'The sitting-room stretched all the way between the two thick walls, as you know,' I said. 'About thirty feet. Above that ...' I sketched, 'there was my room, about eight feet wide, twelve deep, with a window on the short side looking out to the garden. Malcolm's bedroom came next, I suppose about fifteen feet wide and much deeper than mine. The passage outside bent round it ... and then his bathroom, also looking out to the garden, with a sort of dressing-room at the back of it which also led out of the bedroom . . .' I drew it. 'Malcolm's whole suite would have been about twenty-two feet wide facing the garden, by about seventeen or eighteen feet deep.'

Yale studied the drawing. 'Your room and the suite together were more or less identical with the sitting-room, then?'

'Yes, I should think so.'

'A big house,' he commented.

'It used to be bigger. The kitchen was once a morning-room, and where the garage is now there were kitchens and servants' halls. And on the other side, where the passage now goes out into the garden, there were gun-rooms and flower-rooms and music-rooms, a bit of a rabbit warren. I never actually saw the wings, only photographs of them. Malcolm had them pulled down when he inherited the house, to make it easier to deal with without the droves of servants his mother had.'

'Hm,' he said. 'That explains why there are no sideways-facing windows on the ground floor.'

'Yes,' I agreed.

He borrowed my pen and did some calculations and frowned. 'Where exactly was your father's bed?'

I drew it in. 'The bed was against the wall between his room and the large landing, which was a sort of upstairs place to sit in, over the hall.'

'And your bed?'

'Against the wall between my room and Malcolm's.'

Smith considered the plan for some time and then said, 'I think the charge here was placed centrally. Did your father by any chance have a chest, or anything, at the foot of his bed?'

'Yes, he did,' I said, surprised. 'A long box with a padded top for a seat. He kept his tennis things in it, when he used to play.'

'Then I'd think that would be where the explosion occurred. Or under your father's bed. But if there was a box at the foot, I'd bet on that.' Smith borrowed the pen again for some further calculations and looked finally undecided.

'What's the matter?' I asked.

'Mm . . . well, because of your tree roots, I was thinking of an explosive that farmers and landowners use sometimes which is safer than cordite. They blow up tree trunks, clear blocked ditches, that sort of thing. You can buy the ingredients anywhere without restrictions and mix it yourself.'

'That sounds extraordinary,' I said.

He smiled slightly. 'It's not so easy to get the detonators to set it off.'

'What is it, then?' I asked.

Yale, too, was listening with great interest.

'Fertiliser and diesel oil,' Smith said.

'What?' I sounded disappointed and Smith's smile expanded.

'Ammonium nitrate,' he said. 'You can buy it in fine granules from seed merchants and garden centres, places like that. Mix it with fuel oil. Dead simple. As far as I remember, but I'd have to look it up to be sure, it would be sixteen parts fertiliser to one part oil. The only problem is,' he scratched his nose, 'I think you'd need a good deal of it to do the sort of damage we have here. I mean, again I'd have to look it up, but I seem to remember it'll be volume in cubic metres over three, answer in kilos.'

'What volume?' I asked.

'The volume of the space you want cleared by the explosion.'

He looked at the mixed emotions I could feel on my face and dealt at least with the ignorance.

'Say you want effective destruction of everything within a space three metres by three metres by three metres. Twenty-seven cubic metres, OK? Volume of your bedroom, near enough. Divide by three, equals nine. Nine kilos of explosive needed.'

'Is that,' I said slowly, 'why reports of terrorist attacks are often so definite about the weight of the bomb used?'

'Absolutely. The area cleared directly relates to the size of the . . . er . . . bomb. If you can analyse the type of explosive and measure the area affected, you can tell how much explosive was needed.'

Superintendent Yale was nodding as if he knew all that.

'But you don't think this bomb went off in my bedroom,' I said.

'No, I don't. Nine kilos of ammonium nitrate in your bedroom would have annihilated it and made a nasty hole all round, but I wouldn't have thought it would bring half a house down. So if we locate the device in that foot-of-the-bed box, we are looking at something in the region of . . .' he did some more calculations '. . . say at least seventy-five cubic metres for your father's bedroom . . . that's twenty-five kilos of explosive.'

'That's heavy,' I said blankly.

'Yes. A large suitcaseful. But then you'd need a suitcaseful also if you were using cordite. For demolishing this whole house, you'd

169

have needed four times that amount, placed in about four places on the ground floor right against the thickest walls. People often think a small amount of explosive will do a tremendous lot of damage, but it doesn't.'

'What sets it off, then?' I asked.

'Ah.' He smiled the professional smile that wasn't about to give away its secrets. 'Let's just say fulminate of mercury, plus, I should say, an electrical circuit.'

'Please do explain,' I said.

He hesitated, then shrugged. 'ANFO won't explode on its own, it's very stable.'

'What's ANFO?' I interrupted.

'Ammonium nitrate fuel oil. The first letters. ANFO for short.'

'Oh yes. Sorry.'

'So you stick into it a package of something that explodes fast: the detonator, in fact. Then you arrange to heat the detonating substance, either with a burning fuse, or by an electrical circuit which can be achieved by ordinary batteries. The heat sets off the detonator, the detonator detonates the ANFO. And bingo . . .'

'Bang, you're dead.'

'Quite right.'

'At four-thirty in the morning,' I said, 'it would probably be a time-bomb, wouldn't it?'

Mr Smith nodded happily. 'That's what we're looking for. If it was an alarm clock, for instance, we'll probably find the pieces. We usually do if we look hard enough. They don't vaporise in the explosion, they scatter.'

Thirteen

I drove unhurriedly to Epsom but as soon as I let myself into my flat, I knew I wouldn't stay there. It was too negative, too empty, too boring. I wouldn't live there much longer, I thought.

There were a few letters, a few bills, a few messages on the answering machine, but nothing of great interest. If I'd been blown up at Quantum along with Malcolm, it wouldn't have made any vital difference to anybody, and I didn't like that thought very much.

I went into the bedroom to see what I'd got left in the way of clothes and came to the white lace negligée. Well, maybe *she* would have been sorry for a while. I wished I could phone her, but it was forbidden: her husband would answer as he had once before when I'd tried, and too many 'sorry, I've got the wrong number's would raise the suspicions of the dimmest of men, which he reputedly wasn't.

Apart from her, I thought, making a mental inventory, I mostly knew a lot of racing people on the borderline between acquaintance and friend. Enough to be asked to parties, enough for contentment at work. I knew I wasn't in general unpopular. It was enough, I guessed. Or it had seemed enough, up to now.

I had enjoyed being with Malcolm more than I'd realised. I missed him already, and in the twelve days I'd spent with him, I'd developed a taste for spontaneity which made sitting around in my flat impossible. I packed a pair of breeches and a sweater, added some limp old shirts to the new ones in the Simpson's suitcase, closed up the flat and went down to the car-park.

My own car stood there, but I took the hired one again, meaning to turn it in some time and return for my own by train. First stop was at the bank to drop through the letter box an envelope containing Malcolm's cheque, with a paying-in slip to lodge it in my account.

After that, I set off again in the overall direction of Quantum, but without really knowing where I was going.

I felt an awful aversion to the task of searching the psyches of the family, but I ended up in a place from where visiting them all would be easy, taking by impulse a turn onto the road to the village of Cookham and booking a room there in an old inn friendly with dark oak beams and log fires.

Norman West was out. I phoned him on the hour at four and five and reached him at six. He said apologetically that he had stopped working on the Pembroke case, there was nothing else he could do. He was sorry he hadn't been able to solve the . . . er . . . problem, and should he send his account to Mr Pembroke at the Savoy, or at Quantum House?

'Neither,' I said. 'We'd like you to carry on working.' And I told him what had happened to Quantum and very nearly to ourselves.

'Dear me,' he said.

I laughed internally, but I supposed 'dear me' was as apt a comment as any.

'So would you mind traipsing all the way round again to ask what everyone was doing the day before yesterday between three p.m. and midnight?'

He was silent for an appreciable interval. Then he said, 'I don't know that it would be useful, you know. Your family were unhelpful before. They would be doubly unhelpful again. Surely this time the police will make exhaustive enquiries? I think I must leave it to them.'

I was more dismayed than I expected. 'Please do reconsider,' I said. 'If the police go asking the family their movements, and then you do also, I agree they won't like it. But if after that I too go and ask, they may be upset enough or angry enough to let out things that could tell us . . . one way or another.' I paused. 'I suppose I'm not making much sense.'

'Do you remember what you said to me about stepping on a rattlesnake?' he said.

'Well, yes.'

'You're proposing to stir up one with a stick.'

'We absolutely have to know who the rattlesnake is.'

I heard him sigh and could feel his disinclination.

'Look,' I said, 'could you just meet me somewhere? You gave my father and me summaries of what all the family were doing on those

172

two days we asked about, but there must be much more you could tell me. If you don't want to visit them again, could you just . . . help me?'

'I don't mind doing that,' he said. 'When?'

'Tonight? Tomorrow?'

Tonight he was already working. Tomorrow he was taking his wife to visit their grandchildren all day as it was Sunday, but his evening would be free. He knew the pub I was staying in, he would come there, he said; he would meet me in the bar at seven.

I thanked him for that anyway, and next telephoned two stables along on the Downs to ask the trainers if I could ride exercise on their horses for several mornings, if it would be useful to them. The first said no, the second said yes, he was a couple of lads short and he'd be glad of the free help. Start Monday, first lot, pull out at seven-thirty, could I be there by seven-fifteen?

'Yes,' I said appreciatively.

'Stay to breakfast.'

Sanity lay in racing stables, I thought, thanking him. Their brand of insanity was my sort of health. I couldn't stay away for long. I felt unfit, not riding.

I spent the evening in the bar in the pub, mostly listening to a lonely man who felt guilty because his wife was in hospital having her guts rearranged. I never did discover the reason for the guilt but while he grew slowly drunk, I learned a lot about their financial troubles and about his anxieties over her illness. Not a riotously amusing evening for me, though he said he felt better himself from being able to tell a perfect stranger all the things he'd been bottling up. Was there anyone at all, I wondered, going to bed, who went through life feeling happy?

I dawdled Sunday away pleasurably enough, and Norman West, true to his word, appeared at seven.

His age was again very apparent from the grey-white hair downwards, and when I remarked that he looked tired, he said he'd been up most of the previous night but not to worry, he was used to it. Had he been to see his grandchildren? Yes, he had: lively bunch. He accepted a double scotch with water and, under its reviving influence, opened the large envelope he was carrying and pulled out some papers.

'Your photographs of the family are in here,' he said, patting the envelope, 'and I've also brought these copies of all my notes.' He laid the notes on the small table between us. 'You can have them to keep. The originals are in my files. Funny thing,' he smiled fleetingly, 'I used to think that one day I'd write a book about all my cases, but there they are, all those years of work, sitting in their files, and there they'll stay.'

'Why don't you write it?' I asked.

'I'm better at following people.'

I reflected that following people was what he'd been good at when Joyce had first employed him, and that probably we'd expected too much of him, setting him to unravel attempted murders.

He said, 'You'll find there's a definite pattern about the movements of your family, and at the same time an absence of pattern. The murder of Mrs Moira and the gassing of Mr Pembroke both took place at about five in the evening, and at five almost all your family are habitually on the move. Mind you, so is most of the working population. It's a time of day when it's easy to lose an hour or so without anyone noticing. Traffic jams, left work late, stopped for a drink, watched television in shop windows . . . I've heard all those from erring husbands. The list is limitless of things people think up as excuses for getting home late. With a family like yours, where practically no one has a set time for leaving a place of work, it's even easier. That's why it's been almost hopeless establishing alibis, and I'm pretty sure the police found the same thing over Mrs Moira. When there's no expectation of anyone arriving at a regular time, no one looks at the clock.'

'I do understand,' I said thoughtfully.

'Newmarket was a bit different,' he said, 'because it meant someone being away from their normal environment for a whole day, assuming that Mr Pembroke was followed from his hotel when he left at lunchtime for Newmarket. And one has to assume that a follower would be in position much earlier than that, because he wouldn't know when Mr Pembroke would leave, or where he would go.' He cleared his throat and sipped his whisky. 'I thought it would be simple in those circumstances to discover which family member had been away all of that Tuesday, but in fact it wasn't, as you'll read. Now, if the explosive device was planted in Quantum House between four when the gardener usually left and six, when you might have returned from the races, we're back to the . . . er . . .'

'Five o'clock shadow,' I said.

He looked mildly shocked. It wasn't a laughing matter. 'I've no doubt the same pattern will be found,' he said. 'No one will be able, or willing, to say exactly where they were or where anyone else was during that period.'

'We may be lucky,' I said.

He said maybe, and looked unconvinced.

'Couldn't you please tell me,' I said, 'which Mrs Pembroke got you to find Malcolm? I know all about your ethics, but after this bomb . . . can't you? Whose name was on the cheque?'

He considered, staring at his drink as if to find wisdom in the depths. He sighed heavily, and shrugged.

'I didn't get paid,' he said. 'The cheque never came. I'm not sure, but I think . . . I think it was the voice of Mrs Alicia Pembroke.' He shook his head. 'I asked her if it was her, when I interviewed her. She said it wasn't but I think she was lying. But two other people found out on their own account, don't forget, by doing exactly as I did, telephoning around.'

'I won't forget.'

He looked at me sombrely. 'I hope Mr Pembroke can't be found as easily at this moment.'

'I don't think so,' I said.

'Can I give you some advice?'

'Please do.'

'Carry a weapon with you.'

'Mr West!'

'Even if it's only a pot of pepper,' he said, 'or a can of spray paint. There's a good deal of enmity towards you in your family because of your favoured status with Mr Pembroke. You were supposed to die with him in the house, I should imagine. So don't go unprepared.'

I swallowed and thanked him. He nodded and prosaically produced a smaller envelope from an inner pocket, which contained his account. I wrote him his cheque. He took it, inspected it, and put it away.

He rose wearily to his feet and shook my hand. 'Any time you want to,' he said, 'phone me. I don't mind talking, if it will help.'

I thanked him again and he went greyly away, leaving me on my own with his notes and a feeling of nakedness.

I began reading the notes. It so happened that he had reversed his original working order, or perhaps the order had become reversed during the copying: in any event, the eldest-to-youngest progression had been transposed, and it was Serena's notes which came first.

Norman West had written all his notes in longhand with aide-mémoires to himself, and I could almost hear his radio-announcer voice in my head as I read.

Miss Serena Pembroke (26) unmarried, lives at 14 Mossborough Court, Bracknell, a block of flats just off the Easthampstead Road, turn left by the pub. Flats built during Bracknell's new-town expansion, middle-income, business people tenants, keep themselves to themselves. Pretty girl, one of the neighbours said (No 12) but don't know her name. Miss S. has lived there three months. One bedroom, one sitting-room, kit, bath, all small.

Miss S. works at Deanna's Dance and Aerobics Studio, High Street, Bracknell, teaching aerobics. Private business, sloppily run (my opinion), owned by Mrs Deanna Richmond (45?) whose mind is on a younger gent with a hairy chest, gold chain showing, rubbish.

Miss S. works mornings Monday to Friday 8.00 to 1.30 pm, taking classes, first office workers, then housewives. Miss S. and another girl (Sammy Higgs) work in rotation, half hour on, half off. Miss S's times are 8—8.30, 9—9.30, 10— 10.30, 11—11.30, 12—12.30, 1—1.30 most days.

Miss S. and Sammy H. are both good workers. The clients I spoke to said classes v. good. Continuous, therefore popular. A girl can drop in on way to office, on way home after taking children to school, etc. Sign in, pay on way out. Clients come from all over — large clientele.

Evening classes, Monday to Friday, 7 pm—8.30 only. Miss S. does these alone. (S. Higgs does afternoons 1–30–4 pm.) Evenings quite social — rests for clients' drinks etc. Well attended.

Miss S. has bad menstrual cramps every month. Can't dance or exercise. Always two days off. The Tuesday of Newmarket Sales was one of these days — the second. Miss S. called in Monday morning in pain, didn't work, no one expected her Tuesday, she returned Wednesday. Mrs Deanna Richmond's daughter stands in on these occasions and also if either girl especially asks for time off otherwise. No records kept of these times.

Miss S. leads sober, hard-working, regulated life.

Likes pretty clothes, a bit immature (my opinion), has few friends. Goes to her brother's house (Mr Ferdinand) a good deal at weekends, or to her mother's (Mrs Alicia).

176

No ascertainable love life.

Miss S. likes shopping and window-shopping. On the Friday of attack on Mr Pembroke she says she bought food and frilly white blouse at Marks and Spencers, she thinks. (Not sure of the day.) She buys something to wear about four times a week probably — tights, leotards, sweaters, etc. 'Has to look nice for her clients.'

Miss S. owns two-year-old grey/silver Ford Escort, but usually jogs one mile to work to warm up. Drives only if cold or wet. Car clean from automatic car-wash: Miss S. goes through same car-wash approx every two weeks. Car-wash people corroborate, but can't remember exact dates.

Miss S. says Mr Ian must have killed Mrs Moira because she (Mrs Moira) took away both Mr Pembroke and his (Mr Ian's) inheritance, and he hated her. She says Mr Ian must have tried to kill Mr Pembroke for the money. The police are fools not to arrest him, she says. I told her Mr Ian couldn't have killed Moira or attacked his father as he was seeing round a racehorse training stable forty miles away at both times, with thirty or more witnesses. I said he obviously hadn't been driving the car which nearly ran him down. She says he could have arranged it. In my opinion, Miss S. doesn't want to be convinced of Mr Ian's innocence. She wants the killer to be Mr Ian because she doesn't want to find any others in her family guilty. If it is Mr Ian, she can bear it, she says, because it would serve him right for being Daddy's pet. (Muddled thinking!)

End of enquiry.

The three pages of notes on Serena were held together with a paperclip. I shuffled Serena to the bottom of the pack and came to the next paperclip, holding notes on Debs and Ferdinand.

Norman West used grey paperclips, not silver. Most appropriate, I thought.

The first page read:

Mrs Deborah Pembroke (27) second wife of Mr Ferdinand, lives with him at Gables Cottage, Reading Road, Wokingham, Berkshire.

Mrs Deborah works as a photographic model chiefly for mail-order catalogues, and was engaged in London on the Tuesday of Newmarket Sales modelling a succession of swimsuits. There were two other models there, also a photographer and two assistants, also a dresser, a representative of the mail-order firm and a notetaker. The swimsuit session went on until 6 pm. Mrs D. was there until the end. Vouched for without possibility of doubt. Mrs Debs has no firm alibi for the previous Friday evening. She finished work early in London at 3.30 (corroborated by mail-order people) and drove home. No witness to arrival (Mr Ferdinand was out).

Owing to her Tuesday engagement, Mrs Debs could not have been at Newmarket. Friday, inconclusive.

Mrs Debs drives her own car, a scarlet Lancia. When I inspected it, it was dusty overall, with no sign of contact with Mr Ian.

Mrs Debs appeared undisturbed in the main by my questions and gave the following answers. She says her husband is the only good one in the Pembroke family, the only one with any sense of humour. She says he listens to his mother too much, but she'll change that in time. She says they'll be well off one day as long as Mr Ian doesn't queer their pitch. She said that she was happy enough and is in no hurry to have children. She objected to my asking about such a personal matter.

End of enquiry.

I turned over the page and on the next one found:

Mr Ferdinand Pembroke (32) married to Deborah (2nd wife), lives at Gables Cottage, Reading Road, Wokingham, Berks.

Mr Ferdinand is a statistician/actuary for the Merchant General Insurance Company, head office in Reading, Berks. He works about a third of the time at home, where he has a computer with a link to the one in the insurance company offices. Both he and his company like the arrangement, which means he can do exacting work without constant interruption. In addition, his company arranged for him to go on an anti-fraud course, as they are pleased with his ability.

I visited his office and explained to his boss that Mr Pembroke senior wanted to prove his children couldn't have been implicated in attacking him. Mr Ferdinand's boss wanted to be helpful, but in the end couldn't satisfy me.

Mr F. was not in the office on Friday afternoon, nor on the following Tuesday. On the Friday he'd worked at home, on Tuesday he was on the course.

I checked with the course at the Bingham Business Institute, City of London. Mr F. signed in on the first day, Monday, but after that no stringent attendance records were kept. Mr F. couldn't suggest anyone on the course who knew him well enough to swear he was there on Tuesday. I asked if he had made notes on the lectures. He said he didn't take any: the Tuesday lectures were about statistical probabilities and how to calculate them; basic stuff which he knew about. I checked this on the course schedule. The Tuesday lectures were as he said.

Mr Ferdinand drives a cream/grey Audi. It was clean when I saw it. Mr F. says he washes it himself with a brush on a hose (he showed it to me) and he does it frequently. He says he likes things to be clean.

Although he was working at home on the Friday afternoon, he was not in when Mrs Debs arrived from London. He says he had finished the job he'd been working on and decided to drive over to Henley and feed the ducks on the Thames. He found it peaceful. He liked the fresh air. He often did it, had done all his life, he said. He didn't know Mrs Debs was finishing work as early as 3.30 that day, but he said that wouldn't have stopped him going out. They were independent people and not accountable to each other for every minute.

I stopped reading and lifted my head. It was true that Ferdinand had always been attracted to the ducks. I couldn't count the number of times we'd walked along the Henley towpath, scattering bread and listening to the rude laughter of the mallards. Malcolm was the one who took us, whenever Alicia started throwing plates. She squawked rather like the ducks, I'd thought, and had had enough sense not to say so.

I went on reading:

Mr Ferdinand is hard working and successful, going to be more so. (My opinion and his boss's.) He has planning ability and energy. He is physically like his father, stocky and strong. (I remember Mr Pembroke 28 years ago. He threatened to throw me over his car when he found out I'd been following him, and I believed he could do it. Mr Ferdinand is the same.)

Mr F. can be very funny and good company, but his moods change to black disconcertingly fast. He is casual with his wife, not possessive. He is protective of his sister Serena. He is attentive to his mother, Mrs Alicia. He seems to have ambivalent feelings about Mr Pembroke and Mr Ian; I gathered from his inconsistent attitude that he liked them both in the past but no longer trusts them. Mr F. is capable of hate, I think.

End of enquiry.

I put Debs and Ferdinand to the back of the pile but had no mental stamina left for the next section on Ursula and Gervase. I put all the notes into the envelope and ate some pub steak instead and decided I would see the family in the age-reversed order Norman West had handed me, taking the easy ones first. Where was the bravado that had led me to tell Malcolm at Cambridge that I would stay with him just because it was dangerous?

Where indeed.

Somewhere under the rubble of Quantum.

In the morning, I rode out on the windy Downs, grateful for the simplicity of horses and for the physical pleasure of using one's muscles in the way they were trained for. Vigour seemed to flow of its own accord in my arms and legs, and I thought that maybe it was the same for a pianist sitting down after a few days to play; there was no need to work out what to do with one's fingers, it was easy, it was embedded in one's brain, the music came without thought.

I thanked my host sincerely after breakfast and drove towards Quantum thinking of the telephone call I'd made to Malcolm the evening before. It had been nearly midnight for me: nearly six, early evening, for him.

He had arrived safely, he said, and Dave and Sally Cander were true blue cronies. Ramsey Osborn had flown down. The Canders were giving a party, starting in five minutes. He'd seen some good horses. He'd had some great new ideas for spending money (wicked chuckle). How were things in England?

He sounded satisfactorily carefree, having shed depression with the miles, and I said things were the same as when he left except that the house was wrapped up in tarpaulins. The state of the house troubled him for roughly ten seconds, and after that he said he and Ramsey might be leaving Lexington on Tuesday or Wednesday; he wasn't sure.

'Wherever you go,' I said, 'will you please give the Canders a telephone number where I can reach you?'

'I promise,' he said blithely. 'Hurry up with your passport, and come over.'

'Soon.'

'I've got used to you being with me. Keep looking round for you. Odd. Must be senile.'

'Yes, you sound it.'

He laughed. 'It's a different world here, and I like it.'

He said goodbye and disconnected, and I wondered how many horses he would have bought by the time I reached him.

Back at the pub in Cookham, I changed out of riding clothes and dutifully telephoned Superintendent Yale. He had nothing to tell me, nor I to tell him: the call was short.

'Where is your father?' he asked conversationally.

'Safe.'

He grunted. 'Phone me,' he said, and I said, 'Yes.'

With a heavy lack of enthusiasm I returned to the car and pointed its nose towards Bracknell, parking in one of the large featureless car-parks and walking through to the High Street.

The High Street, long before, had been the main road through a minor country town; now it was a pedestrian backwater surrounded by the factories, offices and convoluted ring roads of mushroom progress. 'Deanna's Dance and Aerobics Studio' looked like a wide shop-front flanked by a bright new shiny newsagent on one side and on the other a photographic shop whose window display seemed to consist chiefly of postcard-sized yellow fluorescent labels with prices on, mostly announcing '20% OFF'.

Deanna's studio consisted firstly of a reception area with a staircase on one side leading upwards. A young girl sitting behind the reception desk looked up and brightened when I pushed open the glass entrance door and stepped onto some thick grey carpet, but lost interest when I asked for Serena, explaining I was her brother.

'Back there,' she said. 'She's taking class at the moment.'

Back there was through white-painted double doors. I went through and found myself in a windowless but brightly lit and attractive area of small tables and chairs, where several women sat drinking from polystyrene cups. The air vibrated with the pulse of music being played somewhere else, and when I again asked for Serena and was directed onwards, I came to its source.

The studio itself ran deeply back to end in a wall of windows overlooking a small strip of garden. The floor was of polished wood, sprung somehow so that it almost bounced underfoot. The walls were white except for the long left-hand one, which was entirely of looking-glass. The music, warm and insistent, invited rhythmic response.

Serena herself danced with her back to the mirror. Facing her, in three spread-out rows, was a collection of clients, all female, bouncing in unison on springy ankles, arms and legs swinging in circles and kicks. On every face, concentration and sweat. 'Go for the burn,' Serena commanded, looking happy, and her class with an increase of already frenetic energy, presumably went.

'Great, ladies, that's great,' Serena said eventually, stopping jumping and switching off the music machine which stood in a corner near where I'd come in. She gave me an unfriendly glance but turned with radiance back to the customers. 'If any of you want to continue, Sammy will be here within a minute. Take a rest, ladies.'

A few of the bodies stayed. Most looked at the clock on the wall and filed panting into a door marked 'changing rooms'.

Serena said, 'What do you want?'

'Talk.'

She looked colourful but discouraging. She wore a bright pink long-sleeved body-stocking with white bouncing shoes, pink and white leg-warmers and a scarlet garment like a chopped off vest. 'I'll give you five minutes,' she said.

She was hardly out of breath. A girl who was apparently Sammy Higgs came in in electric blue and started taking charge, and Serena with bad grace led me back through the refreshment area and the entrance hall and up the stairs.

'There are no classes up here just now. Say what you've come for and then go.'

Upstairs, according to a notice on the wall, Deanna offered ballroom dancing tuition, also 'ballet and posture'. Serena stood with her hands on her skinny pink hips and waited.

'Malcolm wants me to find out who bombed Quantum,' I said.

She glowered at me. 'Well, I didn't.'

'Do you remember the day old Fred blew up the tree stump?'

'No,' she said. She didn't bother to think, hadn't tried to remember.

'Thomas gave you a ride on his shoulders out of the field, and the blast of the explosion knocked old Fred over.'

'I don't know what you're talking about.'

'Why are you so hostile?'

'I'm not. Where's Daddy?'

'With friends,' I said. 'It saddens him that you're hostile.'

She said bitterly, 'That's a laugh. He's rejected all of us except you. And I'll bet you killed Moira.'

'He hasn't rejected you,' I said. 'And I didn't.'

'He kicked us all out. I loved him when I was little.' Tears appeared suddenly in her eyes and she shook them angrily away. 'He couldn't wait to get rid of me.'

'He tried to keep you, but Alicia wouldn't have it. She fought him in the courts for custody, and won.'

'He didn't want me,' she said fiercely. 'He only said so to spite Mummy, to make her suffer. I know all about it.'

'Alicia told you?'

'Of course she did. Daddy couldn't wait to get rid of us, to get rid of Mummy, to get married again, to ... to ... throw everything about us out of the house, to tear out all the pretty rooms ... blot us out.'

She was deeply passionate with the old feelings, still smouldering after twenty years. I remembered how upset I'd been when Alicia tore out my own mother's kitchen, how I'd felt betrayed and dispossessed. I had been six, as Serena had been, and I still remembered it clearly.

'Give him a chance,' I suggested.

'I did give him a chance. I offered to help him after Moira died and he still didn't want me. And look at the way he's behaving,' she said. 'Throwing money away. If he thinks I care a tuppenny damn about his stupid scholarships, he's a fool. You can toady up to him all you like, but I'm not going to. He can keep his damned money. I can manage without it.'

She looked hard-eyed and determinedly stubborn. The old man in all of us, I thought.

'You've had your five minutes,' she said. She side-stepped me in swift movements and made for the stairs. 'See you at the funeral.'

'Whose funeral?' I asked, following her.

'Anyone's,' she said darkly, and ran weightlessly down the stairs as if skimming were more normal than walking.

When I reached the entrance hall, she was vanishing through the white double doors. It was pointless to pursue her. I left Deanna's studio feeling I had achieved nothing, and with leaden spirits went back to the car and drove to Wokingham to call on Ferdinand.

I half-hoped he wouldn't be in, but he was. He came to the door frowning because I had interrupted him at his computer, and grudgingly let me in.

'We've nothing to say,' he said, but he sounded more resigned than forbidding; half-relaxed, as he'd been in my flat.

He led the way into the front room of the bungalow he and Debs had bought on the road to Reading. The front room was his office, a perfectly natural arrangement to Ferdinand, since Malcolm's office had always been at home.

The rest of the bungalow, which I'd visited two or three times before, was furnished sparsely in accordance with Debs' and Ferdinand's joint dislike of dirt and clutter. One of the three bedrooms was completely empty, one held a single bed and a chest of drawers (for Serena's visits), and in the third, the couple's own, there was a mattress on a platform and a wall of cupboards and enclosed shelves that Ferdinand had put together himself. The sitting-room held two chairs, a standard lamp, a lot of floor cushions and a television set. In the tidy kitchen, there was a table with four stools. All visible life was in the office, though even there, in direct contrast to Malcolm's comfortable shambles, a spartan order of neatness ruled.

Ferdinand's computer bore a screenful of graphics. He glanced at it and then looked with some impatience back to me.

'What do you want?' he asked. 'I've a lot to do after being away on a course.'

'Can't you save all that,' I gestured to the screen, 'or whatever it is you do? Record it, and come out to a pub for lunch.'

He shook his head and looked at his watch. Then, in indecision, said, 'I suppose I have to eat,' and fiddled about with the computer. 'All right. Half an hour, max.'

I drove us to the town centre and he pointed out a pub with a car-park. The bar was full of business people similarly out for lunch breaks, and I bought scotch and sandwiches after a good deal of polite elbowing. Ferdinand had secured a table from which he was clearing the past customer's detritus with a finicky expression.

'Look,' I said, handing him his drink as we sat down, 'Malcolm wants me to find out who's trying to kill him.'

'It isn't me,' he said. He took a swallow, unconcerned.

'Do you remember old Fred blowing up the tree roots, that time? When we were about twelve or thirteen? When the blast blew old Fred flat?'

He stared. 'Yes, I do,' he said slowly, 'but that's years ago. It can't have anything to do with the house.'

'Why not?' I asked. 'That bang made a big impression on us. Memories last more or less for ever, they just need digging up. The explosives expert working at Quantum asked if I knew what cordite was, and I remembered old Fred.'

Ferdinand did his own digging. 'Black powder . . . in a box.'

'Yes, it's still there in the tool shed. Still viable, but not used on the house. They're working now on its being a homemade explosive called ANFO.'

Ferdinand was visibly shaken and after a minute said, 'I suppose I hadn't considered . . . what it was.'

'Do you know what ANFO is?' I asked.

He said no uncertainly, and I thought he wasn't being truthful. Perhaps he felt that knowing could be considered guilt. I needed to jolt him into being more positive. Into being an ally, if I could.

'Malcolm's made a new will,' I said.

'And left you the lot, I suppose,' he sneered bitterly.

'No,' I said. 'If he dies from normal causes, we all inherit equally.' I paused, and added an invention. 'If someone murders him, it all goes to charities. So how about you getting on the telephone and telling the whole tribe to help me find out who's trying to do them out of their future?'

Fourteen

In my room at Cookham in the evening, I read Norman West's notes on Gervase and Ursula.

Gervase first:

Mr Gervase Pembroke (35) lives with Mrs Ursula at 14 Grant St., Maidenhead, a detached house with a quarter-acre garden in good residential neighbourhood. They have been married for 11 years and have 2 daughters (8 and 6) both attending a private school.

Mr G. is a stockbroker who commutes to the City firm of Wells, Gibson & Cathcart. (Wells, Gibson and Cathcart have all died or retired long ago, but the respected name is kept.) Mr Gervase works for his own commission within the firm: each partner does. He has flexible working hours; he's his own boss to a great extent. He used to work harder than he does now but has become erratic of late, according to the firm's lady receptionist. She didn't like to say outright, but I gathered Mr G. sometimes returns from lunch the worse for drink, and sometimes doesn't return at all.

She didn't of course note down such times. She said she'd heard two of the other partners discussing Mr G., saying he'd lost his nerve and was selling his clients only gilts. They thought that too much playing safe was bad stockbroking. She had no qualms in denigrating Mr G., who she said has a filthy temper when things don't go his way, and never appreciates how hard she works (!)

I requested to interview Mr G. at his place of work. I was shown into his office and explained who I was. He said he knew. I said as a preliminary that I understood he was the illegitimate son of Mrs Alicia Pembroke, and the interview ended immediately. He physically hustled me out (bruise on left arm). He said I'd insulted him. Perhaps I did! I managed to say that if he could produce office records — letters written, brokerage transactions — for the

Tuesday in question, he would be in the clear. He said to consult his secretary, which I did. Mr G. went into the office that morning, she confirmed, and dictated two letters. Mr G. told her he was going to see a new client, and left at 10.30 am. She didn't know who the client was, he was not listed on Mr G's office diary. It was more usual for new clients to come to the office, but not invariable. Mr G. didn't return to the office that day, but returned Wednesday in bad mood (with a hangover?).

Mr G. left the office the previous Friday (secretary's notes) at midday, didn't return. (Mr G. worked normally all day Monday.)

Mr G. commutes by train, leaves off-white Rover in station car-park. His car clean and unmarked when I saw it.

Visited Mr G. at his home to ask about the client on Tuesday re solid alibi. Mr G. said none of my business. Guess: client was either a mistress or a bottle, or else Mr G. wants me to believe that.

Mr G.'s alcohol problem is serious (my opinion) but not incapacitating. He has strong masterful manner, but must have insecurities (illegitimacy??) to make him drink and treat people badly. (His secretary does not love him.) Mr G. appears to make good income, no sign of financial straits.

Attentive to Mrs Alicia. Bossy and possessive with his wife and children. Jealous of Mr Ian and (my judgement) fears him. (I don't know why this is. Something in the past? Mr Pembroke's preference?) Despises but also fears Mr Pembroke. (A lot of bluster when he talked of him.)

Mr G. is physically strong but getting less so, I'd think. Takes little exercise, somewhat overweight. Difficult personality. A bully.

End of enquiry.

I paperclipped Gervase together with a sigh. Norman West, for all his ineffective appearance, had a way of getting to the heart of things pretty smartly.

What had he made of Ursula, I wondered. Ursula, the quiet wife, who had talked in tears to Joyce. Pretty enough in an insipid way, she was like an unfinished painting, without highlights. Pleasant enough to me whenever Gervase allowed, she had never told me her thoughts. I turned with unexpected interest to the West view of Gervase's wife.

Mrs Ursula Pembroke (35) wife of Mr Gervase, lives with him at

14 Grant St., Maidenhead. She has no employment beyond looking after children and household. A cleaner comes in Monday to Friday mornings, 9 am to 1 pm, stays Tuesdays and Thursdays until 4 pm, also baby-sits whenever asked. (I had to make two visits to Mrs U. On the first occasion she had been crying and wouldn't talk. On the second she was cooperative.)

The daughters' school is at the other end of Maidenhead. Mrs U. shares the school-run with a family nearby; Mrs U's mornings are Tuesday and Thursday; afternoons Mon., Wed. and Fri. Mrs U's car is a cream Austin. Clean.

On the Friday of the attack on Mr Pembroke, the daughters were invited to tea by the other school-run family (the mother corroborates). Mrs U. left the daughters there after school (4 pm). Picked them up about 6.30.

On the following Tuesday, Mrs U. arranged for the cleaner to stay and give the daughters their tea as she wanted a day out in London. The cleaner told me Mrs U. did the school run, came back and changed, and drove away to the station to catch the train. She (Mrs U.) said she would be back late as she would go to the cinema after she'd done her shopping. Mrs U. has done this several times lately. She returned at 10 pm. Cleaner went home. (Mrs U. gave me permission to consult the cleaner.) Mrs U. says she didn't go to the cinema, she didn't like the look of the films, she just had dinner in a steak house. She also said she had been into a church to pray. She hadn't bought anything (nothing fitted).

Mrs U. nervous and evasive about trip to London. Did she go to Newmarket? Possible (my opinion) that she goes to London to meet someone, doesn't want cleaner or husband to know. Who? Lover? Not possible, she hasn't the air, they can't hide that inner excitement. Priest? Friend unacceptable to Mr G.? Doctor? Some sort of solace, I would say.

Mrs U. unhappy woman but wouldn't unbutton. Loyal. Any wife of Mr G. liable to be unhappy (my opinion). Mrs U. doesn't like having the cleaner around for so long. Mr G. insists on cleanliness. Mrs U. gets tired of the cleaner's incessant chatter. All adds to Mrs U's stress. Mrs U. would like a job or to do voluntary work. Mr G. won't have it. 'The children come first.' (Mrs U. obviously very fond of the children.)

Mrs U. wishes Mr Pembroke would give all the family a lot of money now so that they would stop griping about it. She sees nothing wrong in Mr Ian, but her husband won't let her talk to him. She could like Mr Pembroke, she thinks he's funny and generous, but her husband ditto. She can't go against her husband. She has no money of her own, I'd say. She's in a trap. (Can't support children herself, couldn't leave without them.)

Does she believe killing Mr Pembroke could solve her problems? Does she believe if Mr G. becomes richer it will make things right? I could tell her it won't.

End of enquiry.

Poor Mrs U. Poor Ursula. Could she have blown up Quantum? Perhaps, if she'd wanted to. She sounded desperate enough for anything, but if she had any sense, her desperation should drive her to beg from Malcolm, not to kill him.

I clipped Ursula behind Gervase: forever in his shadow.

I wondered why she'd married him, but then I'd attended their wedding also, and if one hadn't in the past been on the wrong end of his glowing cigarette, one could have taken him as he seemed on the surface, confident, good looking, positive and strong. A rising young stockbroker. A catch.

I put Gervase and Ursula back in the envelope but they wouldn't stay there, they stuck like burrs in my mind.

There must be thousands, hundreds of thousands of sad marriages like that, I thought, where the unhappiness came from inside. Probably one could more easily withstand disasters that came from without, survive wars, poverty, illness, grief. Much harder to find any good way forward when personality disintegrated. Each of them was disintegrating, Ursula because of Gervase, Gervase because of . . .

Because of Malcolm? Because of Malcolm's boredom with Vivien, his affair with Alicia, his quick marriage to Joyce? Because of illegitimacy? But Ferdinand had been a product of the same process, and Ferdinand was whole.

There were questions without answers. The most likely answers were often wrong. I didn't know why Gervase was disintegrating: I thought only that the process had already begun when we both lived at Quantum; had maybe begun in the womb.

I slept with troubled dreams and went to ride the next morning as if for therapy and release. Solace, Norman West's word, met the case.

The raw morning, the moving horses, the filthy language and the crude jokes, a daily fix of the sort of reality I'd chosen at eighteen. I didn't know why I'd liked horses so much. Choice sprang from deep needs, but where did the needs come from?

I wasn't accustomed to thinking in that way. I usually coasted along, not worrying much, doing my job, enjoying riding in races, making love without strings. Lazy in many respects, I dared say, but uncomplicated. An opt-out that had come to an abrupt end with meeting Malcolm at Newmarket.

It was Tuesday.

Ursula's cleaner, I thought, driving back to Cookham, would currently be chatting away with no respite for Ursula until the girls got back from school. I wondered if Ursula was quietly going bananas at 14 Grant St., Maidenhead. I changed into ordinary clothes and went along there to find out.

The cleaner came to the door; middle-aged, in a flowered overall, with an inquisitive face. Mrs Pembroke was lying down with a headache, she said, and yes, perhaps she could go upstairs and ask her if her brother-in-law might take her out to lunch. Perhaps I would like to wait in the hall.

I waited, and presently Ursula came downstairs looking wan and wearing a coat and gloves.

'Oh!' she said faintly when she saw me. 'I thought it was Ferdinand.'

I'd hoped she would. I said, 'Where would you best like to go?'

'Oh.' She was irresolute. She looked back up the stairs and saw the cleaner watching interestedly from the landing. If she didn't come out with me, she'd be stuck with explaining.

'Come on,' I said persuasively. 'The car's warm.'

It sounded a silly thing to say, but I suppose she listened to the intention, not the words. She continued across the hall and came with me out of the front door, closing it behind us.

'Gervase won't like this,' she said.

'Why should he know?'

'She'll find a way of telling him.' She gestured back to the house, to the cleaner. 'She likes to make trouble. It brightens up her life.'

'Why do you keep her?'

She shrugged. 'I hate housework. If I sack her, I'd have to do it. Gervase thinks she's thorough, and he pays her. He said he wouldn't pay anyone else.'

She spoke matter-of-factly, but I was startled by the picture of domestic tyranny. We got into the car and I drove out of the town and towards the village of Bray, and twice more on the way she said, 'Gervase won't like this.' We stopped at a small roadside restaurant and she chose homemade soup and moussaka, several times looking over her shoulder as if her husband would materialise and pounce.

I ordered a carafe of red wine. Not for her, she protested, but when it came she drank it almost absentmindedly. She had removed the coat and gloves to reveal a well-worn grey skirt topped by a blue sweater with a cream shirt underneath. She wore a string of pearls. Her dark hair was held back at one side by a tortoiseshell slide, and there was no lipstick on her pale mouth. The sort of appearance, I supposed, that Gervase demanded.

When the soup came, she said, 'Ferdinand phoned last night and told Gervase that Malcolm had made a new will, according to you.'

'Yes, he made one,' I agreed. 'He showed it to me.'

'Gervase didn't tell me,' she said. 'He phoned Alicia and told her, and I listened. That's what usually happens. He doesn't tell me things, he tells his mother.'

'How do you get on with Alicia?' I asked.

She very carefully drank the soup already in her spoon. She spoke as if picking her way through a minefield.

'My mother-in-law,' she said intensely, 'has caused more trouble than anyone since Eve. I can't talk about her. Drink your soup.'

I had the impression that if she once started talking about Alicia, she would never stop. I wondered how to start her, but when I tentatively asked what she meant about trouble, she shook her head vehemently.

'Not here,' she said.

I left it. She talked about her children, which she could do without strain, looking almost animated, which saw us through to the moussaka.

'What do you do on your trips to London?' I asked casually.

She looked amazed, then said, 'Oh yes, that wretched Mr West. Gervase was furious with him. Then Gervase was annoyed with me also, and wanted to know where I'd been. I'd been wandering around, that's all.' She ate her moussaka methodically. 'Ferdinand told Gervase and Gervase told Alicia something about a tree stump. What was that all about?'

I explained about the cordite.

She nodded. 'Gervase told Alicia he'd had a good laugh when old Fred was knocked flat.'

She seemed undisturbed by the thought of explosives. We finished the lunch, I paid the bill, and we set off on the short road back to Maidenhead. A little way along there, I stopped the car in a lay-by and switched off the engine.

She didn't ask why we'd stopped. After a pause she said, 'Alicia is ruining our marriage, I suppose you know that?'

I murmured an assent.

'I'd known Gervase for only four months when we got married. I didn't realise . . . She's twisted him from birth, hasn't she? With her awful lies and spite. She sets him against you all the time. Gervase says terrible things about you sometimes . . . I mean, violent . . . I hate it. I try to tell him not to, but he doesn't listen to me, he listens to her. She says you sneer at him, you think you're much superior, because you're legitimate. I know you don't. Gervase believes her though. She tells him over and over that Malcolm threw them out and never loved them. She's wicked. And look what she's done to Serena. Gervase says she was a bright girl, but Alicia wouldn't let her stay on at school, Alicia wanted her to be a little girl, not to grow up. And Serena hates all men, and it's Alicia's fault. The only men Serena will let touch her are Ferdinand and Gervase. It's such a waste. Alicia got rid of Ferdinand's first wife, did you know? Went on and on at her until she couldn't stand it and left. I don't know how Debs puts up with her. It's driving me insane, you know, her drip, drip, drip. She's the worst enemy you'll ever have. If it was you that had been murdered, she would have done it.'

'She wasn't always like that,' I said, as she paused. 'When she lived at Quantum, she treated me the same as Ferdinand and Gervase.'

'Then it must have started when Malcolm kept you there on your own, and as she's got older it's got worse. She's much worse now than she was when we got married, and she was bad enough then. She hated Coochie, you know, and Coochie was nice, wasn't she? I was sorry when Coochie died. But Coochie banned all the family from staying in the house except you, and I should think that's when Alicia turned against you. Or let it all out. I bet it was there inside all the time. Like Gervase keeps things in and lets them out violently . . . so does Serena, and Ferdinand too . . . they're all like that. I wish

192

Alicia would die. I can understand people wanting to kill. I would like to kill Alicia.'

She stopped abruptly, the raw truth quivering in her voice.

'Drive me home,' she said. 'I shouldn't have said that.'

I didn't immediately restart the engine. I said, 'Is it Alicia that's causing Gervase to drink?'

'Oh!' Ursula gulped, the flow of anger ending, the misery flooding back. 'It's just . . . everything. I can see he's unhappy, but he won't let me help him, he won't talk to me, he just talks to *her*, and she makes it worse.'

I sighed and set off towards Grant Street. Alicia hadn't quite reached sixty: the worst of the witches could outlive them all.

'I shouldn't have told you all this,' Ursula said, when I stopped at the door. 'Gervase won't like it.'

'Gervase won't know what you've said.'

She fished a handkerchief out of her handbag and blew her nose. 'Thank you for the lunch. Did your mother tell you we've had lunch a few times in London, she and I? She gives me good advice. I can't tell Gervase, he'd be furious.'

I nodded. 'Joyce told me you were friends.'

'She's awfully catty about Alicia. It cheers me up no end.' She gave me a wan smile and got out of the car. She waved as she opened her front door: I waved back and drove away, and covered the few miles to Cookham.

I thought it might be interesting to see what Norman West had made of Alicia, and I searched through the notes until I came to her. West had written:

Mrs Alicia Pembroke (59) refused to speak to me at all on my first visit and was ungracious and edgy on my second.

Mrs Alicia lives at 25 Lions Court, London Road, Windsor, a block of flats. She still maintains she can't remember what she was doing on the Friday or the Tuesday: she was pottering about, she says. 'One day is much like another.' I think she's being obstructive for the sake of it.

Mrs A. drives a big silver/grey Fiat. Clean, no damage.

Mrs A. antagonistic to me personally because of my following her in Mrs Joyce's divorce case, although in the end she benefited. Twenty-eight years ago! She remembers every detail of that time. Can't remember last Tuesday . . .

I asked her if she had ever engaged me to work for her. She said no. (?)

Mrs A. has changed from the Miss A. I followed. Miss A. was full of giggles, very little-girl. Mrs A. still dresses very young, acts young, but is embittered. Odd how some women flower in love affairs and wither in marriage. Seen it often. Seems as if the spice of secrecy and naughtiness is what they love, not the man himself.

Mrs A. very bitter on subject of Mr Pembroke spending money. Mr Ian's name brought angry looks. Mrs A. turned me out.

End of enquiry.

Short and unsweet, I thought.

I couldn't face going to see Alicia at that moment. I didn't think her physically capable of carrying Malcolm while he was unconscious, and I didn't think her efficient enough to construct a bomb: good enough reasons for avoiding something I wanted to do as much as jump into a crocodile-infested swamp.

I didn't want to talk to Gervase either, but that couldn't be as easily avoided.

I drove back to Grant Street in the early evening and parked along the road from No 14 waiting for the master to return. It wasn't until I was sitting there that I remembered Norman West's advice about defence. Pepper . . . paint . . . I couldn't see myself throwing either in Gervase's eyes, or anyone else's for that matter. Gervase was, goddammit, my brother. Half-brother. Cain killed Abel. Abel hadn't had his pepper ready, or his paint.

Upon that sober reflection, Gervase came home.

His Rover turned into his house's short driveway and pulled up outside the garage. Gervase, carrying a briefcase, let himself in through the front door. Five minutes later, I walked along the road and rang the bell.

The door was opened by one of the children, who called over her shoulder, 'It's Ian.'

Gervase, still in his City suit, came immediately into the hall from his sitting-room, looking inhospitable and carrying a cut-glass tumbler half filled with what I expected was scotch.

'Ferdinand phoned me,' he said authoritatively. 'It's the police's business to look into the bombing of Quantum, not yours.'

'Malcolm asked me to,' I said.

194

'You'd better come in, I suppose.' He was grudging, but pointed me to the room he'd left. 'Do you want a drink?'

'Yes, please.'

He poured from the scotch bottle into a duplicate tumbler, and handed me the glass, gesturing to the matching jug of water which stood on a silver tray. I diluted my drink and sipped it, and said, 'Thanks.'

He nodded, busy with his own.

There was no sign of Ursula, but I could hear the two girls' high voices in the kitchen and supposed she was with them. They would tell her I had come, and she would be worrying about her lunch.

'Ferdinand told me about Malcolm's new will,' Gervase said with annoyance. 'It's ridiculous putting in that clause about being murdered. What if some random mugger bumps him off? Do we all lose our inheritance?'

'Some random mugger is unlikely. A paid assassin might not be.'

Gervase stared. 'That's rubbish.'

'Who killed Moira?' I said. 'Who's tried three times to kill Malcolm?'

'How should I know?'

'I think you should put your mind to it.'

'No. It's for the police to do that.' He drank. 'Where is he now?'

'Staying with friends.'

'I offered him a bed here,' he said angrily, 'but I'm not good enough, I suppose.'

'He wanted to be away from the family,' I said neutrally.

'But he's with you.'

'No, not any more.'

He seemed to relax a little at the news. 'Did you quarrel again?' he said hopefully.

We were still standing in the centre of the room, as the offer of a drink hadn't extended to a chair also. There were fat chintz-covered armchairs in a stylised flower pattern on a mottled grey carpet, heavy red curtains and a brick fireplace with a newly-lit fire burning. I'd been in his house about as seldom as in Ferdinand's, and I'd never been upstairs.

'We haven't quarrelled,' I said. 'Do you remember when old Fred blew up the tree stump?'

195

He found no difficulty in the change of subject. 'Ferdinand said you'd asked that,' he said. 'Yes, of course I remember.'

'Did Fred show you how he set off the explosive?'

'No, he damn well didn't. You're not trying to make out that I blew up the house, are you?' His anger, always near the surface, stoked up a couple of notches.

'No,' I said calmly. 'I should have said, did Fred show you or anyone else how he set off the explosive.'

'I can only speak for myself,' he said distinctly, 'and the answer is no.'

Gervase was heavy and, I thought, getting heavier. His suit looked filled. I had never quite grown to his height. He was the tallest and biggest of all Malcolm's children and easily the most forceful. He looked a strong successful man, and he was cracking up for lack of a piece of paper that no one gave a damn about except himself.

Perhaps, I thought, there was something of that obsessiveness in us all. In some it was healthy, in others destructive, but the gene that had given Malcolm his Midas obsession with gold had been a dominant strain.

Gervase said, 'Will Malcolm ante up anything before he dies?'

His voice was as usual loud and domineering, but I looked at him speculatively over my glass. There had been an odd sub-note of desperation, as if it weren't just of academic interest to him, but essential. Norman West's notes recycled themselves: '... lost his nerve and was selling only gilts. Too much playing safe was bad stockbroking ...' Gervase, who had seemed comfortably fixed, might all of a sudden not be.

I answered the words of the question, not the implications. 'I did ask him to. He said he would think about it.'

'Bloody old fool,' Gervase said violently. 'He's playing bloody games with us. Chucking the stuff away just to spite us. Buying bloody *horses*. I could strangle him.' He stopped as if shocked at what he'd more or less shouted with conviction. 'Figure of speech,' he said, hard-eyed.

'I'll try again,' I said, ignoring it, 'but Vivien tried, and rubbed him up the wrong way so that he stuck his toes in. Malcolm's obstinate, the way we all are, and the more anyone tries to push him, the harder he'll resist.'

'It's you that got him to buy horses. He wouldn't have thought of it on his own.' He was glaring at me. 'Two million pounds for a bloody *colt*. Do you realise what two million pounds means? Have you any idea? *Two million pounds* for a four-legged nothing? He's raving mad. Two million pounds invested in any one of us would give us freedom from worry for the rest of our lives, and he goes and spends it on a *horse*. Retarded children are bad enough, half a million for retarded children . . . but that's not enough for him, is it? Oh no. He buys that bloody horse Blue Clancy, and how many more millions did that cost him? How many?' He was insistent, belligerent, demanding, his chin thrust aggressively forward.

'He can afford it,' I said. 'I think he's very rich.'

'Think!' Gervase grew even angrier. 'How do you know he isn't flinging away every penny? I'll find a way of stopping him. He's *got* to be stopped.'

He suddenly stretched out his free hand and plucked my half-full glass from my grasp.

'Go on, get out of here,' he said. 'I've had enough.'

I didn't move. I said, 'Throwing me out won't solve any problems.'

'It'll make a bloody good start.' He put both glasses on the table and looked ready to put thought into action.

'When Malcolm fled to Cambridge,' I said, 'did Alicia tell you where he was?'

'What?' It stopped him momentarily. 'I don't know what you're talking about. Go on, get out.'

'Did you telephone to Malcolm's hotel in Cambridge?'

He hardly listened. He embarked on a heartfelt tirade. 'I'm fed up with your sneers and your airs and graces. You think you're better than me, you always have, and you're *not*. You've always weaselled into Malcolm's good books and set him against us and he's blind and stupid about you . . . and get out.' He stepped forward threateningly, one hand in a fist.

'But you still want me to plead your case,' I said, standing still.

His mouth opened but no words came out.

'Alicia tells you I sneer at you,' I said, 'but I don't. She tells you lies, you believe them. I've never set Malcolm against you. You hit me now, and I might think of it. If you want me to try to get him to cough up, you'll put that fist down and give me my scotch back, and I'll drink it and go.'

After a long staring pause, he turned his back on me. I took it as agreement to the terms and picked up one of the glasses, not sure whether it was mine or his.

It was his. The drink was much stronger, hardly any water in it at all. I put it down and picked up the other. He didn't turn round, didn't notice.

'Gervase,' I said dispassionately, 'try a psychiatrist.'

'Mind your own bloody business.'

I drank a mouthful of scotch but as a token only, and put the glass down again.

'Goodbye,' I said.

He still showed me his back, and was silent. I shrugged wryly and went out into the hall. Ursula and the two girls stood in the kitchen doorway looking anxious. I smiled at them lopsidedly and said to Ursula, 'We'll get through it somehow.'

'I hope so.' Forlorn hope, she was saying.

'I'll be back,' I said, not knowing if I meant it, but meaning anyway that anything I could do to help her or Gervase, I would do.

I let myself out of the front door quietly, and back at Cookham telephoned to the Canders in Lexington. I talked to Mrs Cander; Sally.

Malcolm had gone to Stamford, Connecticut with Ramsey, she said. She thought they were fixing some kind of deal. She and Dave had really enjoyed Malcolm's visit and Malcolm had just loved the horse farms. Yes, of course she had Ramsey's phone number, he was an old friend. She read it out to me. I thanked her and she said sure thing and to have a nice day.

Ramsey and Malcolm were out. A woman who answered said to try at five-thirty. I tried at five-thirty Connecticut time and they were still out. The woman said Mr Osborn was a busy man and would I like to leave a message. I asked her to tell Mr Pembroke that his son Ian had phoned, but that there was no special news. She would do that, she said.

I went to bed and in the morning rode out on the Downs, and afterwards, from the house of the trainer whose horses I was riding, got through to Superintendent Yale's police station. He was there and came on the line.

'Where are you?'

'At the moment in a racing stable near Lambourn.'

'And your father?'

'I don't know.'

He made a disbelieving grunt. 'What time could you meet me at Quantum House?'.

I looked at my watch. 'In riding clothes,' I said, 'in forty-five minutes. If you want me to change, add on an hour.'

'Come as you are,' he said. 'Mr Smith says there's something to see.'

Fifteen

At Quantum, the heap of rubble had reduced to merely a mess.

I walked round to the back of the house and found two men in hard hats barely ankle deep as they methodically removed debris brick by brick from house to rubbish skip. The wind had abated and the clouds had relented to the extent that a pale sunshine washed the scene, making it to my eyes more of a wasteland than ever.

Superintendent Yale stood beside a trestle table that had been erected on the lawn, with the explosive Smith in his beige overalls and blue hat standing close beside him, heads bent in conference. There were no spectators any more on the far side of the rope across the lawn, not even Arthur Bellbrook. I walked over to the experts and said good morning.

'Good morning,' they said, looking up. 'Glad you came,' Smith said.

He stretched out a casual hand and picked up an object from the table, holding it out to me.

'We've found this,' he said. 'What do you think?'

I took the thing from him. It had been a coil of thin plastic-coated wire, but the coils had been stretched so that the wire was straighter, but still curled. It was about eighteen inches long. The plastic coating had been white, I thought. About an inch of bare wire stuck out of the plastic at each end. Onto the plastic, near one end, someone had bonded a hand from a clock. The hand pointed to the bare wire, so that the wire was an extension of the hand.

I looked at it with despair, though not with shock. I'd been fearing and hoping . . . trying not to believe it possible.

When I didn't ask what it was, Yale said with awakening suspicion, 'Does your silence mean that you know what it is?'

I looked up at the two men. They hadn't expected me to know, were surprised by my reaction, even astonished.

'Yes,' I said drearily. 'I do know. Did you find any other bits?'

Smith pointed to a spot on the table. I took a step sideways and stared down. There were some pieces of metal and plastic, but not those I'd expected. No cogwheels or springs. A grey plastic disc with a small hole in the centre.

'Was this a clock?' I said dubiously.

'A battery-driven clock,' Smith said. 'There's the coil from the electric motor.'

The coil was tiny, about a centimetre in diameter.

'How did you find it in all this rubbish?' I asked.

'We found various remains of the padded box which used to stand at the foot of Mr Pembroke's bed. These small pieces became embedded in the lid when the box blew apart. The wire with the clock's hand on it, and this . . .' he picked up the flat plastic disc '. . . were in the same area.' He turned the plastic disc over to reveal a clock face on the other side. 'There should also be at least one other piece of wire somewhere, and some of the clock case and a battery or two, but we haven't found those yet. This was not actually an alarm clock, I don't think. We've found no sign of an alarm mechanism.'

'No, it won't have been an alarm clock,' I said.

The superintendent had been growing restive during Smith's account and could contain himself no longer.

'Will you please explain your familiarity with this device,' he said formidably. 'Did the gardener use this sort of thing for blowing up the tree trunk?'

'No, I don't think so. This device wasn't meant for setting off bombs. It was a toy.'

'What sort of toy?'

'Well . . . it was for switching things on. Torch bulbs, mostly. Like the lights we had on a station in a train set. A buzzer, sometimes. It was incredibly simple.'

'Explain,' Yale commanded.

I glanced at Smith. He was nodding resignedly.

'You get an old or cheap clock,' I said. 'We had wind-up clocks, not a battery clock. You fix a length of wire to one of the hands, like this, so that a bare bit of wire sticks out and makes the hand much longer.'

'The hands are still on the clock, I take it?'

'Oh yes. Though sometimes we'd pull the minute hand off and just use the hour hand, because it's stronger, even though it's shorter. All you need is for the bare wire to reach out beyond the edge of the clock face. We used glue to stick the wire to the hand. Then you have a long bit of wire coming out from the centre of the front of the clock, and you fasten the free end of that to a battery. One of those nine-volt batteries with things like press-studs at the end.'

Smith was still nodding. Yale looked very much as if I shouldn't know such things.

'We made quite a lot of other gadgets,' I said, hearing the defensiveness in my voice. 'Buzzers for morse codes. Rudimentary telephones. Not just time-switches. I made a lock once which could only be operated with a straight piece of wire.' And it still worked fine, although I wasn't going to show him.

Yale sighed. 'So in this case, we've got the wire fixed to the clock's hand at one end and to a battery at the other, right? Go on from there.'

'You need two more lengths of wire. One goes from the battery to whatever you want to activate. In our case, it was usually a torch bulb screwed into a metal holder. We fastened a bare end of wire to the metal holder. Then the third wire went back from the metal holder to the clock. We fixed this wire with glue to the clock case itself, not to the hands, in such a way that the bare end of wire was pointing out forwards, towards you if you were facing the clock like this.' I demonstrated with the clock face. 'We usually stuck it on over the number twelve, at the top, but you could fix it anywhere you liked. Then you wind up the clock and set the hand with the wire where you want it, and just wait. The wired hand travels round towards the jutting out wire and eventually hits against it at right angles. The circuit is thus complete from the clock wires to the battery to the light and back to the clock, so the light goes on. The clock hand keeps on trying to go round and the jutting wire keeps stopping it, so the light stays on. Well . . .' I finished lamely, 'that's what happened when we made them.'

'Them?' Yale said with apprehension.

'They were easy to make. They were interesting. I don't know how many we had, but quite a few.'

'My God.'

'There might be one still in the playroom,' I said. 'The old train sets are there.'

Yale looked at me balefully. 'How many of your family saw these devices?' he asked.

'Everyone,'

'Who made them?'

'I did, Gervase did, and Ferdinand. Thomas did. I don't remember who else.'

'But your whole family knows how to make a simple time-switch?'

'Yes, I should think so.'

'And why,' he said, 'haven't you mentioned this before?'

I sighed and twisted the wired clock hand round in my fingers. 'Because,' I said, 'for starters I didn't think of it until after I'd left here the other day. After we'd been digging out the black powder and so on, and I'd been looking back to the past. I didn't want you to find this. I wanted you to find something sophisticated, that no one in the family could have thought up.'

'Hm,' he said, seeming to accept it. 'How many people outside your family knew about these clocks?'

'Several did, I suppose, but it was such a long time ago. No one would remember, would they?'

'They might.' Yale turned to Smith. 'This toy, is this really what set off the bomb?'

Smith nodded. 'It sounds just right. Wire in a detonator where the Pembroke children had a torch bulb . . .' He spread his hands. 'It wouldn't need more current than that.'

Not surprisingly, they decided to take a look in the playroom. They picked their way cautiously across the ankle-twisting rubble and headed for the passage which was comparatively clear by this time. The playroom, when we reached it, was shadowy inside, with the windows boarded up. Light of sorts seeped in through the door, but it took a few minutes for eyes to acclimatise, during which Yale bumped into the bicycles, knocking them over. I helped him pick them up. He wanted to know whose they were, and I told him about Peter and Robin.

He made no especial comment but watched while I went over to the shelves and began peering into boxes. I hadn't been in the room at all since the twins had gone, and their own playthings had overlaid those outgrown and abandoned by their elder brothers and sisters so that most of what I was looking at was unfamiliar and seemed to belong to strangers. It took several minutes to locate the box I thought I wanted, and to pick it off the shelves and put it on the table.

Someone, Coochie I dared say, had packed the trains away for good after Gervase and Ferdinand had left and I'd been busy with school and horses. At one time, the tracks had run permanently round half the room, but Peter and Robin had been television-watchers more than the rest of us, and hadn't dragged them out again. I opened the box and found the old treasures undisturbed, looking more battered than I'd thought, with rust on the much-used wheels.

I lifted out a couple of engines and some coaches, then followed them with a tunnel, a signal box with green and red bulbs and a brown plastic railway station adorned with empty bulb-holders among the advertisement stickers. I suppose to any adult, his childhood's rediscovered toys look smaller, deader, less appealing than he remembers. The trains were dusty and sad, relics ready for the skip outside, melancholic. The little lights had long gone out.

I took everything out of the box, but there were no clocks.

'Sorry,' I said. 'They could be in anything, really. If they're here.'

Smith began looking into any box whose contents weren't easily identifiable by the picture on top. Yale, with a no-hope expression, followed suit. I packed the trains back into oblivion with regret.

'Well, just look here,' Smith said suddenly. 'Gold mine.'

He had produced from a jumble of Lego constructions a bright new-looking clock with a Mickey Mouse face in unfaded technicolour. Mickey's hands in fat white gloves were the hands of the clock. To the minute hand was fixed a coil of white plastic-covered wire. A second white coil was stuck to the scarlet clock casing, its bared end jutting out over noon. When Smith held it all up, the white coils stretched out and down like curling streamers.

I looked at it blankly.

'I've never seen that one before,' I said. 'We didn't make them decorative. Ours were . . .' I sought for the word '. . . utilitarian.'

Smith picked away among the Lego. 'Can't find a battery,' he reported. 'Nor a torch bulb, for that matter.' A pause. 'Wait a minute . . .' He rattled around and, finally, triumphantly produced a red and white Lego tower with a bulb-holder lodged inside near the top.

'A lighthouse, wouldn't you say?' he asked, standing it upright. 'Neat.'

'Someone made this for your twin brothers,' Yale said. 'Are you sure you never saw it?'

I shook my head. 'I didn't live here then, only visited. The twins had a short attention span, anyway. They tired of new toys pretty quickly. Always wanted to get on with the next thing.'

'I'll find out who made it,' Yale said. 'Can you sort out a box to put it in? I'll give you a receipt, of course.'

Smith found him an empty Lego box and into it they packed the bright co-star of an act that had brought half the house down. There was room in the box for the lighthouse, so they took that, too. Yale solemnly wrote a receipt on a page of his notebook and gave it to me, and with him carrying the box we went out into the daylight, blinking as our eyes adjusted after the gloom.

As we walked back in the general direction of the trestle table, Smith said, 'We've put all the clothes we've found on a table in the garage. I'm afraid they're mostly torn and unwearable, but you might want to see. All the personal things we've salvaged are in a cardboard carton. Do you want to take those today, or wait until we're finished?'

'Look now, take later,' I said.

Smith half smiled. 'They're in that box under the table.'

I squatted down beside the brown cardboard carton and opened the top flaps. Inside there was quite a good collection of dusty bits and pieces, more than I would have imagined. I picked out one of Malcolm's precious brushes and ran my finger over the gold and silver chased backing. The dust came off and the metal shone in the sunlight. He would be pleased, I thought.

'We've found five of those,' Smith observed. 'Two are badly dented, the others look all right.'

'There were eight,' I said. 'In his dressing-room.'

He shrugged. 'We might find more.'

I turned over a few things in the box. Mostly they were uninteresting, like a bottle of aspirins from the bathroom. At the bottom, I came across one or two things of my own – an empty spongebag and the tape recorder.

I lifted the recorder out, straightened up and put it on the table. Pressed the start button. Absence of results.

'It was just a chance you might want it,' Smith said philosophically. 'It doesn't work as it is, but you might want to get it mended.'

'Probably cheaper to buy a new one,' I said. I pressed the rewind and fast-forward buttons pointlessly, and then the eject button, which worked. The plastic lid staggered open, revealing a tape within. I had to think for a minute which tape it was and then remembered it was only the one from my answering machine; nothing interesting. I shut the lid and put the recorder back in the box under the table.

'If you find my camera, now that would be good news,' I said, straightening again.

Yale had lost interest and was preparing to leave.

'Was it yours?' said Mr Smith. 'It's in the skip, I'm afraid. Badly smashed.'

'Oh well . . .'

'Were you insured?'

I shook my head. 'Never thought of it.'

Smith made sympathetic gestures and went back to the rubble. The superintendent said I should telephone him the following morning without fail. He ran his thumb and finger down his moustache and asked me if I now knew who had bombed the house.

'No,' I said. 'I don't. Do you?'

He wouldn't say he didn't, but he didn't. He picked up the Lego box and marched off with it, and I went to look at the clothes in the garage.

Nothing was worth saving, I thought. All highly depressing. My jodhpur boots with the toes flattened, Malcolm's vicuna coats with triangular tears. I left it all as it lay and started out on a quick hike round the garden to make sure all was well with the gold, and came upon Arthur Bellbrook digging potatoes within six feet of it. My heart jumped a bit. His was undisturbed.

We exchanged good mornings and remarks about the weather. He asked what he should do with the potatoes and I told him to take them home. He nodded his thanks. He complained that the pick-up trucks for the rubbish skips were ruining the lawn. He said souvenir hunters had stripped Mrs Pembroke's fancy greenhouse of every single geranium, including the cuttings, but not to worry, without glass in the windows they would have died in the first frost. It had been a mild autumn, but frost would come soon.

He looked along the length of the kitchen garden, his back towards the end wall. He would dig everything over, he said, ready for winter.

I left him bending again to his task, not sure whether he was a guardian of the gold or a threat to it. Malcolm had a nerve, I thought, hiding his stockpile in that place and seeing Arthur work close to it day after day. Malcolm had more nerve than was good for him.

I drove to the pub in Cookham, where they were getting used to my hours, took a bath, put on trousers, shirt and jersey and, accompanied by Norman West's notes, went down to the bar for a drink before lunch.

I read:

Mr Thomas Pembroke (39) lives with his wife Berenice at 6 Arden Haciendas, Sonning, Nr. Reading, in the strip of new townhouses where old Arden House used to be. Two daughters (9 and 7) go to comprehensive school.

Mr T. used to work as quantity surveyor for Reading firm of biscuit makers, Shutleworth Digby Ltd. He got sacked for wrong estimates several weeks ago. I was told unofficially at the firm that he'd cost them thousands by ordering six times the glacé cherries needed for a run of 'dotted pinks'. (Had to laugh!) No laughing matter when tons of sliced almonds turned up after 'nut fluffs' had been discontinued. Mr T. didn't contest sacking, just left. Firm very relieved. Mr T. had been getting more and more useless, but had long service.

Mr T. didn't tell his wife he'd lost his job, but went off as if to work every day. (Common reaction.) On Newmarket Sales Tuesday he was 'walking about', same as the previous Friday. Pressed, he says he probably went to the public library in Reading, he did that most days; also sat around wherever there were seats, doing nothing. He read the job-offer pages in newspapers, but apparently did little to find work. No heart. (My opinion.)

Mr T. on brink of nervous breakdown (my opinion). I interviewed him in coffee shop. His hands trembled half the time, rattling cup against teeth, and he's not yet forty. Alcohol? Don't think so. Nerves shot to hell.

Mr T. drives old grey Austin 1100. Has slight dent in front wing. Mr T. says it's been there weeks. Car dirty, could do with wash. Mr T. says he has no energy for things like that.

Mr T's opinion of Mr Ian is very muddled (like the rest of him). Mr Ian is 'best of bunch, really', but also Mr T. says Mr Ian is Mr Pembroke's favourite and it isn't fair. (!)

End of enquiry.

With a sigh, I put Thomas to the back and read about Berenice; no happy tale.

Mrs Berenice Pembroke (44 according to Mrs Joyce), wife of Mr Thomas, lives at 6 Arden Haciendas. No job. Looks after daughters, spends her days doing housework and reading trashy romances (according to Mrs Joyce again!).

Mrs B. very hard to interview. First visit, nothing. Second visit, a little, not much. She couldn't produce alibi for either day.

I asked about children and school journeys. Mrs B. doesn't drive them, they go by bus. They walk alone along pavement in residential side-road to and from bus stop, which is about one-third of mile away, on the main thoroughfare. Mrs B's mother lives actually on the bus route. The girls get off the bus there most afternoons and go to their grandmother's for tea.

Interviewed Mrs B's mother. Not helpful. Agreed girls go there most days. Sometimes (if cold, wet or dark) she drives them home at about 7 pm. Other days, they finish journey by bus. I asked why they go there for tea so often and stay so late. Told to mind my own business. Younger girl said Granny makes better teas, Mummy gets cross. Told to shut up by older girl. Mrs B's mother showed me out.

Mrs B. drives old white Morris Maxi, clean, no marks on it.

Mrs B. gave no opinion of Mr Ian when asked, but looked as if she could spit. Says Mr Pembroke is wicked. Mrs B. slammed her front door (she hadn't asked me in!).

End of enquiry.

I put Berenice, too, back in the packet, and cheered myself up just a fraction with a slice of pork pie and a game of darts.

From the outside, Arden Haciendas were dreadful: tiny houses of dark brown-red brick set at odd angles to each other, with dark-framed windows at odd heights and dark front doors leading from walled front gardens one could cross in one stride. Nevertheless, Arden Haciendas, as Joyce had informed me a year earlier when Thomas had moved there, were socially the in thing, as they had won a prize for the architect.

God help architecture, I thought, ringing the bell of No 6. I hadn't been to this house before: had associated Thomas and Berenice always with the rather ordinary bungalow they'd bought at the time of their wedding.

Berenice opened the door and tried to close it again when she saw me, but I pushed from my side and put my shoe over the threshold, and finally, with ill grace, she stepped back.

'We don't want to see you,' she said. 'Dear Thomas isn't well. You've no right to shove your way in here. I hate you.'

'Well, hate or not, I want to talk to Thomas.'

She couldn't say he wasn't there, because I could see him. Inside, the Haciendas were open-plan with rooms at odd angles to each other, which explained the odd-angled exteriors. The front door led into an angled off-shoot of the main room, which had no ceiling where one would expect it, but soared to the rafters. Windows one couldn't see out of let daylight in at random points in the walls. Horrible, I thought, but that was only, as Mr West would say, my opinion.

Thomas rose to his feet from one of the heavily-stuffed armchairs brought from the bungalow, old comfortable chairs looking incongruous in all the aggressive modernity. There was no carpet on the woodblock floor; Thomas's shoes squeaked on it when he moved.

'Come in, old chap,' he said.

'We don't want him,' Berenice objected.

Thomas was looking haggard and I was shocked. I hadn't seen him, I realised, for quite a long time. All youth had left him, and I thought of him as he had been at eighteen or nineteen, laughing and good-humoured, coming for weekends and making Serena giggle.

Twenty years on, he looked middle-aged, the head balder than when I'd last taken his photograph, the ginger moustache less well tended, the desperation all-pervading. Norman West's assessment of early breakdown seemed conservative. It looked to me as if it had already happened. Thomas was a lot further down the line to disintegration than Gervase.

Ferdinand, he confirmed in answer to my question, had told him about Malcolm's will and about Malcolm's wish that I should try to find out who wanted to kill him. Thomas couldn't help, he said.

I reminded him of the day old Fred blew up the tree stump. Ferdinand had mentioned that too, he said. Thomas had been there. He remembered it clearly. He had carried Serena on his shoulders, and Fred had been blown flat.

'And do you remember the time-switches we used to make, with wire on the clocks' hands?'

He stared, his eyes gaunt. After a long pause, he said, 'Yes.'

'Thomas, after Gervase and Ferdinand left Quantum, did you or they make any more of them?'

Berenice interrupted, 'Dear Thomas couldn't make a time-switch to save his life, could you, darling?' Her voice was pitying, sneering, unkind. Thomas sent her a haunted look but no protest.

'Someone gave Robin and Peter a Mickey Mouse clock with white plastic-covered wires stuck on it,' I said. 'Very bright and attractive.'

Thomas shook his head helplessly.

'In the rubble at Quantum, they've found a clock hand stuck onto some white plastic-covered wire.'

'Oh, my God,' Thomas said miserably.

'So what?' Berenice demanded. 'Dear Thomas does over-act so.'

'So,' I said, 'someone who knew how to make these time-switches blew up Quantum.'

'What of it?' she said. 'I can't see Thomas doing it. Not enough nerve, have you, darling?'

Thomas said to me, 'Have a drink?'

Berenice looked disconcerted. Asking me to have a drink had been for Thomas an act of rebellion against her wishes. There hadn't been many of them, I guessed. I accepted with thanks, although it was barely five-thirty and to my mind too early. I'd chosen the hour on purpose, hoping both that Thomas would have returned from his day's wanderings and that the daughters would stop at their grandmother's house on their way home from school.

Thomas squeaked across the floor to the kitchen, which was divided from the main room only by a waist-high counter, and began opening cupboards. He produced three tumblers which he put clumsily on the counter, and then sought in the fridge interminably for mixers. Berenice watched him with her face screwed into an expression of long-suffering impatience and made no move to help.

'We have some gin somewhere,' he said vaguely, having at last found the tonic. 'I don't know where Berenice puts things. She moves them about.'

'Dear Thomas couldn't find a book in a library.'

Thomas gave her a look of black enmity which she either didn't see or chose to ignore. He opened another cupboard, and another, and in his wife's continued unhelpful silence finally found a nearly full bottle of Gordon's gin. He came round into the main room and poured from the bottle into three glasses, topping up inadequately from a single bottle of tonic.

He handed me a glass. I didn't much care for gin, but it was no time to say so.

He held out the second glass to Berenice.

'I don't want any,' she said.

Thomas's hand was trembling. He made an awkward motion as if to raise the glass to his own lips, then put it down with a bang on the counter, and in an uncoordinated movement accidentally knocked the gin bottle over so that it fell to the floor, smashing into green shiny pieces, the liquid spreading in a pool.

Thomas bent down to pick up the bits. Berenice didn't help.

She said, 'Thomas can't get anything right, can you, darling?' The words were no worse than others, but the acid sarcasm in her voice had gone beyond scathing to unbearable.

Thomas straightened with a face filled with passionate hatred, the worm turning at last, and by the neck he held the top part of the green bottle, the broken edges jagged as teeth.

He came up fast with his hand rising. Berenice, cushioned in complacency, wasn't even looking at him and seemed not to begin to understand her danger.

Malcolm said I had fast reactions . . . I dropped my own drink, grasped Berenice by both arms and swung her violently round and out of the slicing track of the razor-sharp weapon. She was furiously indignant, protesting incredulously, sprawling across the floor where I'd almost thrown her, still unaware of what had been happening.

Thomas looked at the damage he'd done to me for a long blank second, then he dropped the fearsome bottle and turned to stumble off blindly towards his front door. I took two strides and caught him by the arm.

'Let me go . . .' He struggled, and I held on. 'Let me go . . . I can't do anything right . . . she's right.'

'She's bloody wrong.'

I was stronger than he. I practically dragged him across the room and flung him into one of the armchairs.

'I've cut you,' he said.

'Yes, well, never mind. You listen to me. You both listen to me. You're over the edge. You're going to have to face some straight facts.'

Berenice had finally realised how close she'd come to needing stitches. She looked with anger at the point of my left shoulder where jersey and shirt had been ripped away, where a couple of cuts were bleeding. She turned to Thomas with a bitterly accusing face and opened her mouth.

'Shut up,' I said roughly. 'If you're going to tell him he's incompetent, don't do it. If you're going to complain that he could have cut you instead, yes he could, he was trying to. Sit down and *shut up*.'

'Trying to?' She couldn't believe it. She sat down weakly, her hair awry, her body slack, eyes shocked.

'You goaded him too far. Don't you understand what you've been doing to him? Putting him down, picking him to pieces every time you open your mouth? You have now completely succeeded. He can't function any more.'

'Dear Thomas – ' she began.

'Don't say that. You don't mean it.'

She stared.

'If he were your dear Thomas,' I said, 'you would help him and encourage him, not sneer.'

'I'm not listening to this.'

'You just think what you stirred up in Thomas today, and if I were you, I'd be careful.' I turned to Thomas, 'And it's not all her fault. You've let her do it, let her carp all this time. You should have stopped her years ago. You should have walked out. You've been loyal to her beyond reason and she's driven you to want to kill her, because that's what I saw in your face.'

Thomas put a hand over his eyes.

'You were dead lucky you didn't connect with her mouth or her throat or whatever you were going for. There would have been no going back. You just think what would have happened, both of you. The consequences to yourselves, and to your girls. *Think!*' I paused. 'Well, it's beyond facing.'

'I didn't mean it,' Thomas mumbled.

'I'm afraid you did,' I said.

'He couldn't have done,' Berenice said.

'He did mean it,' I said to her. 'It takes quite a force to tear away so much woollen jersey. Your only hope is to believe to the depths of your soul that he put all his goaded infuriated strength behind that blow. I'll tell you, I was lucky too. I was moving away fast trying to avoid being cut, and it can have been only the points of the glass that reached my skin, but I'll remember the speed of them . . .' I broke off, not knowing how else to convince her. I didn't want to say, 'It bloody hurts,' but it did.

Thomas put his head in his hands.

'Come on,' I said to him, 'I'm taking you out of here. On your feet, brother.'

'Don't be ridiculous,' Berenice said.

'If I leave him here, will you cuddle him?'

The negative answer filled her whole face. She wouldn't have thought of it. She was aggrieved. It would have taken little time for her to stoke up the recriminations.

'When the firemen have gone,' I said, 'fires often start again from the heat in the embers.'

I went over to Thomas. 'Come on. There's still life ahead.'

Without looking up, he said in a dull sort of agony, 'You don't know . . . It's too late.'

I said 'No' without great conviction, and then the front door opened with a bang to let in the two girls.

'Hello,' they said noisily, bringing in swirls of outside air. 'Granny turned us out early. What's going on? What's all this glass on the floor? What's all the blood on your arm?'

'A bottle got broken,' I said, 'and I fell on it.'

The young one looked at the bowed head of her father, and in a voice that was a devastating mimic of her mother's, vibrating with venom and contempt, she said, 'I'll bet it was Dear Thomas who broke it.'

Berenice heard for herself what she'd been doing to her husband. Heard what she was implanting in her own children. The revelation seemed to overwhelm her, and she sought for excuses.

'If we had more money . . . If only Malcolm . . . It's not fair . . .'

But they had two cars, thanks to their trust fund, and a newly-built townhouse, and Thomas's unemployment had brought no immediate financial disaster: money wasn't their trouble, nor would it cure it.

'Why didn't you get a job?' I said. 'What did you ever expect of Thomas? That he'd set the world alight? He did the best he could.'

Quantum in me fuit . . .

'I wanted a son,' she said flatly. 'Thomas got a vasectomy. He said two children were enough, we couldn't afford any more. It wasn't fair. Malcolm should have given us more money. *I always wanted a son.*'

Dear God, I thought: flat simple words at the absolute heart of things, the suppurating disappointment that she had allowed to poison their lives. Just like Gervase, I thought. So much unhappiness from wanting the unobtainable, so much self-damage.

I could think of nothing to say. Nothing of help. It was too late. I went across to Thomas and touched him on the shoulder. He stood up. He didn't look at his family, or at me. I put my hand lightly under his elbow and steered him to the front door, and in unbroken silence we left the wasteland of his marriage.

Sixteen

I took Thomas to Lucy's house.

It seemed to me, as I drove away from the pretentious Haciendas, that Lucy's particular brand of peace might be just what Thomas needed. I couldn't take him to Vivien, who would demolish him further, and Joyce, who was fond of him, would be insufferably bracing. I frankly didn't want him with me in Cookham; and Donald, influenced by Berenice, tended to despise him.

Lucy was in, to my relief, and opened the front door of the farm cottage where she and Edwin led the simple life near Marlow.

She stared at us. At my red arm. At Thomas's hanging head.

'Sister, dear,' I said cheerfully. 'Two brothers needing succour come knocking at thy gate. Any chance of hot sweet tea? Loving looks? A sticking plaster?'

Edwin appeared behind her, looking peevish. 'What's going on?'

To Lucy, I said, 'We cracked a bottle of gin, and I fell on it.'

'Are you drunk?' she said.

'Not really.'

'You'd better come in.'

'Ferdinand has been on the telephone,' Edwin said without welcome, staring with distaste at my blood as we stepped over his threshold. 'He warned us you'd be turning up some time. You might have had the courtesy to let us know in advance.'

'Sorry,' I said dryly.

Lucy glanced swiftly at my face. 'This is trouble?'

'Just a spot.'

She took Thomas by the arm and led him out of the tiny entrance hall into her book-filled sitting-room. Edwin's and Lucy's cottage consisted of two rooms downstairs, which had been partly knocked into one, with a modern bathroom tacked on at the back. The stairs, which were hidden behind a latched door, led up to three rooms where one had to inch round the beds, bending one's head so as not to knock it on the eaves. Laura Ashley wallpaper everywhere covered uneven old plaster, and rag rugs provided warmth underfoot. Lucy's books were stacked in columns on the floor along one wall in the sitting-room, having overflowed the bookcases, and in the kitchen there were wooden bowls, pestles and mortar, dried herbs hanging.

Lucy's home was unselfconscious, not folksy. Lucy herself, large in dark trousers and thick handknitted sweater, sat Thomas in an armchair and in a very short time thrust a mug of hot liquid into his unwilling hand.

'Drink it, Thomas,' I said. 'How about some gin in it?' I asked Lucy.

'It's in.'

I smiled at her.

'Do you want some yourself?' she said.

'Just with milk.' I followed her into the kitchen. 'Have you got any tissues I could put over this mess?'

She looked at my shoulder. 'Are tissues enough?'

'Aspirins?'

'I don't believe in them.'

'Ah.'

I drank the hot tea. Better than nothing. She had precious few tissues, when it came to the point, and far too small for the job. I said I would leave it and go along to the hospital later to get it cleaned up. She didn't argue.

She said, 'What's all this about?' and dipped into a half-empty packet of raisins and then offered me some, which I ate.

'Thomas has left Berenice. He's in need of a bed.'

'Not here,' she protested. 'Take him with you.'

'I will if you won't keep him, but he'd be better off here.'

She said her son, my nephew, was up in his bedroom doing his homework.

'Thomas won't disturb him,' I said.

She looked at me doubtfully. 'There's something you're not telling me.'

'The last straw,' I said, 'has just broken Thomas. If someone doesn't treat him kindly, he'll end up in the nut house or the suicide statistics and I am not, repeat not, joking.'

'Well . . .'

'That's my girl.'

216

'I'm not your girl,' she said tartly. 'Perhaps I'm Thomas's.' Her face softened slightly. 'All right, he can stay.'

She ate another handful of raisins and went back to the sitting-room, and I again followed. Edwin had taken the second armchair. Lucy lowered her bulk onto a leather stool beside Thomas, which left me on my feet looking around. There were no other seats. Resignedly I sat on the floor and rested my back against a wall. Neither Lucy nor Edwin commented. Neither had invited me to sit.

'As I'm here,' I said, 'I may as well ask the questions I was going to come and ask tomorrow.'

'We don't want to answer,' Edwin said. 'And if you get blood on the wallpaper you can pay for redecorating.'

'The police will come,' I said, twisting slightly out of harm's way. 'Why not practise on me? They'll ask about the timing device that set off the bomb at Quantum.'

Thomas stirred. 'I made it, you know. The Mickey Mouse clock.'

It was the first time he'd spoken since we'd left his house. Lucy looked as if she thought him delirious, then raised her eyebrows and started to concentrate.

'Not that,' she said, troubled.

'Do you remember those clocks?' I asked.

'Of course I do. We've got one upstairs, that Thomas made for our son.'

'What sort of face has it got?'

'A sailing ship. Did the Mickey Mouse clock explode . . .?'

'No,' I said. 'The one actually used had a grey plastic dial with white numbers. The Mickey Mouse clock was intact, in the playroom.'

Thomas said dully, 'I haven't made one for years.'

'When did you make the Mickey Mouse for Robin and Peter?' I asked.

'I didn't make it for them. I made it a long time ago for Serena. She must have given it to them. It made her laugh, when I made it.'

'You were a nice boy, Thomas,' Lucy said. 'Funny and kind.'

Edwin said restlessly, 'I would have thought any timing device would have been blown to unrecognisable fragments by such a big bomb.'

'It seems they often find pieces,' I said.

'Do you mean,' he demanded, 'that they've actually sifted through all those tons of rubbish?'

217

'More or less. They know it was a battery clock. They found part of the motor.'

'It serves Malcolm right the house was blown up,' Edwin said with barely suppressed violence. 'Flinging money about on ridiculous scholarships. Keeping us poor. I suppose *you're* all right, aren't you?' There was a sneer there for me, openly. 'He's never been fair to Lucy. You've always been in the way, smarming him up, taking the lion's share. He gives you whatever you ask for while we have to struggle along on a pittance.'

'Is that the authentic voice of Vivien?' I asked.

'It's the truth!'

'No,' I said. 'It's what you have been told over and over again, but it's not the truth. Most people believe a lie if they're told it often enough. It's easy enough after all to believe a lie if you've heard it only once. Especially if you want to believe it.'

Lucy looked at me intently. 'You care about this, don't you?'

'About being cast perpetually as the family villain? Yes, I dare say I do. But I was thinking also of Thomas. He's been told ad infinitum that he's useless, and now he believes it. I'm going now, Lucy.' I stood up without haste. 'You tell Thomas over and over that he's a worthwhile person, and maybe he'll begin to believe that instead. You have to believe in yourself to get anywhere.'

'Oh yes,' she said quietly. 'You do.'

'What you've written,' I said, 'is for ever.'

Her eyes widened. 'How do you know . . . that I've lost . . .'

'I guessed.' I bent and kissed her cheek, to her surprise. 'Are you seriously in need?'

'Financially?' She was startled. 'No worse than usual.'

'Of course we are,' Edwin said to her waspishly. 'You're earning almost nothing now and you still spend a fortune on books.'

Lucy looked only mildly embarrassed, as if she'd heard that often before.

'If I held the purse-strings,' Edwin complained, 'you'd use the public library, as I do.'

'Why don't you work, Edwin?' I asked.

'Lucy doesn't like bustle.' He seemed to think it explanation enough. 'We'd be perfectly happy if Malcolm trebled Lucy's trust fund, as he ought to. He has millions, we live in a hovel. It's not fair.'

'Doesn't Lucy despise money?' I asked. 'And people who have it? Do you want her to become what she despises?'

218

Edwin glared.

Lucy looked at me blandly. 'There's no such state as perfection,' she said.

I drove back to Reading, to the hospital that had an emergency room open all evening, and there got my shoulder and upper arm cleaned and stitched. There were three cuts, it seemed, variously deep but nothing frightful, and they had long stopped bleeding: with the stitches, they would heal almost instantly. The staff advised pain-killers pro tem. I thanked them and eventually drove to Cookham feeling more than slightly tired but chiefly hungry, and having remedied both conditions satisfactorily, set off again next morning to ride. There was no problem there with the stitches: they were tender to the touch and stiff when I lifted my arm, but that was all.

Restored yet again in spirit by the dose of fresh air, I took a lazy day off from the emotional battering of the family and went to London to get my American and Australian visas. It was only a week since I'd ridden Park Railings at Cheltenham and it felt like eternity. I bought a new sweater and had my hair cut and thought about Ursula 'wandering about' through days of escape. One could wander for hours in London, thinking one's thoughts.

On an impulse, I telephoned Joyce, not expecting her to be in.

'Darling,' she yelled. 'I'm going out. Bridge. Where are you?'

'In a phone box.'

'Where's your father?'

'I don't know.'

'Darling, you're *infuriating*. What did you ring for?'

'I suppose . . . just to hear your voice.'

It seemed to stump her entirely. 'Are you out of your head? You tell that old bugger . . . tell him . . .' She choked on it.

'That you're glad he's alive?' I suggested.

'Don't let the old sod get blown up.'

'No,' I said.

'Must rush, darling. Don't break your neck. 'Bye . . .'

' 'Bye now,' I said.

I wondered if she ever talked on the telephone except at the top of her voice. The decibels were comforting, somehow. At least she never sounded bored. I would rather infuriate her than bore her, I thought.

I went unhurriedly back to Cookham and in the evening bent again to Norman West's notes.

Of Edwin, he had said:

Mr Edwin Pembroke (53) né Bugg, lives with his wife Lucy in No 3 Wrothsay Farm Cottages, near Marlow. One son (15), attends state school, bicycles to school, has latchkey, gets his own tea, goes upstairs, does homework, working for exams, conscientious, doesn't know if his parents were around on the Friday or Tuesday at specified hours, doesn't expect so. He comes downstairs about 8 or 9 pm, they all eat vegetarian meal then. (No TV!) Mrs L. cooks in a wok. Mr E. washes up.

Mr E. does the housework (not much) and shopping, mostly vegetables. He spends hours reading in public library (librarians agree). Goes to pub, spends more hours over one beer (barman indignant). Takes laundry to laundromat. Listens to radio. Spends hours doing crossword puzzles. (The garden's untidy. Mr E. doesn't like gardening. They grow only runner beans, they're easy.)

Mr E. and Mrs L. share an old Hillman, which Mr E. mostly drives. (Mrs L. has licence.) Car dusty and rusty, no dents.

Mr E. good-looking man, complete drone (my opinion). Idle life suits him. Mr E's idle life seems to suit Mrs L. also – no accounting for people. She does less than he does, come to think. Mr E. has sharp sarcastic manner on occasions. Detests Mr Ian, curses Mr Pembroke but at same time wants money from him (!). Definitely thinks of Mr Pembroke's money too much, broods on it, talked about it all the time.

End of enquiry.

Of Lucy, among other things, he had written:

Mrs L. spends large parts of the day unaware of what's going on around her (my opinion). I had to repeat several questions. It seemed she didn't hear me, but nothing wrong with her ears. She listens to things going on in her own head (can't put it very well). Has no alibis for Friday or Tuesday. Can't remember where she was. (I believe it.) Goes for rambling walks. Mrs L. very troubled over something, but wouldn't say what. She ate a tinful of peanuts while I was there, looked surprised when they'd gone.

So much for Lucy and Edwin, I thought. What about Donald and Helen?

Donald Pembroke (44) eldest of Mr Pembroke's offspring, lives at Marblehill House, detached chalet-style house which goes with his job, Secretary, Marblehill Golf Club (rich club, high fees) near Henley-on-Thomas. Long waiting list for membership, rich members.

Mr D. has staff (green keeper, club steward, etc). He himself oversees and runs the whole place, is said to be good at it, members like him, say he gets things done, runs tight ship, decent bar, club rooms, tournaments etc, always listens to and deals with complaints, seen as friend, authority figure, social equal. Mr D. likes his work. His social standing extremely important to him (my opinion). Keeps up high appearances.

As to alibis for the Friday and Tuesday in question: no alibis ascertainable. Is always 'round the place', never at any place at set hours except first thing in the mornings (9 am) to see to post with office staff. Has Mondays off, works Saturdays and Sundays.

Walks to work (barely 100 yds). Usually returns home at 7 pm (much earlier in winter), sometimes stays until bar closes. Often walks round later to see all is well everywhere. Dedicated.

Mr D. has daughter in art school, high fees. Also twin sons who have started this term at Eton, previously at good prep. school. (How does he afford it?)

Mr D. drives silver Mercedes, 2 years old. Clean. No marks of collision with Mr Ian.

Mr D. thinks it's very bad news Mr Ian is back in Mr Pembroke's favour. Certain to mean less inheritance for him (Mr D.). He's angry about that. But he also thinks Mr Ian the only one who can persuade Mr Pembroke to distribute some wealth now. Sees no inconsistency in these beliefs. (He'll use Mr Ian, doesn't have to trust him, he said.) Thinks Mr Pembroke's recent expenditure unreasonable, 'insane' (!). Says he's senile.

Mr D. gave me rapid answers; busy. Says his financial affairs were none of my business, edgy on subject. Is he in debt? (My opinion, considering his expenses, probably.) Champagne lifestyle.

End of enquiry.

And Helen?

Mrs Helen Pembroke (43) wife of Mr D. Very good looking lady. Very worried, wouldn't say what about.

I interviewed her in Marblehill House – big name for fairly ordinary-sized three-bedroom, nice sitting-room, though, over-looking golf course. Good furniture, appearance of wealth.

Mrs H. works at home (on dustsheet in dining-room) painting views of Henley by hand onto plates, jugs, boxes; all china. Very quick, very good (to my eyes), nice pictures. They go off to be glazed, she said, then sell in local shops. Reasonably paid, she says. (What's reasonable? She says her work was to be seen as a hobby. Mr D. refers to it in that way.)

Mrs H. works alone nearly every day, no alibis for Friday or Tuesday. Sometimes drives into Henley to shop, no regular pattern. Mrs H. has white Cavalier, clean, no dents.

No children at home. Daughter shares flat with friends near art school (more expense).

Mrs H. ultra-loyal to Mr D. Says my enquiries unnecessary. Says it's ridiculous to suppose Mr D. would attack his father. Out of the question. (My opinion, she wasn't too sure.) They need more cash badly (my opinion).

Mrs H. mostly shares Mr D's opinion of Mr Ian, but doesn't seem to dislike him personally.

End of enquiry.

On Friday morning, I called in on a public library and looked up 'explosives' in encyclopaedias. Ammonium nitrate was there, also the proportion of fertiliser to diesel oil needed, also the formula for relating volume to kilos. The knowledge was available to anyone who sought it.

On Friday after lunch I went to the Marblehill Golf Club and found Donald in the clubroom placating a foursome who had arrived late and missed their game.

'Go over to the house,' he said when he saw me. 'I can't talk here.' He turned decisively back to the problem in hand and I did what I was told, like a good little brother.

Helen was resigned more than annoyed to see me. 'Ferdinand said you would come, and we had the police here yesterday. Not that we could tell them anything, or you either.'

She was wearing a painter's smock over jeans and looked dressed by Dior. She took me into the sitting-room and pointed to a chair, and with unconscious grace sat herself half-on, half-off a polished table, raising her wrists to keep her paint-smudged hands away from the furniture.

Donald came bustling in, telling me he could give me ten minutes. 'Don't see what you can do,' he said. 'Leave it to the police.'

'What did they ask you?'

'About Fred blowing up the tree stump. I said yes, of course we'd been there. Helen and I weren't then married. It was the first time she'd met Malcolm, she was staying the weekend.'

'Saturday morning,' she said, nodding. 'The gardener came in specially to blow up the tree trunks. Not something one would forget, seeing him knocked flat. I took a photograph of the tree roots afterwards. It's still in one of our albums.'

'And the time-switch clocks, do you remember those?' I asked.

'Naturally,' Donald said.

Helen added, 'Dear Thomas made two for our boys for their birthday once, when they could just tell the time.' She had said Dear Thomas, I noticed, as if she had meant it, not as Berenice said it. 'They got lost in one of our moves.'

'Where's Malcolm?' Donald asked brusquely.

'I don't know.'

'You're lying,' he said, but for once I wasn't. Malcolm and Ramsey Osborn had left the Osborn residence, according to the female voice on the line the evening before, and had given her no number at which they could be reached. I could try again tomorrow, she said. Mr Osborn should have let her know by then; he usually did.

'Did either of you,' I asked, 'trace Malcolm to Cambridge the weekend he was put in the car?'

I hadn't expected any answer but negative, but the question came at them unexpectedly and Helen practically jumped.

'Did you?' I said to her.

'No, of course not,' Donald said quickly. 'We had no way of knowing he would go to Newmarket Sales, if that's what you're inferring.'

'The hotel at Cambridge said three people – two men and a

223

woman – had asked if Malcolm was staying there,' I said. 'One was Norman West, who were the others? I'm not saying you went to Newmarket Sales, just did one of you trace Malcolm?'

They looked at me glumly. Then Helen said, 'I suppose so.'

'Why?' I asked.

Donald cleared his throat. 'I needed his signature on a guarantee.'

'Go on, what guarantee?'

'For a temporary bank loan.' He swallowed. 'I thought he might . . .'

'We had to have the money in a hurry,' Helen said. 'The bank manager told Donald we could borrow it if Malcolm would guarantee it. Then we couldn't get hold of Malcolm. We had to think where he might be, and he's always going to Cambridge. Donald and I just talked about it, guessing, wondering . . . And then, well, Donald went over to the club house and I just picked up the AA book and found those hotels in Cambridge, and without really believing in it I tried two . . . only two . . . and he was there, at the second. When Donald came home I told him and the extraordinary thing was, he'd had the same idea and got the same result.' She paused. 'We were pretty desperate, you see.'

'Don't say that,' Donald said. ' "Desperate" gives the wrong picture.'

'What did you need the money for?' I asked.

They looked at each other, foreheads wrinkled in worry. Finally, reluctantly, but as if coming to a decision, Donald said, 'We had some interest to pay unexpectedly. I had negotiated three months' deferment of interest on a loan, or at least I thought I had, and then I got a threatening demand. I had to pay at once or they'd start proceedings.' The desperation he said wasn't there, definitely had been; it still echoed in his voice. 'I couldn't have it getting around the golf club, could I?' he demanded. 'No one in the family could lend me a large sum in a hurry. Our ordinary bank overdraft is always at maximum. The finance company was inflexible. I knew Malcolm wouldn't *give* me the money, he has those stupid warped views, but I did think he might guarantee . . . just for a short while . . .'

To save the whole pack of cards collapsing, perhaps he might. Malcolm wasn't cruel. He'd lent Edwin money sometimes in the past. Donald, I thought, had stood a good chance.

'But when you'd found where he was, you didn't get in touch with him, did you?'

'No,' Donald said. 'I didn't relish telling Malcolm our troubles. I didn't want to look a fool, and Helen thought of a different way out.'

I looked at her enquiringly.

'Popped my baubles,' she said with a brave attempt at lightness. 'Took them to London. All my lovely rocks.' She held her head high, refusing to cry.

'Pawned them?' I said.

'We'll get them back,' she said valiantly, trying to believe it.

'What day did you pop them?'

'Wednesday. Donald took the money in cash to the finance company, and that gives us a three-months' breather.'

Wednesday, I thought. The day after someone had failed to kill Malcolm at Newmarket.

'When did the finance company start threatening you?'

'The Thursday before,' Helen said. 'They gave us a week. They were utterly beastly, Donald said.'

'Vivien tried to get Malcolm to give us some money,' Donald said with resentment, 'and he flatly refused.'

'Well,' I said, half smiling, 'she called him an evil, wicked, vindictive tyrant, and that's not the best way in the world to persuade Malcolm to be generous. If she'd used honey, she might have succeeded.'

Helen said, 'You're the only one he'll listen to. I don't care if you get millions more than us. All the others are furious about it, they don't believe it about equal shares in his will, but I don't care. If you could just . . . I mean . . .'

'I'll try,' I promised, 'but the equal shares are true.'

It fell on deaf ears. They believed what they believed, the whole lot of them, feeding and reinforcing their fears every time they consulted.

I left Donald and Helen among their antique furniture and behind their shaky façade and trundled along to Quantum to see how things were developing.

Not fast, was the answer. The place was abandoned except for a solitary uniformed policeman sitting in a police car outside what had been the front door. One could see right through the house now. The tarpaulin that had hung from the roof had come down. The policeman was the one who had accompanied me on my tour of peering in through the windows, and I gathered he was pleased to have a visitor to enliven a monotonous stint.

He picked up his car radio and spoke into it to the effect that Mr

Ian Pembroke had come by. A request came back, which he relayed to me: would Mr Pembroke please drop in at the police station when he left? Mr Pembroke would.

The policeman and I walked round to the back of the house. Mr Smith had gone, also his helpers. The last of the rubble was away from the house and overflowing a skip. A flat black plastic sheet, the sort used for roofing hayricks, lay where a week ago the walls of my bedroom had come tumbling down. The interior doors had been sealed with plywood, like the windows, to deter looters, and the broken end of the staircase had been barred off. A house with its centre torn out; a thirty-foot yawn between surviving flanks.

'It looks terrible,' I said, and the policeman agreed.

Arthur Bellbrook was cleaning his spades, getting ready to leave. I gave him a cheque for his wages for that week and the next, and added a chunk for the care of the dogs. He gave me dignified thanks. He hoped Mr Pembroke was all right, poor man, and I said I thought so.

'I had my picture in the paper,' he said. 'Did you see it?'

I said I was sorry I hadn't.

'Oh, well. I did.' He shrugged disappointedly and set off homewards, and I walked down to where he'd earlier been digging potatoes, and then further, to check that the nettles were still untrampled on the far side of the wall.

The green sea looked dusty and ageing but upright. They too, I supposed, would die with the frost.

The policeman was watching me incuriously. I stopped and stared at the house from a distance, giving the impression that that's why I had gone as far as I had, and then walked back and took my leave. The house from a distance looked just as bad, if not worse.

Superintendent Yale shook my hand. Things were almost friendly at the police station but they were no nearer discovering who had planted the bomb. Enquiries were proceeding, the superintendent said, and perhaps I could help.

'Fire away,' I said.

'We interviewed the former gardener, Fred Perkins,' Yale said. 'We asked him about the tree stump and what he used to blow it up. Besides cordite, that is. What sort of a fuse.'

I was interested. 'What did he say? Does he remember?'

226

'He said he'd got the black powder and some detonators and some fuse cord from a quarryman friend of his. The black powder was in the box which we saw, the detonators were in a separate tin with the cord and the instructions.'

'The instructions!' I repeated incredulously.

'Yes.' He sighed. 'Fred Perkins says he followed the instructions because he'd never blown anything up before. He said he used a bit of extra black powder just to make sure.'

'It was quite an explosion.'

'Yes. We asked him what he'd done with the other detonators. He says Mr Pembroke took them away from him that morning, when he came running out of the house. We need to ask Mr Pembroke what he did with them, so . . . er . . . where is he?'

'I really don't know,' I said slowly, 'and that's the truth. I can probably find him, but it'll take a day or two.' I thought for a moment, then said, 'Surely he would have thrown away those detonators years ago.'

'If he had any sense he wouldn't have thrown them anywhere,' Yale said. 'Mr Smith says you handle detonators with extreme caution if you don't want to lose a finger or an eye. They can explode if you knock or drop them or make them too warm. Mr Pembroke's correct course would have been to turn them over to the police.'

'Maybe he did,' I said.

'We'd like to find out.'

'But would detonators still detonate after twenty years?' I asked.

'Mr Smith thinks it possible, perhaps likely. He wouldn't take any liberties, he said.'

'What does a detonator look like?' I asked.

He hesitated, but said, 'Mr Smith said we might be looking for a small aluminium tube about the thickness of a pencil or slightly less, about six centimetres long. He says that's what the army used. He used to be in the Royal Engineers. He says the tube contains fulminate of mercury, and the word "fulminate" means to flash like lightning.'

'He should know.'

'Fred Perkins can't clearly remember what his detonators looked like. He remembers he had to fasten the cord into the end of the tube with pliers. Crimp it in. Mr Smith says civilians who touch explosives should be certified.'

I reflected. 'Did Mr Smith find out exactly what the Quantum bomb was made of?'

'Yes. ANFO, as he thought. He said the whole thing was amateur in the extreme.'

'Amateurs,' I said dryly, 'run faster than anyone else.'

As an amateur, I went to Kempton Park the next day and on Young Higgins beat the hell out of a lot of professionals.

I didn't know what possessed me. It seemed that I rode on a different plane. I knew it was the horse who had to be fast enough; the jockey, however determined, couldn't do it on his own. Young Higgins seemed inspired and against more formidable opponents than at Sandown produced a totally different race.

There were no aunts riding this time, no lieutenant-colonels falling off. No earl's son to chat to. No journalist to make it look easy. For some reason, George and Jo had entered Young Higgins in a high-class open three-mile steeplechase, and I was the only amateur in sight.

I'd ridden against an all-professional field of top jockeys a few times before, and it was usually a humbling experience. I had the basic skills and a good deal of touch. I could get horses settled and balanced. I liked speed, I liked the stretch of one's spirit: but there was always a point against top professionals at which that wasn't enough.

George and Jo were unfussed. Young Higgins was fitter than at Sandown, they thought, and at Kempton there was no hill to tire him. They were bright-eyed and enthusiastic, but not especially hopeful. 'We didn't want to change you for a professional,' they said in explanation. 'It wouldn't have been fair.'

Maybe not fair, but prudent, I thought. The top pros raced with sharper eyes, better tactics, more strength, quicker reactions. Theirs was an intenser determination, a fiercer concentration. Humour was for before and after, not during. Race-riding was their business, besides their pleasure, and some of them thought of amateur opponents as frivolous unfit nuisances who caused accidents and endangered lives.

Perhaps because of an arrogant desire to prove them wrong, perhaps because of the insights and realities I'd faced in a traumatic week, perhaps because of Young Higgins himself: I rode anyway with a new sharp revelationary perception of what was needed for winning, and the horse and I came home in front by four lengths to a fairly stunned silence from the people on the stands who'd backed everything else on the card but us.

George and Jo were vindicated and ecstatic. Young Higgins tossed his head at the modest plaudits. A newspaperman labelled the result as a fluke.

I'd cracked it, I thought. I'd graduated. That had been real professional riding. Satisfactory. But I was already thirty-three. I'd discovered far too late the difference between enjoyment and fire. I'd needed to know it at nineteen or twenty. I'd idled it away.

'This is no time,' Jo said laughing, 'to look sad.'

Seventeen

I flew to New York two days later, still not knowing where to find Malcolm.

The voice at Stamford, Connecticut, always helpful but uninformed, had thought, the previous evening, that the gentlemen might have gone back to Kentucky: they'd been talking of buying a horse that they'd seen there a week earlier. Another horse, not the one they'd bought yesterday.

It was just as well, I thought, that Donald and Helen and Thomas and Berenice and Edwin and Lucy and Vivien and Joyce didn't know. That Gervase, Ursula, Alicia, Ferdinand, Debs and Serena hadn't heard. All fourteen of them would have fallen upon Malcolm and torn him apart.

I chose New York for the twin reasons that Stamford, Connecticut, was barely an hour and a half's drive away (information from the voice) and that everyone should see New York some time. My journeys before that had been only in Europe, to places like Paris, Rome, Athens and Oslo. Beaches and race-meetings and temples. Horses and gods.

I was heading for a hotel on 54th Street, Manhattan, that the voice had recommended: she would tell Mr Pembroke I would be there, as soon as she knew where Mr Pembroke was. It seemed as good an arrangement as any.

Superintendent Yale didn't know I'd left England, nor did any of the family. I sighed with deep relief on the aeroplane and thought about the visits I'd made the day before to Alicia and Vivien. Neither had wanted to see me and both had been abrasive, Alicia in the morning, Vivien in the afternoon.

Alicia's flat outside Windsor was spacious and overlooked the Thames, neither of which pleasures seemed to please her. She did reluctantly let me in, but was unplacated by my admiration of her view.

She was, in fact, looking youthfully pretty in a white wool dress and silver beads. Her hair was pulled high in a velvet bow on the crown, and her neat figure spoke of luck or dieting. She had a visitor with her already when I called, a fortyish substantial-looking man introduced coquettishly as Paul, who behaved with unmistakable lordliness, the master in his domain. How long, I wondered, had this been going on?

'You might have said you were coming,' Alicia complained. 'Ferdinand said you would, some time. I told him to tell you not to.'

'It seemed best to see everyone,' I said neutrally.

'Then hurry up,' she said. 'We're going out to lunch.'

'Did Ferdinand tell you about Malcolm's new will?'

'He did, and I don't believe a word of it. You've always been Malcolm's wretched little pet. He should have sent you back to Joyce when I left. I told him to. But would he listen? No, he wouldn't.'

'That was twenty years ago,' I protested.

'And nothing's changed. He does what he likes. He's utterly selfish.'

Paul listened to the conversation without stirring and with scant apparent interest but he did, it seemed, have his influence. With an arch look at him, Alicia said, 'Paul says Gervase should force Malcolm to give him power of attorney.'

I couldn't off-hand think of anything less likely to happen.

'Have you two known each other long?' I asked.

'No,' Alicia said, and the look she gave Paul was that of a flirt of sixteen.

I asked her if she remembered the tree stump. 'Of course. I was furious with Malcolm for letting Fred do anything so ridiculous. The boys might have been hurt.'

And did she remember the switches? How could she forget them, she said, they'd been all over the house. Not only that, Thomas had made another one for Serena some time later. It had sat in her room gathering dust. Those clocks had all been a pest.

'You were good to me in those old days,' I said.

She stared. There was almost a softening round her eyes, but it was transitory. 'I had to be,' she said acidly. 'Malcolm insisted.'

'Weren't you ever happy?' I asked.

'Oh, yes.' Her mouth curled in a malicious smile. 'When Malcolm came to see me, when he was married to Joyce. Before that weaselly detective spoiled it.

231

I asked her if she had engaged Norman West to find Malcolm in Cambridge.

She looked at me with wide empty eyes and said blandly, 'No, I didn't. Why would I want to? I didn't care where he was.'

'Almost everyone wanted to find him to stop him spending his money.'

'He's insane,' she said. 'Paranoid. He should hand control over to Gervase, and make sure that frightful Ursula isn't included. She's the wrong wife for Gervase, as I've frequently told him.'

'But you didn't ask Norman West to find Malcolm?'

'No, I didn't,' she said very sharply. 'Stop asking that stupid question.' She turned away from me restlessly. 'It's high time you went.'

I thought so too, on the whole. I speculated that perhaps the presence of Paul had inhibited her from saying directly to my face the poison she'd been spreading behind my back. They would dissect me when I'd gone. He nodded coolly to me as I left. No friend of mine, I thought.

If my visit to Alicia had been unfruitful, my call on Vivien was less so. Norman West's notes had been minimal: name, address, sorting magazines, no alibis. She wouldn't answer any of my questions either, or discuss any possibilities. She said several times that Malcolm was a fiend who was determined to destroy his children, and that I was the devil incarnate helping him. She hoped we would both rot in hell. (I thought devils and fiends might flourish there, actually.)

Meanwhile, I said, had she employed Norman West to find Malcolm in Cambridge? Certainly not. She wanted nothing to do with that terrible little man. If I didn't remove myself from her doorstep she would call in the police.

'It can't be much fun,' I said, 'living with so much hatred in your head.'

She was affronted. 'What do you mean?'

'No peace. All anger. Very exhausting. Bad for your health.'

'Go away,' she said, and I obliged her.

I drove back to Cookham and spent a good deal of the evening on the telephone, talking to Lucy about Thomas and to Ferdinand about Gervase. 'We are all our brothers' keepers,' Lucy said, and reported

232

that Thomas was spending most of the time asleep. 'Retreating,' Lucy said.

Lucy had spoken to Berenice. 'Whatever did you say to her, Ian? She sounds quite different. Subdued. Can't see it lasting long, can you? I told her Thomas was all right and she started blubbing.'

Lucy said she would keep Thomas for a while, but not for his natural span.

Ferdinand, when he heard my voice, said, 'Where the hell have you been? All I get is your answering machine. Did you find out who killed Moira?' There was anxiety, possibly, in his voice.

'I found out a few who didn't,' I said.

'That's not what I asked.'

'Well,' I said, 'like you with your computer, I've fed in a lot of data.'

'And the result?'

'The wheels are turning.'

'Computers don't have wheels. Come to think of it, though, I suppose they do. Anyway, you've left a whole trail of disasters behind you, haven't you? I hear Thomas has left Berenice, and as for Gervase, he wants your guts for taking Ursula out to lunch. Did you do that? Whatever for? You know how possessive he is. There's a hell of a row going on.'

'If you want to hang on to Debs,' I said, 'don't listen to Alicia.'

'What the hell's that got to do with Gervase and Ursula having a row?' he demanded.

'Everything.'

He was furious. 'You've always got it in for Alicia.'

'The other way round. She's a dedicated troublemaker who's cost you one wife already.' He didn't immediately answer. I said, 'Gervase is knocking back a fortune in scotch.'

'What's that got to do with anything?'

'How do you cope so well with illegitimacy?'

'*What?*'

'Everything's linked. So long, pal. See you.' I put the receiver down with a sigh, and ate dinner, and packed.

In the morning, having paid a few bills, I took the hired car to Heathrow and turned it in there and, with a feeling of shackles dropping off, hopped into the air.

* * *

233

I spent four nights in New York before I found Malcolm; or before he found me, to be more precise.

In daily consultations, the Stamford voice assured me that I wasn't forgotten, that the message would one day get through. I had a vision of native bearers beating through jungles, but it wasn't like that, it transpired. Malcolm and Ramsey had simply been moving from horse farm to horse farm through deepest Kentucky, and it was from there he finally phoned at eight-ten in the morning.

'What are you doing in New York?' he demanded.

'Looking at skyscrapers,' I said.

'I thought we were meeting in California.'

'Well, we are,' I said. 'When?'

'What's today?'

'Friday.'

'Hang on.'

I heard him talking in the background, then he returned. 'We're just going out to see some horses breeze. Ramsey reserved the rooms from tomorrow through Saturday at the Beverly Wilshire, he says, but he and I are going to spend a few more days here now. You go to California tomorrow and I'll join you, say, on Wednesday.'

'Couldn't you please make it sooner? I do need to talk to you.'

'Did you find something out?' His voice suddenly changed gear, as if he'd remembered almost with shock the world of terrors he'd left behind.

'A few things.'

'Tell me.'

'Not on the telephone. Not in a hurry. Go and see the horses breeze and meet me tomorrow.' I paused. 'There are horses in California. Thousands of them.'

He was quiet for a few moments, then he said, 'I owe it to you. I'll be there,' and disconnected.

I arranged my air ticket and spent the rest of the day as I'd spent all the others in New York, wandering around, filling eyes and ears with the city . . . thinking painful private thoughts and coming to dreadful conclusions.

Malcolm kept his word and, to my relief, came without Ramsey who had decided Stamford needed him if Connecticut were to survive. Ramsey, Malcolm said, would be over on Wednesday, we would all have three days at the races and go to Australia on Saturday night.

He was crackling with energy, the eyes intensely blue. He and Ramsey had bought four more horses in partnership, he said in the first three minutes, and were joining a syndicate to own some others down under.

A forest fire out of control, I thought, and had sympathy for my poor brothers.

The Beverly Wilshire gave us a suite with brilliant red flocked wallpaper in the sitting-room and vivid pink and orange flowers on a turquoise background in the bedrooms. There were ornate crimson curtains, filmy cream inner curtains, a suspicion of lace, an air of Edwardian roguishness brought up to date. Rooms to laugh in, I thought. And with little wrought-iron balconies outside the bowed windows looking down on a pool with a fountain and gardens and orange trees, not much to complain of.

We dined downstairs in a bar that had tables at one end and music, and Malcolm said I looked thinner.

'Tell me about the horses,' I said; and heard about them through the smoked salmon, the salad, the veal and the coffee.

'Don't worry,' he said, near the beginning. 'They're not all as expensive as Blue Clancy and Chrysos. We got all four for under a million dollars, total, and they're two-year-olds ready to run. Good breeding; the best. One's by Alydar, even.'

I listened, amused and impressed. He knew the breeding of all his purchases back three generations, and phrases like 'won a stakes race' and 'his dam's already produced Group I winners' came off his tongue as if he'd been saying them all his life.

'Do you mind if I ask you something?' I said eventually.

'I won't know until you ask.'

'No . . . um . . . just how rich *are* you?'

He laughed. 'Did Joyce put you up to that question?'

'No. I wanted to know for myself.'

'Hm.' He thought. 'I can't tell you to the nearest million. It changes every day. At a rough estimate, about a hundred million pounds. It would grow now of its own accord at the rate of five million a year if I never lifted a finger again, but you know me, that would be boring, I'd be dead in a month.'

'After tax?' I said.

'Sure.' He smiled. 'Capital gains tax usually. I've spent a year's investment income after tax on the horses, that's all. Not as much as

235

that on all those other projects that the family were going bananas about. I'm not raving mad. There'll be plenty for everyone when I pop off. More than there is now. I just have to live longer. You tell them that.'

'I told them you'd said in your will that if you were murdered, it would all go to charity.'

'Why didn't I think of that?'

'Did you think any more of letting the family have some of the lucre before you . . . er . . . pop off?'

'You know my views on that.'

'Yes, I do.'

'And you don't approve.'

'I don't disapprove in theory. The trust funds were generous when they were set up. Many fathers don't do as much. But your children aren't perfect and some of them have got into messes. If someone were bleeding, would you buy them a bandage?'

He sat back in his chair and stared moodily at his coffee.

'Have they sent you here to plead for them?' he asked.

'No. I'll tell you what's been happening, then you can do what you like.'

'Fair enough,' he said, 'but not tonight.'

'All right.' I paused. 'I won a race at Kempton, did you know?'

'Did you really?' He was instantly alive with interest, asking for every detail. He didn't want to hear about his squabbling family with its latent murderer. He was tired of being vilified while at the same time badgered to be bountiful. He felt safe in California although he had, I'd been interested to discover, signed us into the hotel as Watson and Watson.

'Well, you never know, do you?' he'd said. 'It may say in the British papers that Blue Clancy's coming over, and Ramsey says this hotel is the centre for the Breeders' Cup organisers. They're having reception rooms here, and buffets. By Wednesday, he says, this place will be teeming with the international racing crowd. So where, if someone wanted to find me, do you think they'd look first?'

'I think Norman West gave us good advice.'

'So do I.'

The Watsons, father and son, breakfasted the following morning out in the warm air by the pool, sitting in white chairs beside a white

236

table under a yellow sun umbrella, watching the oranges ripen amid dark green leaves, talking of horrors.

I asked him casually enough if he remembered Fred and the tree roots.

'Of course I do,' he said at once. 'Bloody fool could have killed himself.' He frowned. 'What's that got to do with the bomb at Quantum?'

'Superintendent Yale thinks it may have given someone the idea.'

He considered it. 'I suppose it might.'

'The superintendent, or some of his men, asked old Fred what he'd used to set off the cordite . . .' I told Malcolm about the cordite still lying around in the tool shed '. . . and Fred said he had some detonators, but after that first bang, you came out and took them away.'

'Good Lord, I'd forgotten that. Yes, so I did. You were all there, weren't you? Pretty well the whole family?'

'Yes, it was one of those weekends. Helen says it was the first time she met you, she was there too, before she was married to Donald.'

He thought back. 'I don't remember that. I just remember there being a lot of you.'

'The superintendent wonders if you remember what happened to the detonators after you'd taken them away.'

He stared. 'It's twenty years ago, must be,' he protested.

'It might be the sort of thing you wouldn't forget.'

He shook his head doubtfully.

'Did you turn them over to the police?'

'No.' He was definite about that, anyway. 'Old Fred had no business to have them, but I wouldn't have got him into trouble, or the friend he got them from, either. I'll bet they were nicked.'

'Do you remember what they looked like?' I asked.

'Well, yes, I suppose so.' He frowned, thinking, pouring out more coffee. 'There was a row of them in a tin, laid out carefully in cotton wool so that they shouldn't roll about. Small silverish tubes, about two and a half inches long.'

'Fred says they had instructions with them.'

He laughed. 'Did he? A do-it-yourself bomb kit?' He sobered suddenly. 'I suppose it was just that. I don't remember the instructions, but I dare say they were there.'

'You did realise they were dangerous, didn't you?'

'I probably did, but all those years ago ordinary people didn't

237

know so much about bombs. I mean, not terrorist bombs. We'd been bombed from the air, but that was different. I should think I took the detonators away from Fred so he shouldn't set off any more explosions, not because they were dangerous in themselves, if you see what I mean?'

'Mm. But you did know you shouldn't drop them?'

'You mean if I'd dropped them, I wouldn't be here talking about it?'

'According to the explosives expert working at Quantum, quite likely not.'

'I never worked with explosives, being an adjutant.' He buttered a piece of croissant, added marmalade and ate it. His service as a young officer in his war had been spent in arranging details of troop movements and as assistant to camp commanders, often near enough to the enemy but not seeing the whites of their eyes. He never spoke of it much: it had been history before I was born.

'I remembered where the cordite was, even after all this time,' I said. 'If you imagine yourself going into the house with this tin of detonators, where would you be likely to put it? You'd put it where you would think of looking for it first, wouldn't you?'

'Yes,' he nodded, 'always my system.' A faraway unfocused look appeared in his eyes, then he suddenly sat bolt upright.

'I know where they are! I saw the tin not so very long ago, when I was looking for something else. I didn't pay much attention. It didn't even register what was in it, but I'm pretty sure now that that's what it was. It's a sort of sweet tin, not very big, with a picture on top.'

'Where was it, and how long ago?'

'Surely,' he said, troubled, 'they'd be duds by this time?'

'Quite likely not.'

'They're in the office.' He shrugged self-excusingly. 'You know I never tidy that place up. I'd never find anything ever again. I'm always having to stop people tidying it.'

'Like Moira?'

'She could hardly bear to keep her hands off.'

'Where in the office?' I remembered the jumble in his desk drawer when I'd fetched his passport. The whole place was similar.

'On top of some of the books in the breakfront bookcase. Bottom row, right over on the right-hand side, more or less out of sight when the door's closed. On top of the Dickens.' His face suddenly split into a huge grin. 'I remember now, by God. I put it there because the picture on the tin's lid was The Old Curiosity Shop.'

I rubbed my hand over my face, trying not to laugh. Superintendent Yale was going to love it.

'They're safe enough there,' Malcolm said reasonably, 'behind glass. I mean, no one can pick them up accidentally, can they? That's where they are.'

I thought it highly likely that that's where they weren't, but I didn't bother to say so. 'The glass in the breakfront is broken,' I said.

He was sorry about that. It had been his mother's, he said, like all the books.

'When did you see the tin there?' I asked.

'Haven't a clue. Not all that long ago, I wouldn't have thought, but time goes so quickly.'

'Since Moira died?'

He wrinkled his forehead. 'No, probably not. Then, before that, I was away from the house for a week or ten days when I couldn't stand being in the same place with her and she obdurately wouldn't budge. Before that, I was looking for something in a book. Not in Dickens, a shelf or two higher. Can't remember what book, though I suppose I might if I went back and stood in front of them and looked at the titles. Altogether, over three months ago, I should say.'

I reflected a bit and drank my coffee. 'I suppose the bookcase must have been moved now and then for redecorating. The books taken out . . .'

'Don't be ridiculous,' Malcolm interrupted with amusement. 'It weighs more than a ton. The books stay inside it. Redecorating goes on around it, and not at all if I can help it. Moira tried to make me take everything out so she could paint the whole office dark green. I stuck my toes in. She had the rest of the house. That room is mine.'

I nodded lazily. It was pleasant in the sunshine. A few people were sunbathing, a child was swimming, a waiter in a white jacket came along with someone else's breakfast. All a long way away from the ruins of Quantum.

From that quiet Sunday morning and on until Wednesday, Malcolm and I led the same remote existence, being driven round Los Angeles and Hollywood and Beverly Hills in a stretch-limousine Malcolm seemed to have hired by the yard, neck-twisting like tourists, going

239

out to Santa Anita racetrack in the afternoons, dining in restaurants like Le Chardonnay.

I gradually told him what was happening in the family, never pressing, never heated, never too much at one time, stopping at once if he started showing impatience.

'Donald and Helen should send their children to state schools,' he said moderately.

'Maybe they should. But you sent Donald to Marlborough, and you went there yourself. Donald wants the best for his boys. He's suffering to give them what you gave him effortlessly.'

'He's a snob to choose Eton.'

'Maybe, but the Marlborough fees aren't much less.'

'What if it was Donald and Helen who've been trying to kill me?'

'If they had plenty of money they wouldn't be tempted.'

'You've said that before, or something like it.'

'Nothing has changed.'

Malcolm looked out of the long car's window as we were driven up through the hills of Bel Air on the way to the racetrack.

'Do you see those houses perched on the cliffs, hanging out over space? People must be mad to live like that, on the edge.'

I smiled. 'You do,' I said.

He liked Santa Anita racetrack immediately and so did I; it would have been difficult not to. Royal palms near the entrances stretched a hundred feet upward, all bare trunks except for the crowning tufts, green fronds against the blue sky. The buildings were towered and turreted, sea-green in colour, with metal tracery of stylised palm leaves along the balconies and golden shutters over rear-facing windows. It looked more like a château than a racecourse, at first sight.

Ramsey Osborn had given Malcolm fistfuls of instructions and introductions and, as always, Malcolm was welcomed as a kindred spirit upstairs in the Club. He was at home from the first minute, belonging to the scene as if he'd been born there. I envied him his ease and didn't know how to acquire it. Maybe time would do it. Maybe millions. Maybe a sense of achievement.

While he talked easily to almost strangers (soon to be cronies) about the mixing of European and American bloodlines in thorough-breds, I thought of the phone call I'd made at dawn on Monday morning to Superintendent Yale. Because of the eight-hour time difference, it was already afternoon with him, and I thought it unlikely I would reach him at first try. He was there, however, and came on the line with unstifled annoyance.

'It's a week since you telephoned.'

'Yes, sorry.'

'Where are you?'

'Around,' I said. His voice sounded as clear to me as if he were in the next room, and presumably mine to him, as he didn't at all guess I wasn't in England. 'I found my father,' I said.

'Oh. Good.'

I told him where Malcolm had stored the detonators. 'On top of *The Old Curiosity Shop*, as appropriate.'

There was a shattered silence. 'I don't believe it,' he said.

'The books are all old and leatherbound classics standing in full editions. Poets, philosophers, novelists, all bought years ago by my grandmother. We were all allowed to borrow a book occasionally to read, but we had to put it back. My father had us well trained.'

'Are you saying that anyone who borrowed a book from that bookcase could have seen the detonators?'

'Yes, I suppose so, if they've been there for twenty years.'

'Did you know they were there?'

'No. I didn't read those sort of books much. Spent my time riding.'

Lucy, I thought, had in her teens plunged into poets as a fish into its native sea, but twenty years ago she had been twenty-two and writing her own immortality. None of the rest of us had been scholars. Some of grandmother's books had never been opened.

'It is incredible that when someone thought of making a bomb, the detonators were to hand,' Yale complained.

'Other way round, wouldn't you think?' I said. 'The availability of the detonators suggested the bomb.'

'The pool of common knowledge in your family is infuriating,' he said. 'No one can be proved to have special access to explosives. No one has a reliable alibi . . . except Mrs Ferdinand . . . Everyone can make a timing device and nearly all of you have a motive.'

'Irritating,' I agreed.

'That's the wrong word,' he said sourly. 'Where's your father?'

'Safe.'

'You can't stay in hiding for ever.'

'Don't expect to see us for a week or two. What chance is there of your solving the case?'

Enquiries were proceeding, he said with starch. If I came across any further information, I would please give it to him.

Indeed, I said, I would.

'When I was younger,' he said to my surprise, 'I used to think I had a nose for a villain, that I could always tell. But since then, I've met embezzlers I would have trusted my savings to, and murderers I'd have let marry my daughter. Murderers can look like harmless ordinary people.' He paused. 'Does your family know who killed Moira Pembroke?'

'I don't think so.'

'Please enlarge,' he said.

'One or two may suspect they know, but they're not telling. I went to see everyone. No one was even guessing. No one accusing. They don't want to know, don't want to face it, don't want the misery.'

'And you?'

'I don't want the misery either, but I also don't want my father killed, or myself.'

'Do you think you're in danger?'

'Oh, yes,' I said. '*In loco* Moira.'

'As chief beneficiary?'

'Something like that. Only I'm not chief, I'm equal. My father made a new will saying so. I've told the family but they don't believe it.'

'Produce the will. Show it to them.'

'Good idea,' I said. 'Thank you.'

'And you,' he paused, 'do you know, yourself?'

'I don't know.'

'Guess, then.'

'Guessing is one thing, proof is another.'

'I might remind you it's your duty . . .'

'It's not my duty,' I interrupted without heat, 'to go off half-cocked. My duty to my family is to get it right or do nothing.'

I said goodbye to him rather firmly and concluded, from his tone as much as his words, that the police had no more information than I had, and perhaps less: that they hadn't managed (if they'd tried) to find out where the grey plastic clock had come from or who had bought it, which was their only lead as far as I could see and a pretty hopeless proposition. It had been a cheap mass-production clock, probably on sale in droves.

Malcolm said on one of our car journeys, after I'd been telling him about Berenice, 'Vivien, you know, had this thing about sons.'

'But she had a boy first. She had two.'

'Yes, but before Donald was born, she said she wouldn't look at the baby if it was a girl. I couldn't understand it. I'd have liked a girl. Vivien's self-esteem utterly depended on having a boy. She was obsessed with it. You'd have thought she'd come from some dreadful tribe where it really mattered.'

'It did matter,' I said. 'And it matters to Berenice. All obsessions matter because of their results.'

'Vivien never loved Lucy, you know,' he said thoughtfully. 'She shoved her away from her. I always thought that was why Lucy got fat and retreated into poetic fantasies.'

'Berenice shoves off her daughters onto her mother as much as she can.'

'Do you think Berenice murdered Moira?' he said doubtfully.

'I think she thinks that having more money would make her happier, which it probably would. If you were going to think of any . . . er . . . distribution, I'd give it to the wives as well as the husbands. Separately, I mean. So they had independence.'

'Why?' he said.

'Gervase might value Ursula more if she didn't need him financially.'

'Ursula's a mouse.'

'She's desperate.'

'They're all desperate,' he said with irritation. 'It's all their own faults. The fault, dear Brutus, is not in our stars but in ourselves, that we are underlings.'

'I dare say,' I said.

'The bell captain at the hotel gave me a tip for the fourth race.' Back to horses.

Another day, another journey.

Malcolm said, 'What did Serena say, when you saw her?'

'She said you could stuff your money, or words to that effect.'

Malcolm laughed.

'She also said,' I went on, 'that Alicia told her you'd only tried to get custody of her that time so as to be cruel to Alicia.'

'Alicia's a real bitch.'

'She's got a lover, did you know?' I said.

He was thunderstruck. 'Who is he?'

'Someone else's husband, I should think. That's what she likes, isn't it?'

'Don't be so bloody accurate.'

Further down the road we were talking about the time-switch clocks, which had been an unwelcome piece of news to him also.

'Thomas was best at making them, wasn't he?' Malcolm said. 'He could do them in a jiffy. They were his idea originally, I think. Serena brought one over for Robin and Peter which Thomas had made for her years ago.'

I nodded. 'A Mickey Mouse clock. It's still there in the playroom.'

'Serena made them a lighthouse of Lego to go with it, I remember.' He sighed deeply. 'I miss Coochie still, you know. The crash happened not long after that.' He shook his head to rid it of sadness. 'What race shall we choose for the Coochie Memorial Trophy? What do you think?'

On another day, I asked why Ferdinand didn't mind being illegitimate when Gervase did, to the brink of breakdown.

'I don't know,' Malcolm said. 'Gervase always thinks people are sneering and laughing, even now. Someone rubbed his nose in it when he was young, you know. Told him he was rubbish, a mistake, should have been aborted. Boys can be bloody cruel. Gervase got aggressive to compensate, I suppose. Nothing ever worried Ferdinand very much. He's like me in more than looks.'

'Only two wives so far,' I said incautiously.

'Why don't you get married?' he asked.

I was flippant. 'Haven't met the one and only. Don't want five.'

'Don't you trust yourself?' he said.

Christ, I thought, that was sharp, that was penetrating. That was unfair. It was because of him that I didn't trust myself: because in inconstancy, I felt I was very much his son.

His imprint, for better or worse, was on us all.

Eighteen

On Wednesday, the Beverly Wilshire came alive as Ramsey had prophesied and Ramsey himself blew in with gusto and plans. We would go to parties. We would go round the horse barns. We would go to a Hollywood Gala Ball.

The Breeders' Cup organisers opened their reception room where everyone concerned with the races could have breakfast and cocktails (together if they liked) and talk about horses, could arrange cars and tickets and talk about horses, could meet the people they'd met at Epsom and Longchamp and talk about horses. Well-mannered people in good suits and silk dresses, owners whose enthusiasm prompted and funded the sport. Big bucks, big business, big fun.

Malcolm adored it. So did I. Life in high gear. Early on Friday, we went out to the racecourse to see Blue Clancy in his barn and watch him breeze round the track in his last warm-up before the big one. His English trainer was with him, and his English lad. There was heady excitement, a lot of anxiety. The orderly bustle of stable life, the smells, the swear words, the earthy humour, the pride, the affection, the jealousies, the injustices, the dead disappointments, all the same the world over.

Blue Clancy looked fine, worked well, threw Malcolm and Ramsey into back-slapping ecstasies. 'Wait until tomorrow,' the trainer said cautiously, watching them. 'We're taking on the best in the world, don't forget. The hot money is for a California-bred horse.'

'What's hot money?' Malcolm demanded.

'The bets made by people in the know. People with inside information.'

Who cared, Malcolm said. He couldn't remember ever having more fun in his life: and I thought his euphoria was at least partly due to his three close approaches to losing it.

Along with a thousand others, we went to the ball, though in the stretch-limo, not a converted pumpkin, and in the vast sound stage which had lately held a split-open aeroplane for filming cabin dramas, Malcolm danced with several ladies he'd known well for two days. He spent his time laughing. He was infectious. Everyone around him lit up like nightlights, banishing gloom.

We slept, we ate breakfast, we went to the races. The smog that all week had covered the mountains everyone swore were there on the far side of the track, relented and evaporated and disclosed a sunlit rocky backdrop worthy of the occasion. Tables with tablecloths had appeared overnight throughout the Club stands, and overworked black-coated waiters sweated under huge trays of food, threading through ever-moving racegoers, never dropping the lot.

There were seven Breeders' Cup races; various distances, variously aged horses. The first five each offered a total purse (for first, second, third and so on) of one million dollars. Blue Clancy's race, the one-and-a-half-mile Turf, had a purse of two million, and the climactic event, the Breeders' Cup Classic, promised three. They weren't racing for peanuts. The owner of the winner of Blue Clancy's race would be personally richer by six hundred and twenty-nine thousand dollars, enough to keep him in Bollinger for weeks.

We cheered home the first five winners. We went down to the saddling stalls and saw Blue Clancy prepared. We went up to the stands and bit our nails.

Five of the seven races were run on the dirt track, two on grass, of which this was the second; and most of the European horses were running on grass, the green stuff of home. Blue Clancy was taking on the Epsom Derby winner, the Arc de Triomphe winner and the winner of the Italian Derby. On paper, he looked to have an outside chance of coming fourth. In Malcolm's and Ramsey's eyes, he was a shoo-in. (Malcolm had learned the local jargon.)

Blue Clancy broke cleanly from the gate away on the far side of the course and his English jockey held him handily in sixth place all down the far side. Ramsey and Malcolm were looking through binoculars and muttering encouragements. Blue Clancy, not hearing them, swung into the long left-hand bottom bend in no better position and was still lying sixth when the field crossed the dirt track as they turned for home. Malcolm's muttering grew louder. 'Come on, you bugger. Come on.'

There was no clear leader. Three horses raced together in front, followed by a pair together, then Blue Clancy alone. Too much to do,

I thought: and the agile colt immediately proved me wrong. His jockey swung him wide of the others to allow him a clear run and gave him unmistakable signals that now was the time that mattered, now, this half-minute, if never again.

Blue Clancy accelerated. Malcolm was shouting, Ramsey was speechless. Blue Clancy in third place, all the crowds roaring. Blue Clancy still faster, second now. Malcolm silent, mouth open, eyes staring. The incredible was happening, awesome, breathtaking . . . and Blue Clancy had definitely, indubitably won.

Malcolm's eyes were like sapphires lit from inside. He still couldn't speak. Ramsey grabbed him by the arm and pulled him, and the two of them ran, almost dancing, weaving through slowcoaches, making their way down to greet their champion's return. I followed close on their heels, marvelling. Some owners were always lucky, some owners always weren't; it was an inexplicable fact of racing life. Malcolm's luck was stupendous. It always had been, in everything except wives. I should have known, I supposed, that it would come with him onto the track. King Midas had touched him, and Blue Clancy was his latest gold.

I wondered ironically what the family would say. The fortune he'd flung away on horses had already come back: Blue Clancy was worth at least double what he'd been before the Arc.

Chrysos, I daydreamed, would win the Derby. The tadpole film (about sharks actually, Malcolm had told me) would win at Cannes. The Pol Roger would appreciate. Everyone would see the point of not murdering the golden goose (Wrong sex, never mind. It was a lightheaded day.) We could return home to welcomes and safety.

Only it wasn't like that. We would return home to an unassessable danger, and it was essential to be aware of it, and to plan.

Sobered as always by what lay ahead, I nevertheless went to a post-race party in fine spirits, and after that to Los Angeles airport to fly through the night to Australia. The party, the people came with us. Melbourne took up the impetus, pressing forward to its own Cup, always held on the first Tuesday in November. Everything, they told us there, stopped for the race. Schoolchildren had a holiday and the Melbourne shops closed. The Hyatt Hotel, where we stayed (Watson and Watson), had a lobby criss-crossed by people known better in Newmarket, all with the ready grins of kids out of school.

Ramsey had surpassed himself in the matter of reservations. Even to reach our floor, we had to use a special key in the elevator, and there was a private lounge up there for cocktails and breakfast (but separately). Malcolm appreciated it, took it all in his stride, ordered champagne, breathed Melbourne air and became an instant Australian.

Out at Flemington racecourse (no château), there was less sophistication than at Santa Anita, just as much enthusiasm, very good food, a much better parade ring. Malcolm found the day's racing less compulsive than Paris or California through not owning a runner. He'd tried to remedy this on arrival, but no one would sell one of the top bunch, and he wanted nothing less. Instead, he set about gambling with method but only in tens and soon tired of it, win or lose. I left him and Ramsey in the Committee rooms and wandered down to the crowd as in Paris, and wondered how many in the throng struggled with intractable problems in their shirtsleeves, no shirts, carnival hats. When the party was over, Malcolm would grow restless and want to move on, and I wasn't ready. Under the shade trees, surrounded by beer cans, listening to the vigorous down-under language, I searched for the solution that would cause us least grief.

There was no truly easy way out. No overlooking or dodging what had been done to Moira. But if someone could plead guilty and plead diminished responsibility owing to stress, there might be a quiet trial and a lifetime for us of visiting a sort of hospital instead of a rigorous prison. Either way, any way, there were tears in our future.

On top of that I had to be right, and I had to convince Malcolm beyond any doubt that I was. Had to convince all the family, and the police, without any mistake. Had to find a way of doing it that was peaceful and simple, for all our sakes.

I watched the Melbourne Cup from ground level, which meant in effect that I didn't see much of it because of the other thousands doing the same. On the other hand, I was closer to the horses before and after, watching them walk, listening to comments, mostly unflattering, from knowledgeable elbowers striving for a view.

The Melbourne Cup runners were older and more rugged than stars back home. Some were eight or nine. All raced far more often, once a week not being unusual. The favourite for that day's race had won on the course three days earlier.

They were racing for a purse of a million Australian dollars, of which sixty-five per cent went to the winner, besides a handsome gold cup. Thwarted this year, Malcolm, I imagined, would be back next year. He'd met in Paris and California several of the owners now standing in the parade ring and I could guess the envy he was feeling. No one was as passionate as a new convert.

When the race was finally off, I couldn't hear the commentary for the exhortations around me, but it didn't much matter: the winner was owned by one of the international owners and afterwards I found Malcolm beside the winner's enclosure looking broody and thinking expensive thoughts.

'Next year,' he said.

'You're addicted.'

He didn't deny it. He and Ramsey slapped each other on the back, shook hands and promised like blood brothers to meet regularly on every major racecourse in the world. Ramsey, the bulky manufacturer of millions of baseball caps, had somewhere along the line realised what 'metal' really meant in Malcolm's vocabulary and from cronies they had become comfortable friends, neither feeling at an advantage over the other.

They discussed staying on in Australia but Ramsey said the baseball caps needed guidance. Malcolm wavered about going to see some gold mines in Kalgoorlie but decided on a gold share broker in Melbourne instead. We spent Melbourne Cup night in a farewell dinner, and when Ramsey had departed in the morning and left us alone in the quiet breakfast room upstairs, Malcolm looked at me as if coming down to earth for the first time since we'd left England. With a touch of despondency, he asked for how long he was to be exiled for safety's sake.

'But you've enjoyed it,' I said.

'God, yes.' The remembrance flashed in his eyes. 'But it's not real life. We have to go back. I know I've avoided talking about it, it's all dreadful. I know you've been thinking about it all this time. I could see it in your face.'

'I've come to know them all so much better,' I said, 'my brothers and my sisters. I didn't care for them all that much, you know, before Moira died. We've always met of course from time to time, but I'd forgotten to a great extent what we had been like as children.' I paused for a bit, but he didn't comment. 'Since the bomb went off at Quantum,' I said, 'a great deal of the past has come back. And I've seen, you know, how the present has grown out of that past. How my sisters-in-law and my brother-in-law have been affected by it. How people easily believe lies, old and new. How destructive it is to yearn for the unobtainable, to be unsatisfied by anything else. How obsessions don't go away, they get worse.'

He was silent for a while, then said, 'Bleak.' Then he sighed and said, 'How much do they need, then? How much should I give them? I don't believe in it, but I see it's necessary. Their obsessions have got worse as I've grown richer. If the money wasn't there, they'd have sorted themselves out better. Is that what you're saying?'

'Yes, partly.' It hadn't been, entirely, but as it had produced a reaction I'd wanted but hadn't expected, I kept quiet.

'All right, then,' he said. 'I've had a bloody good holiday and I'm feeling generous, so draw up a list of who's to get what.'

'All equal,' I said.

He began to protest, but sighed instead. 'What about you, then?'

'I don't know. We'll decide about that later.'

'I thought you wanted half a million to set up as a trainer.'

'I've changed my mind. For now, anyway. There's something else I want to do first.'

'What's that?'

I hesitated. I'd barely admitted it to myself, had certainly told no one else.

'Go on,' he urged.

'Be a jockey. Turn professional.'

'Good Lord,' he said, astonished, 'haven't you left it too late?'

'Maybe. We'll see. I'll have three or four years, perhaps. Better than not trying.'

'You amaze me.' He reflected. 'Come to think of it, you've constantly amazed me since you came to Newmarket Sales. It seems I hardly knew you before.'

'That's how I feel about you,' I said, 'and about all of the family.'

We set off homewards later the same day, travelling west via Singapore. Malcolm's gold share broker happened to be going there at the same time, so I changed places with him on the aeroplane and let the two of them say things like 'percussion and rotary air blast drilling to get a first idea' and 'diamond core drilling is necessary for estimating reserves accurately', which seemed to entertain them for hours.

I thought meantime about invitations. About invitations like meat over bear pits. The right invitation would bring the right visitor. The problem was how to make the invitation believable.

Part of the trouble was time. When we reached England, Malcolm would have been out of harm's way for four weeks, and I for almost three. We'd been safe, and I'd had time to reflect: those on the plus side. On the minus, as far as the invitation was concerned, was the fact that it would be six weeks since Malcolm had survived in the garage, and ten since Moira had died. Would a classic trap invitation work after so long an interval? Only one thing to do: try it and see.

Malcolm's voice was saying, '. . . a section assaying five point eight grams per tonne' and a bit later, '. . . Big Bell's plant milling oxide and soft rock', and '. . . the future is good in Queensland, with those epithermal gold zones at Woolgar'. The broker listened and nodded and looked impressed. My old man, I thought, really knows his stuff. He'd told me at one point on our journeyings that there were roughly twenty-five hundred active gold mines in Australia and that it would soon rival or even surpass Canada as a producer. I hadn't known gold was big in Canada. I was ignorant, he said. Canada had so far come regularly second to South Africa in the non-communist world.

We'd taught each other quite a lot, I thought, in one way and another.

I would need someone to deliver the invitation. Couldn't do it myself.

'Market capitalisation per ounce . . .' I heard the broker saying in snatches, and '. . . in situ reserves based on geological interpretation . . .'

I knew who could deliver the invitation. The perfect person.

'As open-cut mining cost as little as two hundred Australian dollars an ounce . . .'

Bully for open-cut mining, I thought, and drifted to sleep.

We left spring behind in Australia on Wednesday and came home to winter on Friday in England. Malcolm and I went back to the Ritz as Mr and Mr Watson and he promised with utmost sincerity that he wouldn't telephone anyone, not even his London broker. I went shopping in the afternoon and then confounded him at the brandy and cigar stage late that evening by getting through to Joyce.

'But you said . . .' he hissed as he heard her voice jump as usual out of the receiver.

'Listen,' I hissed back. 'Hello, Joyce.'

'Darling! Where are you? What are you doing? Where's your father?'

'In Australia,' I said.

'*What?*' she yelled.

'Looking at gold mines,' I said.

It made sense to her, as it would make sense to them all.

'He went to California, I saw it in the paper,' she said. 'Blue Clancy won a race.'

'We went to Australia afterwards.'

'*We?* Darling, where are you now?'

'It doesn't matter where I am,' I said. 'To make it safe for us to come home, will you help to find out who killed Moira?'

'But darling, the police have been trying for weeks ... and anyway, Ferdinand says it has to be Arthur Bellbrook.'

'It's not Arthur Bellbrook,' I said.

'Why not?' She sounded argumentative, still wanting it to be Arthur, wanting it to be the intruder from outside. 'He could have done it easily. Ferdinand says he could have done everything. It has to be him. He had a shot-gun, Ferdinand says.'

I said, 'Arthur didn't use his shot-gun. More importantly, he wouldn't have made a timing device exactly like we'd made as children, and he hadn't a motive.'

'He could have detested Moira.'

'Absolutely,' I said, 'but why should he want to kill Malcolm, whom he liked? I saw his face when he found Malcolm was alive that morning after the bomb, and he was genuinely glad.'

'Everyone wants it to be Arthur Bellbrook,' she said obstinately. 'He found her body.'

'If the police thought he'd done it, they wouldn't have been so suspicious of Malcolm.'

'You've got an answer for everything,' she complained.

I had myself for a while wished it to be Arthur. After all, there had been the affair of the prize vegetables (but he'd sounded philosophical about them, and would anyone kill for so little?) and he'd been in the army and might know about explosives. But he stood to lose rather than gain from Malcolm's death, and it was beyond believing that he would trace Malcolm to Cambridge, follow him to Newmarket Sales and try to run him down. That was the work of obsession. Arthur placidly digging potatoes; Arthur enjoying the temporary fame;

Arthur looking after the dogs. Arthur had been the personification of stolid, sensible balance.

Besides, whoever had tried to run Malcolm down at Newmarket had guessed Malcolm would leave the sales with me and would come to the car-park, and at that point Arthur would have had no reason to think so. He didn't know me. Hadn't met me until he came into the house with his shot-gun, thinking I was a burglar. I'd had to exclude Arthur, although with regret.

Joyce said, 'Darling, how do you expect to succeed where the police have failed?'

'The police can't do what we can do.'

'What do you mean? What can we do?'

I told her. Malcolm's mouth opened and there was a long silence from Joyce.

'Let me get this straight,' she said eventually. 'You want me to telephone to everyone in the family . . .'

'*Everyone*,' I said emphatically. 'If a husband answers, tell him, then ask to speak to the wife, and tell her too. And vice versa.'

'Yes,' she said. 'I'm to say you're in Australia, both of you. Right?'

'Yes.'

'I'm to gush. Dreadful word, where *did* you learn it? I'm to let all this drip out as if it were of absolutely no importance but something I've just thought of? Darling, you can't mean I have to ring up *Alicia*?'

'Especially Alicia. Tell her I told you she has a boyfriend. That should stir her up nicely.'

'Darling, you don't mean it!'

'Ask her. And . . . er . . . do you know if the police are still guarding Quantum?'

'They told Donald that if he wanted constant guards, he'd have to get his own now. No one in the family wants to spend the money, so the police just have it on their occasional surveillance list, apparently.'

'And has anything else much happened in the family since we've been away?'

'No, nothing new. Thomas left Berenice, did you know that?'

'Yes . . . Is he still with Lucy?'

'Yes, darling, I think so. Do you want me to tell him too?'

'You might as well.'

'I'm to think of something to phone them about and gossip a bit, and then I'm to say that I don't really care who killed Moira, but I don't think the police were thorough. Is that right? They never thought of looking for her notepad, the one she used to keep in the kitchen, in one of the drawers of those dazzling white cabinets. When anyone telephoned when she was in the kitchen, which was a lot of the time, she doodled their names with stars and things round it and wrote notes like "Donald, Sunday, noon" when people were coming to visit. I'm to say the police could never have found it but I've just remembered it, and I wonder if it's still there. I'm thinking of telling the police about it after the weekend. Is that right?'

'That's right,' I said.

'And I'm to say, what if she wrote down the name of her murderer?'

'Yes,' I said.

'Darling, why do you think her murderer telephoned? To make an appointment to kill her? You don't mean that, do you?'

'To make an appointment to see her, yes. To kill her, I don't know.'

'But why, darling? Why do you think the killer telephoned?'

'Because Malcolm told me she didn't like people just dropping in,' I said. 'She preferred people to telephone first. And because Moira's greenhouse can't be seen from the road, the drive, or from any windows of Quantum. Malcolm made her put it where it was well out of sight on that patch of lawn surrounded by shrubs, because he didn't like it. If anyone had come to see Moira unannounced that evening, they'd have found the house empty. If they'd telephoned first, she'd have said to come round to the greenhouse, that's where she'd be.'

'I suppose that's logical, darling. The police always did say she knew her killer, but I didn't want to believe it unless it was Arthur Bellbrook. He knew her. He fits all round, darling.'

'If Arthur had killed her, why would he go back later and find her body?'

'Darling, are you *sure* it wasn't Arthur Bellbrook?'

'Positive.'

'Oh dear. All right then, darling. You want me to start those phone calls tomorrow but definitely not before ten o'clock, and to go on all day until I've reached everyone? You do realise, I hope, that I'm playing in a sort of exhibition bridge game tomorrow evening?'

'Just keep plugging along.'

'What if they're out, or away?'

'Same thing. If nothing happens and we get no results, I'll phone you on Monday evening.'

'Darling, let me go to Quantum with you.'

'No, definitely not.' I was alarmed. 'Joyce, promise me you'll stay in Surrey. Promise!'

'Darling, don't be so vehement. All right, I promise,' She paused. 'Was that old bugger in good nick when you last saw him?'

'In excellent nick,' I said.

'Can't help being fond of him, darling, but don't bloody tell him I said so. Can't go back, of course. But well, darling, if there's one thing I regret in my life it's getting that frightful man West to catch him with Alicia. If I'd had any bloody *sense*, darling, I'd have turned a blind eye and let him have his bit on the side. But there it is, I was too young to know any better.'

She said goodbye cheerfully, however, promising to do all the phone calls in the morning, and I put the receiver down slowly.

'Did you hear any of that last bit?' I asked Malcolm.

'Not a lot. Something about if she'd had any sense, she wouldn't have done something or other.'

'Wouldn't have divorced you,' I said.

He stared incredulously. 'She insisted on it.'

'Twenty-seven years later, she's changed her mind.'

He laughed. 'Poor old Joyce.' He spent no more thought on it. 'Moira didn't doodle on notepads that I know of.'

'I dare say she didn't. But if you were a murderer, would you bet on it?'

He imagined it briefly. 'I'd be very worried to hear from Joyce. I would think long and hard about going to Quantum to search for the notepad before she told the police.'

'And would you go? Or would you think, if the police didn't find it when Moira was first murdered, then it isn't there? Or if it is there, there's nothing incriminating on it?'

'I don't know if I would risk it. I think I would go. If it turned out to be a silly trap of Joyce's, I could say I'd just come to see how the house was doing.' He looked at me questioningly. 'Are we both going down there?'

'Yes, but not until morning. I'm jet-lagged. Don't know about you. I need a good sleep.'

He nodded. 'Same for me.'

'And that shopping you were doing?' he eyed the several Fortnum & Mason carrier bags with tall parcels inside. 'Essential supplies?'

'Everything I could think of. We'll go down by train and . . .'

He waved his cigar in a negative gesture. 'Car and chauffeur.' He fished out his diary with the phone numbers. 'What time here?'

Accordingly, we went in the morning in great comfort and approached Quantum circumspectly from the far side, not past the eyes of the village.

The chauffeur goggled a bit at the sight of the house, with its missing centre section and boarded-up windows and large new sign saying: 'Keep out. Building unsafe.'

'Reconstructions,' Malcolm said.

The chauffeur nodded and left, and we carried the Fortnum & Mason bags across the windy central expanse and down the passage on the far side of the staircase, going towards the playroom.

Black plastic sheeting still covered all the exposed floor space, not taut and pegged down, but wrinkled and slack. Our feet made soft crunching noises on the grit under the plastic and there were small puddles here and there as if rain had blown in. The boarded-up doors and the barred stairs looked desolate, and far above, over the roof, the second black plastic sheet flapped like sails between the rafters.

Sad, sad house. Malcolm hadn't seen it like that, and was deeply depressed. He looked at the very solid job the police had made of hammering the plywood to the door-frame of the playroom and asked me politely how I proposed to get in.

'With your fingernails?' he suggested.

I produced a few tools from one of the bags. 'There are other shops in Piccadilly,' I said. 'Boy scouts come prepared.'

I'd thought it likely that I wouldn't be able to get the plywood off easily as I understood they'd used four-inch nails, so I'd brought a hammer and chisel and a saw, and before Malcolm's astonished gaze proceeded to dig a hole through the plywood and cut out a head-high, body-wide section instead. Much quicker, less sweat.

'You didn't think of all this since yesterday, did you?' he asked.

'No. On the plane. There were a lot of hours then.'

I freed the cut-out section and put it to one side, and we went into

256

the playroom. Nothing had changed in there. Malcolm fingered the bicycles when his eyes had adjusted to the partial light, and I could see the sorrow in his body.

It was by that time nine-thirty. If Joyce by any chance phoned the right person first, the earliest we could have a visitor was about half past ten. After that, anything was possible. Or nothing.

Malcolm had wanted to know what we would do if someone came.

'All the family have keys to the outside kitchen door,' I said. 'We never had the locks changed, remember? Our visitor will go into the kitchen that way and we will go round and ... er ...'

'Lock him in,' Malcolm said.

'Roughly, yes. And then talk about confessing. Talk about what to do with the future.'

I went round myself to the kitchen door and made sure it did still unlock normally, which it did. I locked it again after a brief look inside. Still a mess in there, unswept.

I returned to the playroom and from the bags produced two stick-on mirrors, each about eight inches by ten.

'I thought you'd brought champagne,' Malcolm grumbled. 'Not saws and bloody looking-glasses.'

'The champagne's there. No ice.'

'It's cold enough without any bloody ice.' He wandered aimlessly round the playroom, finally slumping into one of the armchairs. We had both worn layers of the warmest clothes we had, leaving the suitcases in the Ritz, but the raw November air looked as if it would be a match for the Simpson's vicuna overcoat and my new Barbour, and the gloves I had bought for us in the same shop the day before. We were at least out of the wind which swirled round and through the house, but there was no heat but our own.

I stuck one of the mirrors onto the cut-out piece of plywood, and the other at the same height onto the wall which faced the playroom door, the side wall of the staircase: stuck it not exactly opposite the door but a little further along towards the hall.

'What are you doing?' Malcolm asked.

'Just making it possible for us to see anyone come up the drive without showing ourselves. Would you mind sitting in the other chair, and telling me when the mirrors are at the right angle? Look into the one on the stair wall. I'll move the other. OK?'

He rose and sat in the other chair as I'd asked, and I moved the plywood along and angled it slightly until he said, 'Stop. That's it. I can see a good patch of drive.'

I went and took his place and had a look for myself. It would have been better if the mirrors had been bigger, but they served the purpose. Anyone who came to the house that way would be visible. If they came across the fields we'd have to rely on our ears.

By eleven, Malcolm was bored. By eleven-thirty, we'd temporarily unbolted and unlocked the door at the end of the passage and been out into the bushes to solve the problem posed by no plumbing. By twelve, we were into Bollinger in disposable glasses (disgusting, Malcolm said) and at twelve-thirty ate biscuits and pâté.

No one came. It seemed to get colder. Malcolm huddled inside his overcoat in the armchair and said it had been a rotten idea in the first place.

I had had to promise him that we wouldn't stay overnight. I thought it unlikely anyway that someone would choose darkness rather than daylight for searching for a small piece of paper that could be anywhere in a fairly large room, and I'd agreed to the chauffeur returning to pick us up at abo·.t six. Left to myself, I might have waited all night, but the whole point of the exercise was that Malcolm himself should be there. We would return in the morning by daybreak.

He said, 'This person we're waiting for . . . you know who it is, don't you?'

'Well . . . I think so.'

'How sure are you, expressed as a percentage?'

'Um . . . ninety-five.'

'That's not enough.'

'No, that's why we're here.'

'Edwin,' he said. 'It's Edwin, isn't it?'

I glanced across at him, taking my gaze momentarily off the mirrors. He wanted it to be Edwin. He could bear it to be Edwin. In Edwin's own words, he could have faced it. Edwin might possibly have been capable of killing Moira, I thought: an unplanned killing, shoving her head into the potting compost because the open bag of it gave him the idea. I didn't think he had the driving force, the imagination or the guts to have attempted the rest.

When I didn't contradict him, Malcolm began saying, 'If Edwin comes . . .' and it was easier to leave it that way.

Time crept on. It was cold. By two-thirty, to stoke our internal fires, we were eating rich dark fruit cake and drinking claret. (Heresy, Malcolm said. We should have had the claret with the pâté and the champagne with the cake. As at weddings? I asked. God damn you, he said.)

I didn't feel much like laughing. It was a vigil to which there could be no good end. Malcolm knew as well as I did that he might be going to learn something he fervently didn't want to know. He didn't deep down want anyone to come. And I wanted it profoundly.

By three-thirty, he was restless. 'You don't really mean to go through all this again tomorrow, do you?'

I watched the drive. No change, as before. 'The Ritz might give us a packed lunch.'

'And Monday? Not Monday as well.' He'd agreed on three days before we'd started. The actuality was proving too much.

'We'll give up on Monday when it gets dark,' I said.

'You're so bloody persistent.'

I watched the mirrors. Come, I thought. *Come.*

'Joyce might have forgotten the phone calls,' Malcolm said.

'She wouldn't forget.'

'Edwin might have been out.'

'That's more likely.'

A light-coloured car rolled up the drive, suddenly there.

No attempt at concealment. No creeping about, looking suspicious. All confidence. Not a thought given to entrapment.

I sat still, breathing deeply.

She stood up out of the car, tall and strong. She went round to the passenger side, opened the door, and lifted out a brown cardboard box which she held in front of her, with both arms round it, as one holds groceries. I'd expected her to go straight round to the kitchen door, but she didn't do that, she walked a few steps into the central chasm, looking up and around her as if with awe.

Malcolm noticed my extreme concentration, rose to his feet and put himself between me and the mirrors so that he could see what I was looking at. I thought he would be stunned and miserably silent, but he was not in the least.

'Oh, no,' he said with annoyance. 'What's *she* doing here?'

Before I could stop him, he shot straight out of the playroom and said, 'Serena, do go away, you're spoiling the whole thing.'

I was on his heels, furious with him. Serena whirled round when she heard his voice. She saw him appear in the passage. I glimpsed her face, wide-eyed and scared. She took a step backwards, and tripped on a fold of the black plastic floor covering, and let go of the box. She tried to catch it ... touched it ... knocked it forward.

I saw the panic on her face. I had an instantaneous understanding of what she'd brought.

I yanked Malcolm back with an arm round his neck, twisting and flinging us both to find shelter behind the wall of the staircase.

We were both still falling when the world blew apart.

Nineteen

I lay short of the playroom door trying to breathe. My lungs felt collapsed. My head rang from the appalling noise, and the smell of the explosive remained as a taste as if my mouth were full of it.

Malcolm, on his stomach a few feet away, was unconscious.

The air was thick with dust and seemed to be still reverberating, though it was probably my concussion. I felt pulped. I felt utterly without strength. I felt very lucky indeed.

The house around us was still standing. We weren't under tons of new rubble. The tough old load-bearing walls that had survived the first bomb had survived the second – which hadn't anyway been the size of a suitcase.

My chest gave a heave, and breath came back. I moved, struggled to get up, tried things out. I felt bruised and unwell, but there were no broken bones; no blood. I rolled to my knees and went on them to Malcolm. He was alive, he was breathing, he was not bleeding from ears or nose: at that moment, it was enough.

I got slowly, weakly, to my feet, and walked shakily into the wide centre space. I could wish to shut my eyes, but one couldn't blot it out. One had to live through terrible things if they came one's way.

At the point where the bomb had exploded, the black floor covering had been ripped right away, and the rest was doubled over and convoluted in large torn pieces. Serena – the things that had been Serena – lay among and half under the black folds of plastic: things in emerald and frilly white clothes, pale blue leg-warmers, dark blue tights; torn edges of flesh, scarlet splashes ... a scarlet pool.

I went round covering the parts of her completely with the black folds, hiding the harrowing truth from anyone coming there unprepared. I felt ill. I felt as if my head were full of air. I was trembling uncontrollably. I thought of people who dealt often with such horrors and wondered if they ever got hardened.

Malcolm groaned in the passage. I went back to him fast. He was trying to sit up, to push himself off the floor. There was a large area already beginning to swell on his forehead, and I wondered if he'd simply been knocked out through hitting the wood floor at high speed.

'God,' he said in anguish. 'Serena . . . oh dear God.'

I helped him to his groggy feet and took him out into the garden through the side-door, and round past the office to the front of the house. I eased him into the passenger seat of Serena's car.

Malcolm put his head in his hands and wept for his daughter. I stood with my arms on top of the car and my head on those, and felt wretched and sick and unutterably old.

I'd hardly begun to wonder what to do next when a police car came into the drive and rolled slowly, as if tentatively, towards us.

The policeman I'd looked through the windows with stopped the car and stepped out. He looked young, years younger than I was.

'Someone in the village reported another explosion . . .' He looked from us to the house questioningly.

'Don't go in there,' I said. 'Get word to the superintendent. Another bomb has gone off here, and this time someone's been killed.'

Dreadful days followed, full of questions, formalities, explanations, regrets. Malcolm and I went back to the Ritz where he grieved for the lost child who had tried hard to kill him.

'But you said . . . she didn't care about my money. Why . . . why did she do it all?'

'She wanted . . .' I said, 'to put it at its simplest, I think she wanted to live at Quantum with you. That's what she's longed for since she was six, when Alicia took her away. She might perhaps have grown up sweet and normal if the courts had given you custody, but courts favour mothers, of course. She wanted to have back what had been wrenched away from her. I saw her cry about it, not long ago. It was still sharp and real to her. She wanted to be your little girl again. She refused to grow up. She dressed very often like a child.'

He was listening with stretched eyes, as if seeing familiar country haunted by devils.

'Alicia was no help to her,' I said. 'She filled her with stories of how you'd rejected her, and she actively discouraged her from maturing, because of her own little-girl act.'

'Poor Serena.' He looked tormented. 'She didn't have much luck.'

'No, she didn't.'

'But Moira . . .?' he said.

'I think Serena made herself believe that if she got rid of Moira, you would go back to Quantum and she would live there with you and look after you, and her dream would come true.'

'It doesn't make sense . . .'

'Murder has nothing to do with sense. It has to do with obsession. With compulsion, irresistible impulse, morbid drive. An act beyond reason.'

He shook his head helplessly.

'It's impossible to know,' I said, 'whether she intended to kill Moira on that day. I wish we could know, but we can't . . . she can't have meant to kill her the way she did, because no one could know there'd be a slit-open nearly full sack of potting compost waiting there, handy. If she meant to kill Moira that day, she'd have taken some sort of weapon. I've been wondering, you know, if she meant to hit her over the head and put her in the car, the way she did you.'

'God . . .'

'Anyway, after Moira was out of the way, Serena offered to live with you at Quantum and look after you, but you wouldn't have it.'

'But it wouldn't have worked, you know. I didn't even consider it seriously. It was nice of her, I thought, but I didn't want her, it's true.'

'And I expect you made it clear in a fairly testy way?'

He thought about it. 'I suppose in the end I did. She kept on about it, you see. Asked me several times. Came to Quantum to beg me. I got tired of it and said no pretty definitely. I told her not to keep bothering me . . .' He looked shattered. 'She began to hate me then, do you think?'

I nodded unhappily. 'I'd think so. I think she finally believed she would never have what she craved for. You could have given it to her, and you wouldn't. The rejection was ultimate. Absolute. Extreme. She believed it, as she'd never really believed it before. She told me she'd given you a chance, but you'd turned her down.'

He put a hand over his eyes.

'So she set out to kill you, and finally to kill the house as well . . . to destroy what she couldn't have.'

I still wondered, as I'd wondered in New York, whether it was because I, Ian, had gone back to live at Quantum with Malcolm that she'd come to that great violent protest. I had too often had what she'd yearned for. The bomb had been meant as much for me as for Malcolm, I thought.

'Do you remember that morning when she found we weren't dead?' I asked. 'She practically fainted. Everyone supposed it was from relief, but I'll bet it wasn't. She'd tried three times to kill you and it must have seemed intolerable to her that you were still alive.'

'She must have been . . . well . . . insane.'

Obsessed . . . insane. Sometimes there wasn't much difference.

Malcolm had given up champagne and gone back to scotch. The constant bubbles, I saw, had been a sort of gesture, two fingers held up defiantly in the face of danger, a gallant crutch against fear. He poured a new drink of the old stuff and stood by the window looking over Green Park.

'You knew it was Serena . . . who would come.'

'If anyone did.'

'How did you know?'

'I saw everyone, as you know. I saw what's wrong with their lives. Saw their desperations. Donald and Helen are desperate for money, but they were coping the best way they could. Bravely, really, pawning her jewellery. They thought you might help them with guaranteeing a loan, if they could find you. That's a long way from wanting to kill you.'

Malcolm nodded and drank, and watched life proceeding outside.

'Lucy,' I said, 'may have lost her inspiration but not her marbles. Edwin is petulant but not a planner, not dynamic. Thomas . . .' I paused. 'Thomas was absolutely desperate, but for peace in his house, not for the money itself. Berenice has made him deeply ineffective. He's got a long way to go, to climb back. He seemed to me incapable almost of tying his shoelaces, let alone making a time-bomb, even if he did invent the wired-up clocks.'

'Go on,' Malcolm said.

'Berenice is obsessed with herself and her desires, but her grudge is against Thomas. Money would make her quieter, but it's not money she really wants, it's a son. Killing Moira and you wouldn't achieve that.'

'And Gervase?'

'He's destroying himself. It takes all his energies. He hasn't enough left to go around killing people for money. He's lost his nerve. He drinks. You have to be courageous and sober to mess with explosives. Ursula's desperation takes her to churches and to lunches with Joyce.'

He grunted in his throat, not quite a chuckle.

Joyce had been thanked by us on the telephone on the Saturday night when we'd come back exhausted. She'd been devastated to the point of silence about what had happened and had put the phone down in tears. We phoned her again in the morning. 'I got Serena first,' she said sorrowfully. 'She must have gone out and bought all the stuff . . . I can't bear it. That dear little girl, so sweet when she was little, even though I hated her mother. So *awful*.'

'Go on, then,' Malcolm said. 'You keep stopping.'

'It couldn't have been Alicia or Vivien, they're not strong enough to carry you. Alicia's new boyfriend would be, but why should he think Alicia would be better off with you dead? And I couldn't imagine any of them constructing a bomb.'

'And Ferdinand?'

'I really couldn't see it, could you? He has no particular worries. He's good at his job. He's easy-going most of the time. Not him. Not Debs. That's the lot.'

'So did you come to Serena just by elimination?' He turned from the window, searching my face.

'No,' I said slowly. 'I thought of them all together, all their troubles and heart-aches. To begin with, when Moira died, I thought, like everyone else did, that she was killed to stop her taking half your money. I thought the attacks on you were for money, too. It was the obvious thing. And then, when I'd seen them all, when I understood all the turmoils going on under apparently normal exteriors, I began to wonder whether the money really mattered at all . . . And when I was in New York, I was thinking of them all again but taking the money out . . . and with Serena . . . everything fitted.'

He stirred restlessly and went to sit down.

'It wouldn't have convinced the police,' he said.

'Nor you either,' I agreed. 'You had to see for yourself.' We fell silent, thinking what in fact he had seen, his daughter come to blast out the kitchen rather than search it for a notepad.

'But didn't you have any proof?' he said eventually. 'I mean, any real reason to think it was her? Something you could put your finger on.'

'Not really. Nothing that would stand up in court. Except that I think it was Serena who got Norman West to find you in Cambridge, not Alicia, as West himself thought.'

He stared. 'Why do you think that?'

'Alicia said she hadn't done it. Both West and I thought she was lying, but I think now she was telling the truth. Do you remember the tape from my telephone answering machine? Do you remember Serena's voice? "Mummy wants to know where Daddy is. I told her you wouldn't know, but she insisted I ask." That's what she said. Alicia told me positively that she herself hadn't wanted to know where you were. If Alicia's telling the truth, it was *Serena* who wanted to know, and she wanted to know because she'd lost us after failing to run you over. Lost us because of us scooting up to London in the Rolls.'

'My God,' he said. 'What happened to the tape? I suppose it got lost in the rubble.'

'No, it's in a box in the garage at Quantum. A few things were saved. Several of your gold-and-silver brushes are there too.'

He waved the thought away, although he was pleased enough. 'I suppose Serena did sound like Alicia on the telephone. I sometimes thought it was Alicia, when she phoned. Breathless and girlish. You know. Norman West just got it wrong.'

'She did call herself Mrs Pembroke,' I pointed out. 'Just to confuse matters. Or maybe she said Ms and he didn't hear clearly.'

'It doesn't much matter.' He was quiet for a while. 'Although it was terrible yesterday, it was the best thing, really. We'll grieve and get over this. She couldn't have borne to be locked up, could she, not with all that energy . . . not in drab clothes.'

On that Sunday morning also, we began telephoning to the family to tell them what had happened. I expected to find that Joyce had already told them, but she hadn't. She'd talked to them all the day before, they said, but that was all.

We left a lot of stunned silences behind us. A lot of unstoppable tears.

Malcolm told Alicia first, and asked if she'd like him to come to see her, to comfort her. When she could speak, she said no. She said Serena didn't kill Moira, Ian did. Everything was Ian's fault. Malcolm put the receiver down slowly, rubbed his hand over his face, and told me what she'd said.

'It's very hard,' he said, excusing her, 'to face that you've given birth to a murderer.'

'She helped to make her a murderer,' I said.

I spoke to my four brothers and to Lucy. Malcolm told Vivien last. They all asked where we were: Joyce had told them we were in Australia. In London, we said, but didn't add where. Malcolm said he couldn't face having them all descend on him before he was ready. By the end, I was dropping with fatigue and Malcolm had finished off half a bottle. Long before bedtime, we were asleep.

We went back to Quantum on Monday, as we'd promised the police, and found Mr Smith poking around like old times.

All physical signs of Serena had mercifully been taken away, and all that remained were the torn flaps of black plastic that hadn't been near her.

Mr Smith shook hands with us dustily and after a few commiserating platitudes came out with his true opinions.

'Anyone who carries a fully-wired explosive device from place to place is raving mad. You don't connect the battery until the device is where you want it to go off. If you're me, you don't insert the detonator, either. You keep them separate.'

'I don't suppose she meant to drop it,' I said.

'Mind you, she was also unlucky,' Mr Smith said judiciously. 'It is possible, but I myself wouldn't risk it, to drop ANFO with a detonator in it and have it not explode. But maybe dropping it caused the clock wires to touch.'

'Have you found the clock?' I asked.

'Patience,' he said, and went back to looking.

A policeman fending away a few sensation seekers told us that Superintendent Yale had been detained, and couldn't meet us there: please would we go to the police station. We went, and found him in his office.

He shook hands. He offered sympathy.

He asked if we knew why Serena had gone to Quantum with a second bomb, and we told him. Asked if we knew why she should have killed Moira and tried to kill Malcolm. We told him my theories. He listened broodingly.

'There will be an inquest,' he said. 'Mr Ian can formally identify the remains. You won't need to see them . . . her . . . again, though.

267

The coroner's verdict will be death by misadventure, I've no doubt. You may be needed to give an account of what happened. You'll be informed of all that in due course.' He paused. 'Yesterday, we went to Miss Pembroke's flat and conducted a search. We found a few items of interest. I am going to show you some objects and I'd be glad if you'd say whether you can identify them or not.'

He reached into a carton very like the one Serena had been carrying, which stood on his desk. He brought out a pile of twenty or thirty exercise books with spiral bindings and blue covers and after that a tin large enough to contain a pound of sweets, with a picture on top.

'*The Old Curiosity Shop*,' Malcolm said sadly.

'No possibility of doubt,' Yale nodded. 'The title's printed across the bottom of the picture.'

'Are there any detonators in it?' I asked.

'No, just cotton wool. Mr Smith wonders if she used more than one detonator for each bomb, just to make sure. He says amateurs are mad enough to try anything.'

I picked up one of the notebooks and opened it.

'Have you seen those before, sirs?' Yale asked.

'No,' I said, and Malcolm shook his head.

In Serena's looping handwriting, I read:

'Daddy and I had such fun in the garden this morning. He was teaching the dogs to fetch sticks and I was throwing the sticks. We picked a lot of beautiful daffodils and when we went indoors I put them all in vases in all the rooms. I cooked some lamb chops for lunch and made mint sauce and peas and roast potatoes and gravy and for pudding we had ice-cream and peaches. Daddy is going to buy me some white boots with zips and silver tassels. He calls me his princess, isn't that lovely? In the afternoon, we went down to the stream and picked some watercress for tea. Daddy took his socks off and rolled up his trousers and the boys *no* the boys weren't there I won't have them in my stories it was Daddy who picked the watercress and we washed it and ate it with brown bread. This evening I will sit on his lap and he will stroke my hair and call me his little princess, his little darling, and it will be lovely.'

I flicked through the pages. The whole book was full. Speechlessly I handed it to Malcolm, open where I'd read.

'All the notebooks are like that,' Yale said. 'We've had them all read right through. She's been writing them for years, I would say.'

'But you don't mean . . . they're recent?' I said.

'Some of them are, certainly. I've seen several sets of books like these in my career. Compulsive writing, I believe it's called. These of your sister's are wholesome and innocent by comparison. You can't imagine the pornography and brutality I've read. They make you despair.'

Malcolm, plainly moved, flicking over pages, said, 'She says I bought her a pretty red dress . . . a white sweater with blue flowers on it . . . a bright yellow leotard – I hardly know what a leotard is. Poor girl. Poor girl.'

'She bought them herself,' I said. 'Three or four times a week.'

Yale tilted the stack of notebooks up, brought out the bottom one and handed it to me. 'This is the latest. It changes at the end. You may find it interesting.'

I turned to the last entries in the book and with sorrow read:

'Daddy is going away from me and I don't want him any more. I think perhaps I will kill him. It isn't so difficult. I've done it before.'

There was a space on the page after that, and then, lower down:

'Ian is back with Daddy.'

Another space, and then,

'IAN IS AT QUANTUM WITH DADDY. I CAN'T BEAR IT.'

After yet another space, she had written my name again in larger-still capitals 'IAN' and surrounded it with a circle of little lines radiating outwards: an explosion with my name in the centre.

That was the end. The rest of the notebook was empty.

Malcolm read the page over my arm and sighed deeply. 'Can I have them?' he said to Yale. 'You don't need them, do you? There won't be a trial.'

Yale hesitated but said he saw no reason to retain them. He pushed the pile of books towards Malcolm and put the sweet tin on top.

'And the lighthouse and clock,' I said. 'Could we have those?'

He produced the Lego box from a cupboard, wrote a list of what we were taking on an official-looking receipt and got Malcolm to sign it.

'All very upsetting, Mr Pembroke,' he said, again shaking hands, 'but we can mark our case closed.'

We took the sad trophies back to the Ritz, and that afternoon Malcolm wrote and posted cheques that would solve every financial problem in the Pembrokes' repertoire.

'What about the witches?' he said. 'If Helen and that dreadful Edwin and Berenice and Ursula and Debs are all having their own share, what about those other three?'

'Up to you,' I said. 'They're your wives.'

'*Ex*-wives.' He shrugged and wrote cheques for them also. 'Easy come, easy go,' he said. 'Bloody Alicia doesn't deserve it.'

'Engines work better with a little oil,' I said.

'Greasing their palms, you mean.' He still didn't believe in it. Still felt he was corrupting them by giving them wealth. Still thinking that *he* could stay sane and reasonably sensible when he had millions, but nobody else could.

He wrote a final cheque and gave it to me. I felt awkward taking it, which he found interesting.

'You should have had double,' he said.

I shook my head, reeling at noughts. 'You've post-dated it,' I said.

'Of course I have. I've post-dated all of them. I don't have that much in readies lying around in the bank. Have to sell a few shares. The family can have the promise now and the cash in a month.'

He licked the envelopes. Not a cruel man, I thought.

On Tuesday, because I wished it, we went to see Robin.

'He won't remember Serena,' Malcolm said.

'No, I don't expect so.'

We went in the car I'd hired the day before for going to Quantum, and on the way stopped again to buy toys and chocolate and a packet of balloons.

I had taken with us the Lego lighthouse and the Mickey Mouse clock, thinking they might interest Robin, over which Malcolm shook his head.

'He won't be able to make them work, you know.'

'He might remember them. You never know. They used to be his and Peter's, after all. Serena gave them the clock and made them the lighthouse.'

Robin's room was very cold because of the open french windows. Malcolm tentatively went across and closed them, and Robin at once flung them open. Malcolm patted Robin's shoulder and moved away from the area, and Robin looked at him searchingly, in puzzlement, and at me the same way, as he sometimes did: trying, it seemed, to remember, and never quite getting there.

We gave him the new toys which he looked at and put down again, and after a while I opened the Lego box and brought out the old ones.

He looked at them for only a moment and then went on a long wander round and round the room, several times. Then he came to me, pointed at the packet of balloons and made a puffing noise.

'Good Lord,' Malcolm said.

I opened the packet and blew up several balloons, tying knots in the necks, as I always did. Robin went on making puffing noises until I'd blown up every balloon in the packet. His face looked agitated. He puffed harder to make me go faster.

When they were all scattered round the room, red, yellow, blue, green and white, bobbing about in stray air currents, shiny and festive, he went round bursting them with furious vigour, sticking his forefinger straight into some, pinching others, squashing the last one against the wall with the palm of his hand, letting out the anger he couldn't express.

Most times, after this ritual, he was released and at peace, and would retreat into a corner and sit staring into space or huddled up, rocking.

This time, however, he went over to the table, picked up the lighthouse, pulled it roughly apart into four or five pieces and threw them forcefully out of the wide-open window. Then he picked up the clock and with violence yanked the wires off, including the Mickey Mouse hands.

Malcolm was aghast. Docile Robin's rage shouted out of his mute body. His strength was a revelation.

He took the clock in his hand and walked round the room smashing it against the wall at each step. Step, *smash*, step, *smash*, step, *smash*.

'Stop him,' Malcolm said in distress.

'No . . . he's talking,' I said.

'He's not talking.'

'He's telling us . . .'

Robin reached the window and threw the mangled clock far and high into the garden. Then he started shouting, roaring without words, his voice rough from disuse and hoarse with the change taking place from boy into man. The sound seemed to excite him until his body was reverberating, pouring out sound, the dam of

271

silence swept away. 'Aaah ... aaah ... aaah ...' and then real words, 'No ... No ... No ... Serena ... No ... Serena ... No ... Serena ... No ...' He shouted to the skies, to the fates, to the wicked unfairness of the fog in his brain. Shouted in fury and frenzy. 'Serena ... No ... Serena ... No ...' and on and on until it became mindless, without meaning, just words.

I stepped close beside him in the end and yelled in his ear, 'Serena's dead.'

He stopped shouting immediately. 'Serena's dead,' I repeated. 'Like the clock. Smashed. Finished. Dead.'

He turned and looked at me vaguely, his mouth open, no sound coming out, the sudden silence as unnerving as the shouting had been.

'Serena-is-dead,' I said, making each word separate, giving it weight.

'He doesn't understand,' Malcolm said: and Robin went away and sat in a corner with his arms round his knees and his head down, and began rocking.

'The nurses think he understands quite a lot,' I said. 'Whether he understands that Serena is dead, I don't know. But at least we've tried to tell him.' Robin went on rocking as if we weren't there.

'What does it matter?' Malcolm said helplessly.

'It matters because if he does understand, it may give him rest. I brought the lighthouse and the clock because I wondered if Robin remembered anything at all. I thought it worth trying ... didn't expect quite these results ... but I think he smashed the clock Serena gave him because it reminded him of her, because she gave it to him and Peter shortly before the car crash. Somewhere in that woolly head, things sometimes connect.'

Malcolm nodded, puzzled and instinctively alarmed.

'One could almost think it was that afternoon,' I said, 'seeing the twins happy at Quantum where she hungered to be, seeing you there with them, loving them; perhaps it was that afternoon which finally tipped her over into the insanity of trying to make her fantasy come true. It didn't come true ... you met Moira ... but I'm certain she tried.'

Malcolm was staring, saying 'No! Don't say it! *Don't!*'

I said it anyway. 'I think Robin saw the hit-and-run driver who forced their car off the road. In whatever mangled dreamlike way, he

272

knows who it was. No Serena, no Serena, no . . . You heard him. I've thought ever since New York that it could possibly have happened that way. Serena's obsession was full-blown a long time ago, long before she got rid of Moira. I think she killed Peter . . . and Coochie.'

Epilogue

We all went back to Quantum a year later for the Grand Reopening Ceremony, the house bedecked with garlands and champagne corks popping.

After much soul-searching, Malcolm had decided to rebuild. Without Quantum as its centre, the family would have fallen apart, and he didn't want that to happen. When he told everyone of his intention, there was great communal relief, and he saw without question that it was the right thing to do.

The rancour level lessened dramatically after the arrival of the cheques and the production of his will for inspection, and I was suddenly not everyone's villain, though still and forever Alicia's. Malcolm, having deleted Serena by codicil, sent his will to the Central Probate Office for registration and let everyone know it.

Malcolm still felt that he had pampered and corrupted his children, but he had to admit they were happier because of it. Dramatically happier in some cases, like Donald and Helen whose problems had all been financial. Helen redeemed her baubles and stopped painting china, and Donald paid off the finance company and the bank and ran the golf club with a light heart.

A few weeks after Serena's death, Helen asked me over to Marblehill House. 'A drink before dinner,' she said. I went on a freezing evening in December and she surprised me by kissing me in greeting. Donald was standing with his back to a roaring fire, looking contentedly pompous.

'We wanted to thank you,' Helen said. 'And I suppose ... to apologise.'

'There's no need.'

'Oh, yes. We all know there is. Not everyone will say so, but they know.'

'How's Malcolm?' Donald asked.

'He's fine.'

Donald nodded. Even the fact that Malcolm and I were still together seemed no longer to worry him, and later, when we'd sat round the fire drinking for a while, he asked me to stay on for dinner. I stayed, and although we were never going to be in and out of each other's houses every five minutes, at least on that evening we reached a peaceful plateau as brothers.

Some time later, I went to see Lucy. She and Edwin had made no changes to their cottage and had no plans to move, much to Edwin's disgust.

'We should live somewhere more *suitable*,' he said to her crossly. 'I never thought we would stay here when you inherited.'

Lucy looked at him with affection. 'If you want to leave, Edwin, you can, now that you have money of your own.'

He was disconcerted; open mouthed. 'I don't want to leave,' he said, and it was clearly the truth.

Lucy said to me, 'I'll find a good use for my money: keep the capital, give away most of the income. We have no anxieties now, and that's a relief, I agree, but I haven't changed altogether. I don't believe in luxurious living. It's bad for the soul. I'm staying here.' She ate a handful of raisins determinedly, the old man looking out of her eyes.

Thomas was no longer her guest. Thomas, against all advice, had gone back to Berenice.

I called at Arden Haciendas one dark cold afternoon and Thomas opened the front door himself, looking blank when he saw me.

'Berenice is out,' he said, letting me in.

'I came to see you. How are you doing?'

'Not so bad,' he said, but he still looked defeated.

He gave me a drink. He knew where the gin was, and the tonic. He said Berenice and he had been going to marriage guidance sessions, but he didn't know that they were doing much good.

'You can get vasectomies reversed sometimes,' I said.

'Yes, but I don't really want to. Suppose I did, and we had another girl? Unless Berenice can get over not having sons, I'm going to leave her again. I told her.'

I gazed at him, awestruck. 'What did she say?'

'Nothing much. I think she's afraid of me, really.'

As long as it didn't go to his head, I thought that might not be at all a bad thing.

275

I went to see Gervase and Ursula soon after. The change in Ursula, who let me in, was like unwrapping a brown paper parcel and finding Christmas inside. The old skirt, shirt, pullover and pearls had vanished. She wore narrow scarlet trousers, a huge white sweater and a baroque gold chain. She smiled at me like a shy conspirator and came with me into the sitting-room. Gervase, if not overpoweringly friendly, seemed ready for neutrality and a truce.

'I told Gervase,' Ursula said sweetly, 'that now that I can afford to leave him and take the girls with me, I'm staying because I want to, not because I have to. I'm staying as long as he gets help with this ridiculous fixation about his birth. Who *cares* that Malcolm wasn't married to Alicia at the time? I certainly don't. No one does. Ferdinand doesn't. Ferdinand's been very good, he's been over here several times giving Gervase advice.'

Gervase, who in the past would have shouted her down, listened almost with gratitude. The bear that had run himself into a thicket was being led out by compassionate hands.

Ferdinand, when I called, was in rocketing good spirits. He and Debs had moved immediately from their small bare bungalow into a large bare bungalow with a tennis court, a swimming pool and a three-car garage. Affluence was fun, he said; but one of the new house's rooms was also his office. He was going on with his job.

'I took your remarks to heart, you know,' he said. 'Took a look at what Alicia had done to us. I don't listen to her any more. She won't get rid of Debs and she won't get rid of Ursula. Have you seen Ursula? Transformation! I've told Gervase he has a wife in a million and a mother who's nothing but trouble. I've been talking to him about illegitimacy . . . isn't that what you wanted?' He punched my arm lightly. 'Stay to dinner?' he said.

I didn't go to see either Alicia or Vivien. I stayed a few nights with Joyce.

'Darling, how's that old fool getting along?'

'He spends a lot of time at Quantum with the builders.'

'Don't let him catch pneumonia. It's bitter outside.'

'He does what he likes,' I said.

'Darling, when did he not?'

Joyce rushed busily away to a bridge tournament in Paris, kissing my cheek, patting me with approval, telling me to be careful not to break my neck in those frightful races I insisted on riding.

I gave her the assurances and went back to Lambourn, now my

home instead of Epsom. I'd asked the trainer I'd been riding exercise for if he knew of anyone needing a second-string stable jockey, if I should take the giant step of turning professional.

He stared. 'I heard you don't need to. Didn't you come into money?'

'Forget the money. What chance would I have?'

'I saw you win that race at Kempton,' he said. 'If you turn pro, if you come to Lambourn, I'll give you plenty of rides.'

He was as good as his word, and George and Jo, astonished but happy, entered their few horses to fit in.

I bought a house in Lambourn and Malcolm came to live in it while Quantum was rebuilt. Malcolm loved Lambourn. He went often up to the Downs with the trainer I was riding for to watch the horses work, and far from losing interest in racing, grew more and more involved. When I won my first professional race, the Bollinger ran through Lambourn like a river.

By the day the following November that we all went to the house for the Grand Re-opening (with embossed invitation cards and an army of caterers), everyone's lives had settled into the new patterns.

Malcolm had been to the 'Arc' again, and round the world with Ramsey Osborn. Chrysos had won the Futurity at Doncaster and was tipped for the next year's Derby. Blue Clancy had gone to stud, syndicated for millions.

I had ended my first professional season with a respectable score and at the start of my second had become the chief retained jockey for the stable. I would be a trainer in the end, I supposed. Meantime, I felt alive and fulfilled as never before.

Lucy and Edwin were still eating healthily in the cottage. Lucy, coming to terms with not writing more poetry herself, had started on a scholarly biography and commentary on the Life and Work of Thomas Stearns Eliot. Edwin was still doing the shopping.

Donald and Helen, arm in arm, wandered round the garden like lovers.

Ferdinand fussed over Debs, who was pregnant.

Gervase had recovered most of his bullishness, which seemed to reassure Ursula rather than cow her. She came in a mink coat, laughing with pleasure.

In Berenice, the fire had gone out: in Thomas, it had been faintly rekindled. No longer needing a job, he was learning to play golf. Berenice was house-hunting, with Thomas's approval.

Alicia came looking girlish, trilling away in a voice like an echo of Serena's, and everyone made polite remarks to her with closed teeth.

Vivien complained that Malcolm had re-done the house too much in Coochie's taste. Joyce made diplomatic friends with the married couple he had engaged to look after him. He — and they — had been living in the house for a week.

All of the grandchildren were there, re-exploring the place: children's voices again in the garden. Robin, far away, had fallen silent once more and had never since that violent day wanted me to blow up balloons.

Malcolm and I walked out through the new sitting-room windows and from the lawn looked up at the house. It felt whole again, not just physically, but at peace.

'I don't feel Serena's here, do you?' Malcolm said.

'No, she isn't.'

'I was afraid she might be. I'm glad she's not.'

We went further down the lawn.

'Did you notice I'd taken the golden dolphin and the amethyst tree and so on out of the wall and put them in the sitting-room?' he asked casually.

'Yes, I did.'

'I sold the gold too.'

I glanced at him. He looked quizzically back.

'The price rose sharply this year, as I thought it would. I took the profit. There's nothing in the wall now except spiders and dust.'

'Never mind.'

'I'm leaving the clause in the will though.' The family had been curious about his leaving me the piece of wire, and he'd refused to explain. 'I'll buy more gold, and sell it. Buy and sell. Forward and backward. One of these days . . .' his blue eyes gleamed '. . . you may win on the nod.'

In the Frame

My thanks to two professional artists
Michael Jeffery of Australia
and
Josef Jira of Czechoslovakia

who generously showed me their studios,
their methods, their minds and their lives.

Also to the many art galleries whose experts gave me
information and help, and particularly to Peter Johnson
of Oscar and Peter Johnson, London, SW1, and to the
Stud and Stable gallery, Ascot.

for Caroline
sound asleep

one

I stood on the outside of disaster, looking in.

There were three police cars outside my cousin's house, and an ambulance with its blue turret light revolving ominously, and people bustling in seriously through his open front door. The chill wind of early autumn blew dead brown leaves sadly on to the driveway, and harsh scurrying clouds threatened worse to come. Six o'clock, Friday evening, Shropshire, England.

Intermittent bright white flashes from the windows spoke of photography in progress within. I slid my satchel from my shoulder and dumped both it and my suitcase on the grass verge, and with justifiable foreboding completed my journey to the house.

I had travelled by train to stay for the weekend. No cousin with car to meet me as promised, so I had started to walk the mile and a half of country road, sure he would come tearing along soon in his muddy Peugeot, full of jokes and apologies and plans.

No jokes.

He stood in the hall, dazed and grey. His body inside his neat business suit looked limp, and his arms hung straight down from the shoulders as if his brain had forgotten they were there. His head was turned slightly towards the sitting-room, the source of the flashes, and his eyes were stark with shock.

'Don?' I said. I walked towards him. 'Donald!'

He didn't hear me. A policeman, however, did. He came swiftly from the sitting-room in his dark blue uniform, took me by the arm and swung me strongly and unceremoniously back towards the door.

'Out of here, sir,' he said. 'If you please.'

The strained eyes slid uncertainly our way.

'Charles . . .' His voice was hoarse.

The policeman's grip loosened very slightly. 'Do you know this man, sir?' he asked Donald.

'I'm his cousin,' I said.

'Oh.' He took his hand off, told me to stay where I was and look after Mr Stuart, and returned to the sitting-room to consult.

'What's happened?' I said.

Don was past answering. His head turned again towards the

11

sitting-room door, drawn to a horror he could no longer see. I disobeyed the police instructions, took ten quiet steps, and looked in.

The familiar room was unfamiliarly bare. No pictures, no ornaments, no edge-to-edge floor covering of oriental rugs. Just bare grey walls, chintz-covered sofas, heavy furniture pushed awry, and a great expanse of dusty wood-block flooring.

And on the floor, my cousin's young wife, bloody and dead.

The big room was scattered with busy police, measuring, photographing, dusting for fingerprints. I knew they were there; didn't see them. All I saw was Regina lying on her back, her face the colour of cream.

Her eyes were half open, still faintly bright, and her lower jaw had fallen loose, outlining brutally the shape of the skull. A pool of urine lay wetly on the parquet around her sprawled legs, and one arm was flung out sideways with the dead white fingers curling upwards as if in supplication.

There had been no mercy.

I looked at the scarlet mess of her head and felt the blood draining from my own.

The policeman who had grabbed me before turned round from his consultation with another, saw me swaying in the doorway, and took quick annoyed strides back to my side.

'I told you to wait outside, sir,' he said with exasperation, stating clearly that my faintness was my own fault.

I nodded dumbly and went back into the hall. Donald was sitting on the stairs, looking at nothing. I sat abruptly on the floor near him and put my head between my knees.

'I . . . f . . . found . . . her,' he said.

I swallowed. What could one say? It was bad enough for me, but he had lived with her, and loved her. The faintness passed away slowly, leaving a sour feeling of sickness. I leaned back against the wall behind me and wished I knew how to help him.

'She's . . . never . . . home . . . on F . . . Fridays,' he said.

'I know.'

'S . . . six. S . . . six o'clock . . . she comes b . . . back. Always.'

'I'll get you some brandy,' I said.

'She shouldn't . . . have been . . . here . . .'

12

I pushed myself off the floor and went into the dining-room, and it was there that the significance of the bare sitting-room forced itself into consciousness. In the dining-room too there were bare walls, bare shelves, and empty drawers pulled out and dumped on the floor. No silver ornaments. No silver spoons or forks. No collection of antique china. Just a jumble of table mats and napkins and broken glass.

My cousin's house had been burgled. And Regina . . . Regina, who was never home on Fridays . . . had walked in . . .

I went over to the plundered sideboard, flooding with anger and wanting to smash in the heads of all greedy, callous, vicious people who cynically devastated the lives of total strangers. Compassion was all right for saints. What I felt was plain hatred, fierce and basic.

I found two intact glasses, but all the drink had gone. Furiously I stalked through the swing door into the kitchen and filled the electric kettle.

In that room too, the destruction had continued, with stores swept wholesale off the shelves. What valuables, I wondered, did thieves expect to find in kitchens? I jerkily made two mugs of tea and rummaged in Regina's spice cupboard for the cooking brandy, and felt unreasonably triumphant when it proved to be still there. The sods had missed that, at least.

Donald still sat unmoving on the stairs. I pressed the cup of strong sweet liquid into his hands and told him to drink, and he did, mechanically.

'She's never home . . . on Fridays,' he said.

'No,' I agreed, and wondered just how many people knew there was no one home on Fridays.

We both slowly finished the tea. I took his mug and put it with mine on the floor, and sat near him as before. Most of the hall furniture had gone. The small Sheraton desk . . . the studded leather chair . . . the nineteenth-century carriage clock . . .

'Christ, Charles,' he said.

I glanced at his face. There were tears, and dreadful pain. I could do nothing, nothing, to help him.

*

The impossible evening lengthened to midnight, and beyond.

The police, I suppose, were efficient, polite, and not unsympathetic, but they left a distinct impression that they felt their job was to catch criminals, not to succour the victims. It seemed to me that there was also, in many of their questions, a faint hovering doubt, as if it were not unknown for householders to arrange their own well-insured burglaries, and for smooth-seeming swindles to go horrifically wrong.

Donald didn't seem to notice. He answered wearily, automatically, with long pauses sometimes between question and answer.

Yes, the missing goods were well insured.

Yes, they had been insured for years.

Yes, he had been to his office all day as usual.

Yes, he had been out to lunch. A sandwich in a pub.

He was a wine shipper.

His office was in Shrewsbury.

He was thirty-seven years old.

Yes, his wife was much younger. Twenty-two.

He couldn't speak of Regina without stuttering, as if his tongue and lips were beyond his control. She always s . . . spends F . . . Fridays . . . working . . . in a f . . . friend's . . . flower . . . shop.

'Why?'

Donald looked vaguely at the Detective Inspector, sitting opposite him across the dining-room table. The matched antique dining chairs had gone. Donald sat in a garden armchair brought from the sunroom. The Inspector, a constable and I sat on kitchen stools.

'What?'

'Why did she work in a flower shop on Fridays?'

'She . . . she . . . l . . . likes . . .'

I interrupted brusquely. 'She was a florist before she married Donald. She liked to keep her hand in. She used to spend Fridays making those table arrangement things for dances and weddings and things like that . . .' And wreaths, too, I thought, and couldn't say it.

'Thank you, sir, but I'm sure Mr Stuart can answer for himself.'

'And I'm sure he can't.'

The Detective Inspector diverted his attention my way.

14

'He's too shocked,' I said.

'Are you a doctor, sir?' His voice held polite disbelief, which it was entitled to, no doubt. I shook my head impatiently. He glanced at Donald, pursed his lips, and turned back to me. His gaze wandered briefly over my jeans, faded denim jacket, fawn polo-neck, and desert boots, and returned to my face, unimpressed.

'Very well, sir. Name?'

'Charles Todd.'

'Age?'

'Twenty-nine.'

'Occupation?'

'Painter.'

The constable unemotionally wrote down these scintillating details in his pocket-sized notebook.

'Houses or pictures?' asked the Inspector.

'Pictures.'

'And your movements today, sir?'

'Caught the two-thirty from Paddington and walked from the local station.'

'Purpose of visit?'

'Nothing special. I come here once or twice a year.'

'Good friends, then?'

'Yes.'

He nodded non-committally. Turned his attention again to Donald and asked more questions, but patiently and without pressure.

'And what time do you normally reach home on Fridays, sir?'

Don said tonelessly, 'Five. About.'

'And today?'

'Same.' A spasm twitched the muscles of his face. 'I saw . . . the house had been broken into . . . I telephoned . . .'

'Yes, sir. We received your call at six minutes past five. And after you had telephoned, you went into the sitting-room, to see what had been stolen?'

Donald didn't answer.

'Our sergeant found you there, sir, if you remember.'

'Why?' Don said in anguish. 'Why did she come home?'

15

'I expect we'll find out, sir.'

The careful exploratory questions went on and on, and as far as I could see achieved nothing except to bring Donald ever closer to all-out breakdown.

I, with a certain amount of shame, grew ordinarily hungry, having not bothered to eat earlier in the day. I thought with regret of the dinner I had been looking forward to, with Regina tossing in unmeasured ingredients and herbs and wine and casually producing a gourmet feast. Regina with her cap of dark hair and ready smile, chatty and frivolous and anti-bloodsports. A harmless girl, come to harm.

At some point during the evening her body was loaded into the ambulance and driven away. I heard it happen, but Donald gave no sign of interpreting the sounds. I thought that probably his mind was raising barriers against the unendurable, and one couldn't blame him.

The Inspector rose finally and stretched the kinks caused by the kitchen stool out of legs and spine. He said he would be leaving a constable on duty at the house all night, and that he would return himself in the morning. Donald nodded vaguely, having obviously not listened properly to a word, and when the police had gone still sat like an automaton in the chair, with no energy to move.

'Come on,' I said. 'Let's go to bed.'

I took his arm, persuaded him to his feet, and steered him up the stairs. He came in a daze, unprotesting.

His and Regina's bedroom was a shambles, but the twin-bedded room prepared for me was untouched. He flopped full-length in his clothes and put his arm up over his eyes, and in appalling distress asked the unanswerable question of all the world's sufferers.

'*Why?* Why did it have to happen to *us?*'

I stayed with Donald for a week, during which time some questions, but not that one, were answered.

One of the easiest was the reason for Regina's premature return home. She and the flower-shop friend, who had been repressing annoyance with each other for weeks, had erupted into a quarrel of enough bitterness to make Regina leave at once. She had driven away at about two-thirty, and had probably gone straight home, as it was considered she had been dead for at least two hours by five o'clock.

This information, expressed in semi-formal sentences, was given to Donald by the Detective Inspector on Saturday afternoon. Donald walked out into the autumnal garden and wept.

The Inspector, Frost by name and cool by nature, came quietly into the kitchen and stood beside me watching Donald with his bowed head among the apple trees.

'I would like you to tell me what you can about the relationship between Mr and Mrs Stuart.'

'You'd like *what?*'

'How did they get on?'

'Can't you tell for yourself?'

He answered neutrally after a pause. 'The intensity of grief shown is not always an accurate indication of the intensity of love felt.'

'Do you always talk like that?'

A faint smile flickered and died. 'I was quoting from a book on psychology.'

' "Not always" means it usually is,' I said.

He blinked.

'Your book is bunk,' I said.

'Guilt and remorse can manifest themselves in an excess of mourning.'

'Dangerous bunk,' I added. 'And as far as I could see, the honeymoon was by no means over.'

'After three years?'

'Why not?'

He shrugged and didn't answer. I turned away from the sight of Donald and said, 'What are the chances of getting back any of the stuff from this house?'

'Small, I should think. Where antiques are involved, the goods are likely to be halfway across the Atlantic before the owner returns from his holidays.'

'Not this time, though,' I objected.

He sighed. 'Next best thing. There have been hundreds of

similar break-ins during recent years and very little has been re-covered. Antiques are big business these days.'

'Connoisseur thieves?' I said sceptically.

'The prison library service reports that all their most requested books are on antiques. All the little chummies boning up to jump on the bandwagon as soon as they get out.'

He sounded suddenly quite human. 'Like some coffee?' I said.

He looked at his watch, raised his eyebrows, and accepted. He sat on a kitchen stool while I fixed the mugs, a fortyish man with thin sandy hair and a well-worn grey suit.

'Are you married?' he asked.

'Nope.'

'In love with Mrs Stuart?'

'You do try it on, don't you?'

'If you don't ask, you don't find out.'

I put the milk bottle and a sugar basin on the table and told him to help himself. He stirred his coffee reflectively.

'When did you visit this house last?' he said.

'Last March. Before they went off to Australia.'

'Australia?'

'They went to see the vintage there. Donald had some idea of shipping Australian wine over in bulk. They were away for at least three months. Why didn't their house get robbed *then*, when they were safely out of the way?'

He listened to the bitterness in my voice. 'Life is full of nasty ironies.' He pursed his lips gingerly to the hot coffee, drew back, and blew gently across the top of the mug. 'What would you all have been doing today? In the normal course of events?'

I had to think what day it was. Saturday. It seemed totally unreal.

'Going to the races,' I said. 'We always go to the races when I come to stay.'

'Fond of racing, were they?' The past tense sounded wrong. Yet so much was now past. I found it a great deal more difficult than he did, to change gear.

'Yes ... but I think they only go ... went ... because of me.'

He tried the coffee again and managed a cautious sip. 'In what way do you mean?' he asked.

'What I paint,' I said, 'is mostly horses.'

Donald came in through the back door, looking red-eyed and exhausted.

'The Press are making a hole in the hedge,' he said leadenly.

Inspector Frost clicked his teeth, got to his feet, opened the door to the hall and the interior of the house, and called out loudly.

'Constable? Go and stop those reporters from breaking into the garden.'

A distant voice replied 'Sir', and Frost apologized to Donald. 'Can't get rid of them entirely, you know, sir. They have their editors breathing down their necks. They pester the life out of us at times like these.'

All day long the road outside Donald's house had been lined with cars, which disgorged crowds of reporters, photographers and plain sensation-seekers every time anyone went out of the front door. Like a hungry wolf pack they lay in wait, and I supposed that they would eventually pounce on Donald himself. Regard for his feelings was nowhere in sight.

'Newspapers listen to the radio on the police frequencies,' Frost said gloomily. 'Sometimes the Press arrive at the scene of a crime before we can get there ourselves.'

At any other time I would have laughed, but it wouldn't have been much fun for Donald if it had happened in his case. The police, of course, had thought at first that it more or less had, because I had heard that the constable who had tried to eject me forcibly had taken me for a spearheading scribbler.

Donald sat down heavily on a stool and rested his elbows wearily on the table.

'Charles,' he said, 'If you wouldn't mind heating it, I'd like some of that soup now.'

'Sure,' I said, surprised. He had rejected it earlier as if the thought of food revolted him.

Frost's head went up as if at a signal, and his whole body straightened purposefully, and I realized he had merely been coasting along until then, waiting for some such moment. He waited some more while I opened a can of Campbell's condensed, sloshed it and some water and cooking brandy into a

19

saucepan, and stirred until the lumps dissolved. He drank his coffee and waited while Donald disposed of two platefuls and a chunk of brown bread. Then, politely, he asked me to take myself off, and when I'd gone he began what Donald afterwards referred to as 'serious digging'.

It was three hours later, and growing dark, when the Inspector left. I watched his departure from the upstairs landing window. He and his attendant plain-clothes constable were intercepted immediately outside the front door by a young man with wild hair and a microphone, and before they could dodge round him to reach their car the pack on the road were streaming in full cry into the garden and across the grass.

I went methodically round the house drawing curtains, checking windows, and locking and bolting all the outside doors.

'What are you doing?' Donald asked, looking pale and tired in the kitchen.

'Pulling up the drawbridge.'

'Oh.'

In spite of his long session with the Inspector he seemed a lot calmer and more in command of himself, and when I had finished Fort-Knoxing the kitchen-to-garden door he said, 'The police want a list of what's gone. Will you help me make it?'

'Of course.'

'It'll give us something to do . . .'

'Sure.'

'We did have an inventory, but it was in that desk in the hall. The one they took.'

'Damn silly place to keep it,' I said.

'That's more or less what *he* said. Inspector Frost.'

'What about your insurance company? Haven't they got a list?'

'Only of the more valuable things, like some of the paintings, and her jewellery.' He sighed. 'Everything else was lumped together as "contents".'

We started on the dining-room and made reasonable progress, with him putting the empty drawers back in the sideboard while trying to remember what each had once contained, and me writing down to his dictation. There had been a good deal of solid silver tableware, acquired by Donald's family in its affluent past and handed down routinely. Donald, with his warmth for antiques, had enjoyed using it, but his pleasure in owning it seemed to have vanished with the goods. Instead of being indignant over its loss, he sounded impersonal, and by the time we had finished the sideboard, decidedly bored.

Faced by the ranks of empty shelves where once had stood a fine collection of early nineteenth-century porcelain, he baulked entirely.

'What does it matter?' he said drearily, turning away. 'I simply can't be bothered . . .'

'How about the paintings, then?'

He looked vaguely round the bare walls. The site of each missing frame showed unmistakably in lighter oblong patches of palest olive. In this room they had mostly been works of modern British painters: a Hockney, a Bratby, two Lowrys, and a Spear for openers, all painted on what one might call the artists' less exuberant days. Donald didn't like paintings which he said 'jumped off the wall and made a fuss'.

'You probably remember them better than I do,' he said. 'You do it.'

'I'd miss some.'

'Is there anything to drink?'

'Only the cooking brandy,' I said.

'We could have some of the wine.'

'What wine?'

'In the cellar.' His eyes suddenly opened wide. 'Good God, I'd forgotten about the cellar.'

'I didn't even know you had one.'

He nodded. 'Reason I bought the house. Perfect humidity and temperature for long-term storage. There's a small fortune down there in claret and port.'

There wasn't, of course. There were three floor-to-ceiling rows of empty racks, and a single cardboard box on a plain wooden table.

Donald merely shrugged. 'Oh well . . . that's that.'

I opened the top of the cardboard box and saw the elegant corked shapes of the tops of wine bottles.

'They've left these, anyway,' I said. 'In their rush.'

21

'Probably on purpose,' Don smiled twistedly. 'That's Australian wine. We brought it back with us.'

'Better than nothing,' I said disparagingly, pulling out a bottle and reading the label.

'Better than most, you know. A lot of Australian wine is superb.'

I carried the whole case up to the kitchen and dumped it on the table. The stairs from the cellar led up into the utility room among the washing machines and other domesticities, and I had always had an unclear impression that its door was just another cupboard. I looked at it thoughtfully, an unremarkable white painted panel merging inconspicuously into the general scenery.

'Do you think the burglars *knew* the wine was there?' I asked.

'God knows.'

'I would never have found it.'

'You're not a burglar, though.'

He searched for a corkscrew, opened one of the bottles, and poured the deep red liquid into two kitchen tumblers. I tasted it and it was indeed a marvellous wine, even to my untrained palate. *Wynn's Coonawarra Cabernet Sauvignon*. You could wrap the name round the tongue as lovingly as the product. Donald drank his share absentmindedly as if it were water, the glass clattering once or twice against his teeth. There was still an uncertainty about many of his movements, as if he could not quite remember how to do things, and I knew it was because with half his mind he thought all the time of Regina, and the thoughts were literally paralysing.

The old Donald had been a man of confidence, capably running a middle-sized inherited business and adding his share to the passed-on goodies. He had a blunt uncompromising face lightened by amber eyes which smiled easily, and he had considered his money well-spent on shapely hair-cuts.

The new Donald was a tentative man shattered with shock, a man trying to behave decently but unsure where his feet were when he walked upstairs.

We spent the evening in the kitchen, talking desultorily, eating a scratch meal, and tidying all the stores back on to the shelves.

22

Donald made a good show of being busy but put half the tins back upside down.

The front door bell rang three times during the evening but never in the code pre-arranged with the police. The telephone, with its receiver lying loose beside it, rang not at all. Donald had turned down several offers of refuge with local friends and visibly shook at the prospect of talking to anyone but Frost and me.

'Why don't they go away?' he said despairingly, after the third attempt on the front door.

'They will, once they've seen you,' I said. And sucked you dry, and spat out the husk, I thought.

He shook his head tiredly. 'I simply can't.'

It felt like living through a siege.

We went eventually again upstairs to bed, although it seemed likely that Donald would sleep no more than the night before, which had been hardly at all. The police surgeon had left knock-out pills, which Donald wouldn't take. I pressed him again on that second evening, with equal non-results.

'No, Charles. I'd feel I'd deserted her. D . . . ducked out. Thought only of myself, and not of . . . of how awful it was for her . . . dying like that . . . with n . . . no one near who l . . . loved her.'

He was trying to offer her in some way the comfort of his own pain. I shook my head at him, but tried no more with the pills.

'Do you mind,' he said diffidently, 'if I sleep alone tonight?'

'Of course not.'

'We could make up a bed for you in one of the other rooms.'

'Sure.'

He pulled open the linen-cupboard door on the upstairs landing and gestured indecisively at the contents. 'Could you manage?'

'Of course,' I said.

He turned away and seemed struck by one particular adjacent patch of empty wall.

'They took the Munnings,' he said.

'What Munnings?'

'We bought it in Australia. I hung it just there . . . only a week

23

ago. I wanted you to see it. It was one of the reasons I asked you to come.'

'I'm sorry,' I said. Inadequate words.

'Everything,' he said helplessly. 'Everything's gone.'

two

Frost arrived tirelessly again on Sunday morning with his quiet watchful eyes and non-committal manner. I opened the front door to his signal, and he followed me through to the kitchen, where Donald and I seemed to have taken up permanent residence. I gestured him to a stool, and he sat on it, straightening his spine to avoid future stiffness.

'Two pieces of information you might care to have, sir,' he said to Donald, his voice at its most formal. 'Despite our intensive investigation of this house during yesterday and the previous evening, we have found no fingerprints for which we cannot account.'

'Would you expect to?' I asked.

He flicked me a glance. 'No, sir. Professional housebreakers always wear gloves.'

Donald waited with a grey patient face, as if he would find whatever Frost said unimportant. Nothing, I judged, was of much importance to Donald any more.

'Second,' said Frost, 'our investigations in the district reveal that a removal van was parked outside your front door early on Friday afternoon.'

Donald looked at him blankly.

'Dark coloured, and dusty, sir.'

'Oh,' Donald said, meaninglessly.

Frost sighed. 'What do you know of a bronze statuette of a horse, sir? A horse rearing up on its hind legs?'

'It's in the hall,' Donald said automatically; and then, frowning slightly, 'I mean, it used to be. It's gone.'

'How do you know about it?' I asked Frost curiously, and guessed the answer before I'd finished the question. 'Oh no . . .' I stopped, and swallowed. 'I mean, perhaps you found it . . . fallen off the van . . . ?'

'No, sir.' His face was calm. 'We found it in the sitting-room, near Mrs Stuart.'

Donald understood as clearly as I had done. He stood up abruptly and went to the window, and stared out for a while at the empty garden.

'It is heavy,' he said at last. 'The base of it.'

'Yes, sir.'

'It must have been . . . quick.'

'Yes, sir,' Frost said again, sounding more objective than comforting.

'P . . . poor Regina.' The words were quiet, the desolation immense. When he came back to the table, his hands were trembling. He sat down heavily and stared into space.

Frost started another careful speech about the sitting-room being kept locked by the police for a few days yet and please would neither of us try to go in there.

Neither of us would.

Apart from that, they had finished their enquiries at the house, and Mr Stuart was at liberty to have the other rooms cleaned, if he wished, where the fingerprint dust lay greyish-white on every polished surface.

Mr Stuart gave no sign of having heard.

Had Mr Stuart completed the list of things stolen?

I passed it over. It still consisted only of the dining-room silver and what I could remember of the paintings. Frost raised his eyebrows and pursed his lips.

'We'll need more than this, sir.'

'We'll try again today,' I promised. 'There's a lot of wine missing, as well.'

'Wine?'

I showed him the empty cellar and he came up looking thoughtful.

'It must have taken hours to move that lot,' I said.

'Very likely, sir,' he said primly.

Whatever he was thinking, he wasn't telling. He suggested instead that Donald should prepare a short statement to read to the hungry reporters still waiting outside, so that they could go away and print it.

'No,' Don said.

'Just a short statement,' Frost said reasonably. 'We can prepare it here and now, if you like.'

He wrote it himself, more or less, and I guessed it was as much for his own sake as Donald's that he wanted the Press to depart, as it was he who had to push through them every time. He repeated the statement aloud when he had finished. It sounded like a police account, full of jargon, but because of that so distant from Donald's own raw grief that my cousin agreed in the end to read it out.

'But no photographs,' he said anxiously, and Frost said he would see to it.

They crowded into the hall, a collection of dry-eyed fact-finders, all near the top of their digging profession and inured from sensitivity by a hundred similar intrusions into tragedy. Sure, they were sorry for the guy whose wife had been bashed, but news was news and bad news sold papers, and if they didn't produce the goods they'd lose their jobs to others more tenacious. The Press Council had stopped the brutal bullying of the past, but the leeway still allowed could be a great deal too much for the afflicted.

Donald stood on the stairs, with Frost and myself at the foot, and read without expression, as if the words applied to someone else.

'. . . I returned to the house at approximately five p.m. and observed that during my absence a considerable number of valuable objects had been removed . . . I telephoned immediately for assistance . . . My wife, who was normally absent from the house on Fridays, returned unexpectedly . . . and, it is presumed, disturbed the intruders.'

He stopped. The reporters dutifully wrote down the stilted words and looked disillusioned. One of them, clearly elected by pre-arrangement, started asking questions for them all, in a gentle, coaxing, sympathetic tone of voice.

'Could you tell us which of these closed doors is the one to the room where your wife . . .'

Donald's eyes slid briefly despite himself towards the sitting-room. All the heads turned, the eyes studied the uninformative white painted panels, the pencils wrote.

'And could you tell us what exactly was stolen?'

'Silver. Paintings.'

'Who were the paintings by?'

Donald shook his head and began to look even paler.

'Could you tell us how much they were worth?'

After a pause Don said 'I don't know.'

'Were they insured?'

'Yes.'

'How many bedrooms are there in your house?'

'What?'

'How many bedrooms?'

Donald looked bewildered. 'I suppose . . . five.'

'Do you think you could tell us anything about your wife? About her character, and about her job? And could you let us have a photograph?'

Donald couldn't. He shook his head and said 'I'm sorry,' and turned and walked steadily away upstairs.

'That's all,' Frost said with finality.

'It's not much,' they grumbled.

'What do you want? Blood?' Frost said, opening the front door and encouraging them out. 'Put yourselves in his position.'

'Yeah,' they said cynically; but they went.

'Did you see their eyes?' I said. 'Sucking it all in?'

Frost smiled faintly. 'They'll write long stories from that little lot.'

The interview, however, produced to a great extent the desired results. Most of the cars departed, and the rest, I supposed, would follow as soon as fresher news broke.

'Why did they ask about the bedrooms?' I said.

'To estimate the value of the house.'

'Good grief.'

'They'll all get it different.' Frost was near to amusement. 'They always do.' He looked up the stairs in the direction Donald had taken, and, almost casually, said 'Is your cousin in financial difficulties?'

I knew his catch-them-off-guard technique by now.

'I wouldn't think so,' I said unhurriedly. 'You'd better ask him.'

'I will, sir.' He switched his gaze sharply to my face and studied my lack of expression. 'What do you know?'

I said calmly, 'Only that the police have suspicious minds.'

He disregarded that. 'Is Mr Stuart worried about his business?'

'He's never said so.'

'A great many middle-sized private companies are going bankrupt these days.'

'So I believe.'

'Because of cash flow problems,' he added.

'I can't help you. You'll have to look at his company's books.'

'We will, sir.'

'And even if the firm turns out to be bust, it doesn't follow that Donald would fake a robbery.'

'It's been done before,' Frost said dryly.

'If he needed money he could simply have sold the stuff,' I pointed out.

'Maybe he had. Some of it. Most of it, maybe.'

I took a slow breath and said nothing.

'That wine, sir. As you said yourself, it would have taken a long time to move.'

'The firm is a limited company,' I said. 'If it went bankrupt, Donald's own house and private money would be unaffected.'

'You know a good deal about it, don't you?'

I said neutrally, 'I live in the world.'

'I thought artists were supposed to be unworldly.'

'Some are.'

He peered at me with narrowed eyes as if he were trying to work out a possible way in which I too might have conspired to arrange the theft.

I said mildly, 'My cousin Donald is an honourable man.'

'That's an out-of-date word.'

'There's quite a lot of it about.'

He looked wholly disbelieving. He saw far too much in the way of corruption, day in, day out, all his working life.

Donald came hesitantly down the stairs and Frost took him off immediately to another private session in the kitchen. I thought that if Frost's questions were to be as barbed as those he'd asked me, poor Don was in for a rough time. While they talked I wandered aimlessly round the house, looking into storage spaces, opening cupboards, seeing the inside details of my cousin's life.

Either he or Regina had been a hoarder of empty boxes. I came across dozens of them, all shapes and sizes, shoved into odd corners of shelves or drawers: brown cardboard, bright gift-wrap, beribboned chocolate boxes, all too potentially useful or too pretty to be thrown away. The burglars had opened a lot but had thrown more unopened on the floor. They must, I thought, have had a most frustrating time.

They had largely ignored the big sunroom, which held few antiques and no paintings, and I ended up there sitting on a bamboo armchair among sprawling potted plants looking out into the windy garden. Dead leaves blew in scattered showers from the drying trees and a few late roses clung hardily to thorny stems.

I hated autumn. The time of melancholy, the time of death. My spirits fell each year with the soggy leaves and revived only with crisp winter frost. Psychiatric statistics proved that the highest suicide rate occurred in the spring, the time for rebirth and growth and stretching in the sun. I could never understand it. If ever I jumped over a cliff, it would be in the depressing months of decay.

The sunroom was grey and cold. No sun, that Sunday.

I went upstairs, fetched my suitcase, and brought it down. Over years of wandering journeys I had reversed the painter's traditional luggage: my suitcase now contained the tools of my trade, and my satchel, clothes. The large toughened suitcase, its interior adapted and fitted by me, was in fact a sort of portable studio, containing besides paints and brushes a light collapsible metal easel, unbreakable containers of linseed oil and turpentine, and a rack which would hold four wet paintings safely apart. There were also a dust sheet, a large box of tissues and generous amounts of white spirit, all designed for preventing mess and keeping things clean. The organization of the suitcase had saved and made the price of many a sandwich.

I untelescoped the easel and set out my palette, and on a middling-sized canvas laid in the beginnings of a melancholy landscape, a mixture of Donald's garden as I saw it, against a sweep of bare fields and gloomy woods. Not my usual sort of picture, and not, to be honest, the sort to make headline news a century hence; but it gave me at least something to do. I worked steadily, growing ever colder, until the chillier Frost chose to depart; and he went without seeing me again, the front door closing decisively on his purposeful footsteps.

Donald, in the warm kitchen, looked torn to rags. When I went in he was sitting with his arms folded on the table and his head on his arms, a picture of absolute despair. When he heard me he sat up slowly and wearily, and showed a face suddenly aged and deeply lined.

'Do you know what he thinks?' he said.

'More or less.'

He stared at me sombrely. 'I couldn't convince him. He kept on and on. Kept asking the same questions, over and over. Why doesn't he believe me?'

'A lot of people lie to the police. I think they grow to expect it.'

'He wants me to meet him in my office tomorrow. He says he'll be bringing colleagues. He says they'll want to see the books.'

I nodded. 'Better be grateful he didn't drag you down there today.'

'I suppose so.'

I said awkwardly, 'Don, I'm sorry. I told him the wine was missing. It made him suspicious . . . It was a good deal my fault that he was so bloody to you.'

He shook his head tiredly. 'I would have told him myself. I wouldn't have thought of not telling him.'

'But . . . I even pointed out that it must have taken a fair time to move so many bottles.'

'Mm. Well, he would have worked that out for himself.'

'How long, in fact, do you think it would have taken?'

'Depends how many people were doing it,' he said, rubbing his hand over his face and squeezing his tired eyes. 'They would have to have had proper wine boxes in any case. That means they had to know in advance that the wine was there, and didn't just chance on it. And that means . . . Frost says . . . that I sold it myself some time ago and am now saying it is stolen so I can claim fraudulent insurance, or, if it was stolen last Friday, that I told the thieves they'd need proper boxes, which means that I set up the whole frightful mess myself.'

We thought it over in depressed silence. Eventually, I said, 'Who *did* know you had the wine there? And who knew the house was always empty on Fridays? And was the prime target the wine, the antiques, or the paintings?'

'God, Charles, you sound like Frost.'

'Sorry.'

'Every business nowadays,' he said defensively, 'is going through a cash crisis. Look at the nationalized industries, losing money by the million. Look at the wage rises and the taxes and the inflation . . . How can any small business make the profit it used to? Of *course* we have a cash flow problem. Whoever hasn't?'

'How bad is yours?' I said.

'Not critical. Bad enough. But not within sight of liquidation. It's illegal for a limited company to carry on trading if it can't cover its costs.'

'But it could . . . if you could raise more capital to prop it up?'

He surveyed me with the ghost of a smile. 'It surprises me still that you chose to paint for a living.'

'It gives me a good excuse to go racing whenever I like.'

'Lazy sod.' He sounded for a second like the old Donald, but the lightness passed. 'The absolutely last thing I would do would be to use my own personal assets to prop up a dying business. If my firm was that rocky, I'd wind it up. It would be mad not to.'

I sucked my teeth. 'I suppose Frost asked if the stolen things were insured for more than their worth?'

'Yes, he did. Several times.'

'Not likely you'd tell him, even if they were.'

'They weren't, though.'

'No.'

'Under-insured, if anything.' He sighed. 'God knows if they'll pay up for the Munnings. I'd only arranged the insurance by telephone. I hadn't actually sent the premium.'

'It should be all right, if you can give them proof of purchase, and so on.'

He shook his head listlessly. 'All the papers to do with it were in the desk in the hall. The receipt from the gallery where I bought it, the letter of provenance, and the customs and excise receipt. All gone.'

'Frost won't like that.'

'He doesn't.'

'Well . . . I hope you pointed out that you would hardly be buying expensive pictures and going on world trips if you were down to your last farthing.'

'He said it might be *because* of buying expensive pictures and going on world trips that I might be down to my last farthing.'

Frost had built a brick wall of suspicion for Donald to batter his head against. My cousin needed hauling away before he was punch drunk.

'Have some spaghetti,' I said.

'What?'

'It's about all I can cook.'

'Oh . . .' He focused unclearly on the kitchen clock. It was half past four and long past feeding time according to my stomach.

'If you like,' he said.

The police sent a car the following morning to fetch him to his ordeal in the office. He went lifelessly, having more or less made it clear over coffee that he wouldn't defend himself.

'Don, you must,' I said. 'The only way to deal with the situation is to be firm and reasonable, and decisive, and accurate. In fact, just your own self.'

He smiled faintly. 'You'd better go instead of me. I haven't the energy. And what does it matter?' His smile broke suddenly and the ravaging misery showed deeply like black water under cracked ice. 'Without Regina . . . there's no point in making money.'

'We're not talking about making money, we're talking about suspicion. If you don't defend yourself, they'll assume you can't.'

'I'm too tired. I can't be bothered. They can think what they like.'

'Don,' I said seriously, 'They'll think what you let them.'

'I don't really care,' he said dully: and that was the trouble. He really didn't.

He was gone all day. I spent it painting.

Not the sad landscape. The sunroom seemed even greyer and colder that morning, and I had no mind any more to sink into melancholy. I left the half-finished canvas on the table there and removed myself and trappings to the source of warmth. Maybe the light wasn't so good in the kitchen, but it was the only room in the house with the pulse of life.

I painted Regina standing beside her cooker, with a wooden spoon in one hand and a bottle of wine in the other. I painted the way she held her head back to smile, and I painted the smile, shiny-eyed and guileless and unmistakably happy. I painted the kitchen behind her as I literally saw it in front of my eyes, and I painted Regina herself from the clearest of inner visions. So easily did I see her that I looked up once or twice from her face on the canvas to say something to her, and was disconcerted to find only empty space. An extraordinary feeling of the real and unreal disturbingly tangled.

I seldom ever worked for more than four hours at a stretch because for one thing the actual muscular control required was tiring, and for another the concentration always made me cold and hungry; so I knocked off at around lunch-time and dug out a tin of corned beef to eat with pickles on toast, and after that went for a walk, dodging the front-gate watchers by taking to the apple trees and wriggling through the hedge.

I tramped aimlessly for a while round the scattered shapeless village, thinking about the picture and working off the burst of physical energy I often felt after the constraint of painting. More burnt umber in the folds of the kitchen curtains, I thought; and a purplish shadow on the saucepan. Regina's cream shirt needed yellow ochre under the collar, and probably a touch of green. The cooking stove needed a lot more attention, and I had broken my general rule of working the picture as a whole, background and subject pace by pace.

33

This time, Regina's face stood out clearly, finished except for a gloss on the lips and a line of light along inside the lower eyelids, which one couldn't do until the under paint was dry. I had been afraid of seeing her less clearly if I took too long, but because of it the picture was now out of balance and I'd have to be very careful to get the kitchen into the same key, so that the whole thing looked harmonious and natural and as if it couldn't have been any other way.

The wind was rawly cold, the sky a hurrying jumbled mass of darkening clouds. I huddled my hands inside my anorak pockets and slid back through the hedge with the first drops of rain.

The afternoon session was much shorter because of the light, and I frustratingly could not catch the right mix of colours for the tops of the kitchen fitments. Even after years of experience, what looked right on the palette looked wrong on the painting. I got it wrong three times and decided to stop.

I was cleaning the brushes when Donald came back. I heard the scrunch of the car, the slam of the doors, and, to my surprise, the ring of the front door bell. Donald had taken his keys.

I went through and opened the door. A uniformed policeman stood there, holding Don's arm. Behind, a row of watching faces gazed on hungrily. My cousin, who had looked pale before, now seemed bloodlessly white. The eyes were as lifeless as death.

'Don!' I said, and no doubt looked as appalled as I felt.

He didn't speak. The policeman leant forward, said, 'There we are, sir,' and transferred the support of my cousin from himself to me: and it seemed to me that the action was symbolic as much as practical, because he turned immediately on his heel and methodically drove off in his waiting car.

I helped Donald inside and shut the door. I had never seen anyone in such a frightening state of disintegration.

'I asked,' he said, 'about the funeral.'

His face was stony, and his voice came out in gasps.

'They said . . .' He stopped, dragged in air, tried again. 'They said . . . no funeral.'

'Donald . . .'

'They said . . . she couldn't be buried until they had finished

their enquiries. They said . . . it might be months. They said . . .
they will keep her . . . refrigerated . . .'

The distress was fearful.

'They said . . .' He swayed slightly. 'They said . . . the body of
a murdered person belongs to the State.'

I couldn't hold him. He collapsed at my feet in a deep and total
faint.

three

For two days Donald lay in bed, and I grew to understand what
was meant by prostration.

Whether he liked it or not, this time he was heavily sedated,
his doctor calling morning and evening with pills and injections.
No matter that I was a hopeless nurse and a worse cook, I was
appointed, for lack of anyone else, to look after him.

'I want Charles,' Donald in fact told the doctor. 'He doesn't
fuss.'

I sat with him a good deal when he was awake, seeing him
struggle dazedly to face and come to terms with the horrors in
his mind. He lost weight visibly, the rounded muscles of his face
slackening and the contours changing to the drawn shape of illness. The grey shadows round his eyes darkened to a permanent
charcoal, and all normal strength seemed to have vanished from
arms and legs.

I fed us both from tins and frozen packets, reading the instructions and doing what they said. Donald thanked me punctiliously
and ate what he could, but I doubt if he tasted a thing.

In between times, while he slept, I made progress with both
the paintings. The sad landscape was no longer sad but merely
Octoberish, with three horses standing around in a field, one of
them eating grass. Pictures of this sort, easy to live with and pas-
sably expert, were my bread and butter. They sold quite well,
and I normally churned one off the production line every ten

25

days or so, knowing that they were all technique and no soul.

The portrait of Regina, though, was the best work I'd done for months. She laughed out of the canvas, alive and glowing, and to me at least seemed vividly herself. Pictures often changed as one worked on them, and day by day the emphasis in my mind had shifted, so that the kitchen background was growing darker and less distinct and Regina herself more luminous. One could still see she was cooking, but it was the girl who was important, not the act. In the end I had painted the kitchen, which was still there, as an impression, and the girl, who was not, as the reality.

I hid that picture in my suitcase whenever I wasn't working on it. I didn't want Donald to come face to face with it unawares.

Early Wednesday evening he came shakily down to the kitchen in his dressing-gown, trying to smile and pick up the pieces. He sat at the table, drinking the Scotch I had that day imported, and watching while I cleaned my brushes and tidied the palette.

'You're always so neat,' he said.

'Paint's expensive.'

He waved a limp hand at the horse picture which stood drying on the easel. 'How much does it cost, to paint that?'

'In raw materials, about ten quid. In heat, light, rates, rent, food, Scotch and general wear and tear on the nervous system, about the amount I'd earn in a week if I chucked it in and went back to selling houses.'

'Quite a lot, then,' he said seriously.

I grinned. 'I don't regret it.'

'No. I see that.'

I finished the brushes by washing them in soap and water under the tap, pinching them into shape, and standing them upright in a jar to dry. Good brushes were at least as costly as paint.

'After the digging into the company accounts,' Donald said abruptly, 'they took me along to the police station and tried to prove that I had actually killed her myself.'

'I don't believe it!'

'They'd worked out that I could have got home at lunch time and done it. They said there was time.'

I picked up the Scotch from the table and poured a decent sized shot into a tumbler. Added ice.

'They must be crazy,' I said.

'There was another man, besides Frost. A superintendent. I think his name was Wall. A thin man, with fierce eyes. He never seemed to blink. Just stared and said over and over again that I'd killed her because she'd come back and found me supervising the burglary.'

'For God's sake!' I said disgustedly. 'And anyway, she didn't leave the flower shop until half past two.'

'The girl in the flower shop now says she doesn't know to the minute when Regina left. Only that it was soon after lunch. And I didn't get back from the pub until nearly three. I went to lunch late. I was hung up with a client all morning . . .' He stopped, gripping his tumbler as if it were a support to hold on to. 'I can't tell you . . . how awful it was.'

The mild understatement seemed somehow to make things worse.

'They said,' he added, 'that eighty percent of murdered married women are killed by their husbands.'

That statement had Frost stamped all over it.

'They let me come home, in the end, but I don't think . . .' His voice shook. He swallowed, visibly trying to keep tight control on his hard-won calm. 'I don't think they've finished.'

It was five days since he'd walked in and found Regina dead. When I thought of the mental hammerings he'd taken on top, the punishing assault on his emotional reserves, where common humanity would have suggested kindness and consoling help, it seemed marvellous that he had remained as sane as he had.

'Have they got anywhere with catching the thieves?' I said.

He smiled wanly. 'I don't even know if they're trying.'

'They must be.'

'I suppose so. They haven't said.' He drank some whisky slowly. 'It's ironic, you know. I've always had a regard for the police. I didn't know they could be . . . the way they are.'

A quandary, I thought. Either they leaned on a suspect in the hope of breaking him down, or they asked a few polite questions and got nowhere: and under the only effective system the innocent suffered more than the guilty.

'I see no end to it,' Donald said. 'No end at all.'

*

By midday Friday the police had called twice more at the house, but for my cousin the escalation of agony seemed to have slowed. He was still exhausted, apathetic, and as grey as smoke, but it was as if he were saturated with suffering and could absorb little more. Whatever Frost and his companion said to him, it rolled off without destroying him further.

'You're supposed to be painting someone's horse, aren't you?' he said suddenly, as we shaped up to lunch.

'I told them I'd come later.'

He shook his head. 'I remember you saying, when I asked you to stay, that it would fit in fine before your next commission.' He thought a bit. 'Tuesday. You should have gone to Yorkshire on Tuesday.'

'I telephoned and explained.'

'All the same, you'd better go.'

He said he would be all right alone, now, and thanks for everything. He insisted I look up the times of trains, order a taxi, and alert the people at the other end. I could see in the end that the time had indeed come for him to be by himself, so I packed up my things to depart.

'I suppose,' he said diffidently, as we waited for the taxi to fetch me, 'that you never paint portraits? People, that is, not horses.'

'Sometimes,' I said.

'I just wondered . . . Could you, one day . . . I mean, I've got quite a good photograph of Regina . . .'

I looked searchingly at his face. As far as I could see, it could do no harm. I unclipped the suitcase and took out the picture with its back towards him.

'It's still wet,' I warned. 'And not framed, and I can't varnish it for at least six months. But you can have it, if you like.'

'Let me see.'

I turned the canvas round. He stared and stared, but said nothing at all. The taxi drove up to the front door.

'See you,' I said, propping Regina against a wall.

He nodded and punched my arm, opened the door for me, and sketched a farewell wave. Speechlessly, because his eyes were full of tears.

•

I spent nearly a week in Yorkshire doing my best to immortalize a patient old steeplechaser, and then went home to my noisy flat near Heathrow airport, taking the picture with me to finish.

Saturday I downed tools and went to the races, fed up with too much nose-to-the-grindstone.

Jump racing at Plumpton, and the familiar swelling of excitement at the liquid movement of racehorses. Paintings could never do justice to them: never. The moment caught on canvas was always second best.

I would love to have ridden in races, but hadn't had enough practice or skill; nor, I dare say, nerve. Like Donald, my childhood's background was of middlesized private enterprise, with my father an auctioneer in business on his own account in Sussex. I had spent countless hours in my growing years watching the horses train on the Downs round Findon, and had drawn and painted them from about the age of six. Riding itself had been mostly a matter of begging the wherewithal for an hour's joy from indulgent aunts, never of a pony of my own. Art school later had been fine, but at twenty-two, alone in the world with both parents newly dead, I'd had to face the need to eat. It had been a short meant-to-be-temporary step to the estate agents across the street, but I'd liked it well enough to stay.

Half the horse painters in England seemed to have turned up at Plumpton, which was not surprising, as the latest Grand National winner was due to make his first appearance of the new season. It was a commercial fact that a picture called for instance *Nijinsky on Newmarket Heath* stood a much better chance of being sold than one labelled *A horse on Newmarket Heath*, and *The Grand National winner at the start* won hands down over *A runner at Plumpton before the off*. The economic facts of life had brought many a would-be Rembrandt down to market research.

'Todd!' said a voice in my ear. 'You owe me fifteen smackers.'

'I bloody don't,' I said.

'You said Seesaw was a certainty for Ascot.'

'Never take sweets from a stranger.'

Billy Pyle laughed extravagantly and patted me heavily on the shoulder. Billy Pyle was one of those people you met on racecourses who greeted you as a bosom pal, plied you with drinks and bonhomie, and bored you to death. On and off I'd met Billy Pyle at the races for umpteen years, and had never yet worked out how to duck him without positive rudeness. Ordinary evasions rolled off his thick skin like mercury off glass, and I found it less wearing on the whole to get the drink over quickly than dodge him all afternoon.

I waited for him to say 'how about a beverage', as he always did.

'How about a beverage?' he said.

'Er . . . sure,' I agreed, resignedly.

'Your father would never forgive me if I neglected you.' He always said that, too. They had been business acquaintances, I knew, but I suspected the reported friendship was posthumous.

'Come along, laddie.'

I knew the irritating routine by heart. He would meet his Auntie Sal in the bar, as if by accident, and in my turn I would buy them both a drink. A double brandy and ginger for Auntie Sal.

'Why, there's Auntie Sal,' Billy said, pushing through the door. Surprise, surprise.

Auntie Sal was a compulsive racegoer in her seventies with a perpetual cigarette dangling from the corner of her mouth and one finger permanently inserted in her form book, keeping her place.

'Know anything for the two-thirty?' she demanded.

'Hello,' I said.

'What? Oh, I see. Hello. How are you? Know anything for the two-thirty?'

' 'Fraid not.'

'Huh.'

She peered into the form book. 'Treetops is well in at the weights, but can you trust his leg?' She looked up suddenly and with her free hand prodded her nephew, who was trying to attract service from the bar. 'Billy, get a drink for Mrs Matthews.'

'Mrs Who?'

'Matthews. What do you want, Maisie?'

She turned to a large middle-aged woman who had been standing in the shadows behind her.

40

'Oh . . . gin and tonic, thanks.'

'Got that, Billy? Double brandy and ginger for me, gin and tonic for Mrs Matthews.'

Maisie Matthews' clothes were noticeably new and expensive, and from lacquered hair via crocodile handbag to gold-trimmed shoes she shouted money without saying a word. The hand which accepted the drink carried the weight of a huge opal set in diamonds. The expression on her expertly painted face showed no joy at all.

'How do you do?' I said politely.

'Eh?' said Auntie Sal. 'Oh, yes, Maisie, this is Charles Todd. What do you think of Treetops?'

'Moderate,' I said.

Auntie Sal peered worriedly into the form book and Billy handed round the drinks.

'Cheers,' Maisie Matthews said, looking cheerless.

'Down the hatch,' said Billy, raising his glass.

'Maisie's had a bit of bad luck,' Auntie Sal said.

Billy grinned. 'Backed a loser, then, Mrs Matthews?'

'Her house burned down.'

As a light conversation stopper, it was a daisy.

'Oh . . . I say . . .' said Billy uncomfortably. 'Hard luck.'

'Lost everything, didn't you, Maisie?'

'All but what I stand up in,' she agreed gloomily.

'Have another gin,' I suggested.

'Thanks, dear.'

When I returned with the refills she was in full descriptive flood.

'. . . I wasn't there, of course, I was staying with my sister Betty up in Birmingham, and there was this policeman on the doorstep telling me what a job they'd had finding me. But by that time it was all over, of course. When I got back to Worthing there was just a heap of cinders with the chimney-breast sticking up in the middle. Well, I had a real job finding out what happened, but anyway they finally said it was a flash fire, whatever that is, but they didn't know what started it, because there'd been no one in the house for two days.'

She accepted the gin, gave me a brief unseeing smile, and returned to her story.

'Well, I was spitting mad, I'll tell you, over losing everything like that, and I said why hadn't they used sea water, what with the sea being only the other side of the tamarisk and down the shingle, because of course they said they hadn't been able to save a thing because they hadn't enough water, and this fireman, the one I was complaining to, he said they couldn't use sea water because for one thing it corroded everything and for another the pumps sucked up seaweed and shells and things, and in any case the tide was out.'

I smothered an unseemly desire to laugh. She sensed it, however.

'Well, dear, it may seem funny to you, of course, but then you haven't lost all of your treasures that you'd been collecting since heaven knows when.'

'I'm really sorry, Mrs Matthews. I don't think it's funny. It was just . . .'

'Yes, well, dear. I suppose you can see the funny side of it, all that water and not a drop to put a fire out with, but I was that mad, I can tell you.'

'I think I'll have a bit on Treetops,' Auntie Sal said thoughtfully.

Maisie Matthews looked at her uncertainly and Billy Pyle, who had heard enough of disaster, broke gratefully into geniality, clapped me again on the shoulder, and said yes, it was time to see the next contest.

Duty done, I thought with a sigh, and took myself off to watch the race from the top of the stands, out of sight and earshot.

Treetops broke down and finished last, limping. Too bad for its owner, trainer, and Auntie Sal. I wandered down to the parade ring to see the Grand National winner walk round before his race, but without any thought of drawing him. I reckoned he was just about played out as a subject, and there would shortly be a glut.

The afternoon went quickly, as usual. I won a little, lost a little, and filled my eyes with something better than money. On the stands for the last race, I found myself approached by Maisie Matthews. No mistaking the bright red coat, the air of gloss, and the big, kind-looking, worldly face. She drew to a halt on the step below me, looking up. Entirely self-confident, though registering doubt.

'Aren't you,' she said, 'the young man I had a drink with, with Sal and Billy?'

'Yes, that's right.'

'I wasn't sure,' she said, the doubt disappearing. 'You look older out here.'

'Different light,' I said, agreeing. She too looked older, by about ten years. Fifty-something, I thought. Bar-light always flattered.

'They said you were an artist.' Their mild disapproval coloured the way she spoke.

'Mm,' I said, watching the runners canter past on the way to the post.

'Not very well paid, is it, dear?'

I grinned at her, liking her directness. 'It depends who you are. Picasso didn't grumble.'

'How much would you charge to paint a picture for me?'

'What sort of picture?'

'Well, dear, you may say it sounds morbid and I dare say it is, but I was just thinking this morning when I went over there, and really it makes me that mad every time I see it, well, I was thinking actually that it makes a crazy picture, that burnt ruin with the chimney sticking up, and the burnt hedge behind and all that sea, and I was thinking of getting the local photographer who does all the weddings and things to come along and take a colour picture, because when it's all cleared away and rebuilt, no one will believe how awful it was, and I want to hang it in the new house, just to show them.'

'But . . .'

'So how much would you charge? Because I dare say you can see I am not short of the next quid but if it would be hundreds I might as well get the photographer of course.'

'Of course,' I agreed gravely. 'How about if I came to see the house, or what's left of it, and gave you an estimate?'

She saw nothing odd in that. 'All right, dear. That sounds very businesslike. Of course, it will have to be soon, though, because once the insurance people have been I am having the rubble cleared up.'

'How soon?'

'Well, dear, as you're half-way there, could you come today?'

We discussed it. She said she would drive me in her Jaguar as I hadn't a car, and I could go home by train just as easily from Worthing as from Plumpton.

So I agreed.

One takes the most momentous steps unawares.

The ruin was definitely paintagenic, if there is such a word. On the way there, more or less non-stop, she had talked about her late husband, Archie, who had looked after her very well, dear.

'Well, that's to say, I looked after him, too, dear, because of course I was a nurse. Private, of course. I nursed his first wife all through her illness, cancer it was, dear, of course, and then I stayed on for a bit to look after him, and, well, he asked me to stay on for life, dear, and I did. Of course he was much older, he's been gone more than ten years now. He looked after me very well, Archie did.'

She glanced fondly at the huge opal. Many a man would have liked to have been remembered as kindly.

'Since he went, and left me so well off, dear, it seemed a shame not to get some fun out of it, so I carried on with what we were doing when we were together those few years, which was going round to auction sales in big houses, dear, because you pick up such nice things there, quite cheap sometimes, and of course it's ever so much more interesting when the things have belonged to someone well known or famous.' She changed gear with a jerk and aggressively passed an inoffensive little van. 'And now all those things are burnt to cinders, of course, and all the memories of Archie and the places we went together, and I'll tell you, dear, it makes me mad.'

'It's really horrid for you.'

'Yes, dear, it is.'

I reflected that it was the second time in a fortnight that I'd been cast in the role of comforter; and I felt as inadequate for her as I had for Donald.

She stamped on the brakes outside the remains of her house and rocked us to a standstill. From the opulence of the minor mansions on either side, her property had been far from a slum; but all that was left was an extensive sprawling black heap, with jagged pieces of outside wall defining its former shape, and the thick brick chimney, as she'd said, pointing sturdily skywards from the centre. Ironic, I thought fleetingly, that the fireplace alone had survived the flames.

'There you are, dear,' Maisie said. 'What do you think?'

'A very hot fire.'

She raised her pencilled eyebrows. 'But yes, dear, all fires are hot, aren't they? And of course there was a lot of wood. So many of these old seaside houses were built with a lot of wood.'

Even before we climbed out of her big pale blue car, I could smell the ash.

'How long ago . . . ?' I asked.

'Last weekend, dear. Sunday.'

While we surveyed the mess for a moment in silence a man walked slowly into view from behind the chimney. He was looking down, concentrating, taking a step at a time and then bending to poke into the rubble.

Maisie, for all her scarlet-coated bulk, was nimble on her feet.

'Hey,' she called, hopping out of the car and advancing purposefully. 'What do you think you're doing?'

The man straightened up, looking startled. About forty, I judged, with a raincoat, a crisp-looking trilby and a down-turning moustache.

He raised his hat politely. 'Insurance, madam.'

'I thought you were coming on Monday.'

'I happened to be in the district. No time like the present, don't you think?'

'Well, I suppose not,' Maisie said. 'And I hope there isn't going to be any shilly-shallying over you paying up, though of course nothing is going to get my treasures back and I'd rather have them than any amount of money, as I've got plenty of that in any case.'

The man was unused to Maisie's brand of chat.

'Er . . .' he said. 'Oh yes. I see.'

'Have you found out what started it?' Maisie demanded.

'No, madam.'

'Found anything at all?'

'No, madam.'

'Well, how soon can I get all this cleared away?'

'Any time you like, madam.'

He stepped carefully towards us, picking his way round clumps of blackened debris. He had steady greyish eyes, a strong chin, and an overall air of intelligence.

'What's your name?' Maisie asked.

'Greene, madam.' He paused slightly, and added 'With an "e".'

'Well, Mr Greene with an "e",' Maisie said good-humouredly. 'I'll be glad to have all that in writing.'

He inclined his head. 'As soon as I report back.'

Maisie said 'Good,' and Greene, lifting his hat again, wished her good afternoon and walked along to a white Ford parked a short way along the road.

'That's all right, then,' Maisie said with satisfaction, watching him go. 'Now, how much for that picture?'

'Two hundred plus two nights' expenses in a local hotel.'

'That's a bit steep, dear. *One* hundred, and two nights, and I've got to like the results, or I don't pay.'

'No foal, no fee?'

The generous red mouth smiled widely. 'That's it, dear.'

We settled on one-fifty if she liked the picture, and fifty if she didn't, and I was to start on Monday unless it was raining.

four

Monday came up with a bright breezy day and an echo of summer's warmth. I went to Worthing by train and to the house by taxi, and to the interest of the neighbours set up my easel at about the place where the front gates would have been, had they not been unhinged and transplanted by the firemen. The gates themselves lay flat on the lawn, one of them still pathetically bearing a neat painted nameboard.

Treasure Holme.

Poor Archie. Poor Maisie.

I worked over the whole canvas with an unobtrusive coffee-coloured underpainting of raw umber much thinned with turpentine and linseed oil, and while it was still wet drew in, with a paintbrushful of a darker shade of the same colour, the shape of the ruined house against the horizontals of hedges, shingle, sea and sky. It was easy with a tissue to wipe out mistakes of composition at that stage, and try again: to get the proportions right, and the perspective, and the balance of the main masses.

That done and drying, I strolled right round the whole garden, looking at the house from different angles, and staring out over the blackened stumps of the tamarisk hedge which had marked the end of the grass and the beginning of the shingle. The sea sparkled in the morning sunshine, with the small hurrying cumulus clouds scattering patches of dark slate-grey shadow. All the waves had white frills: distant, because the tide again had receded to the far side of a deserted stretch of wet-looking, wave-rippled sand.

The sea wind chilled my ears. I turned to get back to my task and saw two men in overcoats emerge from a large station wagon and show definite signs of interest in what was left of *Treasure Holme.*

I walked back towards them, reaching them where they stood by the easel appraising my handiwork.

One, heavy and fiftyish. One lean, in the twenties. Both with firm self-confident faces and an air of purpose.

The elder raised his eyes as I approached.

'Do you have permission to be here?' he asked. An enquiry; no belligerence in sight.

'The owner wants her house painted,' I said obligingly.

'I see.' His lips twitched a fraction.

'And you?' I enquired.

He raised his eyebrows slightly. 'Insurance,' he said, as if surprised that anyone should ask.

'Same company as Mr Greene?' I said.

'Mr Who?'

'Greene. With an "e".'

'I don't know who you mean,' he said. 'We are here by arrangement with Mrs Matthews to inspect the damage to her house, which is insured with us.' He looked with some depression at the extent of the so-called damage, glancing about as if expecting Maisie to materialize Phoenix-like from the ashes.

'No Greene?' I repeated.

'Neither with nor without an "e".'

I warmed to him. Half an ounce of a sense of humour, as far as I was concerned, achieved results where thumb-screws wouldn't.

'Well . . . Mrs Matthews is no longer expecting you, because the aforesaid Mr Greene, who said he was in insurance, told her she could roll in the demolition squad as soon as she liked.'

His attention sharpened like a tightened violin string.

'Are you serious?'

'I was here, with her. I saw him and heard him, and that's what he said.'

'Did he show you a card?'

'No, he didn't.' I paused. 'And . . . er . . . nor have you.'

He reached into an inner pocket and did so, with the speed of a conjuror. Producing cards from pockets was a reflex action, no doubt.

'Isn't it illegal to insure the same property with two companies?' I asked idly, reading the card.

Foundation Life and Surety
D. J. Lagland   Area Manager

'Fraud.' He nodded.

'Unless of course Mr Greene with an "e" had nothing to do with insurance.'

'Much more likely.'

I put the card in my trouser pocket, Arran sweaters not having been designed noticeably for business transactions. He looked at me thoughtfully, his eyes observant but judgement suspended. He was the same sort of man my father had been, middle-aged, middle-of-the-road, expert at his chosen job but unlikely to set the world on fire.

Or *Treasure Holme*, for that matter.

'Gary,' he said to his younger side-kick, 'go and find a telephone and ring the Beach Hotel. Tell Mrs Matthews we're here.'

'Will do,' Gary said. He was that sort of man.

While he was away on the errand, D. J. Lagland turned his attention to the ruin, and I, as he seemed not to object, tagged along at his side.

'What do you look for?' I asked.

He shot me a sideways look. 'Evidence of arson. Evidence of the presence of the goods reported destroyed.'

'I didn't expect you to be so frank.'

'I indulge myself, occasionally.'

I grinned. 'Mrs Matthews seems pretty genuine.'

'I've never met the lady.'

Treat in store, I thought. 'Don't the firemen,' I said, 'look for signs of arson?'

'Yes, and also the police, and we ask them for guidance.'

'And what did they say?'

'None of your business, I shouldn't think.'

'Even for a wooden house,' I said, 'it is pretty thoroughly burnt.'

'Expert, are you?' he said with irony.

'I've built a lot of Guy Fawkes bonfires, in my time.'

He turned his head.

'They burn a lot better,' I said, 'if you soak them in paraffin. Especially round the edges.'

'I've been looking at fires since before you were born,' he said. 'Why don't you go over there and paint?'

49

'What I've done is still wet.'

'Then if you stay with me, shut up.'

I stayed with him, silent, and without offence. He was making what appeared to be a preliminary reconnaissance, lifting small solid pieces of debris, inspecting them closely, and carefully returning them to their former positions. None of the things he chose in that way were identifiable to me from a distance of six feet, and as far as I could see none of them gave him much of a thrill.

'Permission to speak?' I said.

'Well?'

'Mr Greene was doing much what you are, though in the area behind the chimney-breast.'

He straightened from replacing yet another black lump. 'Did he take anything?' he said.

'Not while we were watching, which was a very short time. No telling how long he'd been there.'

'No.' He considered. 'Wouldn't you think he was a casual sightseer, poking around out of curiosity?'

'He hadn't the air.'

D. J. frowned. 'Then what did he want?'

A rhetorical question. Gary rolled back, and soon after him, Maisie. In her Jaguar. In her scarlet coat. In a temper.

'What do you mean,' she said, advancing upon D. J. with eyes flashing fortissimo, 'the question of arson isn't yet settled? Don't tell me you're trying to wriggle out of paying my cheque, now. Your man said on Saturday that everything was all right and I could start clearing away and rebuilding, and anyway even if it had been arson you would still have to pay up because the insurance covered arson of course.'

D.J. opened and shut his mouth several times and finally found his voice.

'Didn't our Mr Robinson tell you that the man you saw here on Saturday wasn't from us?'

Our Mr Robinson, in the shape of Gary, nodded vigorously.

'He . . . Mr Greene . . . distinctly said he *was*,' Maisie insisted.

'Well . . . what did he look like?'

'Smarmy,' said Maisie without hesitation. 'Not as young as

Charles . . .' she gestured towards me, 'Or as old as you.' She thought, then shrugged. 'He looked like an insurance man, that's all.'

D.J. swallowed the implied insult manfully.

'About five feet ten,' I said. 'Suntanned skin with a sallow tinge, grey eyes with deep upper eyelids, widish nose, mouth straight under heavy drooping dark moustache, straight brown hair brushed back and retreating from the two top corners of his forehead, ordinary eyebrows, greeny-brown trilby of smooth felt, shirt, tie, fawn unbuttoned raincoat, gold signet ring on little finger of right hand, suntanned hands.'

I could see him in memory as clearly as if he still stood there in the ashes before me, taking off his hat and calling Maisie 'madam'.

'Good God,' D.J. said.

'An artist's eye, dear,' said Maisie admiringly. 'Well I never.'

D.J. said he was certain they had no one like that in their poking-into-claims department, and Gary agreed.

'Well,' said Maisie, with a resurgence of crossness, 'I suppose that still means you are looking for arson, though why you think that anyone in his right senses would want to burn down my lovely home and all my treasures is something I'll never understand.'

Surely Maisie, worldly Maisie, could not be so naïve. I caught a deep glimmer of intelligence in the glance she gave me, and knew that she certainly wasn't. D.J. however, who didn't know, made frustrated little motions with his hands and voted against explaining. I smothered a few more laughs, and Maisie noticed.

'Do you want your picture,' I asked, 'to be sunny like today, or cloudy and sad?'

She looked up at the bright sky.

'A bit more dramatic, dear,' she said.

D.J. and Gary inch-by-inched over the ruin all afternoon, and I tried to infuse it with a little Gothic romance. At five o'clock, on the dot, we all knocked off.

'Union hours?' said D.J. sarcastically, watching me pack my suitcase.

'The light gets too yellow in the evenings.'

'Will you be here tomorrow?'

I nodded. 'And you?'

'Perhaps.'

I went by foot and bus along to the Beach Hotel, cleaned my brushes, thought a bit, and at seven met Maisie downstairs in the bar, as arranged.

'Well, dear,' she said, as her first gin and tonic gravitated comfortably. 'Did they find anything?'

'Nothing at all, as far as I could see.'

'Well, that's good, dear.'

I tackled my pint of draught. Put the glass down carefully.

'Not altogether, Maisie.'

'Why not?'

'What exactly were your treasures, which were burned?'

'I dare say you wouldn't think so much of them of course, but we had ever such fun buying them, and so have I since Archie's gone, and well, dear, things like an antique spear collection that used to belong to old Lord Stequers whose niece I nursed once, and a whole wall of beautiful butterflies, which professors and such came to look at, and a wrought iron gate from Lady Tythe's old home, which divided the hall from the sitting-room, and six warming pans from a castle in Ireland, and two tall vases with eagles on the lids signed by Angelica Kaufman, which once belonged to a cousin of Mata Hari, they really did, dear, and a copper firescreen with silver bosses which was a devil to polish, and a marble table from Greece, and a silver tea urn which was once used by Queen Victoria, and really, dear, that's just the beginning, if I tell you them all I'll go on all night.'

'Did the Foundation insurance company have a full list?'

'Yes, they did, dear, and why do you want to know?'

'Because,' I said regretfully, 'I don't think many of those things were inside the house when it burned down.'

'*What?*' Maisie, as far as I could tell, was genuinely astounded. 'But they must have been.'

'D.J. as good as told me that they were looking for traces of them, and I don't think they found any.'

'D.J.?'

'Mr Lagland. The elder one.'

Alternate disbelief and anger kept Maisie going through two more double gins. Disbelief, eventually, won.

'You got it wrong, dear,' she said finally.

'I hope so.'

'Inexperience of youth, of course.'

'Maybe.'

'Because of course everything was in its place, dear, when I went off last Friday week to stay with Betty, and I only went to Betty's with not having seen her for so long while I'd been away, which is ironic when you think of it, but of course you can't stay at home for ever on the off-chance your house is going to catch fire and you can save it, can you dear, or you'd never go anywhere and I would have missed my trip to Australia.'

She paused for breath. Coincidence, I thought.

'All I can say, dear, is that it's a miracle I took most of my jewellery with me to Betty's, because I don't always, except that Archie always said it was safer and of course he was always so sensible and thoughtful and sweet.'

'Australia?' I said.

'Well, yes, dear, wasn't that nice? I went out there for a visit to Archie's sister who's lived there since heaven knows when and was feeling lonely since she'd been widowed, poor dear, and I went out for a bit of fun, dear, because of course I'd never really met her, only exchanged postcards of course, and I was out there for six weeks with her. She wanted me to stay, and of course we got on together like a house on fire . . . oh dear, I didn't mean that exactly . . . well, anyway, I said I wanted to come back to my little house by the sea and think it over, and of course I took my jewellery with me on that trip too, dear.'

I said idly, 'I don't suppose you bought a Munnings while you were there.'

I didn't know why I'd said it, apart from thinking of Donald in Australia. I was totally unprepared for her reaction.

Astounded she had been before: this time, pole-axed. Before, she had been incredulous and angry. This time, incredulous and frightened.

She knocked over her gin, slid off her bar stool, and covered her open mouth with four trembling red-nailed fingers.

'You didn't!' I said disbelievingly.

'How do you know?'

'I don't . . .'

'Are you from Customs and Excise?'

'Of course not.'

'Oh dear. Oh dear . . .' She was shaking, almost as shattered as Donald.

I took her arm and led her over to an armchair beside a small bar table.

'Sit down,' I said coaxingly, 'and tell me.'

It took ten minutes and a refill double gin.

'Well, dear, I'm not an art expert, as you can probably guess, but there was this picture by Sir Alfred Munnings, signed and everything, dear, and it was such a bargain really, and I thought how tickled Archie would have been to have a real Munnings on the wall, what with us both liking the races, of course, and, well, Archie's sister egged me on a bit, and I felt quite . . . I suppose you might call it *high*, dear, so I bought it.'

She stopped.

'Go on,' I said.

'Well, dear, I suppose you've guessed from what I said just now.'

'You brought it into this country without declaring it?'

She sighed. 'Yes, dear, I did. Of course it was silly of me but I never gave customs duty a thought when I bought the painting, not until just before I came home, a week later, that was, and Archie's sister asked if I was going to declare it, and well, dear, I really *resent* having to pay duty on things, don't you? So anyway I thought I'd better find out just how much the duty would be, and I found it wasn't duty at all in the ordinary way, dear, there isn't duty on second-hand pictures being brought in from Australia, but would you believe it they said I would have to pay Value Added Tax, sort of tax on buying things, you know, dear, and I would have to pay eight per cent on whatever I had bought the picture for. Well, I ask you! I was that mad, dear, I can tell you. So Archie's sister said why didn't I leave the painting with her, because then if I went back to Australia I would have paid the

54

tax for nothing, but I wasn't sure I'd go back and anyway I did want to see Sir Alfred Munnings on the wall where Archie would have loved it, so, well, dear, it was all done up nicely in boards and brown paper so I just camouflaged it a bit with my best nightie and popped it in my suitcase, and pushed it through the "Nothing to Declare" lane at Heathrow when I got back, and nobody stopped me.'

'How much would you have had to pay?' I said.

'Well, dear, to be precise, just over seven hundred pounds. And I know that's not a fortune, dear, but it made me so mad to have to pay tax here because I'd bought something nice in Australia.'

I did some mental arithmetic. 'So the painting cost about nine thousand?'

'That's right, dear. Nine thousand.' She looked anxious. 'I wasn't done, was I? I've asked one or two people since I got back and they say lots of Munningses cost fifteen or more.'

'So they do,' I said absently. And some could be got for fifteen hundred, and others, I dared say, for less.

'Well, anyway, dear, it was only when I began to think about insurance that I wondered if I would be found out, if say, the insurance people wanted a *receipt* or anything, which they probably would, of course, so I didn't do anything about it, because of course if I *did* go back to Australia I could just take the picture with me and no harm done.'

'Awkward,' I agreed.

'So now it's burnt, and I dare say you'll think it serves me right, because the nine thousand's gone up in smoke and I won't see a penny of it back.'

She finished the gin and I bought her another.

'I know it's not my business, Maisie, but how did you happen to have nine thousand handy in Australia? Aren't there rules about exporting that much cash?'

She giggled. 'You don't know much about the world, do you, dear? But anyway, this time it was all hunky-dory. I just toddled along with Archie's sister to a jeweller's and sold him a brooch I had, a nasty sort of *toad*, dear, with a socking big diamond in the middle of its forehead, something to do with Shakespeare, I think, though I never got it clear, anyway I never wore it, it was so ugly, but of course I'd taken it with me because of it being worth so much, and I sold it for nine thousand five, though in Australian dollars of course, so there was no problem, was there?'

Maisie took it for granted I would be eating with her, so we drifted in to dinner. Her appetite seemed healthy, but her spirits were damp.

'You won't *tell* anyone, will you, dear, about the picture?'

'Of course not, Maisie.'

'I could get into such trouble, dear.'

'I know.'

'A fine, of course,' she said. 'And I suppose that might be the least of it. People can be so beastly about a perfectly innocent little bit of smuggling.'

'No one will find out, if you keep quiet.' A thought struck me. 'Unless, that is, you've told anyone already that you'd bought it?'

'No, dear, I didn't, because of thinking I'd better pretend I'd had it for years, and of course I hadn't even hung it on the wall yet because one of the rings was loose in the frame and I thought it might fall down and be damaged, and I couldn't decide who to ask to fix it.' She paused for a mouthful of prawn cocktail. 'I expect you'll think me silly, dear, but I suppose I was feeling a bit scared of being found out, not guilty exactly because I really don't see why we *should* pay that irritating tax but anyway I didn't not only not hang it up, I hid it.'

'You hid it? Still wrapped up?'

'Well, yes, dear, more or less wrapped up. Of course I'd opened it when I got home, and that's when I found the ring coming loose with the cord through it, so I wrapped it up again until I'd decided what to do.'

I was fascinated. 'Where did you hide it?'

She laughed. 'Nowhere very much, dear. I mean, I was only keeping it out of sight to stop people asking about it, of course, so I slipped it behind one of the radiators in the lounge, and don't look so horrified dear, the central heating was turned off.'

I painted at the house all the next day, but neither D.J. nor anyone else turned up.

In between stints at the easel I poked around a good deal on my own account, searching for Maisie's treasures. I found a good many recognizable remains, durables like bed-frames, kitchen machines and radiators, all of them twisted and buckled not merely by heat but by the weight of the whole edifice from roof downwards having collapsed inwards. Occasional remains of heavy rafters lay blackly in the thick ash, but apart from these, everything combustible had totally, as one might say, combusted.

Of all the things Maisie had described, and of all the dozens she hadn't, I found only the wrought iron gate from Lady Tythe's old home, which had divided the hall from the sitting-room. Lady Tythe would never have recognized it.

No copper warming pans, which after all had been designed to withstand red-hot coals. No metal fire screen. No marble table. No antique spears.

Naturally, no Munnings.

When I took my paint-stained fingers back to the Beach at five o'clock I found Maisie waiting for me in the hall. Not the kindly, basically cheerful Maisie I had come to know, but a belligerent woman in a full-blown state of rage.

'I've been waiting for you,' she said, fixing me with a furious eye.

I couldn't think how I could have offended her.

'What's the matter?' I said.

'The bar's shut,' she said. 'So come upstairs to my room. Bring all your stuff with you.' She gestured to the suitcase. 'I'm so *mad* I think I'll absolutely *burst.*'

She did indeed, in the lift, look in danger of it. Her cheeks were bright red with hard outlines of colour against the pale surrounding skin. Her blonde-rinsed hair, normally lacquered into sophistication, stuck out in wispy spikes, and for the first time since I'd met her her mouth was not glistening with lipstick.

She threw open the door of her room and stalked in. I followed, closing it after me.

'You'll never believe it,' she said forcefully, turning to face me and letting go with all guns blazing. 'I've had the police here half the day, and those insurance men here the other half, and *do you know what they're saying?*'

'Oh, Maisie.' I sighed inwardly. It had been inevitable.

'What do you think I am, I asked them,' she said. 'I was so *mad*. There they were, having the nerve to suggest I'd sold all my treasures and over-insured my house, and was trying to take the insurance people for a ride. I told them, I told them over and over, that everything was in its place when I went to Betty's and if it was over-insured it was to allow for inflation and anyway the brokers had advised me to put up the amount pretty high, and I'm glad I took their advice, but that Mr Lagland says they won't be paying out until they have investigated further and he was proper sniffy about it, and no sympathy at all for me having lost everything. They were absolutely *beastly*, and I *hate* them all.'

She paused to regather momentum, vibrating visibly with the strength of her feelings. 'They made me feel so *dirty*, and maybe I *was* screaming at them a bit, I was so mad, but they'd no call to be so *rude*, and making out I was some sort of criminal, and just what *right* have they to tell me to pull myself together when it is because of *them* and their bullying that I am yelling at them at the top of my voice?'

It must, I reflected, have been quite an encounter. I wondered in what state the police and D.J. had retired from the field.

'They say it was definitely arson and I said why did they think so now when they hadn't thought so at first, and it turns out that it was because that Lagland couldn't find any of my treasures in the ashes or any trace of them at all, and they said even if I hadn't sold the things first I had arranged for them to be stolen and the house burnt to cinders while I was away at Betty's, and they kept on and on asking me who I'd paid to do it, and I got more and more furious and if I'd had anything handy I would have *hit* them, I really would.'

'What you need is a stiff gin,' I said.

'I told them they ought to be out looking for whoever had done it instead of hounding helpless women like me, and the more I thought of someone walking into *my* house and stealing *my* treasures and then callously setting fire to everything the madder I got, and somehow that made me even *madder* with those stupid men who couldn't see any further than their stupid noses.'

It struck me after a good deal more of similar diatribe that genuine though Maisie's anger undoubtedly was, she was stoking herself up again every time her temper looked in danger of relapsing to normal. For some reason, she seemed to need to be in the position of the righteous wronged.

I wondered why; and in a breath-catching gap in the flow of hot lava, I said, 'I don't suppose you told them about the Munnings.'

The red spots on her cheeks burned suddenly brighter.

'I'm not *crazy*,' she said bitingly. 'If they found out about that, there would have been a fat chance of convincing them I'm telling the truth about the rest.'

'I've heard,' I said tentatively, 'that nothing infuriates a crook more than being had up for the one job he didn't do.'

It looked for a moment as if I'd just elected myself as the new target for hatred, but suddenly as she glared at me in rage her sense of humour reared its battered head and nudged her in the ribs. The stiffness round her mouth relaxed, her eyes softened and glimmered, and after a second or two, she ruefully smiled.

'I dare say you're right, dear, when I come to think of it.' The smile slowly grew into a giggle. 'How about that gin?'

Little eruptions continued all evening through drinks and dinner, but the red-centred volcano had subsided to manageable heat.

'You didn't seem surprised, dear, when I told you what the police thought I'd done.' She looked sideways at me over her coffee cup, eyes sharp and enquiring.

'No.' I paused. 'You see, something very much the same has just happened to my cousin. Too much the same, in too many ways. I think, if you will come, and he agrees, that I'd like to take you to meet him.'

'But why, dear?'

I told her why. The anger she felt for herself burned up again fiercely for Donald.

'How *dreadful*. How *selfish* you must think *me*, after all that that poor man has suffered.'

'I don't think you're selfish at all. In fact, Maisie, I think you're a proper trouper.'

She looked pleased and almost kittenish, and I had a vivid

impression of what she had been like with Archie.

'There's one thing, though, dear,' she said awkwardly. 'After today, and all that's been said, I don't think I want that picture you're doing. I don't any more want to remember the house as it is now, only like it used to be. So if I give you just the fifty pounds, do you mind?'

five

We went to Shropshire in Maisie's Jaguar, sharing the driving. Donald on the telephone had sounded unenthusiastic at my suggested return, but also too lethargic to raise objections. When he opened his front door to us, I was shocked.

It was two weeks since I'd left him to go to Yorkshire. In that time he had shed at least fourteen pounds and aged ten years. His skin was tinged with bluish shadows, the bones in his face showed starkly, and even his hair seemed speckled with grey.

The ghost of the old Donald put an obvious effort into receiving us with good manners.

'Come in,' he said. 'I'm in the dining-room now. I expect you'd like a drink.'

'That would be very nice, dear,' Maisie said.

He looked at her with dull eyes, seeing, as I saw, a large good-natured lady with glossy hair and expensive clothes, her smart appearance walking a tightrope between vulgarity and elegance and just making it to the safer side.

He waved to me to pour the drinks, as if it would be too much for him, and invited Maisie to sit down. The dining-room had been roughly refurnished, containing now a large rug, all the sunroom armchairs, and a couple of small tables from the bedrooms. We sat in a fairly close group round one of the tables, because I had come to ask questions, and I wanted to write down the answers. My cousin watched the production of notebook and ballpoint with no show of interest.

'Don,' I said, 'I want you to listen to a story.'

'All right.'

Maisie, for once, kept it short. When she came to the bit about buying a Munnings in Australia, Donald's head lifted a couple of inches and he looked from her to me with the first stirring of attention. When she stopped, there was a small silence.

'So,' I said finally, 'you both went to Australia, you both bought a Munnings, and soon after your return you both had your houses burgled.'

'Extraordinary coincidence,' Donald said: but he meant simply that, nothing more. 'Did you come all this way just to tell me that?'

'I wanted to see how you were.'

'Oh. I'm all right. Kind of you, Charles, but I'm all right.'

Even Maisie, who hadn't known him before, could see that he wasn't.

'Where did you buy your picture, Don? Where exactly, I mean.'

'I suppose . . . Melbourne. In the Hilton Hotel. Opposite the cricket ground.'

I looked doubtful. Although hotels quite often sold pictures by local artists, they seldom sold Munnings.

'Fellow met us there,' Don added. 'Brought it up to our room. From the gallery where we saw it first.'

'Which gallery?'

He made a slight attempt to remember. 'Might have been something like Fine Arts.'

'Would you have it on a cheque stub, or anything?'

He shook his head. 'The wine firm I was dealing with paid for it for me, and I sent a cheque to their British office when I got back.'

'Which wine firm?'

'Monga Vineyards Proprietary Limited of Adelaide and Melbourne.'

I wrote it all down.

'And what was the picture like? I mean, could you describe it?'

Donald looked tired. 'One of those "Going down to the start" things. Typical Munnings.'

'So was mine,' said Maisie, surprised. 'A nice long row of jockeys in their colours against a darker sort of sky.'

'Mine had only three horses,' Donald said.

'The biggest, I suppose you might say the *nearest* jockey in my picture had a purple shirt and green cap,' Maisie said, 'and I expect you'll think I was silly but that was one of the reasons I bought it, because when Archie and I were thinking what fun it would be to buy a horse and go to the races as owners, we decided we'd like purple with a green cap for our colours, if no one else already had that, of course.'

'Don?' I said.

'Mm? Oh . . . three bay horses cantering . . . in profile . . . one in front, two slightly overlapping behind. Bright colours on the jockeys. I don't remember exactly. White racetrack rails and a lot of sunny sky."

'What size?'

He frowned slightly. 'Not very big. About twenty-four inches by eighteen, inside the frame.'

'And yours, Maisie?'

'A bit smaller, dear, I should think.'

'Look,' Donald said. 'What are you getting at?'

'Trying to make sure that there are no more coincidences.'

He stared, but without any particular feeling.

'On the way up here,' I said, 'Maisie told me everything' (but *everything*) 'of the way she came to buy her picture. So could you possibly tell us how you came to buy yours. Did you, for example, deliberately go looking for a Munnings?'

Donald passed a weary hand over his face, obviously not wanting the bother of answering.

'Please, Don,' I said.

'Oh . . .' A long sigh. 'No. I wasn't especially wanting to buy anything at all. We just went into the Melbourne Art Gallery for a stroll round. We came to the Munnings they have there . . . and while we were looking at it we just drifted into conversation with a woman near us, as one does in art galleries. She said there was another Munnings, not far away, for sale in a small commercial gallery, and it was worth seeing even if one didn't intend to buy it. We had time to spare, so we went.'

Maisie's mouth had fallen open. 'But, dear,' she said, recovering, 'that was *just* the same as us, my sister-in-law and me, though it was Sydney Art Gallery, not Melbourne. They have this marvellous picture there, *The Coming Storm*, and we were admiring it when this man sort of drifted up to us and joined in . . .'

Donald suddenly looked a great deal more exhausted, like a sick person overdone by healthy visitors.

'Look . . . Charles . . . you aren't going to the police with all this? Because I . . . I don't think . . . I could stand . . . a whole new lot . . . of questions.'

'No, I'm not,' I said.

'Then what . . . does it matter?'

Maisie finished her gin and tonic and smiled a little too brightly.

'Which way to the girls' room, dear?' she asked, and disappeared to the cloakroom.

Donald said faintly, 'I can't concentrate . . . I'm sorry, Charles, but I can't seem to do anything . . . while they still have Regina . . . unburied . . . just *stored* . . .'

Time, far from dulling the agony, seemed to have preserved it, as if the keeping of Regina in a refrigerated drawer had stopped dead the natural progression of mourning. I had been told that the bodies of murdered people could be held in that way for six months or more in unsolved cases. I doubted whether Donald would last that long.

He stood suddenly and walked away out of the door to the hall. I followed. He crossed the hall, opened the door of the sitting-room, and went in.

Hesitantly, I went after him.

The sitting-room still contained only the chintz-covered sofas and chairs, now ranged over-tidily round the walls. The floor where Regina had lain was clean and polished. The air was cold.

Donald stood in front of the empty fireplace looking at my picture of Regina, which was propped on the mantelpiece.

'I stay in here with her, most of the time,' he said. 'It's the only place I can bear to be.'

He walked to one of the armchairs and sat down, directly facing the portrait.

'You wouldn't mind seeing yourselves out, would you Charles?' he said. 'I'm really awfully tired.'

'Take care of yourself.' Useless advice. One could see he wouldn't.

'I'm all right,' he said. 'Quite all right. Don't you worry.'

I looked back from the door. He was sitting immobile, looking at Regina. I didn't know whether it would have been better or worse if I hadn't painted her.

Maisie was quiet for the whole of the first hour of the return journey, a record in itself.

From Donald's house we had driven first to one of the neighbours who had originally offered refuge, because he clearly needed help more now than ever.

Mrs Neighbour had listened with sympathy, but had shaken her head.

'Yes, I know he should have company and get away from the house, but he won't. I've tried several times. Called. So have lots of people round here. He just tells us he's all right. He won't let anyone help him.'

Maisie drove soberly, mile after mile. Eventually she said, 'We shouldn't have bothered him. Not so soon after . . .'

Three weeks, I thought. Only three weeks. To Donald it must have seemed like three months, stretched out in slow motion. You could live a lifetime in three weeks' pain.

'I'm going to Australia,' I said.

'You're very fond of him, dear, aren't you?' Maisie said.

Fond? I wouldn't have used that word, I thought: but perhaps after all it was accurate.

'He's eight years older than me, but we've always got on well together.' I looked back, remembering. 'We were both only children. His mother and mine were sisters. They used to visit each other, with me and Donald in tow. He was always pretty patient about having a young kid under his feet.'

'He looks very ill, dear.'

'Yes.'

She drove another ten miles in silence. Then she said, 'Are you sure it wouldn't be better to tell the police? About the paintings,

I mean? Because you do think they had something to do with the burglaries, don't you, dear, and the police might find out things more easily than you.'

I agreed. 'I'm sure they would, Maisie. But how can I tell them? You heard what Donald said, that he couldn't stand a new lot of questions. Seeing him today, do you think he could? And as for you, it wouldn't just be confessing to a bit of smuggling and paying a fine, but of having a conviction against your name for always, and having the customs search your baggage every time you travelled, and all sorts of other complications and humiliations. Once you get on any blacklist nowadays it is just about impossible to get off.'

'I didn't know you cared, dear.' She tried a giggle, but it didn't sound right.

We stopped after a while to exchange places. I liked driving her car, particularly as for the last three years, since I'd given up a steady income, I'd owned no wheels myself. The power purred elegantly under the pale blue bonnet and ate up the southward miles.

'Can you afford the fare, dear?' Maisie said. 'And hotels, and things?'

'I've a friend out there. Another painter. I'll stay with him.'

She looked at me doubtfully. 'You can't get there by hitch-hiking, though.'

I smiled. 'I'll manage.'

'Yes, well, dear, I dare say you can, but all the same, and I don't want any silly arguments, I've got a great deal of this world's goods thanks to Archie, and you haven't, and as it's partly because of me having gone in for smuggling that you're going your-self at all, I am insisting that you let me buy your ticket.'

'No, Maisie.'

'Yes, dear. Now be a good boy, dear, and do as I say.'

You could see, I thought, why she'd been a good nurse. Swallow the medicine, dear, there's a good boy. I didn't like accepting her offer but the truth was that I would have had to borrow anyway.

'Shall I paint your picture, Maisie, when I get back?'

'That will do very nicely, dear.'

I pulled up outside the house near Heathrow whose attic was my home, and from where Maisie had picked me up that morning.

'How do you stand all this noise, dear?' she said, wincing as a huge jet climbed steeply overhead.

'I concentrate on the cheap rent.'

She smiled, opening the crocodile handbag and producing her chequebook. She wrote out and gave me the slip of paper which was far more than enough for my journey.

'If you're fussed, dear,' she said across my protests, 'you can give me back what you don't spend.' She gazed at me earnestly with grey-blue eyes. 'You will be careful dear, won't you?'

'Yes, Maisie.'

'Because of course, dear, you might turn out to be a nuisance to some really *nasty* people.'

I landed at Mascot airport at noon five days later, wheeling in over Sydney and seeing the harbour bridge and the opera house down below, looking like postcards.

Jik met me on the other side of Customs with a huge grin and a waving bottle of champagne.

'Todd the sod,' he said. 'Who'd have thought it?' His voice soared easily over the din. 'Come to paint Australia red!'

He slapped me on the back with an enthusiastic horny hand, not knowing his own strength. Jik Cassavetes, long-time friend, my opposite in almost everything.

Bearded, which I was not. Exuberant, noisy, extravagant, unpredictable; qualities I envied. Blue eyes and sun-blond hair. Muscles which left mine gasping. An outrageous way with girls. An abrasive tongue; and a wholehearted contempt for the things I painted.

We had met at art school, drawn together by mutual truancy on racetrains. Jik compulsively went racing, but strictly to gamble, never to admire the contestants, and certainly not to paint them. Horse-painters, to him, were the lower orders. No *serious* artist, he frequently said, would be seen dead painting horses.

Jik's paintings, mostly abstract, were the dark reverse of the

66

bright mind: fruits of depression, full of despair at the hatred and pollution destroying the fair world.

Living with Jik was like a toboggan run, downhill, dangerous, and exhilarating. We'd spent the last two years at art school sharing a studio flat and kicking each other out for passing girls. They would have chucked him out of school except for his prodigious talent, because he'd missed weeks in the summer for his other love, which was sailing.

I'd been out with him, deep sea, several times in the years afterwards. I reckoned he'd taken us on several occasions a bit nearer death than was strictly necessary, but it had been a nice change from the office. He was a great sailor, efficient, neat, quick and strong, with an instinctive feeling for wind and waves. I had been sorry when one day he had said he was setting off single-handed round the world. We'd had a paralytic farewell party on his last night ashore; and the next day, when he'd gone, I'd given the estate agent my notice.

He had brought a car to fetch me: his car, it turned out. A British M.G. Sports, dark blue. Both sides of him right there, extrovert and introvert, the flamboyant statement in a sombre colour.

'Are there many of these here?' I asked, surprised, loading suitcase and satchel into the back. 'It's a long way from the birth pangs.'

He grinned. 'A few. They're not popular now because petrol passes through them like salts.' The engine roared to life, agreeing with him, and he switched on the windscreen wiper against a starting shower. 'Welcome to sunny Australia. It rains all the time here. Puts Manchester in the sun.'

'But you like it?'

'Love it, mate. Sydney's like rugger, all guts and go and a bit of grace in the line-out.'

'And how's business?'

'There are thousands of painters in Australia. It's a flourishing cottage industry.' He glanced at me sideways. 'A hell of a lot of competition.'

'I haven't come to seek fame and fortune.'

'But I scent a purpose,' he said.

'How would you feel about harnessing your brawn?'

'To your brain? As in the old days?'

'Those were pastimes.'

His eyebrows rose. 'What are the risks?'

'Arson and murder, to date.'

'Jesus.'

The blue car swept gracefully into the centre of the city. Skyscrapers grew like beanstalks.

'I live right out on the other side,' Jik said. 'God, that sounds banal. Suburban. What has become of me?'

'Contentment oozing from every pore,' I said smiling.

'Yes. So O.K., for the first time in my life I've been actually happy. I dare say you'll soon put that right.'

The car nosed on to the expressway, pointing towards the bridge.

'If you look over your right shoulder,' Jik said, 'You'll see the triumph of imagination over economics. Like the Concorde. Long live madness, it's the only thing that gets us anywhere.'

I looked. It was the opera house, glimpsed, grey with rain.

'Dead in the day,' Jik said. 'It's a night bird. Fantastic.'

The great arch of the bridge rose above us, intricate as steel lace. 'This is the only flat bit of road in Sydney,' Jik said. We climbed again on the other side.

To our left, half-seen at first behind other familiar-looking high-rise blocks, but then revealed in its full glory, stood a huge shiny red-orange building, all its sides set with regular rows of large curve-cornered square windows of bronze-coloured glass.

Jik grinned. 'The shape of the twenty-first century. Imagination and courage. I love this country.'

'Where's your natural pessimism?'

'When the sun sets, those windows glow like gold.' We left the gleaming monster behind. 'It's the water-board offices,' Jik said sardonically. 'The guy at the top moors his boat near mine.'

The road went up and down out of the city through close-packed rows of one-storey houses, whose roofs, from the air, had looked like a great red-squared carpet.

'There's one snag,' Jik said. 'Three weeks ago, I got married.'

The snag was living with him aboard his boat, which was

moored among a colony of others near a headland he called The Spit: and you could see why, temporarily at least, the glooms of the world could take care of themselves.

She was not plain, but not beautiful. Oval-shaped face, mid-brown hair, so-so figure and a practical line in clothes. None of the style or instant vital butterfly quality of Regina. I found myself the critically inspected target of bright brown eyes which looked out with impact-making intelligence.

'Sarah,' Jik said. 'Todd. Todd, Sarah.'

We said hi and did I have a good flight and yes I did. I gathered she would have preferred me to stay at home.

Jik's thirty-foot ketch, which had set out from England as a cross between a studio and a chandler's warehouse, now sported curtains, cushions, and a flowering plant. When Jik opened the champagne he poured it into shining tulip glasses, not plastic mugs.

'By God,' he said. 'It's good to see you.'

Sarah toasted my advent politely, not sure that she agreed. I apologized for gatecrashing the honeymoon.

'Nuts to that,' Jik said, obviously meaning it. 'Too much domestic bliss is bad for the soul.'

'It depends,' said Sarah neutrally, 'on whether you need love or loneliness to get you going.'

For Jik, before, it had always been loneliness. I wondered what he had painted recently: but there was no sign, in the now comfortable cabin, of so much as a brush.

'I walk on air,' Jik said. 'I could bound up Everest and do a handspring on the summit.'

'As far as the galley will do,' Sarah said, 'if you remembered to buy the crayfish.'

Jik, in our shared days, had been the cook; and times, it seemed, had not changed. It was he, not Sarah, who with speed and efficiency chopped open the crayfish, covered them with cheese and mustard, and set them under the grill. He who washed the crisp lettuce and assembled crusty bread and butter. We ate the feast round the cabin table with rain pattering on portholes and roof and the sea-water slapping against the sides in the freshening wind. Over coffee, at Jik's insistence, I told them why I had come to Australia.

They heard me out in concentrated silence. Then Jik, whose politics had not changed much since student pink, muttered darkly about 'pigs', and Sarah looked nakedly apprehensive.

'Don't worry,' I told her. 'I'm not asking for Jik's help, now that I know he's married.'

'You have it. You have it,' he said explosively.

I shook my head. 'No.'

Sarah said, 'What precisely do you plan to do first?'

'Find out where the two Munnings came from.'

'And after?'

'If I knew what I was looking for I wouldn't need to look.'

'That doesn't follow,' she said absently.

'Melbourne,' Jik said suddenly. 'You said one of the pictures came from Melbourne. Well, that settles it. Of course we'll help. We'll go there at once. It couldn't be better. Do you know what next Tuesday is?'

'No,' I said. 'What is it?'

'The day of the Melbourne Cup!'

His voice was triumphant. Sarah stared at me darkly across the table.

'I wish you hadn't come,' she said.

six

I slept that night in the converted boathouse which constituted Jik's postal address. Apart from a bed alcove, new-looking bathroom, and rudimentary kitchen, he was using the whole space as studio.

A huge old easel stood in the centre, with a table to each side holding neat arrays of paints, brushes, knives, pots of linseed and turpentine and cleaning fluid : all the usual paraphernalia.

No work in progress. Everything shut and tidy. Like its counterpart in England, the large rush mat in front of the easel was black with oily dirt, owing to Jik's habit of rubbing his roughly rinsed brushes on it between colours. The tubes of paint were characteristically squeezed flat in the middles, impatience forbidding an orderly progress from the bottom. The palette was a small oblong, not needed any larger because he used most colours straight from the tube and got his effects by overpainting. A huge box of rags stood under one table, ready to wipe clean everything used to apply paint to picture, not just brushes and knives, but fingers, palms, nails, wrists, anything which took his fancy. I smiled to myself. Jik's studio was as identifiable as his pictures.

Along one wall a two-tiered rack held rows of canvasses, which I pulled out one by one. Dark, strong, dramatic colours, leaping to the eye. Still the troubled vision, the perception of doom. Decay and crucifixions, obscurely horrific landscapes, flowers wilting, fish dying, everything to be guessed, nothing explicit.

Jik hated to sell his paintings and seldom did, which I thought was just as well, as they made uncomfortable room-mates, enough to cause depression in a skylark. They had a vigour, though, that couldn't be denied. Everyone who saw his assembled work remembered it, and had their thoughts modified, and perhaps even their basic attitudes changed. He was a major artist in a way I would never be, and he would have looked upon easy popular acclaim as personal failure.

In the morning I walked down to the boat and found Sarah there alone.

'Jik's gone for milk and newspapers,' she said. 'I'll get you some breakfast.'

'I came to say goodbye.'

She looked at me levelly. 'The damage is done.'

'Not if I go.'

'Back to England?'

I shook my head.

'I thought not.' A dim smile appeared briefly in her eyes. 'Jik told me last night that you were the only person he knew who had a head cool enough to calculate a ship's position for a Mayday call by dead reckoning at night after tossing around violently for four hours in a force ten gale with a hole in the hull and the

71

pumps packed up, and get it right.'

I grinned. 'But he patched the hull and mended the pump, and we cancelled the Mayday when it got light.'

'You were both stupid.'

'Better to stay safely at home?' I said.

She turned away. '*Men*,' she said. 'Never happy unless they're risking their necks.'

She was right, to some extent. A little healthy danger wasn't a bad feeling, especially in retrospect. It was only the nerve-breakers which gave you the shakes and put you off repetition.

'Some women, too,' I said.

'Not me.'

'I won't take Jik with me.'

Her back was still turned. 'You'll get him killed,' she said.

Nothing looked less dangerous than the small suburban gallery from which Maisie had bought her picture. It was shut for good. The bare premises could be seen nakedly through the shop-front window, and a succinct and unnecessary card hanging inside the glass door said 'Closed'.

The little shops on each side shrugged their shoulders.

'They were only open for a month or so. Never seemed to do much business. No surprise they folded.'

Did they, I asked, know which estate agent was handling the letting? No, they didn't.

'End of enquiry,' Jik said.

I shook my head. 'Let's try the local agents.'

We split up and spent a fruitless hour. None of the firms on any of the 'For Sale' boards in the district admitted to having the gallery on its books.

We met again outside the uninformative door.

'Where now?'

'Art Gallery?'

'In the Domain,' Jik said, which turned out to be a chunk of park in the city centre. The Art Gallery had a suitable façade of six pillars outside and the Munnings, when we ran it to earth, inside.

No one else was looking at it. No one approached to fall into chat and advise us we could buy another one cheap in a little gallery in an outer suburb.

We stood there for a while with me admiring the absolute mastery which set the two grey ponies in the shaft of pre-storm light at the head of the darker herd, and Jik grudgingly admitting that at least the man knew how to handle paint.

Absolutely nothing else happened. We drove back to the boat in the M.G., and lunch was an anti-climax.

'What now?' Jik said.

'A spot of work with the telephone, if I could borrow the one in the boathouse.'

It took nearly all afternoon, but alphabetically systematic calls to every estate agent as far as Holloway & Son in the classified directory produced the goods in the end. The premises in question, said Holloway & Son, had been let to North Sydney Fine Arts on a short lease.

How short?

Three months, dating from September first.

No, Holloway & Son did not know the premises were now empty. They could not re-let them until December first, because North Sydney Fine Arts had paid all the rent in advance; and they did not feel able to part with the name of any individual concerned. I blarneyed a bit, giving a delicate impression of being in the trade myself, with a client for the empty shop. Holloway & Son mentioned a Mr John Grey, with a post-office box number for an address. I thanked them. Mr Grey, they said, warming up a little, had said he wanted the gallery for a short private exhibition, and they were not really surprised he had already gone.

How could I recognize Mr Grey if I met him? They really couldn't say: all the negotiations had been done by telephone and post. I could write to him myself, if my client wanted the gallery before December first.

Ta ever so, I thought.

All the same, it couldn't do much harm. I unearthed a suitable sheet of paper, and in twee and twirly lettering in black ink told Mr Grey I had been given his name and box number by Holloway & Son, and asked him if he would sell me the last two weeks of his lease so that I could mount an exhibition of a friend's *utterly meaningful* watercolours. Name his own price, I said, within reason. Yours sincerely, I said; Peregrine Smith.

I walked down to the boat to ask if Jik or Sarah would mind me putting their own box number as a return address.

'He won't answer,' Sarah said, reading the letter. 'If he's a crook. I wouldn't.'

'The first principle of fishing,' Jik said, 'is to dangle a bait.'

'This wouldn't attract a starving pirhana.'

I posted it anyway, with Sarah's grudging consent. None of us expected it to bring forth any result.

Jik's own session on the telephone proved more rewarding. Melbourne, it seemed, was crammed to the rooftops for the richest race meeting of the year, but he had been offered last-minute cancellations. Very lucky indeed, he insisted, looking amused.

'Where?' I asked suspiciously.

'In the Hilton,' he said.

I couldn't afford it, but we went anyway. Jik in his student days had lived on cautious hand-outs from a family trust, and it appeared that the source of bread was still flowing. The boat, the boathouse, the M.G. and the wife were none of them supported by paint.

We flew south to Melbourne the following morning, looking down on the Snowy Mountains en route and thinking our own chilly thoughts. Sarah's disapproval from the seat behind froze the back of my head, but she had refused to stay in Sydney. Jik's natural bent and enthusiasm for dicey adventure looked like being curbed by love, and his reaction to danger might not henceforth be uncomplicatedly practical. That was, if I could find any dangers for him to react to. The Sydney trail was dead and cold, and maybe Melbourne too would yield an unlooked-at public Munnings and a gone-away private gallery. And if it did, what then? For Donald the outlook would be bleaker than the strange puckered ranges sliding away underneath.

If I could take home enough to show beyond doubt that the plundering of his house had its roots in the sale of a painting in

Australia, it should get the police off his neck, the life back to his spirit, and Regina into a decent grave.

If.

And I would have to be quick, or it would be too late to matter. Donald, staring hour after hour at a portrait in an empty house ... Donald, on the brink.

Melbourne was cold and wet and blowing a gale. We checked gratefully into the warm plushy bosom of the Hilton, souls cossetted from the door onwards by rich reds and purples and blues, velvety fabrics, copper and gilt and glass. The staff smiled. The lifts worked. There was polite shock when I carried my own suitcase. A long way from the bare boards of home.

I unpacked, which is to say, hung up my one suit, slightly crumpled from the squashy satchel, and then went to work again on the telephone.

The Melbourne office of the Monga Vineyards Proprietary Limited cheerfully told me that the person who dealt with Mr Donald Stuart from England was the managing director, Mr Hudson Taylor, and he could be found at present in his office at the vineyard itself, which was north of Adelaide. Would I like the number?

Thanks very much.

'No sweat,' they said, which I gathered was Australian shorthand for 'It's no trouble, and you're welcome.'

I pulled out the map of Australia I'd acquired on the flight from England. Melbourne, capital of the state of Victoria, lay right down in the south-east corner. Adelaide, capital of South Australia, lay about four hundred and fifty miles north west. Correction, seven hundred and thirty kilometres: the Australians had already gone metric, to the confusion of my mental arithmetic.

Hudson Taylor was not in his vineyard office. An equally cheerful voice there told me he'd left for Melbourne to go to the races. He had a runner in the Cup. Reverence, the voice implied, was due.

Could I reach him anywhere, then?

Sure, if it was important. He would be staying with friends. Number supplied. Ring at nine o'clock.

Sighing a little I went two floors down and found Jik and Sarah bouncing around their room with gleeful satisfaction.

'We've got tickets for the races tomorrow and Tuesday,' he said, 'And a car pass, and a car. And the West Indies play Victoria at cricket on Sunday opposite the hotel and we've tickets for that too.'

'Miracles courtesy of the Hilton,' Sarah said, looking much happier at this programme. 'The whole package was on offer with the cancelled rooms.'

'So what do you want us to do this afternoon?' finished Jik expansively.

'Could you bear the Arts Centre?'

It appeared they could. Even Sarah came without forecasting universal doom, my lack of success so far having cheered her. We went in a taxi to keep her curled hair dry.

The Victoria Arts Centre was huge, modern, inventive and endowed with the largest stained-glass roof in the world. Jik took deep breaths as if drawing the living spirit of the place into his lungs and declaimed at the top of his voice that Australia was the greatest, the greatest, the only adventurous country left in the corrupt, stagnating, militant, greedy, freedom-hating, mean-minded, strait-jacketed, rotting, polluted world. Passers-by stared in amazement and Sarah showed no surprise at all.

We ran the Munnings to earth, eventually, deep in the labyrinth of galleries. It glowed in the remarkable light which suffused the whole building; the *Departure of the Hop Pickers*, with its great wide sky and the dignified gypsies with their ponies, caravans and children.

A young man was sitting at an easel slightly to one side, painstakingly working on a copy. On a table beside him stood large pots of linseed oil and turps, and a jar with brushes in cleaning fluid. A comprehensive box of paints lay open to hand. Two or three people stood about, watching him and pretending not to, in the manner of gallery-goers the world over.

Jik and I went round behind him to take a look. The young man glanced at Jik's face, but saw nothing there except raised eyebrows and blandness. We watched him squeeze flake white

76

and cadmium yellow from tubes on to his palette and mix them together into a nice pale colour with a hogshair brush.

On the easel stood his study, barely started. The outlines were there, as precise as tracings, and a small amount of blue had been laid on the sky.

Jik and I watched in interest while he applied the pale yellow to the shirt of the nearest figure.

'Hey,' Jik said loudly, suddenly slapping him on the shoulder and shattering the reverent gallery hush into kaleidoscopic fragments, 'You're a fraud. If you're an artist I'm a gas-fitter's mate.'

Hardly polite, but not a hanging matter. The faces of the scattered onlookers registered embarrassment, not affront.

On the young man, though, the effect was galvanic. He leapt to his feet, overturning the easel and staring at Jik with wild eyes: and Jik, with huge enjoyment put in the clincher.

'What you're doing is *criminal*,' he said.

The young man reacted to that with ruthless reptilian speed, snatching up the pots of linseed and turps and flinging the liquids at Jik's eyes.

I grabbed his left arm. He scooped up the paint-laden palette in his right and swung round fiercely, aiming at my face. I ducked instinctively. The palette missed me and struck Jik, who had his hands to his eyes and was yelling very loudly.

Sarah rushed towards him, knocking into me hard in her anxiety and loosening my grip on the young man. He tore his arm free, ran precipitously for the exit, dodged round behind two open-mouthed middle-aged spectators who were on their way in, and pushed them violently into my chasing path. By the time I'd disentangled myself, he had vanished from sight. I ran through several halls and passages, but couldn't find him. He knew his way, and I did not: and it took me long enough, when I finally gave up the hunt, to work out the route back to Jik.

A fair-sized crowd had surrounded him, and Sarah was in a roaring fury based on fear, which she unleashed on me as soon as she saw me return.

'Do something,' she screamed. 'Do something, he's going blind . . . He's going *blind* . . . I knew we should never have listened to you . . .'

I caught her wrists as she advanced in near hysteria to do at least some damage to my face in payment for Jik's. Her strength was no joke.

'Sarah,' I said fiercely. 'Jik is *not* going blind.'

'He is. He is,' she insisted, kicking my shins.

'Do you *want* him to?' I shouted.

She gasped sharply in outrage. What I'd said was at least as good as a slap in the face. Sense reasserted itself suddenly like a drench of cold water, and the manic power receded back to normal angry girl proportions.

'Linseed oil will do no harm at all,' I said positively. 'The turps is painful, but that's all. It absolutely will not affect his eyesight.'

She glared at me, pulled her wrists out of my grasp, and turned back to Jik, who was rocking around in agony and cupping his fingers over his eyes with rigid knuckles. Also, being Jik, he was exercising his tongue.

'The slimy little bugger ... wait till I catch him ... Jesus Christ Almighty I can't bloody see ... Sarah ... where's that bloody Todd ... I'll strangle him ... get an ambulance ... my eyes are burning out ... bloody buggering hell ...'

I spoke loudly in his ear. 'Your eyes are O.K.'

'They're my bloody eyes and if I say they're not O.K. they're bloody not.'

'You know damn well you're not going blind, so stop hamming it up.'

'They're not your eyes, you sod.'

'And you're frightening Sarah,' I said.

That message got through. He took his hands away and stopped rolling about.

At the sight of his face a murmur of pleasant horror rippled through the riveted audience. Blobs of bright paint from the young man's palette had streaked one side of his jaw yellow and blue: and his eyes were red with inflammation and pouring with tears, and looked very sore indeed.

'Jesus, Sarah,' he said blinking painfully. 'Sorry, love. The bastard's right. Turps never blinded anybody.'

'Not permanently,' I said, because to do him justice he obviously couldn't see anything but tears at the moment.

Sarah's animosity was unabated. 'Get him an ambulance, then.'

I shook my head. 'All he needs is water and time.'

'You're a stupid heartless *pig*. He obviously needs a doctor, and hospital care.'

Jik, having abandoned histrionics, produced a handkerchief and gently mopped his streaming eyes.

'He's right, love. Lots of water, as the man said. Washes the sting away. Lead me to the nearest gents.'

With Sarah unconvinced but holding one arm, and a sympathetic male spectator the other, he was solicitously helped away like an amateur production of *Samson*. The chorus in the shape of the audience bent reproachful looks on me, and cheerfully awaited the next act.

I looked at the overturned mess of paints and easel which the young man had left. The onlookers looked at them too.

'I suppose,' I said slowly, 'that no one here was talking to the young artist before any of this happened?'

'We were,' said one woman, surprised at the question.

'So were we,' said another.

'What about?'

'Munnings,' said one, and 'Munnings,' said the other, both looking immediately at the painting on the wall.

'Not about his own work?' I said, bending down to pick it up. A slash of yellow lay wildly across the careful outlines, result of Jik's slap on the back.

Both of the ladies, and also their accompanying husbands, shook their heads and said they had talked with him about the pleasure of hanging a Munnings on their own walls, back home.

I smiled slowly.

'I suppose,' I said, 'that he didn't happen to know where you could get one?'

'Well, yeah,' they said. 'As a matter of fact, he sure did.'

'Where?'

'Well, look here, young fellow . . .' The elder of the husbands, a seventyish American with the unmistakable stamp of wealth, began shushing the others to silence with a practised damping movement of his right hand. Don't give information away, it said, you may lose by it. '. . . You're asking a lot of questions.'

'I'll explain,' I said. 'Would you like some coffee?'

They all looked at their watches and said doubtfully they possibly would.

'There's a coffee shop just down the hall,' I said. 'I saw it when I was trying to catch that young man . . . to make him tell why he flung turps in my friend's eyes.'

Curiosity sharpened in their faces. They were hooked.

The rest of the spectators drifted away, and I, asking the others to wait a moment, started moving the jumbled painting stuff off the centre of the floor to a tidier wallside heap.

None of it was marked with its owner's name. All regulation kit, obtainable from art shops. Artists' quality, not students' cheaper equivalents. None of it new, but not old, either. The picture itself was on a standard sized piece of commercially prepared hardboard, not on stretched canvas. I stacked everything together, added the empty jars which had held linseed and turps, and wiped my hands on a piece of rag.

'Right,' I said. 'Shall we go?'

They were all Americans, all rich, retired, and fond of racing. Mr and Mrs Howard K. Petrovitch of Ridgeville, New Jersey, and Mr and Mrs Wyatt L. Minchless from Carter, Illinois.

Wyatt Minchless, the one who had shushed the others, called the meeting to order over four richly creamed iced coffees and one plain black. The black was for himself. Heart condition, he murmured, patting the relevant area of suiting. A white-haired man, black-framed specs, pale indoor complexion, pompous manner.

'Now, young fellow, let's hear it from the top.'

'Um,' I said. Where exactly was the top? 'The artist boy attacked my friend Jik because Jik called him a criminal.'

'Yuh,' Mrs Petrovitch nodded, 'I heard him. Just as we were leaving the gallery. Now why would he do that?'

'It isn't criminal to copy good painting,' Mrs Minchless said knowledgeably. 'In the Louvre in Paris, France, you can't get near the Mona Lisa for those irritating students.'

She had blue-rinsed puffed-up hair, uncreasable navy and green clothes, and enough diamonds to attract a top-rank thief. Deep lines of automatic disapproval ran downwards from the corner of her mouth. Thin body. Thick mind.

'It depends what you are copying *for*,' I said. 'If you're going to try to pass your copy off as an original, then that definitely is a fraud.'

Mrs Petrovitch began to say, 'Do you think the young man was *forging* . . .' but was interrupted by Wyatt Minchless, who smothered her question both by the damping hand and his louder voice.

'Are you saying that this young artist boy was painting a Munnings he later intended to sell as the real thing?'

'Er . . .' I said.

Wyatt Minchless swept on. 'Are you saying that the Munnings picture he told us we might be able to buy is itself a forgery?'

The others looked both horrified at the possibility and admiring of Wyatt L. for his perspicacity.

'I don't know,' I said. 'I just thought I'd like to see it.'

'You don't want to buy a Munnings yourself? You are not acting as an agent for anyone else?' Wyatt's questions sounded severe and inquisitorial.

'Absolutely not,' I said.

'Well, then.' Wyatt looked round the other three, collected silent assents. 'He told Ruthie and me there was a good Munnings racing picture at a very reasonable price in a little gallery not far away . . .' He fished with forefinger and thumb into his outer breast pocket. 'Yes, here we are. Yarra River Fine Arts. Third turning off Swanston Street, about twenty yards along.'

Mr and Mrs Petrovitch looked resigned. 'He told us, exactly the same.'

'He seemed such a nice young man,' Mrs Petrovitch added sadly. 'So interested in our trip. Asked us what we'd be betting on in the Cup.'

'He asked where we would be going after Melbourne,' Mr Petrovitch nodded. 'We told him Adelaide and Alice Springs, and he said Alice Springs was a Mecca for artists and to be sure to visit the Yarra River gallery there. The same firm, he said. Always had good pictures.'

Mr Petrovitch would have misunderstood if I had leaned across and hugged him. I concentrated on my fancy coffee and kept my excitement to myself.

'We're going on to Sydney,' pronounced Wyatt L. 'He didn't offer any suggestions for Sydney.'

The tall glasses were nearly empty. Wyatt looked at his watch and swallowed the last of his plain black.

'You didn't tell us,' Mrs Petrovitch said, looking puzzled, 'why your friend called the young man a criminal. I mean . . . I can see why the young man attacked your friend and ran away if he *was* a criminal, but why did your friend *think* he was?'

'Just what I was about to ask,' said Wyatt, nodding away heavily. Pompous liar, I thought.

'My friend Jik,' I said, 'is an artist himself. He didn't think much of the young man's effort. He called it criminal. He might just as well have said lousy.'

'Is that all?' said Mrs Petrovitch, looking disappointed.

'Well . . . the young man was painting with paints which won't really mix. Jik's a perfectionist. He can't stand seeing paint misused.'

'What do you mean, won't mix?'

'Paints are chemicals,' I said apologetically. 'Most of them don't have any effect on each other, but you have to be careful.'

'What happens if you aren't?' demanded Ruthie Minchless.

'Um . . . nothing explodes,' I said, smiling. 'It's just that . . . well, if you mix flake white, which is lead, with cadmium yellow, which contains sulphur, like the young man was doing, you get a nice pale colour to start with but the two minerals react against each other and in time darken and alter the picture.'

'And your friend called this criminal?' Wyatt said in disbelief. 'It couldn't possibly make that much difference.'

'Er . . .' I said. 'Well, Van Gogh used a light bright new yellow made of chrome when he painted a picture of sunflowers. Cadmium yellow hadn't been developed then. But chrome yellow has shown that over a couple of hundred years it decomposes and in the end turns greenish black, and the sunflowers are already an odd colour, and I don't think anyone has found a way of stopping it.'

'But the young man wasn't painting for posterity,' said Ruthie with irritation. 'Unless he's another Van Gogh, surely it doesn't matter.'

I didn't think they'd want to hear that Jik hoped for recognition in the twenty-third century. The permanence of colours had always been an obsession with him, and he'd dragged me along once to a course on their chemistry.

The Americans got up to go.

'All very interesting,' Wyatt said with a dismissive smile. 'I guess I'll keep my money in regular stocks.'

seven

Jik had gone from the gents, gone from the whole Arts Centre. I found him back with Sarah in their hotel room, being attended by the Hilton's attractive resident nurse. The door to the corridor stood open, ready for her to leave.

'Try not to rub them, Mr Cassavetes,' she was saying. 'If you have any trouble, call the reception desk, and I'll come back.'

She gave me a professional half-smile in the open doorway and walked briskly away, leaving me to go in.

'How are the eyes?' I said, advancing tentatively.

'Ruddy awful.' They were bright pink, but dry. Getting better.

Sarah said with tight lips, 'This has all gone far enough. I know that this time Jik will be all right again in a day or two, but we are not taking any more risks.'

Jik said nothing and didn't look at me.

It wasn't exactly unexpected. I said, 'O.K. . . . Well, have a nice weekend, and thanks anyway.'

'Todd . . .' Jik said.

Sarah leapt in fast. 'No, Jik. It's not our responsibility. Todd can think what he likes, but his cousin's troubles are nothing to do with us. We are not getting involved any further. I've been against all this silly poking around all along, and this is where it stops.'

'Todd will go on with it,' Jik said.

'Then he's a fool.' She was angry, scornful, biting.

'Sure,' I said. 'Anyone who tries to right a wrong these days is a fool. Much better not to meddle, not to get involved, not to think it's your responsibility. I really ought to be painting away safely in my attic at Heathrow, minding my own business and letting Donald rot. Much more sensible, I agree. The trouble is that I simply can't do it. I see the hell he's in. How can I just turn my back? Not when there's a chance of getting him out. True enough, I may not manage it, but what I can't face is not having tried.'

I came to a halt.

A blank pause.

'Well,' I said, raising a smile. 'Here endeth the lesson according to the world's foremost nit. Have fun at the races. I might go too, you never know.'

I sketched a farewell and eased myself out. Neither of them said a word. I shut the door quietly and took the lift up to my own room.

A pity about Sarah, I thought. She would have Jik in cotton-wool and slippers if he didn't look out; and he'd never paint those magnificent brooding pictures any more, because they sprang from a torment he would no longer be allowed. Security, to him, would be a sort of abdication; a sort of death.

I looked at my watch and decided the Yarra River Fine Arts set-up might still have its doors open. Worth trying.

I wondered, as I walked along Wellington Parade and up Swanston Street, whether the young turps-flinger would be there, and if he was, whether he would know me. I'd seen only glimpses of his face, as I'd mostly been standing behind him. All one could swear to was light-brown hair, acne on the chin, a round jaw-line and a full-lipped mouth. Under twenty. Perhaps not more than seventeen. Dressed in blue jeans, white tee-shirt, and tennis shoes. About five-foot-eight, a hundred and thirty pounds. Quick on his feet, and liable to panic. And no artist.

The gallery was open, brightly lit, with a horse painting on a gilt display easel in the centre of the window. Not a Munnings. A portrait picture of an Australian horse and jockey, every detail sharp-edged, emphatic, and, to my taste, overpainted. Beside it a notice, gold embossed on black, announced a special display of distinguished equine art; and beside that, less well-produced but with larger letters, stood a display card saying 'Welcome to the Melbourne Cup'.

The gallery looked typical of hundreds of others round the world; narrow frontage, with premises stretching back a good way from the street. Two or three people were wandering about inside, looking at the merchandise on the well-lit neutral grey walls.

I had gone there intending to go in. To go in was still what I intended, but I hesitated outside in the street feeling as if I were at the top of a ski jump. Stupid, I thought. Nothing venture, nothing gain, and all that. If you don't look, you won't see.

I took a ruefully deep breath and stepped over the welcoming threshold.

Greeny-grey carpet within, and an antique desk strategically placed near the door, with a youngish woman handing out small catalogues and large smiles.

'Feel free to look around,' she said. 'More pictures downstairs.'

She handed me a catalogue, a folded glazed white card with several typed sheets clipped into it. I flipped them over. One hundred and sixty-three items, numbered consecutively, with titles, artists' names, and asking price. A painting already sold, it said, would have a red spot on the frame.

I thanked her. 'Just passing by,' I said.

She nodded and smiled professionally, eyes sliding in a rapid summing up over my denim clothes and general air of not belonging to the jet set. She herself wore the latest trendy fashion with careless ease and radiated tycoon-catching sincerity. Australian, assured, too big a personality to be simply a receptionist.

'You're welcome anyway,' she said.

I walked slowly down the long room, checking the pictures against their notes. Most were by Australian artists, and I could see what Jik had meant about the hot competition. The field was just as crowded as at home, if not more so, and the standard in some respects better. As usual when faced with other people's flourishing talents I began to have doubts of my own.

At the far end of the ground-floor display there was a staircase leading downwards, adorned with a large arrow and a notice repeating 'More Pictures Downstairs'.

I went down. Same carpet, same lighting, but no scatter of customers looking from pictures to catalogues and back again.

Below stairs, the gallery was not one straight room but a series of small rooms off a long corridor, apparently the result of not being able to knock down all the dividing and load-bearing walls. A room to the rear of the stairs was an office, furnished with another distinguished desk, two or three comfortable chairs for prospective clients, and a civilized row of teak-faced filing cabinets. Heavily framed pictures adorned the walls, and an equally substantial man was writing in a ledger at the desk.

He raised his head, conscious of my presence outside his door. 'Can I help you?' he said.

'Just looking.'

He gave me an uninterested nod and went back to his work. He, like the whole place, had an air of permanence and respectability quite unlike the fly-by-night suburban affair in Sydney. This reputable business, I thought, could not be what I was looking for. I had got the whole thing wrong. I would have to wait until I could get Hudson Taylor to look up Donald's cheque and point me in a new direction.

Sighing, I continued down the line of rooms, thinking I might as well finish taking stock of the opposition. A few of the frames were adorned with red spots, but the prices on everything good were a mile from a bargain and a deterrent to all but the rich.

In the end room, which was larger than the others, I came across the Munnings. Three of them. All with horses; one racing scene, one hunting, one of gypsies.

They were not in the catalogue.

They hung without ballyhoo in a row of similar subjects, and to my eyes stuck out like thoroughbreds among hacks.

Prickles began up my spine. It wasn't just the workmanship, but one of the pictures itself. Horses going down to the start. A long line of jockeys, bright against a dark sky. The silks of the nearest rider, purple with a green cap.

Maisie's chatty voice reverberated in my inner ear, describing what I saw. '. . . I expect you'll think I was silly but that was one of the reasons I bought it . . . because Archie and I decided we'd like purple with a green cap for our colours, if no one already had that . . .'

Munnings had always used a good deal of purple and green in shadows and distances. All the same . . . This picture, size, subject, and colouring, was exactly like Maisie's, which had been hidden behind a radiator, and, presumably, burned.

The picture in front of me looked authentic. The right sort of patina for the time since Munnings' death, the right excellence of draughtsmanship, the right indefinable something which separated the great from the good. I put out a gentle finger to feel the surface of canvas and paint. Nothing there that shouldn't be.

An English voice from behind me said, 'Can I help you?'

'Isn't that a Munnings?' I said casually, turning round.

He was standing in the doorway, looking in, his expression full of the guarded helpfulness of one whose best piece of stock is being appraised by someone apparently too poor to buy it.

I knew him instantly. Brown receding hair combed back, grey eyes, down-drooping moustache, suntanned skin: all last on view thirteen days ago beside the sea in Sussex, England, prodding around in a smoky ruin.

Mr Greene. With an 'e'.

It took him only a fraction longer. Puzzlement as he glanced from me to the picture and back, then the shocking realization of where he'd seen me. He took a sharp step backwards and raised his hand to the wall outside.

I was on my way to the door, but I wasn't quick enough. A steel mesh gate slid down very fast in the doorway and clicked into some sort of bolt in the floor. Mr Greene stood on the outside, disbelief still stamped on every feature and his mouth hanging open. I revised all my easy theories about danger being good for the soul and felt as frightened as I'd ever been in my life.

'What's the matter?' called a deeper voice from up the corridor.

Mr Greene's tongue was stuck. The man from the office appeared at his shoulder and looked at me through the imprisoning steel.

'A thief?' he asked with irritation.

Mr Greene shook his head. A third person arrived outside, his young face bright with curiosity, and his acne showing like measles.

'Hey,' he said in loud Australian surprise. 'He was the one at the Arts Centre. The one who chased me. I swear he didn't follow me. I swear it.'

'Shut up,' said the man from the office briefly. He stared at me steadily. I stared back.

I was standing in the centre of a brightly lit room of about fifteen feet square. No windows. No way out except through the guarded door. Nowhere to hide, no weapons to hand. A long way down the ski jump and no promise of a soft landing.

'I say,' I said plaintively. 'Just what is all this about?' I walked up to the steel gate and tapped on it. 'Open this up, I want to get out.'

'What are you doing here?' the office man said. He was bigger than Greene and obviously more senior in the gallery. Heavy dark spectacle frames over unfriendly eyes, and a blue bow tie with polka dots under a double chin. Small mouth with a full lower lip. Thinning hair.

'Looking,' I said, trying to sound bewildered. 'Just looking at pictures.' An innocent at large, I thought, and a bit dim.

'He chased me in the Arts Centre,' the boy repeated.

'You threw some stuff in that man's eyes,' I said indignantly. 'You might have blinded him.'

'Friend of yours, was he?' the office man said.

'No,' I said. 'I was just there, that was all. Same as I'm here. Just looking at pictures. Nothing wrong in that, is there? I go to lots of galleries, all the time.'

Mr Greene got his voice back. 'I saw him in England,' he said to the office man. His eyes returned to the Munnings, then he put his hand on the office man's arm and pulled him up the corridor out of my sight.

'Open the door,' I said to the boy, who still gazed in.

'I don't know how,' he said. 'And I don't reckon I'd be popular, somehow.'

The two other men returned. All three gazed in. I began to feel sympathy for creatures in cages.

'Who *are* you?' said the office man.

'Nobody. I mean, I'm just here for the racing, of course, and the cricket.'

'Name?'

'Charles Neil.' Charles Neil Todd.

'What were you doing in England?'

'I live there!' I said. 'Look,' I went on, as if trying to be reasonable under great provocation. 'I saw this man here,' I nodded to Greene, 'at the home of a woman I know slightly in Sussex. She was giving me a lift home from the races, see, as I'd missed my train to Worthing and was thumbing along the road from the Members' car park. Well, she stopped and picked me up, and then said she wanted to make a detour to see her house which had lately been burnt, and when we got there, this man was there. He said his name was Greene and that he was from an insurance company, and that's all I know about him. So what's going on?'

'It is a coincidence that you should meet here again, so soon.'

'It certainly is,' I agreed fervently. 'But that's no bloody reason to lock me up.'

I read indecision on all their faces. I hoped the sweat wasn't running visibly down my own.

I shrugged exasperatedly. 'Fetch the police or something, then,' I said. 'If you think I've done anything wrong.'

The man from the office put his hand to the switch on the outside wall and carefully fiddled with it, and the steel gate slid up out of sight, a good deal more slowly than it had come down.

'Sorry,' he said perfunctorily. 'But we have to be careful, with so many valuable paintings on the premises.'

'Well, I see that,' I said, stepping forward and resisting a strong impulse to make a dash for it. 'But all the same . . .' I managed an aggrieved tone. 'Still, no harm done, I suppose.' Magnanimous, as well.

They all walked behind me along the corridor and up the stairs and through the upper gallery, doing my nerves no slightest good. All the other visitors seemed to have left. The receptionist was locking the front door.

My throat was dry beyond swallowing.

'I thought everyone had gone,' she said in surprise.

'Slight delay,' I said, with a feeble laugh.

She gave me the professional smile and reversed the locks. Opened the door. Held it, waiting for me.

Six steps.

Out in the fresh air.

God almighty, it smelled good. I half turned. All four stood in the gallery watching me go. I shrugged and nodded and trudged away into the drizzle, feeling as weak as a fieldmouse dropped by a hawk.

I caught a passing tram and travelled a good way into unknown regions of the huge city, conscious only of an urgent desire to put a lot of distance between myself and that basement prison.

They would have second thoughts. They were bound to. They would wish they had found out more about me before letting me go. They couldn't be certain it wasn't a coincidence that I'd turned up at their gallery, because far more amazing coincidences did exist, like Lincoln at the time of his assassination having a secretary called Kennedy and Kennedy having a secretary called Lincoln; but the more they thought about it the less they would believe it.

If they wanted to find me, where would they look? Not at the Hilton, I thought in amusement. At the races: I had told them I would be there. On the whole I wished I hadn't.

At the end of the tramline I got off and found myself opposite a small interesting-looking restaurant with B.Y.O. in large letters on the door. Hunger as usual rearing its healthy head, I went in and ordered a steak, and asked for a look at the wine list.

The waitress looked surprised. 'It's B.Y.O.,' she said.

'What's B.Y.O.?'

Her eyebrows went still higher. 'You are a stranger? Bring Your Own. We don't sell drinks here, only food.'

'Oh.'

'If you want something to drink, there's a drive-in bottle shop a hundred yards down the road that'll still be open. I could hold the steak until you get back.'

I shook my head and settled for a teetotal dinner, grinning all through coffee at a notice on the wall saying 'We have an arrangement with our bank. They don't fry steaks and we don't cash cheques.'

When I set off back to the city centre on the tram, I passed the bottle shop, which at first sight looked so like a garage that if I hadn't known I would have thought the line of cars was queuing for petrol. I could see why Jik liked the Australian imagination: both sense and fun.

The rain had stopped. I left the tram and walked the last couple of miles through the bright streets and dark parks, asking the way. Thinking of Donald and Maisie and Greene with an 'e', and of paintings and burglaries and violent minds.

The overall plan had all along seemed fairly simple: to sell pictures in Australia and steal them back in England, together with everything else lying handy. As I had come across two instances within three weeks, I had been sure there had to be more, because it was surely impossible that I could have stumbled on the *only* two, even given the double link of racing and painting. Since I'd met the Petrovitches and the Minchlesses, it seemed I'd been wrong to think of all the robberies taking place in England. Why not in America? Why not anywhere that was worth the risk?

Why not a mobile force of thieves shuttling containerfuls of antiques from continent to continent, selling briskly to a ravenous market. As Inspector Frost had said, few antiques were ever recovered. The demand was insatiable and the supply, by definition, limited.

Suppose I were a villain, I thought, and I didn't want to waste weeks in foreign countries finding out exactly which houses were worth robbing. I could just stay quietly at home in Melbourne selling paintings to rich visitors who could afford an impulse-buy of ten thousand pounds or so. I could chat away with them about their picture collections back home, and I could shift the conversation easily to their silver and china and objets d'art.

I wouldn't want the sort of customers who had Rembrandts or

Fabergés or anything well-known and unsaleable like that. Just the middling wealthy with Georgian silver and lesser Gauguins and Chippendale chairs.

When they bought my paintings, they would give me their addresses. Nice and easy. Just like that.

I would be a supermarket type of villain, with a large turnover of small goods. I would reckon that if I kept the victims reasonably well scattered, the fact that they had been to Australia within the past year or so would mean nothing to each regional police force. I would reckon that among the thousands of burglary claims they had to settle, Australian visits would bear no significance to insurance companies.

I would not, though, reckon on a crossed wire like Charles Neil Todd.

If I were a villain, I thought, with a well-established business and a good reputation, I wouldn't put myself at risk by selling fakes. Forged oil paintings were almost always detectable under a microscope, even if one discounted that the majority of experienced dealers could tell them at a glance. A painter left his signature all over a painting, not just in the corner, because the way he held his brush was as individual as handwriting. Brush strokes could be matched as conclusively as grooves on bullets.

If I were a villain I'd wait in my spider's web with a real Munnings, or maybe a real Picasso drawing, or a genuine work by a recently dead good artist whose output had been voluminous, and along would come the rich little flies, carefully steered my way by talkative accomplices who stood around in the states' capitals' art galleries for the purpose. Both Donald and Maisie had been hooked that way.

Supposing when I'd sold a picture to a man from England and robbed him, and got my picture back again, I then sold it to someone from America. And then robbed him, and got it back, and so on and round.

Suppose I sold a picture to Maisie in Sydney, and got it back, and started to sell it again in Melbourne . . . My supposing stopped right there, because it didn't fit.

If Maisie had left her picture in full view it would have been stolen like her other things. Maybe it even had been, and was right now glowing in the Yarra River Fine Arts, but if so, why had the house been burnt, and why had Mr Greene turned up to search the ruins?

It only made sense if Maisie's picture had been a copy, and if the thieves hadn't been able to find it. Rather than leave it around, they'd burned the house. But I'd just decided that I wouldn't risk fakes. Except that ... would Maisie know an expert copy if she saw one? No, she wouldn't.

I sighed. To fool even Maisie you'd have to find an accomplished artist willing to copy instead of pressing on with his own work, and they weren't that thick on the ground. All the same, she'd bought her picture in the short-lived Sydney gallery, not in Melbourne, so maybe in other places besides Melbourne they would take a risk with fakes.

The huge bulk of the hotel rose ahead of me across the last stretch of park. The night air blew cool on my head. I had a vivid feeling of being disconnected, a stranger in a vast continent, a speck under the stars. The noise and warmth of the Hilton brought the expanding universe down to imaginable size.

Upstairs, I telephoned to Hudson Taylor at the number his secretary had given me. Nine o'clock on the dot. He sounded mellow and full of good dinner, his voice strong, courteous and vibrantly Australian.

'Donald Stuart's cousin? Is it true about little Regina being killed?'

'I'm afraid so.'

'It's a real tragedy. A real nice lass, that Regina.'

'Yes.'

'Lookee here, then, what can I do for you? Is it tickets for the races?'

'Er, no,' I said. 'It was just that since the receipt and provenance letter of the Munnings had been stolen along with the picture, Donald would like to get in touch with the people who had sold it to him, for insurance purposes, but he had forgotten their name. And as I was coming to Melbourne for the Cup . . .'

'That's easy enough,' Hudson Taylor said pleasantly. 'I remember the place well. I went with Donald to see the picture there, and the guy in charge brought it along to the Hilton afterwards, when we arranged the finance. Now let's see . . .' There was a pause for thought. 'I can't remember the name of the place just now. Or the manager. It was some months ago, do you see? But I've got him on record here in the Melbourne office, and I'm calling in there anyway in the morning, so I'll look them up. You'll be at the races tomorrow?'

'Yes,' I said.

'How about meeting for a drink, then? You can tell me about poor Donald and Regina, and I'll have the information he wants.'

I said that would be fine, and he gave me detailed instructions as to where I would find him, and when. 'There will be a huge crowd,' he said, 'But if you stand on that exact spot I shouldn't miss you.'

The spot he had described sounded public and exposed. I hoped that it would only be he who found me on it.

'I'll be there,' I said.

eight

Jik called through on the telephone at eight next morning.

'Come down to the coffee shop and have breakfast.'

'O.K.'

I went down in the lift and along the foyer to the hotel's informal restaurant. He was sitting at a table alone, wearing dark glasses and making inroads into a mountain of scrambled egg.

'They bring you coffee,' he said, 'But you have to fetch everything else from that buffet.' He nodded towards a large well-laden table in the centre of the breezy blue and sharp green decor. 'How's things?'

'Not what they used to be.'

He made a face. 'Bastard.'

'How are the eyes?'

He whipped off the glasses with a theatrical flourish and leaned forward to give me a good look. Pink, they were, and still inflamed, but on the definite mend.

'Has Sarah relented?' I asked.

'She's feeling sick.'

'Oh?'

'God knows,' he said. 'I hope not. I don't want a kid yet. She isn't overdue or anything.'

'She's a nice girl,' I said.

He slid me a glance. 'She says she's got nothing against you personally.'

'But,' I said.

He nodded. 'The mother hen syndrome.'

'Wouldn't have cast you as a chick.'

He put down his knife and fork. 'Nor would I, by God. I told her to cheer up and get this little enterprise over as soon as possible and face the fact she hadn't married a marshmallow.'

'And she said?'

He gave a twisted grin. 'From my performance in bed last night, that she had.'

I wondered idly about the success or otherwise of their sex life. From the testimony of one or two past girls who had let their hair down to me while waiting hours in the flat for Jik's unpredictable return, he was a moody lover, quick to arousal and easily put off. 'It only takes a dog barking, and he's gone.' Not much, I dared say, had changed.

'Anyway,' he said. 'There's this car we've got. Damned silly if you didn't come with us to the races.'

'Would Sarah ...' I asked carefully, '... scowl?'

'She says not.'

I accepted this offer and inwardly sighed. It looked as if he wouldn't take the smallest step henceforth without the nod from Sarah. When the wildest ones got married, was it always like that? Wedded bliss putting nets over the eagles.

'Where did you get to, last night?' he said.

'Aladdin's cave,' I said. 'Treasures galore and damned lucky to escape the boiling oil.'

I told him about the gallery, the Munnings, and my brief moment of captivity. I told him what I thought of the burglaries.

It pleased him. His eyes gleamed with humour and the familiar excitement rose.

'How are we going to prove it?' he said.

He heard the 'we' as soon as he said it. He laughed ruefully, the fizz dying away. 'Well, how?'

'Don't know yet.'

'I'd like to help,' he said apologetically.

I thought of a dozen sarcastic replies and stifled the lot. It was I who was the one out of step, not them. The voice of the past had no right to break up the future.

'You'll do what pleases Sarah,' I said with finality, and as an order, not a prodding satire.

'Don't sound so bloody bossy.'

We finished breakfast amicably trying to build a suitable new relationship on the ruins of the old, and both knowing well what we were about.

When I met them later in the hall at setting-off time it was clear that Sarah too had made a reassessment and put her mind to work on her emotions. She greeted me with an attempted smile and an outstretched hand. I shook the hand lightly and also gave her a token kiss on the cheek. She took it as it was meant.

Truce made, terms agreed, pact signed. Jik the mediator stood around looking smug.

'Take a look at him,' he said, flapping a hand in my direction. 'The complete stockbroker. Suit, tie, leather shoes. If he isn't careful they'll have him in the Royal Academy.'

Sarah looked bewildered. 'I thought that was an honour.'

'It depends,' said Jik, sneering happily. 'Passable artists with polished social graces get elected in their thirties. Masters with average social graces, in their forties; masters with no social graces, in their fifties. Geniuses who don't give a damn about being elected are ignored as long as possible.'

'Putting Todd in the first category and yourself in the last?' Sarah said.

'Of course.'

'Stands to reason,' I said. 'You never hear about young masters. Masters are always old.'

'For God's sake,' Sarah said. 'Let's go to the races.'

We went slowly, on account of a continuous stream of traffic going the same way. The car park at Flemington racecourse, when we arrived, looked like a giant picnic ground, with hundreds of full-scale lunch parties going on between the cars. Tables, chairs, cloths, china, silver, glass. Sun umbrellas optimistically raised in defiance of the rain-clouds threatening above. A lot of gaiety and booze and a giant overall statement that 'This Was The Life.'

To my mild astonishment Jik and Sarah had come prepared. They whipped out table, chairs, drinks and food from the rented car's boot and said it was easy when you knew how, you just ordered the whole works.

'I have an uncle,' Sarah said, 'who holds the title of Fastest Bar in the West. It takes him roughly ten seconds from putting the brakes on to pouring the first drink.'

She was really trying, I thought. Not just putting up with an arrangement for Jik's sake, but actually trying to make it work. If it was an effort, it didn't show. She was wearing an interesting olive green linen coat, with a broad brimmed hat of the same colour, which she held on from time to time against little gusts of wind. Overall, a new Sarah, prettier, more relaxed, less afraid.

'Champagne?' Jik offered, popping the cork. 'Steak and oyster pie?'

'How will I go back to cocoa and chips?'

'Fatter.'

We demolished the goodies, repacked the boot, and with a sense of taking part in some vast semi-religious ritual, squeezed along with the crowd through the gate to the holy of holies.

'It'll be much worse than this on Tuesday,' observed Sarah, who had been to these junkets several times in the past. 'Melbourne Cup day is a public holiday. The city has three million inhabitants and half of them will try to get here.' She was shouting above the crowd noises and holding grimly on to her hat against the careless buffeting all around.

'If they've got any sense they'll stay at home and watch it on the box,' I said breathlessly, receiving a hefty kidney punch from the elbow of a man fighting his way into a can of beer.

'It won't be on the television in Melbourne, only on the radio.'

97

'Good grief. Why ever not?'

'Because they want everyone to come. It's televised all over the rest of Australia, but not on its own doorstep.'

'Same with the golf and the cricket,' Jik said with a touch of gloom. 'And you can't even have a decent bet on those.'

We went through the bottleneck and, by virtue of the inherited badges, through a second gate and round into the calmer waters of the green oblong of Members' lawn. Much like on many a Derby Day at home, I thought. Same triumph of will over weather. Bright faces under grey skies. Warm coats over the pretty silks, umbrellas at the ready for the occasional top hat. When I painted pictures of racegoers in the rain, which I sometimes did, most people laughed. I never minded. I reckoned it meant they understood that the inner warmth of a pleasure couldn't be externally damped; that they too might play a trumpet in a thunderstorm.

Come to think of it, I thought, why didn't I paint a racegoer playing a trumpet in a thunderstorm? It might be symbolic enough even for Jik.

My friends were deep in a cross-talking assessment of the form of the first race. Sarah, it appeared, had a betting pedigree as long as her husband's, and didn't agree with him.

'I know it was soft going at Randwick last week. But it's pretty soft here too after all this rain, and he likes it on top.'

'He was only beaten by Boyblue at Randwick, and Boyblue was out of sight in the Caulfield Cup.'

'Please your silly self,' Sarah said loftily. 'But it's still too soft for Grapevine.'

'Want to bet?' Jik asked me.

'Don't know the horses.'

'As if that mattered.'

'Right.' I consulted the racecard. 'Two dollars on Generator.'

They both looked up, and they both said 'Why?'

'If in doubt, back number eleven. I once went nearly through the card on number eleven.'

They made clucking and pooh-poohing noises and told me I could make a gift of my two dollars to the bookies or the T.A.B.

'The what?'

'Totalizator Agency Board.'

The bookmakers, it seemed, were strictly on-course only, with no big firms as in England. All off-course betting shops were run by the T.A.B., which returned a good share of the lolly to racing. Racing was rich, rock-solid, and flourishing. Bully for Australia, Jik said.

We took our choice and paid our money, and Generator won at twenty-fives.

'Beginners' luck,' Sarah said.

Jik laughed. 'He's no beginner. He got kicked out of playschool for running a book.'

They tore up their tickets, set their minds to race two, and made expeditions to place their bets. I settled for four dollars on number one.

'Why?'

'Double my stake on half of eleven.'

'Oh God,' said Sarah. 'You're something else.'

One of the more aggressive clouds started scattering rain, and the less hardy began to make for shelter.

'Come on,' I said. 'Let's go and sit up there in the dry.'

'You two go,' Sarah said. 'I can't.'

'Why not?'

'Because those seats are only for men.'

I laughed. I thought she was joking, but it appeared it was no joke. Very unfunny, in fact. About two thirds of the best seats in the Members' stands were reserved for males.

'What about their wives and girl friends?' I said incredulously.

'They can go up on the roof.'

Sarah, being Australian, saw nothing very odd in it. To me, and surely to Jik, it was ludicrous.

He said with a carefully straight face, 'On a lot of the bigger courses the men who run Australian racing give themselves leather armchairs behind glass to watch from, and thick-carpeted restaurants and bars to eat and drink like kings in, and let their women eat in the cafeterias and sit on hard plastic chairs on the open stands among the rest of the crowd. They consider this be-haviour quite normal. All anthropological groups consider their most bizarre tribal customs quite normal.'

99

'I thought you were in love with all things Australian.'

Jik sighed heavily. 'Nowhere's perfect.'

'I'm getting wet,' Sarah said.

We escalated to the roof which had a proportion of two women to one man and was windy and damp, with bench seating.

'Don't worry about it,' Sarah said, amused at my aghastness on behalf of womenkind. 'I'm used to it.'

'I thought this country made a big thing about equality for all.'

'For all except half the population,' Jik said.

We could see the whole race superbly from our eyrie. Sarah and Jik screamed encouragement to their fancies but number one finished in front by two lengths, at eight to one.

'It's disgusting,' Sarah said, tearing up more tickets. 'What number do you fancy for the third?'

'I won't be with you for the third. I've got an appointment to have a drink with someone who knows Donald.'

She took it in, and the lightness went out of her manner. 'More . . . investigating?'

'I have to.'

'Yes.' She swallowed and made a visible effort. 'Well . . . Good luck.'

'You're a great girl.'

She looked surprised that I should think so and suspicious that I was intending sarcasm, and also partly pleased. I returned earthwards with her multiple expression amusing my mind.

The Members' lawn was bounded on one long side by the stands and on the opposite side by the path taken by the horses on their way from the saddling boxes to the parade ring. One short side of the lawn lay alongside part of the parade ring itself : and it was at the corner of lawn where the horses' path reached the parade ring that I was to meet Hudson Taylor.

The rain had almost stopped, which was good news for my suit. I reached the appointed spot and stood there waiting, admiring the brilliant scarlet of the long bedful of flowers which lined the railing between horse-walk and lawn. Cadmium red mixtures with highlights of orange and white and maybe a streak or two of expensive vermilion . . .

'Charles Todd?'

'Yes . . . Mr Taylor?'.

'Hudson. Glad to know you.' He shook hands, his grip dry and firm. Late forties, medium height, comfortable build, with affable, slightly sad eyes sloping downwards at the outer corners. He was one of the minority of men in morning suits, and he wore it as comfortably as a sweater.

'Let's find somewhere dry,' he said. 'Come this way.'

He led me steadily up the bank of steps, in through an entrance door, down a wide interior corridor running the whole length of the stands, past a uniformed guard and a notice saying 'Committee Only', and into a large square comfortable room fitted out as a small-scale bar. The journey had been one long polite push through expensively dressed cohorts, but the bar was comparatively quiet and empty. A group of four, two men, two women, stood chatting with half-filled glasess held close to their chests, and two women in furs were complaining loudly of the cold.

'They love to bring out the sables,' Hudson Taylor chuckled, fetching two glasses of Scotch and gesturing to me to sit by a small table. 'Spoils their fun, the years it's hot for this meeting.'

'Is it usually hot?'

'Melbourne's weather can change twenty degrees in an hour.' He sounded proud of it. 'Now then, this business of yours.' He delved into an inner breast pocket and surfaced with a folded paper. 'Here you are, typed out for Donald. The gallery was called Yarra River Fine Arts.'

I would have been astounded if it hadn't been.

'And the man we dealt with was someone called Ivor Wexford.'

'What did he look like?' I asked.

'I don't remember very clearly. It was back in April, do you see?'

I thought briefly and pulled a small slim sketchbook out of my pocket.

'If I draw him, might you know him?'

He looked amused. 'You never know.'

I drew quickly in soft pencil a reasonable likeness of Greene, but without the moustache.

'Was it him?'

Hudson Taylor looked doubtful. I drew in the moustache. He

shook his head decisively. 'No, that wasn't him.'

'How about this?'

I flipped over the page and started again. Hudson Taylor looked pensive as I did my best with the man from the basement office.

'Maybe,' he said.

I made the lower lip fuller, added heavy-framed spectacles, and a bow tie with spots.

'That's him,' said Hudson in surprise. 'I remember the bow tie, anyway. You don't see many of those these days. How did you know? You must have met him.'

'I walked round a couple of galleries yesterday afternoon.'

'That's quite a gift you have there,' he said with interest, watching me put the notebook away.

'Practice, that's all.' Years of seeing people's faces as matters of shapes and proportions and planes, and remembering which way the lines slanted. I could already have drawn Hudson's eyes from memory. It was a knack I'd had from childhood.

'Sketching is your hobby?' Hudson asked.

'And my work. I mostly paint horses.'

'Really?' He glanced at the equine portraits decorating the wall. 'Like these?'

I nodded, and we talked a little about painting for a living.

'Maybe I can give you a commission, if my horse runs well in the Cup.' He smiled, the outer edges of his eyes crinkling finely. 'If he's down the field, I'll feel more like shooting him.'

He stood up and gestured me still to follow. 'Time for the next race. Care to watch it with me?'

We emerged into daylight in the prime part of the stands, overlooking the big square enclosure which served both for parading the runners before the race and unsaddling the winners after. I was amused to see that the front rows of seats were all for men: two couples walking in front of us split like amoebas, the husbands going down left, the women up right.

'Down here,' Hudson said, pointing.

'May we only go up there if accompanied by a lady?' I asked.

He glanced at me sideways, and smiled. 'You find our ways odd? We'll go up, by all means.'

He led the way and settled comfortably among the predominantly female company, greeting several people and introducing me companionably as his friend Charles from England. Instant first names, instant acceptance, Australian style.

'Regina hated all this division of the sexes, poor lass,' he said. 'But it has interesting historical roots.' He chuckled. 'Australia was governed nearly all last century with the help of the British Army. The officers and gentlemen left their wives back in England, but such is nature, they all set up liaisons here with women of low repute. They didn't want their fellow officers to see the vulgarity of their choice, so they invented a rule that the officers' enclosures were for men only, which effectively silenced their popsies' pleas to be taken.'

I laughed. 'Very neat.'

'It's easier to establish a tradition,' Hudson said, 'than to get rid of it.'

'You're establishing a great tradition for fine wines, Donald says.'

The sad-looking eyes twinkled with civilized pleasure. 'He was most enthusiastic. He travelled round all the big vineyards, of course, besides visiting us.'

The horses for the third race cantered away to the start, led by a fractious chestnut colt with too much white about his head.

'Ugly brute,' Hudson said. 'But he'll win.'

'Are you backing it?'

He smiled. 'I've a little bit on.'

The race started and the field sprinted, and Hudson's knuckles whitened so much from his grip as he gazed intently through his binoculars that I wondered just how big the little bit was. The chestnut colt was beaten into fourth place. Hudson put his race-glasses down slowly and watched the unsatisfactory finish with a blank expression.

'Oh well,' he said, his sad eyes looking even sadder. 'Always another day.' He shrugged resignedly, cheered up, shook my hand, told me to remember him to Donald, and asked if I could find my own way out.

'Thank you for your help,' I said.

He smiled. 'Any time. Any time.'

With only a couple of wrong turnings I reached ground level, listening on the way to fascinating snippets of Australian conversation.

'. . . They say he's an embarrassment as a Committee man. He only opens his mouth to change feet . . .'

'. . . a beastly stomach wog, so he couldn't come . . .'

'. . . told him to stop whingeing like a bloody Pommie, and get on with it . . .'

'. . . won twenty dollars? Good on yer, Joanie . . .'

And everywhere the diphthong vowels which gave the word 'No' about five separate sounds, defying my attempts to copy it. I'd been told on the flight over, by an Australian, that all Australians spoke with one single accent. It was about as true as saying all Americans spoke alike, or all British. English was infinitely elastic; and alive, well and living in Melbourne.

Jik and Sarah, when I rejoined them, were arguing about their fancies for the Victoria Derby, next race on the card.

'Ivory Ball is out of his class and has as much chance as a blind man in a blizzard.'

Sarah ignored this. 'He won at Moonee Valley last week and two of the tipsters pick him.'

'Those tipsters must have been drunk.'

'Hello Todd,' Sarah said, 'Pick a number, for God's sake.'

'Ten.'

'Why ten?'

'Eleven minus one.'

'Jesus,' Jik said. 'You used to have more sense.'

Sarah looked it up. 'Royal Road. Compared with Royal Road, Ivory Ball's a certainty.'

We bought our tickets and went up to the roof, and none of our bets came up. Sarah disgustedly yelled at Ivory Ball who had at least managed fifth, but Royal Road fell entirely by the wayside. The winner was number twelve.

'You should have *added* eleven and one,' Sarah said. 'You make such silly mistakes.'

'What are you staring at?' Jik said.

I was looking attentively down at the crowd which had watched the race from ground level on the Members' lawn.

'Lend me your raceglasses . . .'

Jik handed them over. I raised them, took a long look, and slowly put them down.

'What is it?' Sarah said anxiously. 'What's the matter?'

'That,' I said, 'has not only torn it, but ripped the bloody works apart.'

'What has?'

'Do you see those two men . . . about twenty yards along from the parade ring railing . . . one of them in a grey morning suit?'

'What about them?' Jik said.

'The man in the morning suit is Hudson Taylor, the man I just had a drink with. He's the managing director of a wine-making firm, and he saw a lot of my cousin Donald when he was over here. And the other man is called Ivor Wexford, and he's the manager of the Yarra River Fine Arts Gallery.'

'So what?' Sarah said.

'So I can just about imagine the conversation that's going on down there,' I said. 'Something like, "Excuse me, sir, but didn't I sell a picture to you recently?" "Not to me, Mr Wexford, but to my friend Donald Stuart." "And who was that young man I saw you talking to just now?" "That was Donald Stuart's cousin, Mr Wexford." "And what do you know about him?" "That he's a painter by trade and drew a picture of you, Mr Wexford, and asked me for your name." '

I stopped. 'Go on,' Jik said.

I watched Wexford and Hudson Taylor stop talking, nod casually to each other, and walk their separate ways.

'Ivor Wexford now knows he made a horrible mistake in letting me out of his gallery last night.'

Sarah looked searchingly at my face. 'You really do think that's very serious.'

'Yes I really do.' I loosened a few tightened muscles and tried a smile. 'At the least, he'll be on his guard.'

'And at the most,' Jik said, 'he'll come looking for you.'

'Er . . .' I said thoughtfully. 'What do either of you feel about a spot of instant travel?'

'Where to?'

'Alice Springs?' I said.

nine

Jik complained all the way to the airport on various counts. One, that he would be missing the cricket. Two, that I hadn't let him go back to the Hilton for his paints. Three, that his Derby clothes would be too hot in Alice. Four, that he wasn't missing the Melbourne Cup for any little ponce with a bow tie.

None of the colourful gripes touched on the fact that he was paying for all our fares with his credit card, as I had left my travellers cheques in the hotel.

It had been Sarah's idea not to go back there.

'If we're going to vanish, let's get on with it,' she said. 'It's running back into fires for handbags that gets people burnt.'

'You don't have to come,' I said tentatively.

'We've been through all that. What do you think the rest of my life would be like if I stopped Jik helping you, and you came to grief?'

'You'd never forgive me.'

She smiled ruefully. 'You're dead right.'

As far as I could tell we had left the racecourse unobserved, and certainly no one car had followed us to the airport. Neither Greene with an 'e' nor the boy non-artist appeared underfoot to trip us up, and we travelled uneventfully on a half-full aircraft on the first leg to Adelaide, and an even emptier one from there to Alice Springs.

The country beneath us from Adelaide northwards turned gradually from fresh green to grey-green, and finally to a fierce brick red.

'Gaba,' said Jik, pointing downwards.

'What?'

'G.A.B.A.,' he said. 'Gaba. Stands for Great Australian Bugger All.'

I laughed. The land did indeed look baked, deserted, and older than time, but there were track-like roads here and there, and incredibly isolated homesteads. I watched in fascination until it grew dark, the purple shadows rushing in like a tide as we swept north into the central wastelands.

The night air at Alice was hot, as if someone had forgotten to switch off the oven. The luck which had presented us with an available flight as soon as we reached Melbourne airport seemed still to be functioning: a taciturn taxi driver took us straight to a new-looking motel which proved to have room for us.

'The season is over,' he grunted, when we congratulated and thanked him. 'It will soon be too hot for tourists.'

Our rooms were air-conditioned, however. Jik and Sarah's was down on the ground floor, their door opening directly on to a shady covered walk which bordered a small garden with a pool. Mine, in an adjacent wing across the car park, was two tall floors up, reached by an outside tree-shaded staircase and a long open gallery. The whole place looked greenly peaceful in the scattered spotlights which shone unobtrusively from palms and gums.

The motel restaurant had closed for the night at eight o'clock, so we walked along the main street to another. The road surface itself was tarmacadamed, but some of the side roads were not, nor were the footpaths uniformly paved. Often enough we were walking on bare fine grit, and we could see from the dust haze in the headlights of passing cars that the grit was bright red.

'Bull dust,' Sarah said. 'I've never seen it before. My aunt swore it got inside her locked trunk once when she and my uncle drove out to Ayers Rock.'

'What's Ayers Rock?' I said.

'Ignorant pommie,' Sarah said. 'It's a chunk of sandstone two miles long and a third of a mile high left behind by some careless glacier in the ice age.'

'Miles out in the desert,' Jik added. 'A place of ancient magic regularly desecrated by the plastic society.'

'Have you been there?' I asked dryly.

He grinned. 'Nope.'

'What difference does that make?' Sarah asked.

'He means,' Jik said, 'our pompous friend here means that one shouldn't make judgments from afar.'

'You haven't actually got to be swallowed by a shark before you believe it's got sharp teeth,' Sarah said. 'You can believe what other people see.'

107

'It depends from where they're looking.'

'Facts are not judgments, and judgments are not facts,' Jik said. 'A bit of Todd's Law from way back.'

Sarah gave me a glance. 'Have you got iced water in that head?'

'Emotion is a rotten base for politics. He used to say that too,' Jik said. 'Envy is the root of all evil. What have I left out?'

'The most damaging lies are told by those who believe they're true.'

'There you are,' Jik said. 'Such a pity you can't paint.'

'Thanks very much.'

We reached the restaurant and ate a meal of such excellence that one wondered at the organization it took to bring every item of food and clothing and everyday life to an expanding town of thirteen and a half thousand inhabitants surrounded by hundreds of miles of desert in every direction.

'It was started here, a hundred years ago, as a relay station for sending cables across Australia,' Sarah said. 'And now they're bouncing messages off the stars.'

Jik said, 'Bet the messages aren't worth the technology. Think of "See you Friday, Ethel", chattering round the eternal spheres.'

With instructions from the restaurant we walked back a different way and sought out the Yarra River Fine Arts gallery, Alice Springs variety.

It was located in a paved shopping arcade closed to traffic, one of several small but prosperous-looking boutiques. There were no lights on in the gallery, nor in the other shops. From what we could see in the single dim street light the merchandise in the gallery window consisted of two bright orange landscapes of desert scenes.

'Crude,' said Jik, whose own colours were not noted for pastel subtlety.

'The whole place,' he said, 'will be full of local copies of Albert Namatjira. Tourists buy them by the ton.'

We strolled back to the motel more companionably than at any time since my arrival. Maybe the desert distances all around us invoked their own peace. At any rate when I kissed Sarah's cheek to say goodnight it was no longer as a sort of pact, as in the morning, but with affection.

At breakfast she said, 'You'll never guess. The main street here is Todd Street. So is the river. Todd River.'

'Such is fame,' I said modestly.

'And there are eleven art galleries.'

'She's been reading the Alice Springs Tourist Promotion Association Inc.'s handout,' Jik explained.

'There's also a Chinese takeaway.'

Jik made a face. 'Just imagine all this lot dumped down in the middle of the Sahara.'

The daytime heat, in fact, was fierce. The radio was cheerfully forecasting a noon temperature of thirty-nine, which was a hundred and two in the old Fahrenheit shade. The single step from a cool room to the sun-roasting balcony was a sensuous pleasure, but the walk to the Yarra River gallery, though less than half a mile, was surprisingly exhausting.

'I suppose one would get used to it, if one lived here,' Jik said. 'Thank God Sarah's got her hat.'

We dodged in and out of the shadows of overhanging trees and the local inhabitants marched around bareheaded as if the branding-iron in the sky was pointing another way. The Yarra River gallery was quiet and air-conditioned and provided chairs near the entrance for flaked-out visitors.

As Jik had prophesied, all visible space was knee deep in the hard clear watercolour paintings typical of the disciples of Namatjira. They were fine if you liked that sort of thing, which on the whole I didn't. I preferred the occasional fuzzy outline, indistinct edge, shadows encroaching, suggestion, impression, and ambiguity. Namatjira, given his due as the first and greatest of the Aboriginal artists, had had a vision as sharp as a diamond. I vaguely remembered reading somewhere that he'd produced more than two thousand paintings himself, and certainly his influence on the town where he'd been born had been extraordinary. Eleven art galleries. Mecca for artists. Tourists buying pictures by the ton. He had died, a plaque on the wall said, in Alice Springs hospital on August 8th 1959.

We had been wandering around for a good five minutes before anyone came. Then the plastic strip curtain over a recessed doorway parted, and the gallery keeper came gently through.

'See anything you fancy?' he said.

His voice managed to convey an utter boredom with tourists and a feeling that we should pay up quickly and go away. He was small, languid, long-haired and pale, and had large dark eyes with drooping tired-looking lids. About the same age as Jik and myself, though a lot less robust.

'Do you have any other pictures?' I asked.

He glanced at our clothes. Jik and I wore the trousers and shirts in which we'd gone to the races: no ties and no jackets, but more promising to picture-sellers than denims. Without discernible enthusiasm he held back half of the strip curtain, inviting us to go through.

'In here,' he said.

The inner room was bright from skylights, and its walls were almost entirely covered with dozens of pictures which hung closely together. Our eyes opened wide. At first sight we were surrounded by an incredible feast of Dutch interiors, French impressionists and Gainsborough portraits. At second blink one could see that although they were original oil paintings, they were basically second rate. The sort sold as 'school of' because the artists hadn't bothered to sign them.

'All European, in this room,' the gallery keeper said. He still sounded bored. He wasn't Australian, I thought. Nor British. Maybe American. Difficult to tell.

'Do you have any pictures of horses?' I asked.

He gave me a long steady peaceful gaze. 'Yes we do, but this month we are displaying works by native Australians and lesser Europeans.' His voice had the faintest of lisps. 'If you wish to see horse paintings, they are in racks through there.' He pointed to a second plastic strip curtain directly opposite the first. 'Are you looking for anything in particular?'

I murmured the names of some of the Australians whose work I had seen in Melbourne. There was a slight brightening of the lack-lustre eyes.

'Yes, we do have a few by those artists.'

He led us through the second curtain into the third, and from our point of view, most interesting room. Half of it, as promised,

110

was occupied by well-filled double tiers of racks. The other half was the office and packing and framing department. Directly ahead a glass door led out to a dusty parched-looking garden, but most of the lighting in here too came from the roof.

Beside the glass door stood an easel bearing a small canvas with its back towards us. Various unmistakable signs showed work currently in progress and recently interrupted.

'Your own effort?' asked Jik inquisitively, walking over for a look.

The pale gallery keeper made a fluttering movement with his hand as if he would have stopped Jik if he could, and something in Jik's expression attracted me to his side like a magnet.

A chestnut horse, three-quarters view, its elegant head raised as if listening. In the background, the noble lines of a mansion. The rest, a harmonious composition of trees and meadow. The painting, as far as I could judge, was more or less finished.

'That's great,' I said with enthusiasm. 'Is that for sale? I'd like to buy that.'

After the briefest hesitation he said, 'Sorry. That's commissioned.'

'What a pity! Couldn't you sell me that one, and paint another?'

He gave me a small regretful smile. 'I'm afraid not.'

'Do tell me your name,' I said earnestly.

He was unwillingly flattered. 'Harley Renbo.'

'Is there anything else of yours here?'

He gestured towards the racks. 'One or two. The horse paintings are all in the bottom row, against the wall.'

We all three of us pulled out the paintings one by one, making amateur-type comments.

'That's nice,' said Sarah, holding a small picture of a fat grey pony with two old-fashioned country boys. 'Do you like that?' She showed it to Jik and me.

We looked at it.

'Very nice,' I said kindly.

Jik turned away as if uninterested. Harley Renbo stood motionless.

'Oh well,' Sarah said, shrugging. 'I just thought it looked nice.'

She put it back in the rack and pulled out the next. 'How about this mare and foal? I think it's pretty.'

Jik could hardly bear it. 'Sentimental tosh,' he said.

Sarah looked downcast. 'It may not be Art, but I like it.'

We found one with a flourishing signature; Harley Renbo. Large canvas, varnished, unframed.

'Ah,' I said appreciatively. 'Your~.'

Harley Renbo inclined his head. Jik, Sarah and I gazed at his acknowledged work.

Derivative Stubbs-type. Elongated horses set in a Capability Brown landscape. Composition fair, anatomy poor, execution good, originality nil.

'Great,' I said. 'Where did you paint it?'

'Oh . . . here.'

'From memory?' Sarah said admiringly. 'How clever.'

Harley Renbo, at our urging, brought out two more examples of his work. Neither was better than the first, but one was a great deal smaller.

'How much is this?' I asked.

Jik glanced at me sharply, but kept quiet.

Harley Renbo mentioned a sum which had me shaking my head at once.

'Awfully sorry,' I said. 'I like your work, but . . .'

The haggling continued politely for quite a long time, but we came to the usual conclusion, higher than the buyer wanted, lower than the painter hoped. Jik resignedly lent his credit card and we bore our trophy away.

'Jesus Christ,' Jik exploded when we were safely out of ear-shot. 'You could paint better than that when you were in your cradle. Why the hell did you want to buy that rubbish?'

'Because,' I said contentedly, 'Harley Renbo is the copier.'

'But this,' Jik pointed to the parcel under my arm, 'is his own abysmal original work.'

'Like fingerprints?' Sarah said. 'You can check other things he paints against this?'

'Got brains, my wife,' Jik said. 'But that picture he wouldn't sell was nothing like any Munnings I've ever seen.'

'You never look at horse paintings if you can help it.'

'I've seen more of your pathetic daubs than I care to.'

'How about Raoul Millais?' I said.

'Jesus.'

We walked along the scorching street almost without feeling it.

'I don't know about you two,' Sarah said, 'But I'm going to buy a bikini and spend the rest of the day in the pool.'

We all bought swimming things, changed into them, splashed around for ages, and laid ourselves out on towels to dry. It was peaceful and quiet in the shady little garden. We were the only people there.

'That picture of a pony and two boys, that you thought was nice,' I said to Sarah.

'Well, it was,' she repeated defensively. 'I liked it.'

'It was a Munnings.'

She sat up abruptly on her towel.

'Why ever didn't you say so?'

'I was waiting for our friend Renbo to tell us, but he didn't.'

'A real one?' Sarah asked. 'Or a copy?'

'Real,' Jik said, with his eyes shut against the sun dappling through palm leaves.

I nodded lazily. 'I thought so, too,' I said. 'An old painting. Munnings had that grey pony for years when he was young, and painted it dozens of times. It's the same one you saw in Sydney in *The Coming Storm*.'

'You two do know a lot,' Sarah said, sighing and lying down again.

'Engineers know all about nuts and bolts,' Jik said. 'Do we get lunch in this place?'

I looked at my watch. Nearly two o'clock. 'I'll go and ask,' I said.

I put shirt and trousers on over my sun-dried trunks and ambled from the outdoor heat into the refrigerated air of the lobby. No lunch, said the reception desk. We could buy lunch nearby at a takeaway and eat in the garden. Drink? Same thing. Buy your own at a bottle shop. There was an ice-making machine and plastic glasses just outside the door to the pool.

'Thanks,' I said.

'You're welcome.'

I looked at the ice-making machine on the way out. Beside it swung a neat notice: 'We don't swim in your toilet. Please don't pee in our pool.' I laughed across to Jik and Sarah and told them the food situation.

'I'll go and get it,' I said. 'What do you want?'

Anything, they said.

'And drink?'

'Cinzano,' Sarah said, and Jik nodded. 'Dry white.'

'O.K.'

I picked up my room key from the grass and set off to collect some cash for shopping. Walked along to the tree-shaded outside staircase, went up two storeys, and turned on to the blazing hot balcony.

There was a man walking along it towards me, about my own height, build and age; and I heard someone else coming up the stairs at my back.

Thought nothing of it. Motel guests like me. What else?

I was totally unprepared both for the attack itself, and for its ferocity.

ten

They simply walked up to me, one from in front, one from behind.

They reached me together. They sprang into action like cats. They snatched the dangling room key out of my hand.

The struggle, if you could call it that, lasted less than five seconds. Between them, with Jik's type of strength, they simply picked me up by my legs and armpits and threw me over the balcony.

It probably takes a very short time to fall two storeys. I found it long enough for thinking that my body, which was still whole, was going to be smashed. That disaster, not yet reached, was inevitable. Very odd, and very nasty.

What I actually hit first was one of the young trees growing round the staircase. Its boughs bent and broke and I crashed on through them to the hard driveway beneath.

The monstrous impact was like being wiped out. Like fusing electrical circuits. A flash into chaos. I lay in a semi-conscious daze, not knowing if I were alive or dead.

I felt warm. Simply a feeling, not a thought.

I wasn't aware of anything else at all. I couldn't move any muscle. Couldn't remember I had muscles to move. I felt like pulp.

It was ten minutes, Jik told me later, before he came looking for me: and he came only because he wanted to ask me to buy a lemon to go with the Cinzano, if I had not gone already.

'Jesus Christ Almighty,' Jik's voice, low and horrified, near my ear.

I heard him clearly. The words made sense.

I'm alive, I thought. I think, therefore I exist.

Eventually, I opened my eyes. The light was brilliant. Blinding. There was no one where Jik's voice had been. Perhaps I'd imagined it. No I hadn't. The world began coming back fast, very sharp and clear.

I knew also that I hadn't imagined the fall. I knew, with increasing insistence, that I hadn't broken my neck and hadn't broken my back. Sensation, which had been crushed out, came flooding back with vigour from every insulted tissue. It wasn't so much a matter of which bits of me hurt, as of finding out which didn't. I remembered hitting the tree. Remembered the ripping of its branches. I felt both torn to shreds and pulverized. Frightfully jolly.

After a while I heard Jik's voice returning. 'He's alive,' he said, 'and that's about all.'

'It's impossible for anyone to fall off our balcony. It's more than waist high.' The voice of the reception desk, sharp with anger and anxiety. A bad business for motels, people falling off their balconies.

'Don't ... panic,' I said. It sounded a bit croaky.

'Todd!' Sarah appeared, kneeling on the ground and looking pale.

'If you give me time . . .' I said. '. . . I'll fetch . . . the Cinzano.' How much time? A million years should be enough.

'You sod,' Jik said, standing at my feet and staring down. 'You gave us a shocking fright.' He was holding a broken-off branch of tree.

'Sorry.'

'Get up, then.'

'Yeah . . . in a minute.'

'Shall I cancel the ambulance?' said the reception desk hopefully.

'No,' I said. 'I think I'm bleeding.'

Alice Springs hospital, even on a Sunday, was as efficient as one would expect from a Flying Doctor base. They investigated and X-rayed and stitched, and presented me with a list.

One broken shoulder blade. (Left).
Two broken ribs. (Left side, no lung puncture).
Large contusion, left side of head. (No skull fracture).
Four jagged tears in skin of trunk, thigh, and left leg. (Stitched).
Several other small cuts.
Grazes and contusions on practically all of left side of body.

'Thanks,' I said, sighing.

'Thank the tree. You'd've been in a right mess if you'd missed it.'

They suggested I stop there for the rest of the day and also all night. Better, they said, a little too meaningfully.

'O.K.' I said resignedly. 'Are my friends still here?'

They were. In the waiting room. Arguing over my near-dead body about the favourite for the Melbourne Cup.

'Newshound *stays* . . .'

'Stays in the same place . . .'

'Jesus,' Jik said, as I shuffled stiffly in. 'He's on his feet.'

'Yeah.' I perched gingerly on the arm of a chair, feeling a bit like a mummy, wrapped in bandages from neck to waist with my left arm totally immersed, as it were, and anchored firmly inside.

116

'Don't damn well laugh,' I said.

'No one but a raving lunatic would fall off that balcony,' Jik said.

'Mm,' I agreed. 'I was pushed.'

Their mouths opened like landed fish. I told them exactly what had happened.

'Who were they?' Jik said.

'I don't know. Never seen them before. They didn't introduce themselves.'

Sarah said, definitely, 'You must tell the police.'

'Yes,' I said. 'But . . . I don't know your procedures here, or what the police are like. I wondered . . . if you would explain to the hospital, and start things rolling in an orderly and unsensational manner.'

'Sure,' she said, 'if anything about being pushed off a balcony could be considered orderly and unsensational.'

'They took my room key first,' I said. 'Would you see if they've pinched my wallet?'

They stared at me in awakening unwelcome awareness.

I nodded. 'Or that picture,' I said.

Two policemen came, listened, took notes, and departed. Very non-committal. Nothing like that had happened in The Alice before. The locals wouldn't have done it. The town had a constant stream of visitors so, by the law of averages, some would be muggers. I gathered that there would have been much more fuss if I'd been dead. Their downbeat attitude suited me fine.

By the time Jik and Sarah came back I'd been given a bed, climbed into it, and felt absolutely rotten. Shivering. Cold deep inside. Gripped by the system's aggrieved reaction to injury, or in other words, shock.

'They did take the painting,' Jik said. 'And your wallet as well.'

'And the gallery's shut,' Sarah said. 'The girl in the boutique opposite said she saw Harley close early today, but she didn't see him actually leave. He goes out the back way, because he parks his car there.'

'The police've been to the motel,' Jik said. 'We told them about the picture being missing, but I don't think they'll do much more about it unless you tell them the whole story.'

'I'll think about it,' I said.

'So what do we do now?' Sarah asked.

'Well . . . there's no point in staying here any more. Tomorrow we'll go back to Melbourne.'

'Thank God,' she said, smiling widely. 'I thought you were going to want us to miss the Cup.'

In spite of a battery of pills and various ministering angels I spent a viciously uncomfortable and wideawake night. Unable to lie flat. Feverishly hot on the pendulum from shock. Throbbing in fifteen places. Every little movement screechingly sticky, like an engine without oil. No wonder the hospital had told me it would be better to stay.

I counted my blessings until daybreak. It could have been so very much worse.

What was most alarming was not the murderous nature of the attackers, but the speed with which they'd found us. I'd known ever since I'd seen Regina's head that the directing mind was ruthlessly violent. The acts of the team always reflected the nature of the boss. A less savage attitude would have left Regina gagged and bound, not brutally dead.

I had to conclude that it was chiefly this pervading callousness which had led to my being thrown over the balcony. As a positive means of murder, it was too chancy. It was quite possible to survive a fall from such a height, even without a cushioning tree. The two men had not as far as I could remember bothered to see whether I was alive or dead, and they had not, while I lay half-unconscious and immobile, come along to finish the job.

So it had either been simply a shattering way of getting rid of me while they robbed my room, or they'd had the deliberate intention of injuring me so badly that I would have to stop poking my nose into their affairs.

Or both.

And how had they found us?

I puzzled over it for some time but could arrive at no definite answer. It seemed most likely that Wexford or Greene had telephoned from Melbourne and told Harley Renbo to be on his guard in case I turned up. Even the panic which would have followed the realization that I'd seen the Munnings and the fresh Millais copy, and actually carried away a specimen of Renbo's work, could not have transported two toughs from Melbourne to Alice Springs in the time available.

There had only been about four hours between purchase and attack, and some of that would have had to be spent on finding out which motel we were in, and which rooms, and waiting for me to go upstairs from the pool.

Perhaps we had after all been followed all the way from Flemington racecourse, or traced from the aeroplane passenger lists. But if that were the case, surely Renbo would have been warned we were on our way, and would never have let us see what we had.

I gave it up. I didn't even know if I would recognize my attackers again if I saw them. Certainly not the one who had been behind me, because I hadn't had a single straight look at him.

They could, though, reasonably believe they had done a good job of putting me out of action: and indeed, if I had any sense, they had.

If they wanted time, what for?

To tighten up their security, and cover their tracks, so that any investigation I might persuade the police to make into a paintings-robbery link would come up against the most respectable of brick walls.

Even if they knew I'd survived, they would not expect any action from me in the immediate future: therefore the immediate future was the best time to act.

Right.

Easy enough to convince my brain. From the neck down, a different story.

Jik and Sarah didn't turn up until eleven, and I was still in bed. Sitting up, but not exactly perky.

'God,' Sarah said, 'You look much worse than yesterday.'

'So kind.'

'You're never going to make it to Melbourne.' She sounded despondent. 'So goodbye Cup.'

'Nothing to stop you going,' I said.

She stood beside the bed. 'Do you expect us just to leave you here . . . like this . . . and go and enjoy ourselves?'

'Why not?'

'Don't be so bloody stupid.'

Jik sprawled in a visitor's chair. 'It isn't our responsibility if he gets himself thrown from heights,' he said.

Sarah whirled on him. 'How *can* you say such a thing?'

'We don't want to be involved,' Jik said.

I grinned. Sarah heard the sardonic echo of what she'd said so passionately herself only three days ago. She flung out her arms in exasperated realization.

'You absolutely bloody beast,' she said.

Jik smiled like a cream-fed cat. 'We went round to the gallery,' he said. 'It's still shut. We also found our way round into the back garden, and looked in through the glass door, and you can guess what we saw.'

'Nothing.'

'Dead right. No easel with imitation Millais. Everything dodgy carefully hidden out of sight. Everything else, respectable and normal.'

I shifted a bit to relieve one lot of aches, and set up protests from another. 'Even if you'd got in, I doubt if you'd've found anything dodgy. I'll bet everything the least bit incriminating disappeared yesterday afternoon.'

Jik nodded. 'Sure to.'

Sarah said, 'We asked the girl in the reception desk at the motel if anyone had been asking for us.'

'And they had?'

She nodded. 'A man telephoned. She thought it was soon after ten o'clock. He asked if a Mr Charles Todd was staying there with two friends, and when she said yes, he asked for your room number. He said he had something to deliver to you.'

'Christ.' Some delivery. Express. Downwards.

'She told him the room number but said if he left the package at the desk, she would see you got it.'

'He must have laughed.'

'He wouldn't have that much sense of humour,' Jik said.

'Soon after ten?' I said, considering.

'While we were out,' Sarah said, nodding. 'It must have been fairly soon after we'd left the gallery ... and while we were buying the swimming things.'

'Why didn't the girl tell us someone had been enquiring for us?'

'She went off for a coffee break, and didn't see us when we came back. And after that, she forgot. She hadn't anyway thought it of any importance.'

'There aren't all that many motels in Alice,' Jik said. 'It wouldn't have taken long to find us, once they knew we were in the town. I suppose the Melbourne lot telephoned Renbo, and that set the bomb ticking.'

'They must have been apoplectic when they heard you'd bought that picture.'

'I wish I'd hidden it,' I said. The words reminded me briefly of Maisie, who had hidden her picture, and had her house burnt.

Sarah sighed. 'Well ... what are we going to do?'

'Last chance to go home,' I said.

'Are you going?' she demanded.

I listened briefly to the fierce plea from my battered shell, and I thought too of Donald in his cold house. I didn't actually answer her at all.

She listened to my silence. 'Quite,' she said. 'So what do we do next?'

'Well ...' I said. 'First of all, tell the girl in the reception desk at the motel that I'm in a pretty poor state and likely to be in hospital for at least a week.'

'No exaggeration,' Jik murmured.

'Tell her it's O.K. to pass on that news, if anyone enquires. Tell her you're leaving for Melbourne, pay all our bills, confirm your bookings on the afternoon flight, and cancel mine, and make a normal exit to the airport bus.'

'But what about you?' Sarah said. 'When will you be fit to go?'

'With you,' I said. 'If between you you can think of some un-obtrusive way of getting a bandaged mummy on to an aeroplane without anyone noticing.'

'Jesus,' Jik said. He looked delighted. 'I'll do that.'

'Telephone the airport and book a seat for me under a different name.'

'Right.'

'Buy me a shirt and some trousers. Mine are in the dustbin.'

'It shall be done.'

'And reckon all the time that you may be watched.'

'Put on sad faces, do you mean?' Sarah said.

I grinned. 'I'd be honoured.'

'And after we get to Melbourne, what then?' Jik said.

I chewed my lip. 'I think we'll have to go back to the Hilton. All our clothes are there, not to mention my passport and money. We don't know if Wexford and Greene ever knew we were staying there, so it may well be a hundred per cent safe. And anyway, where else in Melbourne are we likely to get beds on the night before the Melbourne Cup?'

'If you get thrown out of the Hilton's windows, you won't be alive to tell the tale,' he said cheerfully.

'They don't open far enough,' I said. 'It's imposssible.'

'How reassuring.'

'And tomorrow,' Sarah said. 'What about tomorrow?'

Hesitantly, with a pause or two, I outlined what I had in mind for Cup day. When I had finished, they were both silent.

'So now,' I said. 'Do you want to go home?'

Sarah stood up. 'We'll talk it over,' she said soberly. 'We'll come back and let you know.'

Jik stood also, but I knew from the jut of his beard which way he'd vote. It had been he who'd chosen the bad-weather routes we'd taken into the Atlantic and the North Sea. At heart he was more reckless than I.

They came back at two o'clock lugging a large fruit-shop carrier with a bottle of scotch and a pineapple sticking out of the top.

'Provisions for hospitalized friend,' said Jik, whisking them out and putting them on the end of the bed. 'How do you feel?'

'With every nerve ending.'

'You don't say. Well, Sarah says we go ahead.'

I looked searchingly at her face. Her dark eyes stared steadily back, giving assent without joy. There was no antagonism, but no excitement. She was committed, but from determination, not conviction.

'O.K.,' I said.

'Item,' said Jik, busy with the carrier, 'One pair of medium grey trousers. One light blue cotton shirt.'

'Great.'

'You won't be wearing those, though, until you get to Melbourne. For leaving Alice Springs, we bought something else.'

I saw the amusement in both their faces. I said with misgiving, 'What else?'

With rising glee they laid out what they had brought for my unobtrusive exit from Alice Springs.

Which was how I came to stroll around the little airport, in the time-gap between signing in and boarding, with the full attention of everyone in the place. Wearing faded jeans cut-off and busily frayed at mid-calf. No socks. Flip-flop rope-soled sandals. A brilliant orange, red and magenta poncho-type garment which hung loosely over both arms like a cape from shoulders to crutch. A sloppy white T-shirt underneath. A large pair of sunglasses. Artificial suntan on every bit of skin. And to top it all, a large straw sunhat with a two-inch raffia fringe round the brim, the sort of hat in favour out in the bush for keeping flies away. Flies were the torment of Australia. The brushing-away-of-flies movement of the right hand was known as the great Australian salute.

On this hat there was a tourist-type hat-band, bright and distinctly legible. It said 'I Climbed Ayers Rock'.

Accompanying all this jazz I carried the Trans-Australian airline bag Sarah had bought on the way up. Inside it, the garments of sanity and discretion.

'No one,' Jik had said with satisfaction, laying out my wardrobe, 'will guess you're a walking stretcher case, if you're wearing these.'

'More like a nut case.'

'Not far out,' Sarah said dryly.

They were both at the airport, sitting down and looking glum, when I arrived. They gave me a flickering glance and gazed thereafter at the floor, both of them, they told me later, fighting off terrible fits of giggles at seeing all that finery on the march.

I walked composedly down to the postcard stand and waited there on my feet, for truth to tell it was more comfortable than sitting. Most of the postcards seemed to be endless views of the huge crouching orange monolith out in the desert: Ayers Rock at dawn, at sunset, and every five minutes in between.

Alternatively with inspecting the merchandise I took stock of the room. About fifty prospective passengers, highly assorted. Some airline groundstaff, calm and unhurried. A couple of aborigines with shadowed eyes and patient black faces, waiting for the airport bus back to dreamtime. Air-conditioning doing fine, but everyone inside still moving with the slow walk of life out in the sun.

No one remotely threatening.

The flight was called. The assorted passengers, including Jik and Sarah, stood up, picked up their hand luggage and straggled out to the tarmac.

It was then, and then only, that I saw him.

The man who had come towards me on the balcony to throw me over.

I was almost sure at once, and then certain. He had been sitting among the waiting passengers, reading a newspaper which he was now folding up. He stood still, watching Jik and Sarah present their boarding passes at the door and go through to the tarmac. His eyes followed them right across to the aircraft. When they'd filed up the steps and vanished, he peeled off and made a bee-line in my direction.

My heart lurched painfully. I absolutely could not run.

He looked just the same. Exactly the same. Young, strong, purposeful, as well co-ordinated as a cat. Coming towards me.

As Jik would have said, *Jesus*.

He didn't even give me a glance. Three yards before he reached me he came to a stop beside a wall telephone, and fished in his pocket for coins.

My feet didn't want to move. I was still sure he would see me, look at me carefully, recognize me . . . and do something I would regret. I could feel the sweat prickling under the bandages.

'Last call for flight to Adelaide and Melbourne.'

I would have to, I thought. Have to walk past him to get to the door.

I unstuck my feet. Walked. Waiting with every awful step to hear his voice shouting after me. Or even worse, his heavy hand.

I got to the door, presented the boarding pass, made it out on to the tarmac.

Couldn't resist glancing back. I could see him through the glass, earnestly telephoning, and not even looking my way.

The walk to the aircraft was all the same quite far enough. God help us all, I thought, if the slightest fright is going to leave me so weak.

eleven

I had a window seat near the rear of the aircraft, and spent the first part of the journey in the same sort of fascination as on the way up, watching the empty red miles of the ancient land roll away underneath. A desert with water underneath it in most places; with huge lakes and many rock pools. A desert which could carry dormant seed for years in its burning dust, and bloom like a garden when it rained. A place of pulverizing heat, harsh and unforgiving, and in scattered places, beautiful.

GABA, I thought. I found it awesome, but it didn't move me in terms of paint.

After a while I took off the exaggerated hat, laid it on the empty seat beside me, and tried to find a comfortable way to sit, my main frustration being that if I leaned back in the ordinary way my broken shoulder blade didn't care for it. You wouldn't think, I thought, that one *could* break a shoulder blade. Mine, it appeared, had suffered from the full thud of my five-eleven frame hitting terra extremely firma.

Oh well . . . I shut my eyes for a bit and wished I didn't still feel so shaky.

My exit from hospital had been the gift of one of the doctors, who had said he couldn't stop me if I chose to go, but another day's rest would be better.

'I'd miss the Cup,' I said, protesting.

'You're crazy.'

'Yeah . . . Would it be possible for you to arrange that the hospital said I was "satisfactory", and "progressing" if anyone telephones to ask, and not on any account to say that I'd left?'

'Whatever for?'

'I'd just like those muggers who put me here to think I'm still flat out. For several days, if you don't mind. Until I'm long gone.'

'But they won't try again.'

'You never know.'

He shrugged. 'You mean you're nervous?'

'You could say so.'

'All right. For a couple of days, anyway. I don't see any harm in it, if it will set your mind at rest.'

'It would indeed,' I said gratefully.

'Whatever are these?' He gestured to Jik's shopping, still lying on the bed.

'My friend's idea of suitable travelling gear.'

'You're having me on?'

'He's an artist,' I said, as if that explained any excesses.

He returned an hour later with a paper for me to sign before I left, Jik's credit card having again come up trumps, and at the sight of me, nearly choked. I had struggled slowly into the clothes and was trying on the hat.

'Are you going to the airport dressed like that?' he said incredulously.

'I sure am.'

'How?'

'Taxi, I suppose.'

'You'd better let me drive you,' he said, sighing. 'Then if you feel too rotten I can bring you back.'

He drove carefully, his lips twitching. 'Anyone who has the courage to go around like that shouldn't worry about a couple of thugs.' He dropped me solicitously at the airport door, and departed laughing.

Sarah's voice interrupted the memory.

'Todd?'

I opened my eyes. She had walked towards the back of the aeroplane and was standing in the aisle beside my seat.

'Are you all right?'

'Mm.'

She gave me a worried look and went on into the toilet compartment. By the time she came out, I'd assembled a few more wits, and stopped her with the flap of the hand. 'Sarah . . . You were followed to the airport. I think you'll very likely be followed from Melbourne. Tell Jik . . . tell Jik to take a taxi, spot the tail, lose him, and take a taxi back to the airport, to collect the hired car. O.K.?'

'Is this . . . this tail . . . on the aeroplane?' She looked alarmed at the thought.

'No. He telephoned . . . from Alice.'

'All right.'

She went away up front to her seat. The aeroplane landed at Adelaide, people got off, people got on, and we took off again for the hour's flight to Melbourne. Halfway there, Jik himself came back to make use of the facilities.

He too paused briefly beside me on the way back.

'Here are the car keys,' he said. 'Sit in it, and wait for us. You can't go into the Hilton like that, and you're not fit enough to change on your own.'

'Of course I am.'

'Don't argue. I'll lose any tail, and come back. You wait.'

He went without looking back. I picked up the keys and put them in my jeans pocket, and thought grateful thoughts to pass the time.

I dawdled a long way behind Jik and Sarah at disembarkation. My gear attracted more scandalized attention in this solemn financial city, but I didn't care in the least. Nothing like fatigue and anxiety for killing off embarrassment.

Jik and Sarah, with only hand-baggage, walked without ado past the suitcase-unloading areas and straight out towards the waiting queue of taxis. The whole airport was bustling with Cup eve arrivals, but only one person, that I could see, was bustling exclusively after my fast-departing friends.

I smiled briefly. Young and eel-like, he slithered through the throng, pushing a young woman with a baby out of the way to grab the next taxi behind Jik's. They'd sent him, I supposed, because he knew Jik by sight. He'd flung turps in his eyes at the Arts Centre.

Not too bad, I thought. The boy wasn't over-intelligent, and Jik should have little trouble in losing him. I wandered around for a bit looking gormless, but as there was no one else who seemed the remotest threat, I eventually eased out to the car park.

The night was chilly after Alice Springs. I unlocked the car, climbed into the back, took off the successful hat, and settled to wait for Jik's return.

They were gone nearly two hours, during which time I grew stiffer and ever more uncomfortable and started swearing.

'Sorry,' Sarah said breathlessly, pulling open the car door and tumbling into the front seat.

'We had the devil's own job losing the little bugger,' Jik said, getting in beside me in the back. 'Are you all right?'

'Cold, hungry, and cross.'

'That's all right, then,' he said cheerfully. 'He stuck like a bloody little leech. That boy from the Arts Centre.'

'Yes, I saw him.'

'We hopped into the Victoria Royal, meaning to go straight out again by the side door and grab another cab, and there he was following us in through the front. So we peeled off for a drink in the bar and he hovered around in the lobby looking at the book-stall.'

'We thought it would be better not to let him know we'd spotted him, if we could,' Sarah said. 'So we did a re-think, went outside, called another taxi, and set off to The Naughty Ninety, which is about the only noisy big dine, dance and cabaret place in Melbourne.'

'It was absolutely packed,' Jik said. 'It cost me ten dollars to get a table. Marvellous for us, though. All dark corners and psychedelic coloured lights. We ordered and paid for some drinks, and read the menu, and then got up and danced.'

'He was still there, when we saw him last, standing in the queue for tables just inside the entrance door. We got out through an emergency exit down a passage past some cloakrooms. We'd dumped our bags there when we arrived, and simply collected them again on the way out.'

'I don't think he'll know we ducked him on purpose,' Jik said. 'It's a proper scrum there tonight.'

'Great.'

With Jik's efficient help I exchanged Tourist, Alice Style, for Racing Man, Melbourne Cup. He drove us all back to the Hilton, parked in its car park, and we walked into the front hall as if we'd never been away.

No one took any notice of us. The place was alive with pre-race excitement. People in evening dress flooding downstairs from the ballroom to stand in loud-talking groups before dispersing home. People returning from eating out, and calling for one more nightcap. Everyone discussing the chances of the next day's race.

Jik collected our room keys from the long desk.

'No messages,' he said. 'And they don't seem to have missed us.'

'Fair enough.'

'Todd,' Sarah said. 'Jik and I are going to have some food sent up. You'll come as well?'

I nodded. We went up in the lift and along to their rooms, and ate a subdued supper out of collective tiredness.

'Night,' I said eventually, getting up to go. 'And thanks for everything.'

'Thank us tomorrow,' Sarah said.

The night passed. Well, it passed.

In the morning I did a spot of one-handed shaving and some highly selective washing, and Jik came up, as he'd insisted, to help with my tie. I opened the door to him in underpants and dressing gown and endured his comments when I took the latter off.

'Jesus God Almighty, is there any bit of you neither blue nor patched?'

'I could have landed face first.'

He stared at the thought. *'Jesus.'*

'Help me rearrange these bandages,' I said.

'I'm not touching that lot.'

'Oh come on, Jik. Unwrap the swaddling bands. I'm itching like hell underneath and I've forgotten what my left hand looks like.'

With a variety of blasphemous oaths he undid the expert handiwork of the Alice hospital. The outer bandages proved to be large strong pieces of linen, fastened with clips, and placed so as to support my left elbow and hold my whole arm statically in one position, with my hand across my chest and pointing up towards my right shoulder. Under the top layer there was a system of crêpe bandages tying my arm in that position. Also a sort of tight cummerbund of adhesive strapping, presumably to deal with the broken ribs. Also, just below my shoulder blade, a large padded wound dressing, which, Jik kindly told me after a delicate inspection from one corner, covered a mucky looking bit of darning.

'You damn near tore a whole flap of skin off. There are four lots of stitching. Looks like Clapham Junction.'

'Fasten it up again.'

'I have, mate, don't you worry.'

There were three similar dressings, two on my left thigh and one, a bit smaller, just below the knee: all fastened both with adhesive strips and tapes with clips. We left them all untouched.

'What the eye doesn't see doesn't scare the patient,' Jik said. 'What else do you want done?'

'Untie my arm.'

'You'll fall apart.'

'Risk it.'

He laughed and undid another series of clips and knots. I tentatively straightened my elbow. Nothing much happened except that the hovering ache and soreness stopped hovering and came down to earth.

'That's not so good,' Jik observed.

'It's my muscles as much as anything. Protesting about being stuck in one position all that time.'

'What now, then?'

From the bits and pieces we designed a new and simpler sling

130

which gave my elbow good support but was less of a strait-jacket. I could get my hand out easily, and also my whole arm, if I wanted. When we'd finished, we had a small heap of bandages and clips left over.

'That's fine,' I said.

We all met downstairs in the hall at ten-thirty.

Around us a buzzing atmosphere of anticipation pervaded the chattering throng of would-be winners, who were filling the morning with celebratory drinks. The hotel, I saw, had raised a veritable fountain of champagne at the entrance to the bar-lounge end of the lobby, and Jik, his eyes lighting up, decided it was too good to be missed.

'Free booze,' he said reverently, picking up a glass and holding it under the prodigal bubbly which flowed in delicate gold streams from a pressure-fed height. 'Not bad, either,' he added, tasting. He raised his glass. 'Here's to Art. God rest his soul.'

'Life's short. Art's long,' I said.

'I don't like that,' Sarah said, looking at me uneasily.

'It was Alfred Munnings's favourite saying. And don't worry, love, he lived to be eighty plus.'

'Let's hope you do.'

I drank to it. She was wearing a cream dress with gold buttons; neat, tailored, a touch severe. An impression of the military for a day in the front line.

'Don't forget,' I said. 'If you think you see Wexford or Greene, make sure they see you.'

'Give me another look at their faces,' she said.

I pulled the small sketch book out of my pocket and handed it to her again, though she'd studied it on and off all the previous evening through supper.

'As long as they look like this, maybe I'll know them,' she said, sighing. 'Can I take it?' She put the sketch book in her handbag.

Jik laughed. 'Give Todd his due, he can catch a likeness. No imagination, of course. He can only paint what he sees.' His voice as usual was full of disparagement.

Sarah said, 'Don't you mind the awful things Jik says of your work, Todd?'

I grinned. 'I know exactly what he thinks of it.'

'If it makes you feel any better,' Jik said to his wife, 'He was the star pupil of our year. The Art School lacked judgment, of course.'

'You're both crazy.'

I glanced at the clock. We all finished the champagne and put down the glasses.

'Back a winner for me,' I said to Sarah, kissing her cheek.

'Your luck might run out.'

I grinned. 'Back number eleven.'

Her eyes were dark with apprehension. Jik's beard was at the bad-weather angle for possible storms ahead.

'Off you go,' I said cheerfully. 'See you later.'

I watched them through the door and wished strongly that we were all three going for a simple day out to the Melbourne Cup. The effort ahead was something I would have been pleased to avoid. I wondered if others ever quaked before the task they'd set themselves, and wished they'd never thought of it. The beginning, I supposed, was the worst. Once you were in, you were committed. But before, when there was still time to turn back, to rethink, to cancel, the temptation to retreat was demoralizing.

Why climb Everest if at its foot you could lie in the sun?

Sighing, I went to the cashier's end of the reception desk and changed a good many travellers' cheques into cash. Maisie's generosity had been far-sighted. There would be little enough left by the time I got home.

Four hours to wait. I spent them upstairs in my room calming my nerves by drawing the view from the window. Black clouds still hung around the sky like cobwebs, especially in the direction of Flemington racecourse. I hoped it would stay dry for the Cup.

Half an hour before it was due to be run I left the Hilton on foot, walking unhurriedly along towards Swanston Street and the main area of shops. They were all shut, of course. Melbourne Cup day was a national public holiday. Everything stopped for the Cup

I had taken my left arm out of its sling and threaded it gingerly through the sleeves of my shirt and jacket. A man with his jacket hunched over one shoulder was too memorable for sense. I found that by hooking my thumb into the waistband of my trousers I got quite good support.

Swanston Street was far from its usual bustling self. People still strode along with the breakneck speed which seemed to characterize all Melbourne pedestrians, but they strode in tens, not thousands. Trams ran up and down the central tracks with more vacant seats than passengers. Cars sped along with the drivers, eyes down, fiddling dangerously with radio dials. Fifteen minutes to the race which annually stopped Australia in its tracks.

Jik arrived exactly on time, driving up Swanston Street in the hired grey car and turning smoothly around the corner where I stood waiting. He stopped outside the Yarra River Fine Arts gallery, got out, opened the boot, and put on a brown coat-over-all, of the sort worn by storemen.

I walked quietly along towards him. He brought out a small radio, switched it on, and stood it on top of the car. The commentator's voice emerged tinnily, giving details of the runners currently walking round the parade ring at Flemington races.

'Hello,' he said unemotionally, when I reached him. 'All set?' I nodded, and walked to the door of the gallery. Pushed it. It was solidly shut. Jik dived again into the boot, which held further fruits of his second shopping expedition in Alice Springs.

'Gloves,' he said, handing me some, and putting some on himself. They were of white cotton, with ribbed wristbands, and looked a lot too new and clean. I wiped the backs of mine along the wings of Jik's car, and he gave me a glance and did the same with his.

'Handles and impact adhesive.'

He gave me the two handles to hold. They were simple chromium plated handles, with flattened pieces at each end, pierced by screw holes for fixing. Sturdy handles, big enough for gripping with the whole hand. I held one steady, bottom side up, while Jik covered the screw-plate areas at each end with adhesive. We couldn't screw these handles where we wanted them. They had to be stuck.

'Now the other. Can you hold it in your left hand?'

I nodded. Jik attended to it. One or two people passed, paying no attention. We were not supposed to park there, but no one told us to move.

We walked across the pavement to the gallery. Its frontage was not one unbroken line across its whole width, but was recessed at the right-hand end to form a doorway. Between the front-facing display window and the front-facing glass door, there was a joining window at right angles to the street.

To this sheet of glass we stuck the handles, or rather, Jik did, at just above waist height. He tested them after a minute, and he couldn't pull them off. We returned to the car.

One or two more people passed, turning their heads to listen to the radio on the car roof, smiling in brotherhood at the universal national interest. The street was noticeably emptying as the crucial time drew near.

'. . . *Vinery carries the colours of Mr Hudson Taylor of Adelaide and must be in with a good outside chance. Fourth in the Caulfield Cup and before that, second at Randwick against Brain-Teaser, who went on to beat Afternoon Tea . . .*'

'Stop listening to the damn race!' Jik said sharply.

'Sorry.'

'Ready?'

'Yes.'

We walked back to the entrance to the gallery, Jik carrying the sort of glass-cutter used by, among others, picture framers. Without casting a glance around for possible onlookers, he applied the diamond cutting edge to the matter in hand, using considerable strength as he pushed the professional tool round the outside of the pane. I stood behind him to block any passing curious glances.

'Hold the right-hand handle,' he said, as he started on the last of the four sides, the left-hand vertical.

I stepped past him and slotted my hand through the grip. None of the few people left in the street paid the slightest attention.

'When it goes,' Jik said, 'for God's sake don't drop it.'

'No.'

'Put your knee against the glass. Gently, for God's sake.'

134

I did what he said. He finished the fourth long cut.

'Press smoothly.'

I did that. Jik's knee, too, was firmly against the glass. With his left hand he gripped the chromium handle, and with the palm of his right he began jolting the top perimeter of the heavy pane.

Jik had cut a lot of glass in his time, even if not in exactly these circumstances. The big flat sheet cracked away evenly all round under our pressure and parted with hardly a splinter. The weight fell suddenly on to the handle I held in my right hand, and Jik steadied the now free sheet of glass with hands and knees and blasphemy.

'Jesus, don't let go.'

'No.'

The heavy vibrations set up in the glass by the breaking process subsided, and Jik took over the right-hand handle from me. Without any seeming inconvenience he pivoted the sheet of glass so that it opened like a door. He stepped through the hole, lifted the glass up wholesale by the two handles, carried it several feet, and propped it against the wall to the right of the more conventional way in.

He came out, and we went over to the car. From there, barely ten feet away, one could not see that the gallery was not still securely shut. There were by now in any case very few to look.

'. . . Most jockeys have now mounted and the horses will soon be going out onto the course . . .'

I picked up the radio. Jik exchanged the glass-cutter for a metal saw, a hammer and a chisel, and shut the boot, and we walked through the unorthodox entrance as if it was all in the day's work. Often only the furtive manner gave away the crook. If you behaved as if you had every right to, it took longer for anyone to suspect.

It would really have been best had we next been able to open the real door, but a quick inspection proved it impossible. There were two useful locks, and no keys.

'The stairs are at the back,' I said.

'Lead on.'

We walked the length of the plushy green carpet and down the

135

beckoning stairs. There was a bank of electric switches at the top: we pressed those lighting the basement and left the upstairs lot off.

Heart-thumping time, I thought. It would take only a policeman to walk along and start fussing about a car parked in the wrong place to set Cassavetes and Todd on the road to jail.

'... *horses are now going out on to the course. Foursquare in front, sweating up and fighting jockey Ted Nester for control ...*'

We reached the front of the stairs. I turned back towards the office, but Jik took off fast down the corridor.

'Come back,' I said urgently. 'If that steel gate shuts down ...'

'Relax,' Jik said. 'You told me.' He stopped before reaching the threshold of the furthest room. Stood still, and looked. Came back rapidly.

'O.K. The Munnings are all there. Three of them. Also something else which will stun you. Go and look while I get this door open.'

'... *cantering down to the start, and the excitement is mounting here now ...*'

With a feeling of urgency I trekked down the passage, stopped safely short of any electric gadgets which might trigger the gate and set off alarms, and looked into the Munnings room. The three paintings still hung there, as they had before. But along the row from them was something which, as Jik had said, stunned me. Chestnut horse with head raised, listening. Stately home in the background. The Raoul Millais picture we'd seen in Alice.

I went back to Jik who with hammer and chisel had bypassed the lock on the office door.

'Which is it?' he said. 'Original or copy?'

'Can't tell from that distance. Looks like real.'

He nodded. We went into the office and started work.

'... *Derriby and Special Bet coming down to the start now, and all the runners circling while the girths are checked ...*'

I put the radio on Wexford's desk, where it sat like an hourglass, ticking away the minutes as the sands ran out.

Jik turned his practical attention to the desk drawers, but they were all unlocked. One of the waist-high line of filing cabinets, however, proved to be secure. Jik's strength and knowhow soon ensured that it didn't remain that way.

In his wake I looked through the drawers. Nothing much in them except catalogues and stationery.

In the broken-open filing cabinet, a gold mine.

Not that I realized it at first. The contents looked merely like ordinary files with ordinary headings.

'... moved very freely coming down to the start and is prime fit to run for that hundred and ten thousand dollar prize ...'

There were a good many framed pictures in the office, some on the walls but even more standing in a row on the floor. Jik began looking through them at high speed, almost like flicking through a rack of record albums.

'... handlers are beginning to load the runners into the starting stalls, and I see Vinery playing up ...'

Half of the files in the upper of the two drawers seemed to deal in varying ways with insurance. Letters, policies, revaluations and security. I didn't really know what I was looking for, which made it all a bit difficult.

'Jesus Almighty,' Jik said.

'What is it?'

'Look at this.'

'... more than a hundred thousand people here today to see the twenty-three runners fight it out over the three thousand two hundred metres ...'

Jik had reached the end of the row and was looking at the foremost of three unframed canvasses tied loosely together with string. I peered over his shoulder. The picture had Munnings written all over it. It had Alfred Munnings written large and clear in the right hand bottom corner. It was a picture of four horses with jockeys cantering on a racecourse: and the paint wasn't dry.

'What are the others?' I said.

Jik ripped off the string. The two other pictures were exactly the same.

'God Almighty,' Jik said in awe.

'... Vinery carries only fifty-one kilograms and has a good barrier position so it's not impossible ...'

'Keep looking,' I said, and went back to the files.

Names. Dates. Places. I shook my head impatiently. We needed more than those Munnings copies and I couldn't find a thing.

'Jesus!' Jik said.

He was looking inside the sort of large flat two-foot by three-foot folder which was used in galleries to store prints.

'. . . only Derriby now to enter the stalls . . .'

The print-folder had stood between the end of the desk and the nearby wall. Jik seemed transfixed.

Overseas Customers. My eyes flicked over the heading and then went back. Overseas Customers. I opened the file. Lists of people, sorted into countries. Pages of them. Names and addresses.

England.

A long list. Not alphabetical. Too many to read through in the shortage of time.

A good many of the names had been crossed out.

'. . . They're running! This is the moment you've all been waiting for, and Special Bet is out in front . . .'

'Look at this,' Jik said.

Donald Stuart. Donald Stuart, crossed out. Shropshire, England. Crossed out.

I practically stopped breathing.

'. . . as they pass the stands for the first time it's Special Bet, Foursquare, Newshound, Derriby, Wonderbug, Vinery . . .'

'Look at this,' Jik said again, insistently.

'Bring it,' I said. 'We've got less than three minutes before the race ends and Melbourne comes back to life.'

'But—'

'Bring it,' I said. 'And also those three copies.'

'. . . Special Bet still making it, from Newshound close second, then Wonderbug . . .'

I shoved the filing-drawer shut.

'Put this file in the print-folder and let's get out.'

I picked up the radio and Jik's tools, as he himself had enough trouble managing all three of the untied paintings and the large print-folder.

'. . . down the backstretch by the Maribyrnong River it's still

138

Special Bet with Vinery second now . . .'

We went up the stairs. Switched off the lights. Eased round into a view of the car.

It stood there, quiet and unattended, just as we'd left it. No policeman. Everyone elsewhere, listening to the race.

Jik was calling on the Deity under his breath.

'. . . rounding the turn towards home Special Bet is dropping back now and its Derriby with Newhound . . .'

We walked steadily down the gallery.

The commentator's voice rose in excitement against a background of shouting crowds.

'. . . Vinery in third with Wonderbug, and here comes Ringwood very fast on the stands side . . .'

Nothing stirred out on the street. I went first through our hole in the glass and stood once more, with a great feeling of relief, on the outside of the beehive. Jik carried out the plundered honey and stacked it in the boot. He took the tools from my hands and stored them also.

'Right?'

I nodded with a dry mouth. We climbed normally into the car. The commentator was yelling to be heard.

'. . . Coming to the line it's Ringwood by a length from Wonderbug, with Newshound third, then Derriby, then Vinery . . .'

The cheers echoed inside the car as Jik started the engine and drove away.

'. . . Might be a record time. Just listen to the cheers. The result again. The result of the Melbourne Cup. In the frame . . . first Ringwood, owned by Mr Robert Khami . . . second Wonderbug . . .'

'Phew,' Jik said, his beard jaunty and a smile stretching to show an expanse of gum. 'That wasn't a bad effort. We might hire ourselves out some time for stealing politicians' papers.' He chuckled fiercely.

'It's an overcrowded field,' I said, smiling broadly myself.

We were both feeling the euphoria which follows the safe deliverance from danger. 'Take it easy,' I said. 'We've a long way to go.'

He drove to the Hilton, parked, and carried the folder and pictures up to my room. He moved with his sailing speed, economically and fast, losing as little time as possible before returning to Sarah on the racecourse and acting as if he'd never been away.

'We'll be back here as soon as we can,' he promised, sketching a farewell.

Two seconds after he'd shut my door there was a knock on it. I opened it. Jik stood there.

'I'd better know,' he said, 'What won the Cup?'

twelve

When he'd gone I looked closely at the spoils.

The more I saw, the more certain it became that we had hit the absolute jackpot. I began to wish most insistently that we hadn't wasted time in establishing that Jik and Sarah were at the races. It made me nervous, waiting for them in the Hilton with so much dynamite in my hands. Every instinct urged immediate departure.

The list of Overseas Customers would to any other eyes have seemed the most harmless of documents. Wexford would not have needed to keep it in better security than a locked filing-cabinet, for the chances of anyone seeing its significance in ordinary circumstances were millions to one against.

Donald Stuart, Wrenstone House, Shropshire.

Crossed out.

Each page had three columns, a narrow one at each side with a broad one in the centre. The narrow left-hand column was for dates and the centre for names and addresses. In the narrow right-hand column, against each name, was a short line of apparently random letters and numbers. Those against Donald's entry, for instance, were MM3109T: and these figures had not been crossed out with his name. Maybe a sort of stock list, I thought, identifying the picture he'd bought.

I searched rapidly down all the other crossed-out names in the

140

England sector. Maisie Matthews' name was not among them.

Damn, I thought. Why wasn't it?

I turned all the papers over rapidly. As far as I could see all the overseas customers came from basically English-speaking countries, and the proportion of crossed-out names was about one in three. If every crossing-out represented a robbery, there had been literally hundreds since the scheme began.

At the back of the file I found there was a second and separate section, again divided into pages for each country. The lists in this section were much shorter.

England.

Half way down. My eyes positively leapt at it.

Mrs M. Matthews, Treasure Holme, Worthing, Sussex.

Crossed out.

I almost trembled. The date in the left-hand column looked like the date on which Maisie had bought her picture. The uncrossed-out numbers in the right hand column were SMC29R.

I put down the file and sat for five minutes staring unseeingly at the wall, thinking.

My first and last conclusions were that I had a great deal to do before Jik and Sarah came back from the races, and that instincts were not always right.

The large print-folder, which had so excited Jik, lay on my bed. I opened it flat and inspected the contents.

I daresay I looked completely loony standing there with my mouth open. The folder contained a number of simplified line drawings like the one the boy-artist had been colouring in the Arts Centre. Full-sized outline drawings, on flat white canvas, as neat and accurate as tracings.

There were seven of them, all basically of horses. As they were only black and white line drawings I couldn't be sure, but I guessed that three were Munnings, two Raoul Millais, and the other two . . . I stared at the old-fashioned shapes of the horses . . . They couldn't be Stubbs, he was too well documented . . . How about Herring? Herring, I thought, nodding. The last two had a look of Herring.

Attached to one of these two canvases by an ordinary paper

clip was a small handwritten memo on a piece of scrap paper.

'Don't forget to send the original. Also find out what palette he used, if different from usual.'

I looked again at the three identical finished paintings which we had also brought away. These canvases, tacked on to wooden stretchers, looked very much as if they might have started out themselves as the same sort of outlines. The canvas used was of the same weave and finish.

The technical standard of the work couldn't be faulted. The paintings did look very much like Munnings' own, and would do much more so after they had dried and been varnished. Different coloured paints dried at different speeds, and also the drying time of paints depended very much on the amount of oil or turps used to thin them, but at a rough guess all three pictures had been completed between three and six days earlier. The paint was at the same stage on all of them. They must, I thought, have all been painted at once, in a row, like a production line. Red hat, red hat, red hat . . . It would have saved time and paint.

The brushwork throughout was painstaking and controlled. Nothing slapdash. No time skimped. The quality of care was the same as in the Millais copy at Alice.

I was looking, I knew, at the true worth of Harley Renbo.

All three paintings were perfectly legal. It was never illegal to copy : only to attempt to sell the copy as real.

I thought it all over for a bit longer, and then set rapidly to work.

The Hilton, when I went downstairs an hour later, were most amiable and helpful.

Certainly, they could do what I asked. Certainly, I could use the photo-copying machine, come this way. Certainly, I could pay my bill now, and leave later.

I thanked them for their many excellent services.

'Our pleasure,' they said; and, incredibly, they meant it.

Upstairs again, waiting for Jik and Sarah, I packed all my things. That done, I took off my jacket and shirt and did my best at rigging the spare bandages and clips back into something like the Alice shape, with my hand inside across my chest. No use pretending that it wasn't a good deal more comfortable that way than the dragging soreness of letting it all swing free. I buttoned my shirt over the top and calculated that if the traffic was bad Jik might still be struggling out of the racecourse.

A little anxiously, and still faintly feeling unwell, I settled to wait.

I waited precisely five minutes. Then the telephone by the bed rang, and I picked up the receiver.

Jik's voice, sounding hard and dictatorial.

'Charles, will you please come down to our room at once.'

'Well . . .' I said hesitantly. 'Is it important?'

'Bloody chromicoxide!' he said explosively. 'Can't you do anything without arguing?'

Christ, I thought.

I took a breath. 'Give me ten minutes,' I said. 'I need ten minutes. I'm . . . er . . . I've just had a shower. I'm in my underpants.'

'Thank you, Charles,' he said. The telephone clicked as he disconnected.

A lot of Jik's great oaths galloped across my mind, wasting precious time. If ever we needed divine help, it was now.

Stifling a gut-twisting lurch of plain fear I picked up the telephone and made a series of internal calls.

'Please could you send a porter up right away to room seventeen eighteen to collect Mr Cassavetes' bags?'

'Housekeeper . . . ? Please will you send someone along urgently to seventeen eighteen to clean the room as Mr Cassavetes has been sick . . .'

'Please will you send the nurse along to seventeen eighteen at once as Mr Cassavetes has a severe pain . . .'

'Please will you send four bottles of your best champagne and ten glasses up to seventeen eighteen immediately . . .'

'Please bring coffee for three to seventeen eighteen at once . . .'

'Electrician? All the electrics have fused in room seventeen eighteen, please come at once.'

'. . . the water is overflowing in the bathroom, please send the plumber urgently.'

Who else was there? I ran my eye down the list of possible

services. One wouldn't be able to summon chiropodists, masseuses, secretaries, barbers or clothespressers in a hurry . . . but television, why not?

'. . . Please would you see to the television in room seventeen eighteen. There is smoke coming from the back and it smells like burning . . .'

That should do it, I thought. I made one final call for myself, asking for a porter to collect my bags. Right on, they said. Ten dollar tip I said if the bags could be down in the hall within five minutes. No sweat, an Australian voice assured me happily. Coming right that second.

I left my door ajar for the porter and rode down two storeys in the lift to floor seventeen. The corridor outside Jik and Sarah's room was still a broad empty expanse of no one doing anything in a hurry.

The ten minutes had gone.

I fretted.

The first to arrive was the waiter with the champagne, and he came not with a tray but a trolley, complete with ice buckets and spotless white cloths. It couldn't possibly have been better.

As he slowed to a stop outside Jik's door, two other figures turned into the corridor, hurrying, and behind them, distantly, came a cleaner slowly pushing another trolley of linen and buckets and brooms.

I said to the waiter, 'Thank you so much for coming so quickly.' I gave him a ten dollar note, which surprised him. 'Please go and serve the champagne straight away.'

He grinned, and knocked on Jik's door.

After a pause, Jik opened it. He looked tense and strained.

'Your champagne, sir,' said the waiter.

'But I didn't . . .' Jik began. He caught sight of me suddenly, where I stood a little back from his door. I made waving-in motions with my hand, and a faint grin appeared to lighten the anxiety.

Jik retreated into the room followed by trolley and waiter.

At a rush, after that, came the electrician, the plumber and the television man. I gave them each ten dollars and thanked them for coming so promptly. 'I had a winner,' I said. They took the money with more grins and Jik opened the door to their knock.

'Electrics . . . plumbing . . . television . . .' His eyebrows rose. He looked across to me in rising comprehension. He flung wide his door and invited them in with all his heart.

'Give them some champagne,' I said.

'God Almighty.'

After that, in quick succession, came the porter, the man with the coffee, and the nurse. I gave them all ten dollars from my mythical winnings and invited them to join the party. Finally came the cleaner, pushing her top-heavy-looking load. She took the ten dollars, congratulated me on my good fortune, and entered the crowded and noisy fray.

It was up to Jik, I thought. I couldn't do any more.

He and Sarah suddenly popped out like the corks from the gold-topped bottles, and stood undecided in the corridor. I gripped Sarah's wrist and tugged her towards me.

'Push the cleaning trolley through the door, and turn it over,' I said to Jik.

He wasted no time deliberating. The brooms crashed to the carpet inside the room, and Jik pulled the door shut after him.

Sarah and I were already running on our way to the lifts. She looked extremely pale and wild-eyed, and I knew that whatever had happened in their room had been almost too much for her.

Jik sprinted along after us. There were six lifts from the seventeenth floor, and one never had to wait more than a few seconds for one to arrive. The seconds this time seemed like hours but were actually very few indeed. The welcoming doors slid open, and we leapt inside and pushed the 'doors closed' button like maniacs.

The doors closed.

The lift descended, smooth and fast.

'Where's the car?' I said.

'Car park.'

'Get it and come round to the side door.'

'Right.'

'Sarah . . .'

She stared at me in fright.

'My satchel will be in the hall. Will you carry it for me?'

She looked vaguely at my one-armed state, my jacket swinging loosely over my left shoulder.

'Sarah!'

'Yes . . . all right.'

We erupted into the hall, which had filled with people returning from the Cup. Talkative groups mixed and mingled, and it was impossible to see easily from one side to the other. All to the good, I thought.

My suitcase and satchel stood waiting near the front entrance, guarded by a young man in porter's uniform.

I parted with the ten dollars. 'Thank you very much,' I said.

'No sweat,' he said cheerfully. 'Can I get you a taxi?'

I shook my head. I picked up the suitcase and Sarah the satchel and we headed out of the door.

Turned right. Hurried. Turned right again, round to the side where I'd told Jik we'd meet him.

'He's not here,' Sarah said with rising panic.

'He'll come,' I said encouragingly. 'We'll just go on walking to meet him.'

We walked. I kept looking back nervously for signs of pursuit, but there were none. Jik came round the corner on two wheels and tore millimetres off the tyres stopping beside us. Sarah scrambled into the front and I and my suitcase filled the back. Jik made a hair-raising U turn and took us away from the Hilton at an illegal speed.

'Wowee,' he said, laughing with released tension. 'Whatever gave you that idea?'

'The Marx brothers.'

He nodded. 'Pure crazy comedy.'

'Where are we going?' Sarah said.

'Have you noticed,' Jik said, 'how my wife always brings us back to basics?'

The city of Melbourne covered a great deal of land.

We drove randomly north and east through seemingly endless suburban developments of houses, shops, garages and light industry, all looking prosperous, haphazard, and, to my eyes, American.

146

'Where are we?' Jik said.

'Somewhere called Box Hill,' I said, reading it on shop fronts.

'As good as anywhere.'

We drove a few miles further and stopped at a modern middle-rank motel which had bright coloured strings of triangular flags fluttering across the forecourt. A far cry from the Hilton, though the rooms we presently took were cleaner than nature intended.

There were plain divans, a square of thin carpet nailed at the edges, and a table lamp screwed to an immovable table. The looking glass was stuck flat to the wall and the swivelling armchair was bolted to the floor. Apart from that, the curtains were bright and the hot tap ran hot in the shower.

'They don't mean you to pinch much,' Jik said. 'Let's paint them a mural.'

'No!' Sarah said, horrorstruck.

'There's a great Australian saying,' Jik said. 'If it moves, shoot it, and if it grows, chop it down.'

'What's that got to do with it?' Sarah said.

'Nothing. I just thought Todd might like to hear it.'

'Give me strength.'

We were trying to, in our inconsequential way.

Jik sat in the armchair in my room, swivelling. Sarah sat on one of the divans, I on the other. My suitcase and satchel stood side by side on the floor.

'You do realize we skipped out of the Hilton without paying,' Sarah said.

'No we didn't,' Jik said. 'According to our clothes, we are still resident. I'll ring them up later.'

'But Todd . . .'

'I did pay,' I said. 'Before you got back.'

She looked slightly happier.

'How did Greene find you?' I said.

'God knows,' Jik said gloomily.

Sarah was astonished. 'How did you know about Greene? How did you know there was anyone in our room besides Jik and me? How did you know we were in such awful trouble?'

'Jik told me.'

'But he couldn't! He couldn't risk warning you. He just had to

147

tell you to come. He really did . . .' Her voice quivered. The tears weren't far from the surface. 'They made him . . .'

'Jik told me,' I said matter-of-factly. 'First, he called me Charles, which he never does, so I knew something was wrong. Second, he was rude to me, and I know you think he is most of the time, but he isn't, not like that. And third, he told me the name of the man who I was to guess was in your room putting pressure on you both to get me to come down and walk into a nasty little hole. He told me it was chromic oxide, which is the pigment in green paint.'

'Green paint!' The tearful moment passed. 'You really are both extraordinary,' she said.

'Long practice,' Jik said cheerfully.

'Tell me what happened,' I said.

'We left before the last race, to avoid the traffic, and we just came back normally to the Hilton. I parked the car, and we went up to our room. We'd only been there about a minute when there was this knock on the door, and when I opened it they just pushed in . . .'

'They?'

'Three of them. One was Greene. We both knew him straight away, from your drawing. Another was the boy from the Arts Centre. The third was all biceps and beetle brows, with his brains in his fists.'

He absentmindedly rubbed an area south of his heart.

'He punched you?' I said.

'It was all so quick . . .' he said apologetically. 'They just crammed in . . . and biff bang . . . The next thing I knew they'd got hold of Sarah and were twisting her arm and saying that she wouldn't just get turps in her eyes if I didn't get you to come at once.'

'Did they have a gun?' I asked.

'No . . . a cigarette lighter. Look, I'm sorry, mate. I guess it sounds pretty feeble, but Beetle-brows had her in a pretty rough grasp and the boy had this ruddy great cigarette lighter with a flame like a blow torch just a couple of inches from her cheek . . . and I was a bit groggy . . . and Greene said they'd burn her if I didn't get you . . . and I couldn't fight them all at once.'

148

'Stop apologizing,' I said.

'Yeah . . . well, so I rang you. I told Greene you'd be ten minutes because you were in your underpants, but I think he heard you anyway because he was standing right beside me, very wary and sharp. I didn't know really whether you'd cottoned on, but I hoped to God . . . and you should have seen their faces when the waiter pushed the trolley in. Beetle-brows let go of Sarah and the boy just stood there with his mouth open and the cigarette lighter flaring up like an oil refinery . . .'

'Greene said we didn't want the champagne and to take it away,' Sarah said. 'But Jik and I said yes we did, and Jik asked the waiter to open it at once.'

'Before he got the first cork out the others all began coming . . . and then they were all picking up glasses . . . and the room was filling up . . . and Greene and the boy and Beetle-brows were all on the window side of the room, sort of pinned in by the trolley and all those people . . . and I just grabbed Sarah and we ducked round the edge. The last I saw, Greene and the others were trying to push through, but our guests were pretty thick on the ground by then and keen to get their champagne . . . and I should think the cleaning trolley was just about enough to give us that start to the lift.'

'I wonder how long the party lasted,' I said.

'Until the bubbles ran out.'

'They must all have thought you mad,' Sarah said.

'Anything goes on Cup day,' I said, 'and the staff of the Hilton would be used to eccentric guests.'

'What if Greene had had a gun?' Sarah said.

I smiled at her twistedly. 'He would have had to wave it around in front of a hell of a lot of witnesses.'

'But he might have done.'

'He might . . . but he was a long way from the front door.' I bit my thumbnail. 'Er . . . how did he know I was in the Hilton?'

There was a tangible silence.

'I told him,' Sarah said finally, in a small mixed outburst of shame and defiance. 'Jik didn't tell you it all, just now. At first they said . . . Greene said . . . they'd burn my face if Jik didn't tell them where you were. He didn't want to . . . but he had to . . . so

I told them, so that it wouldn't be him . . . I suppose that sounds stupid.'

I thought it sounded extraordinarily moving. Love of an exceptional order, and a depth of understanding.

I smiled at her. 'So they didn't know I was there, to begin with?'

Jik shook his head. 'I don't think they knew you were even in Melbourne. They seemed surprised when Sarah said you were upstairs. I think all they knew was that you weren't still in hospital in Alice Springs.'

'Did they know about our robbery?'

'I'm sure they didn't.'

I grinned. 'They'll be schizophrenic when they find out.'

Jik and I both carefully shied away from what would have happened if I'd gone straight down to their room, though I saw from his eyes that he knew. With Sarah held as a hostage I would have had to leave the Hilton with Greene and taken my chance. The uncomfortably slim chance that they would have let me off again with my life.

'I'm hungry,' I said.

Sarah smiled. 'Whenever are you not?'

We ate in a small Bring Your Own restaurant nearby, with people at tables all around us talking about what they'd backed in the Cup.

'Good heavens,' Sarah exclaimed. 'I'd forgotten about that.'

'About what?'

'Your winnings,' she said. 'On Ringwood.'

'But . . .' I began.

'It was number eleven!'

'I don't believe it.'

She opened her handbag and produced a fat wad of notes. Somehow, in all the mêlée in the Hilton, she had managed to emerge from fiery danger with the cream leather pouch swinging from her arm. The strength of the instinct which kept women attached to their handbags had often astounded me, but never more than that day.

'It was forty to one,' she said. 'I put twenty dollars on for you, so you've got eight hundred dollars, and I think it's disgusting.'

'Share it,' I said, laughing.

She shook her head. 'Not a cent . . . To be honest, I thought it had no chance at all, and I thought I'd teach you not to bet that way by losing you twenty dollars, otherwise I'd only have staked you ten.'

'I owe most of it to Jik, anyway,' I said.

'Keep it,' he said. 'We'll add and subtract later. Do you want me to cut your steak?'

'Please.'

He sliced away neatly at my plate, and pushed it back with the fork placed ready.

'What else happened at the races?' I said, spearing the first succulent piece. 'Who did you see?' The steak tasted as good as it looked, and I realized that in spite of all the sore patches I had at last lost the overall feeling of unsettled shaky sickness. Things were on the mend, it seemed.

'We didn't see Greene,' Jik said. 'Or the boy, or Beetle-brows.'

'I'd guess they saw you.'

'Do you think so?' Sarah said worriedly.

'I'd guess,' I said, 'that they saw you at the races and simply followed you back to the Hilton.'

'Jesus,' Jik groaned. 'We never spotted them. There was a whole mass of traffic.'

I nodded. 'And all moving very slowly. If Greene was perhaps three cars behind you, you'd never have seen him, but he could have kept you in sight easily.'

'I'm bloody sorry, Todd.'

'Don't be silly. And no harm done.'

'Except for the fact,' Sarah said, 'that I've still got no clothes.'

'You look fine,' I said absently.

'We saw a girl I know in Sydney,' Sarah said. 'We watched the first two races together and talked to her aunt. And Jik and I were talking to a photographer we both knew just after he got back . . . so it would be pretty easy to prove Jik was at the races all afternoon, like you wanted.'

'No sign of Wexford?'

'Not if he looked like your drawing,' Sarah said. 'Though of

151

course he might have been there. It's awfully difficult to recognize a complete stranger just from a drawing, in a huge crowd like that.'

'We talked to a lot of people,' Jik said. 'To everyone Sarah knew even slightly She used the excuse of introducing me as her newly-bagged husband.'

'We even talked to that man you met on Saturday,' Sarah agreed, nodding. 'Or rather, he came over and talked to us.'

'Hudson Taylor?' I asked.

'The one you saw talking to Wexford,' Jik said.

'He asked if you were at the Cup,' Sarah said. 'He said he'd been going to ask you along for another drink. We said we'd tell you he'd asked.'

'His horse ran quite well, didn't it?' I said.

'We saw him earlier than that. We wished him luck and he said he'd need it.'

'He bets a bit,' I said, remembering.

'Who doesn't?'

'Another commission down the drain,' I said. 'He would have had Vinery painted if he'd won.'

'You hire yourself out like a prostitute,' Jik said. 'It's obscene.'

'And anyway,' added Sarah cheerfully, 'You won more on Ringwood than you'd've got for the painting.'

I looked pained, and Jik laughed.

We drank coffee, went back to the motel, and divided to our separate rooms. Five minutes later Jik knocked on my door.

'Come in,' I said, opening it.

He grinned. 'You were expecting me.'

'Thought you might come.'

He sat in the armchair and swivelled. His gaze fell on my suitcase, which lay flat on one of the divans.

'What did you do with all the stuff we took from the gallery?' I told him.

He stopped swivelling and sat still.

'You don't mess about, do you?' he said eventually.

'A few days from now,' I said, 'I'm going home.'

'And until then?'

'Um . . . until then, I aim to stay one jump ahead of Wexford,

152

Greene, Beetle-brows, the Arts Centre boy, and the tough who met me on the balcony at Alice.'

'Not to mention our copy artist, Harley Renbo.'

I considered it. 'Him too,' I said.

'Do you think we can?'

'Not we. Not from hereon. This is where you take Sarah home.'

He slowly shook his head. 'I don't reckon it would be any safer than staying with you. We're too easy to find. For one thing, we're in the Sydney phone book. What's to stop Wexford from marching on to the boat with a bigger threat than a cigarette lighter?'

'You could tell him what I've just told you.'

'And waste all your efforts.'

'Retreat is sometimes necessary.'

He shook his head. 'If we stay with you, retreat may never be necessary. It's the better of two risks. And anyway . . .' the old fire gleamed in his eye . . . 'It will be a great game. Cat and mouse. With cats who don't know they are mice chasing a mouse who knows he's a cat.'

More like a bull fight, I thought, with myself waving the cape to invite the charge. Or a conjuror, attracting attention to one hand while he did the trick with the other. On the whole I preferred the notion of the conjuror. There seemed less likelihood of being gored.

thirteen

I spent a good deal of the night studying the list of Overseas Customers, mostly because I still found it difficult to lie comfortably to sleep, and partly because I had nothing else to read.

It became more and more obvious that I hadn't really pinched *enough*. The list I'd taken was fine in its way, but would have been doubly useful with a stock list to match the letters and numbers in the right hand column.

On the other hand, all stock numbers were a form of code, and if I looked at them long enough, maybe some sort of recognizable pattern might emerge.

By far the majority began with the letter M, particularly in the first and much larger section. In the smaller section, which I had found at the back of the file, the M prefixes were few, and S, A, W and B were much commoner.

Donald's number began with M. Maisie's began with S.

Suppose, I thought, that the M simply stood for Melbourne, and the S for Sydney, the cities where each had bought their pictures.

Then A, W and B were where? Adelaide, Wagga Wagga and Brisbane?

Alice?

In the first section the letters and numbers following the initial M seemed to have no clear pattern. In the second section, though, the third letter was always C, the last letter always R, and the numbers, divided though they were between several countries, progressed more or less consecutively. The highest number of all was 54, which had been sold to a Mr Norman Updike, living in Auckland, New Zealand. The stock number against his name was WHC54R The date in the left hand column was only a week old, and Mr Updike had not been crossed out.

All the pictures in the shorter section had been sold within the past three years. The first dates in the long first section were five and a half years old.

I wondered which had come first, five and a half years ago: the gallery or the idea. Had Wexford originally been a full-time crook deliberately setting up an imposing front, or a formerly honest art dealer struck by criminal possibilities? Judging from the respectable air of the gallery and what little I'd seen of Wexford himself, I would have guessed the latter. But the violence lying just below the surface didn't match.

I sighed, put down the lists, and switched off the light. Lay in the dark, thinking of the telephone call I'd made after Jik had gone back to Sarah.

It had been harder to arrange from the motel than it would

154

have been from the Hilton, but the line had been loud and clear.

'You got my cable?' I said.

'I've been waiting for your call for half an hour.'

'Sorry.'

'What do you want?'

'I've sent you a letter,' I said. 'I want to tell you what's in it.'

'But . . .'

'Just listen,' I said. 'And talk after.' I spoke for quite a long time to a response of grunts from the far end.

'Are you sure of all this?'

'Positive about most,' I said. 'Some of it's a guess.'

'Repeat it.'

'Very well.' I did so, at much the same length.

'I have recorded all that.'

'Good.'

'Hm . . . What do you intend doing now?'

'I'm going home soon. Before that, I think I'll keep looking into things that aren't my business.'

'I don't approve of that.'

I grinned at the telephone. 'I don't suppose you do, but if I'd stayed in England we wouldn't have got this far. There's one other thing . . . Can I reach you by telex if I want to get a message to you in a hurry?'

'Telex? Wait a minute.'

I waited.

'Yes, here you are.' A number followed. I wrote it down. 'Address any message to me personally and head it urgent.'

'Right,' I said. 'And could you get answers to three questions for me?' He listened and said he could. 'Thank you very much,' I said. 'And goodnight.'

Sarah and Jik both looked heavy-eyed and languorous in the morning. A successful night, I judged.

We checked out of the motel, packed my suitcase into the boot of the car, and sat in the passenger seats to plan the day.

'Can't we please get our clothes from the Hilton?' Sarah said, sounding depressed.

Jik and I said 'No' together.

'I'll ring them now,' Jik said. 'I'll get them to pack all our things and keep them safe for us, and I'll tell them I'll send a cheque for the bill.' He levered himself out of the car again and went off on the errand.

'Buy what you need out of my winnings,' I said to Sarah.

She shook her head. 'I've got some money. It's not that. It's just . . . I wish all this was over.'

'It will be, soon,' I said neutrally. She sighed heavily. 'What's your idea of a perfect life?' I asked.

'Oh . . .' she seemed surprised. 'I suppose right now I just want to be with Jik on the boat and have fun, like before you came.'

'And for ever?'

She looked at me broodingly. 'You may think, Todd, that I don't know Jik is a complicated character, but you've only got to look at his paintings . . . They make me shudder. They're a side of Jik I don't know because he hasn't painted anything since we met. You may think that this world will be worse off if Jik is happy for a bit, but I'm no fool, I know that in the end whatever it is that drives him to paint like that will come back again . . . I think these first few months together are frantically precious . . . and it isn't just the physical dangers you've dragged us into that I hate, but the feeling that I've lost the rest of that golden time . . . that you remind him of his painting, and that after you've gone he'll go straight back to it . . . weeks and weeks before he might have done.'

'Get him to go sailing,' I said. 'He's always happy at sea.'

'You don't care, do you?'

I looked straight into her clouded brown eyes. 'I care for you both, very much.'

'Then God help the people you hate.'

And God help me, I thought, if I become any fonder of my oldest friend's wife. I looked away from her, out of the window. Affection wouldn't matter. Anything else would be a mess.

Jik came back with a satisfied air. 'That's all fixed. They said there's a letter for you, Todd, delivered by hand a few minutes ago. They asked me for a forwarding address.'

'What did you say?'

'I said you'd call them yourself.'

'Right . . . Well, let's get going.'

'Where to?'

'New Zealand, don't you think?'

'That should be far enough,' Jik said dryly.

He drove us to the airport, which was packed with people going home from the Cup.

'If Wexford and Greene are looking for us,' Sarah said, 'they will surely be watching at the airport.'

If they weren't, I thought, we'd have to lay a trail: but Jik, who knew that, didn't tell her.

'They can't do much in public,' he said comfortingly.

We bought tickets and found we could either fly to Auckland direct at lunchtime, or via Sydney leaving within half an hour.

'Sydney,' said Sarah positively, clearly drawing strength from the chance of putting her feet down on her own safe doorstep.

I shook my head. 'Auckland direct. Let's see if the restaurant's still open for breakfast.'

We squeezed in under the waitresses' pointed consultation of clocks and watches and ordered bacon and eggs lavishly.

'Why are we going to New Zealand?' Sarah said.

'To see a man about a painting and advise him to take out extra insurance.'

'Are you actually making sense?'

'Actually,' I said, 'yes.'

'I don't see why we have to go so far, when Jik said you found enough in the gallery to blow the whole thing wide open.'

'Um . . .' I said. 'Because we don't want to blow it wide open. Because we want to hand it to the police in full working order.'

She studied my face. 'You are very devious.'

'Not on canvas,' Jik said.

After we'd eaten we wandered around the airport shops, buying yet more toothbrushes and so on for Jik and Sarah, and another airline bag. There was no sign of Wexford or Greene or the boy or Beetle-brows or Renbo, or the tough who'd been on watch at Alice Springs. If they'd seen us without us seeing them, we couldn't tell.

157

'I think I'll ring the Hilton,' I said.

Jik nodded. I put the call through with him and Sarah sitting near, within sound and sight.

'I called about a forwarding address . . .' I told the reception desk. 'I can't really give you one. I'll be in New Zealand. I'm flying to Auckland in an hour or two.'

They asked for instructions about the hand-delivered letter.

'Er . . . Would you mind opening it, and reading it to me?'

Certainly, they said. Their pleasure. The letter was from Hudson Taylor saying he was sorry to have missed me at the races, and that if while I was in Australia I would like to see round a vineyard, he would be pleased to show me his.

Thanks, I said. Our pleasure, sir, they said. If anyone asked for me, I said, would they please mention where I'd gone. They would. Certainly. Their pleasure.

During the next hour Jik called the car-hire firm about settling their account and leaving the car in the airport car park, and I checked my suitcase through with Air New Zealand. Passports were no problem: I had mine with me in any case, but for Jik and Sarah they were unnecessary, as passage between New Zealand and Australia was as unrestricted as between England and Ireland.

Still no sign of Wexford or Greene. We sat in the departure bay thinking private thoughts.

It was again only when our flight was called that I spotted a spotter. The prickles rose again on my skin. I'd been blind, I thought. Dumb and blind.

Not Wexford, nor Greene, nor the boy, nor Renbo, nor any rough set of muscles A neat day dress, neat hair, unremarkable handbag and shoes. A calm concentrated face. I saw her because she was staring at Sarah. She was standing outside the departure bay, looking in. The woman who had welcomed me into the Yarra River Fine Arts, and given me a catalogue, and let me out again afterwards.

As if she felt my eyes upon her she switched her gaze abruptly to my face. I looked away instantly, blankly, hoping she wouldn't know I'd seen her, or wouldn't know at least that I'd recognized her.

158

Jik, Sarah and I stood up and drifted with everyone else towards the departure doors. In their glass I could see the woman's reflection: standing still, watching us go. I walked out towards the aircraft and didn't look back.

Mrs Norman Updike stood in her doorway, shook her head, and said that her husband would not be home until six.

She was thin and sharp-featured and talked with tight New Zealand vowels. If we wanted to speak to her husband, we would have to come back.

She looked us over; Jik with his rakish blond beard, Sarah in her slightly crumpled but still military cream dress, I with my arm in its sling under my shirt, and jacket loose over my shoulder. Hardly a trio one would easily forget. She watched us retreat down her front path with a sharply turned-down mouth.

'Dear gentle soul,' murmured Jik.

We drove away in the car we had hired at the airport.

'Where now?' Jik said.

'Shops.' Sarah was adamant. 'I must have some clothes.'

The shops, it appeared, were in Queen Street, and still open for another half hour. Jik and I sat in the car, waiting and watching the world go by.

'The dolly-birds fly out of their office cages about now,' Jik said happily.

'What of it?'

'I sit and count the ones with no bras.'

'And you a married man.'

'Old habits die hard.'

We had counted eight definites and one doubtful by the time Sarah returned. She was wearing a light olive skirt with a pink shirt, and reminded me of pistachio ice cream.

'That's better,' she said, tossing two well-filled carriers onto the back seat. 'Off we go, then.'

The therapeutic value of the new clothes lasted all the time we spent in New Zealand and totally amazed me. She seemed to feel safer if she looked fresh and clean, her spirits rising accordingly. Armourplated cotton, I thought. Drip-dry bullet-proofing. Security is a new pin.

We dawdled back to the hill overlooking the bay where Norman Updike's house stood in a crowded suburban street. The Updike residence was large but squashed by neighbours, and it was not until one was inside that one realized that the jostling was due to the view. As many houses as could be crammed on to the land had been built to share it. The city itself seemed to sprawl endlessly round miles of indented coastline, but all the building plots looked tiny.

Norman Updike proved as expansive as his wife was closed in. He had a round shiny bald head on a round short body, and he called his spouse Chuckles without apparently intending satire.

We said, Jik and I, that we were professional artists who would be intensely interested and grateful if we could briefly admire the noted picture he had just bought.

'Did the gallery send you?' he asked, beaming at the implied compliments to his taste and wealth.

'Sort of,' we said, and Jik added: 'My friend here is well known in England for his painting of horses, and is represented in many top galleries, and has been hung often at the Royal Academy ...'

I thought he was laying it on a bit too thick, but Norman Updike was impressed and pulled wide his door.

'Come in then. Come in. The picture's in the lounge. This way, lass, this way.'

He showed us into a large over-stuffed room with dark ankle-deep carpet, big dark cupboards, and the glorious view of sunlit water.

Chuckles, sitting solidly in front of a television busy with a moronic British comic show, gave us a sour look and no greeting.

'Over here,' Norman Updike beamed, threading his portly way round a battery of fat armchairs. 'What do you think of that, eh?' He waved his hand with proprietorial pride at the canvas on his wall.

A smallish painting, fourteen inches by eighteen. A black horse, with an elongated neck curving against a blue and white sky; a chopped-off tail; the grass in the foreground yellow; and the whole covered with an old-looking varnish.

'Herring,' I murmured reverently.

160

Norman Updike's beam broadened. 'I see you know your stuff. Worth a bit, that is.'

'A good deal,' I agreed.

'I reckon I got a bargain. The gallery said I'd always make a profit if I wanted to sell.'

'May I look at the brushwork?' I asked politely.

'Go right ahead.'

I looked closely. It was very good. It did look like Herring, dead since 1865. It also, indefinably, looked like the meticulous Renbo. One would need a microscope and chemical analysis, to make sure.

I stepped back and glanced round the rest of the room. There was nothing of obvious value, and the few other pictures were all prints.

'Beautiful,' I said admiringly, turning back to the Herring. 'Unmistakable style. A real master.'

Updike beamed.

'You'd better beware of burglars,' I said.

He laughed. 'Chuckles, dear, do you hear what this young man says? He says we'd better beware of burglars!'

Chuckles' eyes gave me two seconds' sour attention and returned to the screen.

Updike patted Sarah on the shoulder. 'Tell your friend not to worry about burglars.'

'Why not?' I said.

'We've got alarms all over this house,' he beamed. 'Don't you worry, a burglar wouldn't get far.'

Jik and Sarah, as I had done, looked round the room and saw nothing much worth stealing. Nothing, certainly, worth alarms all over the house. Updike watched them looking and his beam grew wider.

'Shall I show these young people our little treasures, Chuckles?' he said.

Chuckles didn't even reply. The television cackled with tinned laughter.

'We'd be most interested,' I said.

He smiled with the fat anticipatory smirk of one about to show

161

what will certainly be admired. Two or three steps took him to one of the big dark cupboards which seemed built into the walls, and he pulled open the double doors with a flourish.

Inside, there were about six deep shelves, each bearing several complicated pieces of carved jade. Pale pink, creamy white and pale green, smooth, polished, intricate, expensive; each piece standing upon its own heavy-looking black base-support. Jik, Sarah and I made appreciative noises and Norman Updike smiled ever wider.

'Hong Kong, of course,' he said. 'I worked there for years, you know. Quite a nice little collection, eh?' He walked along to the next dark cupboard and pulled open a duplicate set of doors. Inside, more shelves, more carvings, as before.

'I'm afraid I don't know much about jade,' I said, apologetically. 'Can't appreciate your collection to the full.'

He told us a good deal more about the ornate goodies than we actually wanted to know. There were four cupboards full in the lounge and overflows in bedroom and hall.

'You used to be able to pick them up very cheap in Hong Kong,' he said. 'I worked there more than twenty years, you know.'

Jik and I exchanged glances. I nodded slightly.

Jik immediately shook Norman Updike by the hand, put his arm round Sarah, and said we must be leaving. Updike looked enquiringly at Chuckles, who was still glued to the telly and still abdicating from the role of hostess. When she refused to look our way he shrugged good-humouredly and came with us to his front door. Jik and Sarah walked out as soon as he opened it, and left me alone with him in the hall.

'Mr Updike,' I said. 'At the gallery . . . which man was it who sold you the Herring?'

'Mr Grey,' he said promptly.

Mr Grey . . . Mr Grey . . .

I frowned.

'Such a pleasant man,' nodded Updike, beaming. 'I told him I knew very little about pictures, but he assured me I would get as much pleasure from my little Herring as from all my jade.'

'You did tell him about your jade, then?'

162

'Naturally I did. I mean . . . if you don't know anything about one thing, well . . . you try and show you do know about something else. Don't you? Only human, isn't it?'

'Only human,' I agreed, smiling. 'What was the name of Mr Grey's gallery?'

'Eh?' He looked puzzled. 'I thought you said he sent you, to see my picture.'

'I go to so many galleries, I've foolishly forgotten which one it was.'

'Ruapehu Fine Arts,' he said. 'I was down there last week.'

'Down . . . ?'

'In Wellington.' His smile was slipping. 'Look here, what is all this?' Suspicion flitted across his rounded face. 'Why did you come here? I don't think Mr Grey sent you at all.'

'No,' I said. 'But Mr Updike, we mean you no harm. We really are painters, my friend and I. But . . . now we've seen your jade collection . . . we do think we must warn you. We've heard of several people who've bought paintings and had their houses burgled soon after. You say you've got burglar alarms fitted, so if I were you I'd make sure they are working properly.'

'But . . . good gracious . . .'

'There's a bunch of thieves about,' I said. 'Who follow up the sales of paintings and burgle the houses of those who buy. I suppose they reckon that if anyone can afford, say, a Herring, they have other things worth stealing.'

He looked at me with awakening shrewdness. 'You mean, young man, that I told Mr Grey about my jade . . .'

'Let's just say,' I said, 'that it would be sensible to take more precautions than usual.'

'But . . . for how long?'

I shook my head. 'I don't know, Mr Updike. Maybe for ever.'

His round jolly face looked troubled.

'Why did you bother to come and tell me all this?' he said.

'I'd do a great deal more to break up this bunch.'

He asked 'Why?' again, so I told him. 'My cousin bought a painting. My cousin's house was burgled. My cousin's wife disturbed the burglars, and they killed her.'

Norman Updike took a long slow look at my face. I couldn't

163

have stopped him seeing the abiding anger, even if I'd tried. He shivered convulsively.

'I'm glad you're not after *me*,' he said.

I managed a smile. 'Mr Updike . . . please take care. And one day, perhaps, the police may come to see your picture, and ask where you bought it . . . anyway, they will if I have anything to do with it.'

The round smile returned with understanding and conviction. 'I'll expect them,' he said.

fourteen

Jik drove us from Auckland to Wellington; eight hours in the car.

We stopped overnight in a motel in the town of Hamilton, south of Auckland, and went on in the morning. No one followed us, molested us or spied on us. As far as I could be, I was sure no one had picked us up in the northern city, and no one knew we had called at the Updikes.

Wexford must know, all the same, that I had the Overseas Customers list, and he knew there were several New Zealand addresses on it. He couldn't guess which one I'd pick to visit, but he could and would guess that any I picked with the prefix W would steer me straight to the gallery in Wellington.

So in the gallery in Wellington, he'd be ready . . .

'You're looking awfully grim, Todd,' Sarah said.

'Sorry.'

'What were you thinking?'

'How soon we could stop for lunch.'

She laughed. 'We've only just had breakfast.'

We passed the turning to Rotorua and the land of hot springs. Anyone for a boiling mud pack? Jik asked. There was a power station further on run by steam jets from underground, Sarah

164

said, and horrid black craters stinking of sulphur, and the earth's crust was so thin in places that it vibrated and sounded hollow. She had been taken round a place called Waiotapu when she was a child, she said, and had had terrible nightmares afterwards, and she didn't want to go back.

'Pooh,' Jik said dismissively. 'They only have earthquakes every other Friday.'

'Somebody told me they have so many earthquakes in Wellington that all the new office blocks are built in cradles,' Sarah said.

'Rock-a-bye skyscraper . . .' sang Jik, in fine voice.

The sun shone bravely, and the countryside was green with leaves I didn't know. There were fierce bright patches and deep mysterious shadows; gorges and rocks and heaven-stretching tree trunks; feathery waving grasses, shoulder high. An alien land, wild and beautiful.

'Get that chiaroscuro,' Jik said, as we sped into one particularly spectacular curving valley.

'What's chiaroscuro?' Sarah said.

'Light and shade,' Jik said. 'Contrast and balance. Technical term. All the world's a chiaroscuro, and all the men and women merely blobs of light and shade.'

'Every life's a chiaroscuro,' I said.

'And every soul.'

'The enemy,' I said, 'is grey.'

'And you get grey,' Jik nodded, 'by muddling together red, white and blue.'

'Grey lives, grey deaths, all levelled out into equal grey nothing.'

'No one,' Sarah sighed, 'would ever call you two grey.'

'Grey!' I said suddenly. 'Of bloody course.'

'What are you on about?' Jik said.

'Grey was the name of the man who hired the suburban art gallery in Sydney, and Grey is the name of the man who sold Updike his quote Herring unquote.'

'Oh dear.' Sarah's sigh took the lift out of the spirits and the dazzle from the day.

'Sorry,' I said.

*

There were so many of them, I thought. Wexford and Greene. The boy. The woman. Harley Renbo. Two toughs at Alice Springs, one of whom I knew by sight, and one (the one who'd been behind me) whom I didn't. The one I didn't know might, or might not, be Beetle-brows. If he wasn't, Beetle-brows was extra.

And now Grey. And another one, somewhere.

Nine at least. Maybe ten. How could I possibly tangle all that lot up without getting crunched? Or worse, getting Sarah crunched, or Jik. Every time I moved, the serpent grew another head.

I wondered who did the actual robberies. Did they send their own two (or three) toughs overseas, or did they contract out to local labour, so to speak?

If they sent their own toughs, was it one of them who had killed Regina?

Had I already met Regina's killer? Had he thrown me over the balcony at Alice?

I pondered uselessly, and added one more twist . . .

Was he waiting ahead in Wellington?

We reached the capital in the afternoon and booked into the Townhouse Hotel because of its splendid view over the harbour. With such marvellous coastal scenery, I thought, it would have been a disgrace if the cities of New Zealand had been ugly. I still thought there were no big towns more captivating than flat old marshy London, but that was another story. Wellington, new and cared for, had life and character to spare.

I looked up the Ruapehu Fine Arts in the telephone directory and asked the hotel's reception desk how to get there. They had never heard of the gallery, but the road it was in, that must be up past the old town, they thought: past Thorndon.

They sold me a local area road map, which they said would help, and told me that Mount Ruapehu was a (with luck) extinct volcano, with a warm lake in its crater. If we'd come from Auckland, we must have passed nearby.

I thanked them and carried the map to Jik and Sarah upstairs in their room.

'We could find the gallery,' Jik said. 'But what would we do when we got there?'

'Make faces at them through the window?'

'You'd be crazy enough for that, too,' Sarah said.

'Let's just go and look,' I said. 'They won't see us in the car, if we simply drive past.'

'And after all,' Jik said incautiously, 'we do want them to know we're here.'

'Why?' asked Sarah in amazement.

'Oh Jesus,' Jik said.

'Why?' she demanded, the anxiety crowding back.

'Ask Todd, it's his idea.'

'You're a sod,' I said.

'Why, Todd?'

'Because,' I said, 'I want them to spend all their energies looking for us over here and not clearing away every vestige of evidence in Melbourne. We do want the police to deal with them finally, don't we, because we can't exactly arrest them ourselves? Well . . . when the police start moving, it would be hopeless if there was no one left for them to find.'

She nodded. 'That's what you meant by leaving it all in working order. But . . . you didn't say anything about deliberately enticing them to follow us.'

'Todd's got that list, and the pictures we took,' Jik said, 'and they'll want them back. Todd wants them to concentrate exclusively on getting them back, because if they think they can get them back and shut us up . . .'

'Jik,' I interrupted. 'You do go on a bit.'

Sarah looked from me to him and back again. A sort of hopeless calm took over from the anxiety.

'If they think they can get everything back and shut us up,' she said, 'they will be actively searching for us in order to kill us. And you intend to give them every encouragement. Is that right?'

'No,' I said. 'Or rather, yes.'

'They'd be looking for us anyway,' Jik pointed out.

'And we are going to say "Coo-ee, we're over here"?'

'Um,' I said. 'I think they may know already.'

'God give me strength,' she said. 'All right. I see what you're doing, and I see why you didn't tell me. And I think you're a louse. But I'll grant you you've been a damn sight more successful than I thought you'd be, and here we all still are, safe and moderately sound, so all right, we'll let them know we're definitely here. On the strict understanding that we then keep our heads down until you've fixed the police in Melbourne.'

I kissed her cheek. 'Done,' I said.

'So how do we do it?'

I grinned at her. 'We address ourselves to the telephone.'

In the end Sarah herself made the call, on the basis that her Australian voice would be less remarkable than Jik's Englishness, or mine.

'Is that the Ruapehu Fine Arts gallery? It is? I wonder if you can help me . . .' she said. 'I would like to speak to whoever is in charge. Yes, I know, but it is important. Yes, I'll wait.' She rolled her eyes and put her hand over the mouthpiece. 'She sounded like a secretary. New Zealand, anyway.'

'You're doing great,' I said.

'Oh . . . Hello? Yes. Could you tell me your name, please?' Her eyes suddenly opened wide. '*Wexford*. Oh, er . . . Mr Wexford, I've just had a visit from three extraordinary people who wanted to see a painting I bought from you some time ago. Quite extraordinary people. They said you'd sent them. I didn't believe them. I wouldn't let them in. But I thought perhaps I'd better check with you. Did you send them to see my painting?'

There was some agitated squawking from the receiver.

'Describe them? A young man with fair hair and a beard, and another young man with an injured arm, and a bedraggled looking girl. I sent them away. I didn't like the look of them.'

She grimaced over the phone and listened to some more squawks.

'No of course I didn't give them any information. I told you I didn't like the look of them. Where do I live? Why, right here in Wellington. Well, thank you so much Mr Wexford, I am so pleased I called you.'

She put the receiver down while it was still squawking.

'He was asking me for my name,' she said.

168

'What a girl,' Jik said. 'What an actress, my wife.'

Wexford. Wexford himself.

It had *worked*.

I raised a small internal cheer.

'So now that they know we're here,' I said, 'would you like to go off somewhere else?'

'Oh no,' Sarah said instinctively. She looked out of the window across the busy harbour. 'It's lovely here, and we've been travelling all day already.'

I didn't argue. I thought it might take more than a single telephone call to keep the enemy interested in Wellington, and it had only been for Sarah's sake that I would have been prepared to move on.

'They won't find us just by checking the hotels by telephone,' Jik pointed out. 'Even if it occurred to them to try the Town-house, they'd be asking for Cassavetes and Todd, not Andrews and Peel.'

'Are we Andrews and Peel?' Sarah asked.

'We're Andrews. Todd's Peel.'

'So nice to know,' she said.

Mr and Mrs Andrews and Mr Peel took dinner in the hotel restaurant without mishap, Mr Peel having discarded his sling for the evening on the grounds that it was in general a bit too easy to notice. Mr Andrews had declined, on the same consideration, to remove his beard.

We went in time to our separate rooms, and so to bed. I spent a jolly hour unsticking the Alice bandages from my leg and admiring the hemstitching. The tree had made tears that were far from the orderly cuts of operations, and as I inspected the long curving railway lines on a ridged backing of crimson, black and yellow skin, I reckoned that those doctors had done an expert job. It was four days since the fall, during which time I hadn't exactly led an inactive life, but none of their handiwork had come adrift. I realized I had progressed almost without noticing it from feeling terrible all the time to scarcely feeling anything worth mentioning. It was astonishing, I thought, how quickly the human body repaired itself, given the chance.

I covered the mementoes with fresh adhesive plaster bought

that morning in Hamilton for the purpose, and even found a way of lying in bed that drew no strike action from mending bones. Things, I thought complacently as I drifted to sleep, were altogether looking up.

I suppose one could say that I underestimated on too many counts. I underestimated the desperation with which Wexford had come to New Zealand. Underestimated the rage and the thoroughness with which he searched for us.

Underestimated the effect of our amateur robbery on professional thieves. Underestimated our success. Underestimated the fear and the fury we had unleashed.

My picture of Wexford tearing his remaining hair in almost comic frustration was all wrong. He was pursuing us with a determination bordering on obsession, grimly, ruthlessly, and fast.

In the morning I woke late to a day of warm windy spring sunshine and made coffee from the fixings provided by the hotel in each room; and Jik rang through on the telephone.

'Sarah says she must wash her hair today. Apparently it's sticking together.'

'It looks all right to me.'

His grin came down the wire. 'Marriage opens vast new feminine horizons. Anyway, she's waiting down in the hall for me to drive her to the shops to buy some shampoo, but I thought I'd better let you know we were going.'

I said uneasily, 'You will be careful . . .'

'Oh sure,' he said. 'We won't go anywhere near the gallery. We won't go far. Only as far as the nearest shampoo shop. I'll call you as soon as we get back.'

He disconnected cheerfully, and five minutes later the bell rang again. I lifted the receiver.

It was the girl from the reception desk. 'Your friends say would you join them downstairs in the car.'

'O.K.,' I said.

I went jacketless down in the lift, left my room key at the desk, and walked out through the front door to the sun-baked and windy car park. I looked around for Jik and Sarah; but they were not, as it happened, the friends who were waiting.

It might have been fractionally better if I hadn't had my left arm slung up inside my shirt. As it was they simply clutched my clothes, lifted me off balance and off my feet, and ignominiously bundled me into the back of their car.

Wexford was sitting inside it; a one-man reception committee. The eyes behind the heavy spectacles were as hostile as forty below, and there was no indecision this time in his manner. This time he as good as had me again behind his steel mesh door, and this time he was intent on not making mistakes.

He still wore a bow tie. The jaunty polka-dots went oddly with the unfunny matter in hand.

The muscles propelling me towards him turned out to belong to Greene with an 'e', and to a thug I'd never met but who answered the general description of Beetle-brows.

My spirits descended faster than the Hilton lifts. I ended up sitting between Beetle-brows and Wexford, with Greene climbing in front into the driving seat.

'How did you find me?' I said.

Greene, with a wolfish smile, took a polaroid photograph from his pocket and held it for me to see. It was a picture of the three of us, Jik, Sarah and me, standing by the shops in Melbourne airport. The woman from the gallery, I guessed, had not been wasting the time she spent watching us depart.

'We went round asking the hotels,' Greene said. 'It was easy.'

There didn't seem to be much else to say, so I didn't say anything. A slight shortage of breath might have had something to do with it.

None of the others, either, seemed over-talkative. Greene started the car and drove out into the city. Wexford stared at me with a mixture of anger and satisfaction: and Beetle-brows began twisting my free right arm behind my back in a grip which left no room for debate. He wouldn't let me remain upright. My head went practically down to my knees. It was all most undignified and excruciating.

Wexford said finally, 'We want our list back.'

There was nothing gentlemanly in his voice. He wasn't making light conversation. His heavy vindictive rage had no trouble at all in communicating itself to me without possibility of misunderstanding.

Oh Christ, I thought miserably; I'd been such a bloody fool, just walking into it like that.

'Do you hear? We want our list back, and everything else you took.'

I didn't answer. Too busy suffering.

From external sounds I guessed we were travelling through busy workaday Friday morning city streets, but as my head was below window-level, I couldn't actually see.

After some time the car turned sharply left and ground uphill for what seemed like miles. The engine sighed from overwork at the top, and the road began to descend.

Almost nothing was said on the journey. My thoughts about what very likely lay at the end of it were so unwelcome that I did my best not to allow them houseroom. I could give Wexford his list back, but what then? What then, indeed.

After a long descent the car halted briefly and then turned to the right. We had exchanged city sounds for those of the sea. There were also no more Doppler-effects from cars passing us from the opposite direction. I came to the sad conclusion that we had turned off the highway and were on our way along an infrequently used side road.

The car stopped eventually with a jerk.

Beetle-brows removed his hands. I sat up stiffly, wrenched and unenthusiastic.

They could hardly have picked a lonelier place. The road ran along beside the sea so closely that it was more or less part of the shore, and the shore was a jungle of sharply pointed rough black rocks, with frothy white waves slapping among them, a far cry from the gentle beaches of home.

On the right rose jagged cliffs, steeply towering. Ahead, the road ended blindly in some workings which looked like a sort of quarry. Slabs had been cut from the cliffs, and there were dusty clearings, and huge heaps of small jagged rocks, and graded stones, and sifted chips. All raw and harsh and blackly volcanic.

No people. No machinery. No sign of occupation.

'Where's the list?' Wexford said.

Greene twisted round in the driving seat and looked seriously at my face.

'You'll tell us,' he said. 'With or without a beating. And we won't hit you with our fists, but with pieces of rock.'

Beetle-brows said aggrievedly, 'What's wrong with fists?' But what was wrong with Greene's fists was the same as with mine: I would never have been able to hit anyone hard enough to get the desired results. The local rocks, by the look of them, were something else.

'What if I tell you?' I said.

They hadn't expected anything so easy. I could see the surprise on their faces, and it was flattering, in a way. There was also a furtiveness in their expressions which boded no good at all. Regina, I thought. Regina, with her head bashed in.

I looked at the cliffs, the quarry, the sea. No easy exit. And behind us, the road. If I ran that way, they would drive after me, and mow me down. If I could run. And even that was problematical.

I swallowed and looked dejected, which wasn't awfully difficult.

'I'll tell you . . .' I said. 'Out of the car.'

There was a small silence while they considered it; but as they weren't anyway going to have room for much crashing around with rocks in that crowded interior, they weren't entirely against.

Greene leaned over towards the glove compartment on the passenger side, opened it, and drew out a pistol. I knew just about enough about firearms to distinguish a revolver from an automatic, and this was a revolver, a gun whose main advantage, I had read, was that it never jammed.

Greene handled it with a great deal more respect than familiarity. He showed it to me silently, and returned it to the glove compartment, leaving the hinged flap door open so that we all had a clear view of his ultimate threat.

'Get out, then,' Wexford said.

We all got out, and I made sure that I ended up on the side of the sea. The wind was much stronger on this exposed coast, and chilling in the bright sunshine. It lifted the thin carefully combed hair away from Wexford's crown, and left him straggly bald, and intensified the stupid look of Beetle-brows. Greene's eyes stayed as watchful and sharp as the harsh terrain around us.

'All right then,' Wexford said roughly, shouting a little to bring his voice above the din of sea and sky. 'Where's the list?'

I whirled away from them and did my best to sprint for the sea.

I thrust my right hand inside my shirt and tugged at the sling-forming bandages.

Wexford, Greene and Beetle-brows shouted furiously and almost trampled on my heels.

I pulled the lists of Overseas Customers out of the sling, whirled again with them in my hand, and flung them with a bowling action as far out to sea as I could manage.

The pages fluttered apart in mid-air, but the offshore winds caught most of them beautifully and blew them like great leaves out to sea.

I didn't stop at the water's edge. I went straight on into the cold inhospitable battlefield of shark-teeth rocks and green water and white foaming waves. Slipping, falling, getting up, staggering on, finding that the current was much stronger than I'd expected, and the rocks more abrasive, and the footing more treacherous. Finding I'd fled from one deadly danger to embrace another.

For one second, I looked back.

Wexford had followed me a step or two into the sea, but only, it seemed, to reach one of the pages which had fallen shorter than the others. He was standing there with the frothy water swirling round his trouser legs, peering at the sodden paper.

Greene was beside the car, leaning in; by the front passenger seat.

Beetle-brows had his mouth open.

I reapplied myself to the problem of survival.

The shore shelved, as most shores do. Every forward step led into a stronger current, which sucked and pulled and shoved me around like a piece of flotsam. Hip-deep between waves, I found it difficult to stay on my feet, and every time I didn't I was in dire trouble, because of the black needle-sharp rocks waiting in ranks above and below the surface to scratch and tear.

The rocks were not the kind I was used to: not the hard familiar lumpy rocks of Britain, polished by the sea. These were the raw stuff of volcanoes, as scratchy as pumice. One's groping hand

174

didn't slide over them: one's skin stuck to them, and tore off. Clothes fared no better. Before I'd gone thirty yards I was running with blood from a dozen superficial grazes: and no blood vessels bleed more convincingly than the small surface capillaries.

My left arm was still tangled inside the sling, which had housed the Overseas Customers since Cup day as an insurance against having my room robbed, as at Alice. Soaking wet, the bandages now clung like leeches, and my shirt also. Muscles weakened by a fracture and inactivity couldn't deal with them. I rolled around a lot from not having two hands free.

My foot stepped awkwardly on the side of a submerged rock and I felt it scrape my shin: lost my balance, fell forward, tried to save myself with my hand, failed, crashed chest first against a small jagged peak dead ahead, and jerked my head sharply sideways to avoid connecting with my nose.

The rock beside my cheek splintered suddenly as if exploding. Slivers of it prickled in my face. For a flicker of time I couldn't understand it: and then I struggled round and looked back to the shore with a flood of foreboding.

Greene was standing there, aiming the pistol, shooting to kill.

fifteen

Thirty to thirty-five yards is a long way for a pistol; but Greene seemed so close.

I could see his drooping moustache and the lanky hair blowing in the wind. I could see his eyes and the concentration in his body. He was standing with his legs straddled and his arms out straight ahead, aiming the pistol with both hands.

I couldn't hear the shots above the crash of the waves on the rocks. I couldn't see him squeeze the trigger. But I did see the upward jerk of the arms at the recoil, and I reckoned it would be just plain silly to give him a stationary target.

I was, in all honesty, pretty frightened. I must have looked as close to him as he to me. He must have been quite certain he would hit me, even though his tenderness with the pistol in the car had made me think he was not an expert.

I turned and stumbled a yard or two onwards, though the going became even rougher, and the relentless fight against current and waves and rocks was draining me to dish-rags.

There would have to be an end to it.

Have to be.

I stumbled and fell on a jagged edge and gashed the inside of my forearm, and out poured more good red life. Christ, I thought, I must be scarlet all over, leaking from a hundred tiny nicks.

It gave me at least an idea.

I was waist-deep in dangerous green water, with most of the shore-line rocks now submerged beneath the surface. Close to one side a row of bigger rock-teeth ran out from the shore like a nightmarish breakwater, and I'd shied away from it, because of the even fiercer waves crashing against it. But it represented the only cover in sight. Three stumbling efforts took me nearer; and the current helped.

I looked back at Greene. He was reloading the gun. Wexford was practically dancing up and down beside him, urging him on; and Beetle-brows, from his disinclination to chase me, probably couldn't swim.

Greene slapped shut the gun and raised it again in my direction.

I took a frightful chance.

I held my fast-bleeding forearm close across my chest: and I stood up, swaying in the current, visible to him from the waist up.

I watched him aim, with both arms straight. It would take a marksman, I believed, to hit me with that pistol from that distance, in that wind. A marksman whose arms didn't jerk upwards when he fired.

The gun was pointing straight at me.

I saw the jerk as he squeezed the trigger.

For an absolutely petrifying second I was convinced he had shot accurately; but I didn't feel or see or even hear the passing of the flying death.

I flung my own right arm wide and high, and paused there facing him for a frozen second, letting him see that most of the front of my shirt was scarlet with blood.

Then I twisted artistically and fell flat, face downwards, into the water; and hoped to God he would think he had killed me.

The sea wasn't much better than bullets. Nothing less than extreme fear of the alternative would have kept me down in it, tumbling and crashing against the submerged razor edges like a piece of cheese in a grater.

The waves themselves swept me towards the taller breakwater teeth, and with a fair amount of desperation I tried to get a grip on them, to avoid being alternately sucked off and flung back, and losing a lot more skin.

There was also the problem of not struggling too visibly. If Wexford or Greene saw me threshing about, all my histrionics would have been in vain.

As much by luck as trying I found the sea shoving me into a wedge-shaped crevice between the rocks, from where I was unable to see the shore. I clutched for a hand-hold, and then with bent knees found a good foothold, and clung there precariously while the sea tried to drag me out again. Every time the wave rolled in it tended to float my foot out of the niche it was lodged in, and every time it receded it tried to suck me with it, with a syphonic action. I clung, and see-sawed in the chest-high water, and clung, and see-sawed, and grew progressively more exhausted.

I could hear nothing except the waves on the rocks. I wondered forlornly how long Wexford and Greene would stay there, staring out to sea for signs of life. I didn't dare to look, in case they spotted my moving head.

The water was cold, and the grazes gradually stopped bleeding, including the useful gash on my forearm. Absolutely nothing, I thought, like having a young strong healthy body. Absolutely nothing like having a young strong healthy body on dry land with a paintbrush in one hand and a beer in the other, with the nice friendly airliners thundering overhead and no money to pay the gas.

Fatigue, in the end, made me look. It was either that or cling like a limpet until I literally fell off nervelessly, too weak to struggle back to life.

To look, I had to leave go. I tried to find other holds, but they weren't as good. The first out-going wave took me with it in no uncertain terms; and its incoming fellow threw me back.

In the tumbling interval I caught a glimpse of the shore.

The road, the cliffs, the quarry, as before. Also the car. Also people.

Bloody damn, I thought.

My hand scrambled for its former hold. My fingers were cramped, bleeding again, and cold. Oh Christ, I thought. How much longer.

It was a measure of my tiredness that it took the space of three in and out waves for me to realize that it wasn't Wexford's car, and it wasn't Wexford standing on the road.

If it wasn't Wexford, it didn't matter who it was.

I let go again of the hand-hold and tried to ride the wave as far out of the crevice as possible, and to swim away from the return force flinging me back. All the other rocks were still there under the surface. A few yards was a heck of a long way.

I stood up gingerly, feeling for my footing more carefully than on the outward flight, and took a longer look at the road.

A grey-white car. A couple beside it, standing close, the man with his arms round the girl.

A nice quiet spot for it, I thought sardonically. I hoped they would drive me somewhere dry.

They moved apart and stared out to sea.

I stared back.

For an instant it seemed impossible. Then they started waving their arms furiously and ran towards the water; and it was Sarah and Jik.

Throwing off his jacket, Jik ploughed into the waves with enthusiasm, and came to a smart halt as the realities of the situation scraped his legs. All the same, he came on after a pause towards me, taking care.

I made my slow way back. Even without haste driving like a fury, any passage through those wave-swept rocks was ruin to the epidermis. By the time we met we were both streaked with red.

We looked at each other's blood. Jik said 'Jesus' and I said 'Christ', and it occurred to me that maybe the Almighty would think we had been calling for His help a bit too often.

Jik put his arm round my waist and I held on to his shoulders, and together we stumbled slowly to land. We fell now and then. Got up gasping. Reclutched, and went on.

He let go when we reached the road. I sat down on the edge of it with my feet pointing out to sea, and positively drooped.

'Todd,' Sarah said anxiously. She came nearer. '*Todd.*' Her voice was incredulous. 'Are you *laughing*?'

'Sure.' I looked up at her, grinning. 'Why ever not?'

Jik's shirt was torn, and mine was in tatters. We took them off and used them to mop up the grazes which were still persistently oozing. From the expression on Sarah's face, we must have looked crazy.

'What a damn silly place to bathe,' Jik said.

'Free back-scratchers,' I said.

He glanced round behind me. 'Your Alice Springs dressing has come off.'

'How're the stitches?'

'Intact.'

'Bully for them.'

'You'll both get pneumonia, sitting there,' Sarah said.

I took off the remnants of the sling. All in all, I thought, it had served me pretty well. The adhesive rib-supporting cummerbund was still more or less in place, but had mostly come unstuck through too much immersion. I pulled that off also. That only left the plasters on my leg, and they too, I found, had floated off in the mêlée. The trousers I'd worn over them had windows everywhere.

'Quite a dust-up,' Jik observed, pouring water out of his shoes and shivering.

'We need a telephone,' I said, doing the same.

'Give me strength,' Sarah said. 'What you need is hot baths, warm clothes, and half a dozen psychiatrists.'

'How did you get here?' I asked.

'How come you aren't dead?' Jik said.

'You first.'

'I came out of the shop where I'd bought the shampoo,' Sarah said, 'and I saw Greene drive past. I nearly died on the spot. I just stood still, hoping he wouldn't look my way, and he didn't ... The car turned to the left just past where I was ... and I could see there were two other people in the back ... and I went back to our car and told Jik.'

'We thought it damn lucky he hadn't spotted her,' Jik said, dabbing at persistent scarlet trickles. 'We went back to the hotel, and you weren't there, so we asked the girl at the desk if you'd left a message, and she said you'd gone off in a car with some friends ... With a man with a droopy moustache.'

'Friends!' Sarah said.

'Anyway,' Jik continued, 'Choking down our rage, sorrow, indignation and what not, we thought we'd better look for your body.'

'Jik!' Sarah protested.

He grinned. 'And who was crying?'

'Shut up.'

'Sarah hadn't seen any sign of you in Greene's car but we thought you might be imitating a sack of potatoes in the boot or something, so we got out the road map, applied our feet to the accelerator, and set off in pursuit. Turned left where Greene had gone, and found ourselves climbing a ruddy mountain.'

I surveyed our extensive grazes and scratches. 'I think we'd better get some disinfectant,' I said.

'We could bath in it.'

'Good idea.'

I could hear his teeth chattering even above the din of my own.

'Let's get out of this wind,' I said. 'And bleed in the car.'

We crawled stiffly into the seats. Sarah said it was lucky the upholstery was plastic. Jik automatically took his place behind the wheel.

'We drove for miles,' he said. 'Growing, I may say, a little frantic. Over the top of the mountain and down this side. At the bottom of the hill the road swings round to the left and we could see from the map that it follows the coastline round a whole lot of bays and eventually ends up right back in Wellington.'

He started the car, turned it, and rolled gently ahead. Naked to the waist, wet from there down, and still with beads of blood forming and overflowing, he looked an unorthodox chauffeur. The beard, above, was undaunted.

'We went that way,' Sarah said. 'There was nothing but miles of craggy rocks and sea.'

'I'll paint those rocks,' Jik said.

Sarah glanced at his face, and then at me. She'd heard the fervour in that statement of intent. The golden time was almost over.

'After a bit we turned back,' Jik said. 'There was this bit of road saying "no through road", so we came down it. No you, of course. We stopped here on this spot and Sarah got out of the car and started bawling her eyes out.'

'You weren't exactly cheering yourself,' she said.

'Huh,' he smiled. 'Anyway, I kicked a few stones about, wondering what to do next, and there were those cartridges.'

'Those what?'

'On the edge of the road. All close together. Maybe dropped out of one of those spider-ejection revolvers, or something like that.'

'When we saw them,' Sarah said, 'we thought . . .'

'It could have been anyone popping off at seabirds,' I said. 'And I think we might go back and pick them up.'

'Are you serious?' Jik said.

'Yeah.'

We stopped, turned again, and retraced our tyre treads.

'No one shoots seabirds with a revolver,' he said. 'But bloody awful painters of slow horses, that's different.'

The quarry came in sight again. Jik drew up and stopped, and Sarah, hopping out quickly, told us to stay where we were, she would fetch the bullet cases.

'They really did shoot at you?' Jik said.

'Greene. He missed.'

'Inefficient.' He shifted in his seat, wincing. 'They must have gone back over the hill while we were looking for you round the bays.' He glanced at Sarah as she searched along the side of the road. 'Did they take the list?'

'I threw it in the sea.' I smiled lopsidedly. 'It seemed too tame just to hand it over . . . and it made a handy diversion. They salvaged enough to see that they'd got what they wanted.'

'It must all have been a bugger.'

'Hilarious.'

Sarah found the cases, picked them up, and came running back. 'Here they are . . . I'll put them in my handbag.' She slid into the passenger seat. 'What now?'

'Telephone,' I said.

'Like that?' She looked me over. 'Have you any idea . . .' She stopped. 'Well,' she said. 'I'll buy you each a shirt at the first shop we come to.' She swallowed. 'And don't say what if it's a grocery.'

'What if it's a grocery?' Jik said.

We set off again, and at the intersection turned left to go back over the hill, because it was about a quarter of the distance.

Near the top there was a large village with the sort of store which sold everything from hammers to hairpins. Also groceries. Also, upon enquiry, shirts. Sarah made a face at Jik and vanished inside.

I pulled on the resulting navy tee-shirt and made wobbly tracks for the telephone, clutching Sarah's purse.

'Operator . . . which hotels have a telex?'

She told me three. One was the Townhouse. I thanked her and rang off.

I called the Townhouse. Remembered, with an effort, that my name was Peel.

'But, Mr Peel . . .' said the girl, sounding bewildered. 'Your friend . . . the one with the moustache, not the one with the beard . . . He paid your account not half an hour ago and collected all your things . . Yes, I suppose it is irregular, but he brought your note, asking us to let him have your room key . . . I'm sorry but I didn't know you hadn't written it . . . Yes, he took all your things, the room's being cleaned at this minute . . .'

'Look,' I said, 'Can you send a telex for me? Put it on my friend Mr . . . er . . . Andrew's bill.'

She said she would. I dictated the message. She repeated it, and said she would send it at once.

'I'll call again soon for the reply,' I said.

Sarah had bought jeans for us, and dry socks. Jik drove out of the village to a more modest spot, and we put them on: hardly the world's best fit, but they hid the damage.

'Where now?' he said. 'Intensive Care Unit?'

'Back to the telephone.'

'Jesus God Almighty.'

He drove back and I called the Townhouse. The girl said she'd received an answer, and read it out. 'Telephone at once, reverse charges,' she said, 'And there's a number . . .' She read it out, twice. I repeated it. 'That's right.'

I thanked her.

'No sweat,' she said. 'Sorry about your things.'

I called the international exchange and gave them the number. It had a priority rating, they said. The call would be through in ten minutes. They would ring back.

The telephone was on the wall of a booth inside the general store. There was nothing to sit on. I wished to God there was.

The ten minutes dragged slowly by. Nine and a half, to be exact.

The bell rang, and I picked up the receiver.

'Your call to England . . .'

The modern miracle. Half-way round the world, and I was talking to Inspector Frost as if he were in the next room. Eleven-thirty in the morning at Wellington: eleven-thirty at night in Shropshire.

'Your letter arrived today, sir,' he said. 'And action has already been started.'

'Stop calling me sir. I'm used to Todd.'

'All right. Well, we telexed Melbourne to alert them and we've started checking on all the people on the England list. The results are already incredible. All the crossed-out names we've checked so far have been the victims of break-ins. We're alerting the police in all the other countries concerned. The only thing is, we see the list you sent us is a photo-copy. Do you have the original?'

'No . . . Most of it got destroyed. Does it matter?'

'Not really. Can you tell us how it came into your possession?'

'Er . . . I think we'd better say it just did.'

A dry laugh travelled twelve thousand miles.

'All right. Now what's so urgent that you're keeping me from my bed?'

'Are you at home?' I said contritely.

'On duty, as it happens. Fire away.'

'Two things . . . One is, I can save you time with the stock list numbers. But first . . .' I told him about Wexford and Greene being in Wellington, and about them stealing my things. 'They've got my passport and travellers' cheques, and also my suitcase which contains painting equipment.'

'I saw it at your cousin's,' he said.

'That's right. I think they may also have a page or two of the list . . .'

'Say that again.'

I said it again. 'Most of it got thrown into the sea, but I know Wexford regained at least one page. Well . . . I thought . . . they'd be going back to Melbourne, probably today, any minute really, and when they land there, there's a good chance they'll have at least some of those things with them . . .'

'I can fix a Customs search,' he said. 'But why should they risk stealing . . . ?'

'They don't know I know,' I said. 'I think they think I'm dead.'

'Good God. Why?'

'They took a pot shot at me. Would bullet cases be of any use? Fortunately I didn't collect a bullet, but I've got six shells.'

'They may be . . .' He sounded faint. 'What about the stock list?'

'In the shorter list . . . Got it?'

'Yes, in front of me.'

'Right. The first letter is for the city the painting was sold in; M for Melbourne, S for Sydney, W for Wellington. The second letter identifies the painter; M for Munnings, H for Herring, and I think R for Raoul Millais. The letter C stands for copy. All the paintings on that list are copies. All the ones on the longer list are originals. Got that?'

'Yes. Go on.'

'The numbers are just numbers. They'd sold 54 copies when I . . . er . . . when the list reached me. The last letter R stands for

Renbo. That's Harley Renbo, who was working at Alice Springs. If you remember, I told you about him last time.'

'I remember,' he said.

'Wexford and Greene have spent the last couple of days chasing around in New Zealand, so with a bit of luck they will not have destroyed anything dodgy in the Melbourne gallery. If the Melbourne police can arrange a search, there might be a harvest.'

'It's their belief that the disappearance of the list from the gallery will have already led to the immediate destruction of anything else incriminating.'

'They may be wrong. Wexford and Greene don't know I photocopied the list and sent it to you. They think the list is floating safely out to sea, and me with it.'

'I'll pass your message to Melbourne.'

'There's also another gallery here in Wellington, and an imitation Herring they sold to a man in Auckland . . .'

'For heaven's sake . . .'

I gave him the Ruapehu address, and mentioned Norman Updike.

'There's also a recurring B on the long stock list, so there's probably another gallery. In Brisbane, maybe. There may also be another one in Sydney. I shouldn't think the suburban place I told you about had proved central enough, so they shut it.'

'Stop,' he said.

'Sorry,' I said. 'But the organization is like a mushroom . . . it burrows along underground and pops up everywhere.'

'I only said stop so I could change the tape on the recorder. You can carry right on now.'

'Oh.' I half laughed. 'Well . . . did you get any answers from Donald to my questions?'

'Yes, we did.'

'Carefully?'

'Rest assured,' he said dryly. 'We carried out your wishes to the letter. Mr Stuart's answers were "Yes, of course" to the first question, and "No, whyever should I" to the second, and "Yes" to the third.'

'Was he absolutely certain?'

'Absolutely.' He cleared his throat. 'He seems distant and withdrawn. Uninterested. But quite definite.'

'How is he?' I asked.

'He spends all his time looking at a picture of his wife. Every time we call at his house, we can see him through the front window, just sitting there.'

'He is still . . . sane?'

'I'm no judge.'

'You can at least let him know that he's no longer suspected of engineering the robbery and killing Regina.'

'That's a decision for my superiors,' he said.

'Well, kick them into it,' I said. 'Do the police positively yearn for bad publicity?'

'You were quick enough to ask our help,' he said tartly.

To do your job, I thought. I didn't say it aloud. The silence spoke for itself.

'Well . . .' his voice carried a mild apology. 'Our co-operation, then.' He paused. 'Where are you now? When I've telexed Melbourne, I may need to talk to you again.'

'I'm in a phone booth in a country store in a village on the hills above Wellington.'

'Where are you going next?'

'I'm staying right here. Wexford and Greene are still around in the city and I don't want to risk the outside chance of their seeing me.'

'Give me the number, then.'

I read it off the telephone.

'I want to come home as soon as possible,' I said. 'Can you do anything about my passport?'

'You'll have to find a consul.'

Oh ta, I thought tiredly. I hung up the receiver and wobbled back to the car.

'Tell you what,' I said, dragging into the back seat, 'I could do with a double hamburger and a bottle of brandy.'

We sat in the car for two hours.

The store didn't sell liquor or hot food. Sarah bought a packet of biscuits. We ate them.

'We can't stay here all day,' she said explosively, after a lengthy glum silence.

I couldn't be sure that Wexford wasn't out searching for her and Jik with murderous intent, and I didn't think she'd be happy to know it.

'We're perfectly safe here,' I said.

'Just quietly dying of blood-poisoning,' Jik agreed.

'I left my pills in the Hilton,' Sarah said.

Jik stared. 'What's that got to do with it?'

'Nothing. I just thought you might like to know.'

'*The* pill?' I asked.

'Yes.'

'Jesus,' Jik said.

A delivery van struggled up the hill and stopped outside the shop. A man in an overall opened the back, took out a large bakery tray, and carried it in.

'Food,' I said hopefully.

Sarah went in to investigate. Jik took the opportunity to un-stick his tee-shirt from his healing grazes, but I didn't bother.

'You'll be glued to those clothes, if you don't,' Jik said, grimacing over his task.

'I'll soak them off.'

'All those cuts and things didn't feel so bad when we were in the sea.'

'No.'

'Catches up with you a bit, doesn't it?'

'Mm.'

He glanced at me. 'Why don't you just scream or something?'

'Can't be bothered. Why don't you?'

He grinned. 'I'll scream in paint.'

Sarah came back with fresh doughnuts and cans of Coke. We made inroads, and I at least felt healthier.

After another half hour, the storekeeper appeared in the door-way, shouting and beckoning.

'A call for you . . .'

I went stiffly to the telephone. It was Frost, clear as a bell.

'Wexford, Greene and Snell have booked a flight to Melbourne. They will be met at Melbourne airport . . .'

'Who's Snell?' I said.

'How do I know? He was travelling with the other two.'

Beetle-brows, I thought.

'Now listen,' Frost said. 'The telex has been red-hot between here and Melbourne, and the police there want your co-operation, just to clinch things . . .' He went on talking for a long time. At the end he said, 'Will you do that?'

I'm tired, I thought. I'm battered, and I hurt. I've done just about enough.

'All right.'

Might as well finish it, I supposed.

'The Melbourne police want to know for sure that the three Munnings copies you . . . er . . . acquired from the gallery are still where you told me.'

'Yes, they are.'

'Right. Well . . . good luck.'

sixteen

We flew Air New Zealand back to Melbourne, tended by angels in sea-green. Sarah looked fresh, Jik definitely shop-worn, and I apparently like a mixture (Jik said) of yellow ochre, Payne's grey, and white, which I didn't think was possible.

Our passage had been oiled by telexes from above. When we arrived at the airport after collecting Sarah's belongings in their carrier bags from the Townhouse, we found ourselves whisked into a private room, plied with strong drink, and subsequently taken by car straight out across the tarmac to the aeroplane.

A thousand miles across the Tasman Sea and an afternoon tea later we were driven straight from the aircraft's steps to another small airport room, which contained no strong drink but only a large hard Australian plain-clothes policeman.

'Porter,' he said, introducing himself and squeezing our bones in a blacksmith's grip. 'Which of you is Charles Todd?'

'I am.'

'Right on, Mr Todd.' He looked at me without favour. 'Are you ill, or something?' He had a strong rough voice and a strong rough manner, natural aids to putting the fear of God into chummy and bringing on breakdowns in the nervous. To me, I gradually gathered, he was grudgingly offering the status of temporary inferior colleague.

'No,' I said, sighing slightly. Time and airline schedules waited for no man. If I'd spent time on first aid we'd have missed the only possible flight.

'His clothes are sticking to him,' Jik observed, giving the familiar phrase the usual meaning of being hot. It was cool in Melbourne. Porter looked at him uncertainly.

I grinned. 'Did you manage what you planned?' I asked him. He decided Jik was nuts and switched his gaze back to me.

'We decided not to go ahead until you had arrived,' he said, shrugging. 'There's a car waiting outside.' He wheeled out of the door without holding it for Sarah and marched briskly off.

The car had a chauffeur. Porter sat in front, talking on a radio, saying in stiltedly guarded sentences that the party had arrived and the proposals should be implemented.

'Where are we going?' Sarah said.

'To reunite you with your clothes,' I said.

Her face lit up. 'Are we really?'

'And what for?' Jik asked.

'To bring the mouse to the cheese.' And the bull to the sword, I thought: and the moment of truth to the conjuror.

'We got your things back, Todd,' Porter said with satisfaction. 'Wexford, Greene and Snell were turned over on entry, and they copped them with the lot. The locks on your suitcase were scratched and dented but they hadn't burst open. Everything inside should be O.K. You can collect everything in the morning.'

'That's great,' I said. 'Did they still have any of the lists of customers?'

'Yeah. Damp but readable. Names of guys in Canada.'

'Good.'

'We're turning over that Yarra gallery right this minute, and Wexford is there helping. We've let him overhear what we wanted him to, and as soon as I give the go-ahead we'll let him take action.'

'Do you think he will?' I said.

'Look, mister, wouldn't you?'

I thought I might be wary of gifts from the Greeks, but then I wasn't Wexford, and I didn't have a jail sentence breathing down my neck.

We pulled up at the side door of the Hilton. Porter raised himself agilely to the pavement and stood like a solid pillar, watching with half-concealed impatience while Jik, Sarah, and I eased ourselves slowly out. We all went across the familiar red-and-blue opulence of the great entrance hall, and from there through a gate in the reception desk, and into the hotel manager's office at the rear.

A tall dark-suited member of the hotel staff there offered us chairs, coffee, and sandwiches. Porter looked at his watch and offered us an indeterminate wait.

It was six o'clock. After ten minutes a man in shirt and necktie brought a two-way personal radio for Porter, who slipped the ear-plug into place and began listening to disembodied voices.

The office was a working room, lit by neon strips and furnished functionally, with a wall-papering of charts and duty rosters. There were no outside windows: nothing to show the fade of day to night.

We sat, and drank coffee, and waited. Porter ate three of the sandwiches simultaneously. Time passed.

Seven o'clock.

Sarah was looking pale in the artificial light, and tired also. So was Jik, his beard on his chest. I sat and thought about life and death and polka dots.

At seven eleven Porter clutched his ear and concentrated intently on the ceiling. When he relaxed, he passed to us the galvanic message.

'Wexford did just what we reckoned he would, and the engine's turning over.'

'What engine?' Sarah said.

Porter stared at her blankly. 'What we planned,' he said painstakingly, 'is happening.'

'Oh.'

Porter listened again to his private ear and spoke directly to me. 'He's taken the bait.'

'He's a fool,' I said.

Porter came as near to a smile as he could. 'All crooks are fools, one way or another.'

Seven-thirty came and went. I raised my eyebrows at Porter. He shook his head.

'We can't say too much on the radio,' he said. 'Because you get all sorts of ears listening in.'

Just like England, I thought. The Press could turn up at a crime before the police; and the mouse might hear of the trap.

We waited. The time dragged. Jik yawned and Sarah's eyes were dark with fatigue. Outside, in the lobby, the busy rich life of the hotel chattered on unruffled, with guests' spirits rising towards the next day's race meeting, the last of the carnival.

The Derby on Saturday, the Cup on Tuesday, the Oaks (which we'd missed) on Thursday, and the International on Saturday. No serious racegoers went home before the end of things, if they could help it.

Porter clutched his ear again, and stiffened.

'He's here,' he said.

My heart, for some unaccountable reason, began beating overtime. We were in no danger that I could see, yet there it was, thumping away like a steam organ.

Porter disconnected himself from the radio, put it on the manager's desk, and went out into the foyer.

'What do we do?' Sarah said.

'Nothing much except listen.'

We all three went over to the door and held it six inches open. We listened to people asking for their room keys, asking for letters and messages, asking for Mr and Mrs So-and-So, and which way to Toorak, and how did you get to Fanny's.

Then suddenly, the familiar voice, sending electric fizzes to my fingertips. Confident: not expecting trouble. 'I've come to collect a package left here last Tuesday by a Mr Charles Todd. He says he checked it into the baggage room. I have a letter here from him, authorizing you to release it to me.'

There was a crackle of paper as the letter was handed over. Sarah's eyes were round and startled.

'Did you write it?' she whispered.

I shook my head. 'No.'

The desk clerk outside said, 'Thank you, sir. If you'll just wait a moment I'll fetch the package.'

There was a long pause. My heart made a lot of noise, but nothing much else happened.

The desk clerk came back. 'Here you are, sir. Paintings, sir.'

'That's right.'

There were vague sounds of the bundle of paintings and the print-folder being carried along outside the door.

'I'll bring them round for you,' said the clerk, suddenly closer to us. 'Here we are, sir.' He went past the office, through the door in the desk, and round to the front. 'Can you manage them, sir?'

'Yes. Yes. Thank you.' There was haste in his voice, now that he'd got his hands on the goods. 'Thank you. Goodbye.'

Sarah had begun to say 'Is that all?' in disappointment when Porter's loud voice chopped into the Hilton velvet like a hatchet.

'I guess we'll take care of those paintings, if you don't mind,' he said. 'Porter, Melbourne city police.'

I opened the door a little, and looked out. Porter stood four-square in the lobby, large and rough, holding out a demanding hand.

At his elbows, two plain-clothes policemen. At the front door, two more, in uniform. There would be others, I supposed, at the other exits. They weren't taking any chances.

'Why ... er ... Inspector ... I'm only on an errand ... er ... for my young friend, Charles Todd.'

'And these paintings?'

'I've no idea what they are. He asked me to fetch them for him.'

I walked quietly out of the office, through the gate and round to the front. I leaned a little wearily against the reception desk. He was only six feet away, in front of me to my right. I could have stretched forward and touched him. I hoped Porter would think it near enough, as requested.

A certain amount of unease had pervaded the Hilton guests. They stood around in an uneven semicircle, eyeing the proceedings sideways.

'Mr Charles Todd asked you to fetch them?' Porter said loudly.

'Yes, that's right.'

Porter's gaze switched abruptly to my face.

'Did you ask him?'

'No,' I said.

The explosive effect was all that the Melbourne police could have asked, and a good deal more than I expected. There was no polite quiet identification followed by a polite quiet arrest. I should have remembered all my own theories about the basic brutality of the directing mind.

I found myself staring straight into the eyes of the bull. He realized that he'd been tricked. Had convicted himself out of his own mouth and by his own presence on such an errand. The fury rose in him like a geyser and his hands reached out to grab my neck.

'*You're dead,*' he yelled. '*You're fucking dead.*'

His plunging weight took me off balance and down on to one knee, smothering under his choking grip and two hundred pounds of city suiting; trying to beat him off with my fists and not succeeding. His anger poured over me like lava. Heaven knows what he intended, but Porter's men pulled him off before he did bloody murder on the plushy carpet. As I got creakily to my feet, I heard the handcuffs click.

He was standing there, close to me, quivering in the restraining hands, breathing heavily, dishevelled and bitter-eyed. Civilized exterior all stripped away by one instant of ungovernable rage. The violent core plain to see.

'Hello, Hudson,' I said.

'Sorry,' Porter said perfunctorily. 'Didn't reckon he'd turn wild.'

'Revert,' I said.

'Uh?'

'He always was wild,' I said, 'Underneath.'

'You'd know,' he said. 'I never saw the guy before.' He nodded to Jik and Sarah and finally to me, and hurried away after his departing prisoner.

We looked at each other a little blankly. The hotel guests stared at us curiously and began to drift away. We sat down weakly on the nearest blue velvet seat, Sarah in the middle.

Jik took her hand and squeezed it. She put her fingers over mine.

It had taken nine days.

It had been a long haul.

'Don't know about you,' Jik said. 'But I could do with a beer.'

'Todd,' said Sarah, 'Start talking.'

We were upstairs in a bedroom (mine) with both of them in a relaxed mood, and me in Jik's dressing gown, and he and I in a cloud of Dettol.

I yawned. 'About Hudson?'

'Who else? And don't go to sleep before you've told us.'

'Well . . . I was looking for him, or someone like him, before I ever met him.'

'But why?'

'Because of the wine,' I said. 'Because of the wine which was stolen from Donald's cellar. Whoever stole it not only knew it was there, down some stairs behind an inconspicuous cupboard-like door . . . and I'd stayed several times in the house and never knew the cellar existed . . . but according to Donald they would have had to come prepared with proper cases to pack it in. Wine is usually packed twelve bottles in a case . . . and Donald had two thousand or more bottles stolen. In bulk alone it would have taken a lot of shifting. A lot of time, too, and time for housebreakers is risky. But also it was special wine. A small fortune, Donald said. The sort of wine that's bought and sold as an asset and ends up at a week's wage a bottle, if it's ever drunk at all. Anyway, it was the sort of wine that needed expert handling and marketing if it was to be worth the difficulty of stealing it in the first place . . . and as Donald's business is wine, and the reason for his journey to Australia was wine, I started looking right away for someone who knew Donald, knew he'd bought a Munnings,

194

and knew about good wine and how to sell it. And there, straight-away, was Hudson Taylor, who matched like a glove. But it seem-ed too easy . . . because he didn't *look* right.'

'Smooth and friendly,' said Sarah, nodding.

'And rich,' Jik added.

'Probably a moneyholic,' I said, pulling open the bed and looking longingly at the cool white sheets.

'A what?'

'Moneyholic. A word I've just made up to describe someone with an uncontrollable addiction to money.'

'The world's full of them,' Jik said, laughing.

I shook my head. 'The world is full of drinkers, but alcoholics are obsessive. Moneyholics are obsessive. They never have enough. They *cannot* have enough. However much they have, they want more. And I'm not talking about the average hard-up man, but about real screwballs. Money, money, money. Like a drug. Moneyholics will do anything to get it . . . Kidnap, murder, cook the computer, rob banks, sell their grandmothers . . . You name it.'

I sat on the bed with my feet up, feeling less than fit. Sore from too many bruises, on fire from too many cuts. Jik too, I guessed. They had been wicked rocks.

'Moneyholism,' Jik said, like a lecturer to a dimmish class, 'is a widespread disease easily understood by everyone who has ever felt a twinge of greed, which is everyone.'

'Go on about Hudson,' Sarah said.

'Hudson had the organizing ability . . . I didn't know when I came that the organization was so huge, but I did know it was *organized*, if you see what I mean. It was an overseas operation. It took some doing. Knowhow.'

Jik tugged the ring off a can of beer and passed it to me, winc-ing as he stretched.

'But he convinced me I was wrong about him,' I said, drinking through the triangular hole. 'Because he was so careful. He pre-tended he had to look up the name of the gallery where Donald bought his picture. He didn't think of me as a threat, of course, but just as Donald's cousin. Not until he talked to Wexford down on the lawn.'

'I remember,' Sarah said. 'When you said it had ripped the whole works apart.'

'Mm . . . I thought it was only that he had told Wexford I was Donald's cousin, but of course Wexford also told *him* that I'd met Greene in Maisie's ruins in Sussex and then turned up in the gallery looking at the original of Maisie's burnt painting.'

'Jesus Almighty,' Jik said. 'No wonder we beat it to Alice Springs.'

'Yes, but by then I didn't think it could be Hudson I was look-ing' for. I was looking for someone brutal, who passed on his violence through his employees. Hudson didn't look or act brutal.' I paused. 'The only slightest crack was when his gamble went down the drain at the races. He gripped his binoculars so hard that his knuckles showed white. But you can't think a man is a big-time thug just because he gets upset over losing a bet.'

Jik grinned. 'I'd qualify.'

'In spades, redoubled,' Sarah said.

'I was thinking about it in the Alice Springs hospital . . . There hadn't been time for the musclemen to get to Alice from Mel-bourne between us buying Renbo's picture and me diving off the balcony, but there had been time for them to come from *Adelaide*, and Hudson's base was at Adelaide . . . but it was much too flimsy.'

'They might have been in Alice to start with,' Jik said reason-ably.

'They might, but what for?' I yawned. 'Then on the night of the Cup you said Hudson had made a point of asking you about me . . . and I wondered how he knew you.'

'Do you know,' Sarah said, 'I did wonder too at the time, but it didn't seem important. I mean, *we'd* seen *him* from the top of the stands, so it didn't seem impossible that somewhere he'd seen you with us.'

'The boy knew you,' I said. 'And he was at the races, because he followed you, with Greene, to the Hilton. The boy must have pointed you out to Greene.'

'And Greene to Wexford, and Wexford to Hudson?' Jik asked.

'Quite likely.'

'And by then,' he said, 'they all knew they wanted to silence you pretty badly, and they'd had a chance and muffed it . . . I'd love to have heard what happened when they found we'd robbed the gallery.' He chuckled, tipping up his beer can to catch the last few drops.

'On the morning after,' I said, 'a letter from Hudson was delivered by hand to the Hilton. How did he know we were there?'

They stared. 'Greene must have told him,' Jik said. 'We certainly didn't. We didn't tell anybody. We were careful about it.'

'So was I,' I said. 'That letter offered to show me round a vineyard. Well . . . if I hadn't been so doubtful of him, I might have gone. He was a friend of Donald's . . . and a vineyard would be interesting. From his point of view, anyway, it was worth a try.'

'Jesus!'

'On the night of the Cup, when we were in that motel near Box Hill, I telephoned the police in England and spoke to the man in charge of Donald's case, Inspector Frost. I asked him to ask Donald some questions . . . and this morning outside Wellington I got the answers.'

'This morning seems several light years away,' Sarah said.

'Mm . . .'

'What questions and what answers?' Jik said.

'The questions were, did Donald tell Hudson all about the wine in his cellar, and did Donald tell *Wexford* about the wine in the cellar, and was it Hudson who had suggested to Donald that he and Regina should go and look at the Munnings in the Arts Centre. And the answers were "Yes, of course", and "No, why-ever should I?", and "Yes".'

They thought about it in silence. Jik fiddled with the dispenser in the room's in-built refrigerator and liberated another can of Fosters.

'So what then?' Sarah said.

'So the Melbourne police said it was too insubstantial, but if they could tie Hudson in definitely with the gallery they might believe it. So they dangled in front of Hudson the pictures and stuff we stole from the gallery, and along he came to collect them.'

'How? How did they dangle them?'

'They let Wexford accidentally overhear snippets from a fake report from several hotels about odd deposits in their baggage

197

rooms, including the paintings at the Hilton. Then after we got here they gave him an opportunity to use the telephone when he thought no one was listening, and he rang Hudson at the house he's been staying in here for the races, and told him. So Hudson wrote himself a letter to the Hilton from me, and zoomed along to remove the incriminating evidence.'

'He must have been crazy.'

'Stupid. But he thought I was dead . . . and he'd no idea anyone suspected him. He should have had the sense to know that Wexford's call to him would be bugged by the police . . . but Frost told me that Wexford would think he was using a public phone booth.'

'Sneaky,' Sarah said.

I yawned. 'It takes a sneak to catch a sneak.'

'You'd never have thought Hudson would blaze up like that,' she said. 'He looked so . . . so dangerous.' She shivered. 'You wouldn't think people could hide such really frightening violence under a friendly public face.'

'The nice Irish bloke next door,' Jik said, standing up, 'can leave a bomb to blow the legs off children.'

He pulled Sarah to her feet. 'What do you think I paint?' he said. 'Vases of flowers?' He looked down at me. 'Horses?'

We parted the next morning at Melbourne airport, where we seemed to have spent a good deal of our lives.

'It seems strange, saying goodbye,' Sarah said.

'I'll be coming back,' I said.

They nodded.

'Well . . .' We looked at watches.

It was like all partings. There wasn't much to say. I saw in their eyes, as they must have seen in mine, that the past ten days would quickly become a nostalgic memory. Something we did in our crazy youth. Distant.

'Would you do it all again?' Jik said.

I thought inconsequentially of surviving wartime pilots looking back from forty years on. Had their achievements been worth the blood and sweat and risk of death: did they regret?

I smiled. Forty years on didn't matter. What the future made of the past was its own tragedy. What we ourselves did on the day was all that counted.

'I guess I would.'

I leaned forward and kissed Sarah, my oldest friend's wife.

'Hey,' he said. 'Find one of your own.'

seventeen

Maisie saw me before I saw her, and came sweeping down like a great scarlet bird, wings outstretched.

Monday lunchtime at Wolverhampton races, misty and cold.

'Hello, dear, I'm so glad you've come. Did you have a good trip back, because of course it's such a long way, isn't it, with all that wretched jet lag?' She patted my arm and peered acutely at my face. 'You don't really look awfully well, dear, if you don't mind me saying so, and you don't seem to have collected any sun-tan, though I suppose as you haven't been away two weeks it isn't surprising, but those are nasty gashes on your hand, dear, aren't they, and you were walking very *carefully* just now.'

She stopped to watch a row of jockeys canter past on their way to the start. Bright shirts against the thin grey mist. A subject for Munnings.

'Have you backed anything, dear? And are you sure you're warm enough in that anorak? I never think jeans are good for people in the winter, they're only cotton, dear, don't forget, and how did you get on in Australia? I mean, dear, did you find out anything useful?'

'It's an awfully long story . . .'

'Best told in the bar, then, don't you think, dear?'

She bought us immense brandies with ginger ale and settled herself at a small table, her kind eyes alert and waiting.

I told her about Hudson's organization, about the Melbourne gallery, and about the list of robbable customers.

'Was I on it?'

I nodded. 'Yes, you were.'

'And you gave it to the police?' she said anxiously.

I grinned. 'Don't look so worried, Maisie. Your name was crossed out already. I just crossed it out more thoroughly. By the time I'd finished, no one could ever disentangle it, particularly on a photocopy.'

She smiled broadly. 'No one could call you a fool, dear.'

I wasn't so sure about that. 'I'm afraid, though,' I said, 'that you've lost your nine thousand quid.'

'Oh yes, dear,' she said cheerfully. 'Serves me right, doesn't it, for trying to cheat the Customs, though frankly, dear, in the same circumstances I'd probably do it again, because that tax makes me so mad, dear. But I'm ever so glad, dear, that they won't come knocking on my door this time, or rather my sister Betty's, because of course I'm staying with her again up here at the moment, as of course the Beach told you, until my house is ready.'

I blinked. 'What house?'

'Well, dear, I decided not to rebuild the house at Worthing because it wouldn't be the same without the things Archie and I bought together, so I'm selling that plot of seaside land for a fortune, dear, and I've chosen a nice place just down the road from Sandown Park racecourse.'

'You're not going to live in Australia?'

'Oh no, dear, that would be too far away. From Archie, you see, dear.'

I saw. I liked Maisie very much.

'I'm afraid I spent all your money,' I said.

She smiled at me with her well-kept head on one side and absentmindedly stroked her crocodile handbag.

'Never mind, dear. You can paint me *two* pictures. One of me, and one of my new house.'

I left after the third race, took the train along the main line to Shrewsbury, and from there travelled by bus to Inspector Frost's official doorstep.

He was in an office, chin deep in papers. Also present, the unblinking Superintendent Wall, who had so unnerved Donald, and whom I'd not previously met. Both men shook hands in a cool and businesslike manner, Wall's eyes traversing the anorak, jeans and desert boots, and remaining unimpressed. They offered me a chair, moulded plastic and armless.

Frost said, faintly smiling, 'You sure kicked open an ant-hill.'

Wall frowned, disliking such frivolity. 'It appears you stumbled on an organization of some size.'

The gaze of both men swept the mountain of paper.

'What about Donald?' I asked.

Frost kept his eyes down. His mouth twitched.

Wall said, 'We have informed Mr Stuart that we are satisfied the break-in at his house and the death of Mrs Stuart were the work of outside agencies, beyond his knowledge or control.'

Cold comfort words. 'Did he understand what he was hearing?'

The Wall eyebrows rose. 'I went to see him myself, this morning. He appeared to understand perfectly.'

'And what about Regina?'

'The body of Mrs Stuart,' Wall said correctively.

'Donald wants her buried,' I said.

Frost looked up with an almost human look of compassion. 'The difficulty is,' he said, 'that in a murder case, one has to preserve the victim's body in case the defence wishes to call for its own post mortem. In this case, we have not been able to accuse anyone of her murder, let alone get as far as them arranging a defence.' He cleared his throat. 'We'll release Mrs Stuart's body for burial as soon as official requirements have been met.'

I looked at my fingers, interlacing them.

Frost said, 'Your cousin already owes you a lot. You can't be expected to do more.'

I smiled twistedly and stood up. 'I'll go and see him,' I said.

Wall shook hands again, and Frost came with me through the hall and out into the street. The lights shone bright in the early winter evening.

'Unofficially,' he said, walking slowly with me along the pavement, 'I'll tell you that the Melbourne police found a list of names in the gallery which it turns out are of known housebreakers. Divided into countries, like the Overseas Customers.

There were four names for England. I suppose I shouldn't guess and I certainly ought not to be saying this to you, but there's a good chance Mrs Stuart's killer may be one of them.'

'Really?'

'Yes. But don't quote me.' He looked worried.

'I won't,' I said. 'So the robberies were local labour?'

'It seems to have been their normal method.'

Greene, I thought. With an 'e'. Greene could have recruited them. And checked afterwards, in burnt houses, on work done.

I stopped walking. We were standing outside the flower shop where Regina had worked. Frost looked at the big bronze chrysanthemums in the brightly lit window, and then enquiringly at my face.

I put my hand in my pocket and pulled out the six revolver shell cases. Gave them to Frost.

'These came from the gun which the man called Greene fired at me,' I said. 'He dropped them when he was reloading. I told you about them on the telephone.'

He nodded.

'I don't imagine they're of much practical use,' I said. 'But they might persuade you that Greene is capable of murder.'

'Well . . . what of it?'

'It's only a feeling . . .'

'Get on with it.'

'Greene,' I said, 'was in England at about the time Regina died.' He stared.

'Maybe Regina knew him,' I said. 'She had been in the gallery in Australia. Maybe she saw him helping to rob her house . . . supervising, perhaps . . . and maybe that's why she was killed, because it wouldn't have been enough just to tie her up and gag her . . . she could identify him for certain if she was alive.'

He looked as if he was trying to draw breath.

'That's all . . . guessing,' he said.

'I know for certain that Greene was in England two weeks after Regina's death. I know for certain he was up to his neck in selling paintings and stealing them back. I know for certain that he would kill someone who could get him convicted. The rest . . . well . . . it's over to you.'

'My God,' Frost said. 'My God.'

I started off again, towards the bus-stop. He came with me, looking glazed.

'What everyone wants to know,' he said, 'is what put you on to the organization in the first place.'

I smiled. 'A hot tip from an informer.'

'What informer?'

A smuggler in a scarlet coat, glossy hair-do and crocodile handbag. 'You can't grass on informers,' I said.

He sighed, shook his head, stopped walking, and pulled a piece of torn-off telex paper out of his jacket.

'Did you meet an Australian policeman called Porter?'

'I sure did.'

'He sent you a message.' He handed me the paper. I read the neatly typed words.

'Tell that Pommie painter Thanks.'

'Will you send a message back?'

He nodded. 'What is it?'

'No sweat,' I said.

I stood in the dark outside my cousin's house, looking in.

He sat in his lighted drawing-room, facing Regina, unframed on the mantelshelf. I sighed, and rang the bell.

Donald came slowly. Opened the door.

'Charles!' He was mildly surprised. 'I thought you were in Australia.'

'Got back yesterday.'

'Come in.'

We went into the kitchen, where at least it was warm, and sat one each side of the table. He looked gaunt and fifty, a shell of a man, retreating from life.

'How's business?' I said.

'Business?'

'The wine trade.'

'I haven't been to the office.'

'If you didn't have a critical cash flow problem before,' I said, 'you'll have one soon.'

'I don't really care.'

'You've got stuck,' I said. 'Like a needle in a record. Playing the same little bit of track over and over again.'

He looked blank.

'The police know you didn't fix the robbery,' I said.

He nodded slowly. 'That man Wall . . . came and told me so. This morning.'

'Well, then.'

'It doesn't seem to make much difference.'

'Because of Regina?'

He didn't answer.

'You've got to stop it, Donald,' I said. 'She's dead. She's been dead five weeks and three days. Do you want to see her?'

He looked absolutely horrified. 'No! Of course not.'

'Then stop thinking about her body.'

'Charles!' He stood up violently, knocking over his chair. He was somewhere between outrage and anger, and clearly shocked.

'She's in a cold drawer,' I said, 'And you want her in a box in the cold ground. So where's the difference?'

'Get out,' he said loudly. 'I don't want to hear you.'

'The bit of Regina you're obsessed about,' I said, not moving, 'is just a collection of minerals. That . . . that *shape* lying in storage isn't Regina. The real girl is in your head. In your memory. The only life you can give her is to remember her. That's her immortality, in your head. You're killing her all over again with your refusal to go on living.'

He turned on his heel and walked out. I heard him go across the hall, and guessed he was making for the sitting-room.

After a minute I followed him. The white-panelled door was shut.

I opened the door. Went in.

He was sitting in his chair, in the usual place.

'Go away,' he said.

What did it profit a man, I thought, if he got flung over balconies and shot at and mangled by rocks, and couldn't save his cousin's soul.

'I'm taking that picture with me to London,' I said.

He was alarmed. He stood up. 'You're *not*.'

'I am.'

'You can't. You gave it to me.'

'It needs a frame,' I said. 'Or it will warp.'

'You can't take it.'

'You can come as well.'

'I can't leave here,' he said.

'Why not?'

'Don't be stupid,' he said explosively. 'You know why not. Because of . . .' His voice died away.

I said, 'Regina will be with you wherever you are. Whenever
you think of her, she'll be there.'

Nothing.

'She isn't in this room. She's in your head. You can go out of
here and take her with you.'

Nothing.

'She was a great girl. It must be bloody without her. But she
deserves the best you can do.'

Nothing.

I went over to the fireplace and picked up the picture. Regina's
face smiled out, vitally alive. I hadn't done her left nostril too
well, I thought.

Donald didn't try to stop me.

I put my hand on his arm.

'Let's get your car out,' I said, 'And drive down to my flat.
Right this minute.'

A little silence.

'Come on,' I said.

He began, with difficulty, to cry.

I took a long breath and waited. 'O.K.,' I said. 'How are you off
for petrol?'

'We can get some more . . .' he said, sniffing, '. . . on the motor-
way.'

Colin Forbes
Special limited edition
The Stockholm Syndicate/
The Stone Leopard £0.00
Two bestsellers for the price of one!

The struggle for power, global conspiracy and the deadly workings of
international terrorism are just some of the hallmarks of Colin
Forbes's classic adventure thrillers – bestseller in over thirty countries
around the world.

. . . thrill to blackmail, bribery and calculated murder in *The Stockholm
Syndicate*, as a devastating secret strike force seeks out an enemy
attempting to control the West's economy – by any means at its
disposal . . .

. . . follow the hunt for a Resistance hero turned international
conspirator in *The Stone Leopard*, the gripping thriller which
introduced fictional hero Marc Grelle, Prefect of the Paris Police.

COLIN FORBES
'Has no equal' *Sunday Mirror*

All Pan Books are available at your local bookshop or newsagent, or can be ordered direct from the publisher. Indicate the number of copies required and fill in the form below.

Send to: Pan C. S. Dept
               Macmillan Distribution Ltd
               Houndmills Basingstoke RG21 2XS

or phone: 0256 29242, quoting title, author and Credit Card number.

Please enclose a remittance* to the value of the cover price plus £1.00 for the first book plus 50p per copy for each additional book ordered.

*Payment may be made in sterling by UK personal cheque, postal order, sterling draft or international money order, made payable to Pan Books Ltd.

Alternatively by Barclaycard/Access/Amex/Diners

Card No.

Expiry Date

Signature

Applicable only in the UK and BFPO addresses.

While every effort is made to keep prices low, it is sometimes necessary to increase prices at short notice. Pan Books reserve the right to show on covers and charge new retail prices which may differ from those advertised in the text or elsewhere.

NAME AND ADDRESS IN BLOCK LETTERS PLEASE

. . . .

Name _____

Address _____

_____

_____

_____

6/92